Lucinda's Mountain

Book 1 in the Lucinda Harmon Saga

Cover art by Rhonda Whited

Adda Leah Davis

Accolades

"In her excellent novel, *Lucinda's Mountain,* Adda Leah Davis beautifully captures the intricately confining lifestyles of a young Appalachian woman growing to maturity among complicated social and religious family values... Readers will be inspired by Lucinda Harmon as she struggles to work through relationships... I was overjoyed when I found that the author plans to extend Lucinda's story into a trilogy. I don't want to leave this woman's story so quickly."

> - Howard Dorgan, author of four University of Tennessee volumes on Appalachian religious traditions and the Religious Section Editor of the recent *Encyclopedia of Appalachia*. Professor Emeritus at Appalachian State University.

"*Lucinda's Mountain*" is a compelling story set in West Virginia around the 1950s in such locales as Bradshaw, Iaeger, JoLo, War, and Welch. Highly individualistic in style, tone, and treatment of characters and place it is firmly rooted in great American traditions of realism... Realism succeeds by depiction of the familiar, the ordinary, the commonplace, how life is (or was) lived on a daily basis in a particular place and time... This is precisely the case in "*Lucinda's Mountain*".

> - Dr. Robert J. Higgs recently retired from the Appalachian Literature Department of East Tennessee State University

"Adda Leah Davis has written a book with characters that are realistic and compelling without being overly romantic or idealized- not an easy task... Her historical research gives the setting accuracy and a lifelike artistic representation. The dialect and the authentic Appalachian expressions create a language of practicality and pragmatism that is hard to miss. I can't wait for the next installment."

> - Dr. Thomas Keats McKnight, Professor of English, Southwest Virginia Community College, Richlands, Virginia

Dedication

This book is dedicated to the McDowell County of my
youth:

Forested peaks and fertile soil
Sparkling creeks and rivers rush
Sounds carried from peak to peak
Nothing disturbs the peaceful hush.
Extended families in sharing homes
Helping neighbors and trusting friends
Brush arbor shades where neighbors come
To hear the preacher who's long of wind.
Horses, mules, and dogs abound
Brought for the purposes of trade
Ending up at the jockey ground
Where men divest their religious shade
Life and death and passing time
Weave a treasured tapestry in my mind.
Adda Leah Davis

Introduction

You are about to read a love story. In superficial ways, it is like many other love stories, even those set in the hills of Appalachia. John Knowles and William Hoffman wrote their mountain versions on the Romeo and Juliet theme, lovers from different subcultures whose star-crossed lives, invited trouble from the beginning. Conventional wisdom holds that sons and daughters from the opposing camps of union and management simply had too much ideological baggage to make it together as husband and wife. Success of such pairings was even less likely if one of the lovers was an "outsider".

When reading *Lucinda's Mountain*, students of rural education will be reminded of two books from the genre that peered inside the one room schoolhouse- Jesse Stuart's *The Thread That Runs So True* and Edward Eggleston's *Hoosier Schoolmaster*.

But one should not be early deceived by the seeming similarities in these tales. Here is not only a love story but a song to a people and a place that have seeped down into the author's soul and reappeared on these pages. While McDowell County, West Virginia invites song and story, only a keen and careful observer, aware of the unspoken language that passes between people who have lived for generations in places like Panther and Estep Ridge, should dare attempt it. Ms. Davis has found the language to express the ineffable, something that Jack Weller (*Yesterday's People*) and others of his stripe never quite "got". Her story is a confession of a love affair with home and its people who are linked to one another and the land in a manner seldom understood by mainstream America, frenetic in its zeal to get somewhere else.

Two decades ago, geographers asked research subjects to draw what they considered to be the boundaries of Appalachia. When they averaged the results to determine the perceived center of the region, McDowell County lay at the perceptual heart of the resulting map. The county in other ways has come to symbolize the plight of an entire region whose principal and most prized product has been its people who have fled to the cities of the upper Midwest and more recently to states along the Atlantic seaboard.

McDowell became the heart of what promoters called the "billion dollar Pocahontas coal field". Before the discovery of coal, before the opening of the region by railroad, and before the Civil War, fewer than 2,000 people were scattered on isolated farms across the county. But coal and the railroads brought explosive growth. From 1900 to 1915, it was the state's fastest growing county and by 1950, its population neared 100,000. A dearth of able hands to mine the high quality metallurgical and steam coal beneath its tortuous topography sent agents of mine owners scrambling to recruit men for this grueling and dangerous work. And, it was a diverse lot who answered the "help wanted" ads: freedmen from plantations in the South, fiercely independent Scotch-Irish farmers who had tried too long to scratch a living from barren highland soil, Italian stone masons just off the boat at Ellis Island or the Port of Boston, and Poles and Hungarians who had previous mining experience.

Place names came to reflect the new influences. Some say that Big Four was named for the principal labor unions that organized the area, while others contend that is was for the financiers who developed across the country: Collis P. Huntington, Leland Stanford, and others. Gary was named for Elbert Gary, president of U.S. Steel, who also provided his name for Gary, Indiana, site of the company's major mills. Names familiar to people in Pittsburgh, Pennsylvania and Boston found their way in company towns.

Nowadays, a drive along U.S. Route 52 across the county reveals the discarded husks of a once robust string of communities. Outsiders would be quick to spy evidences of despair at every turn of the road. Where still standing, a row or two of company houses compete with the road, the railroad tracks, and Elkhorn Creek for space in the narrow valley where a "bullfrog would need a flashlight at noon to see" allow some of the old timers. Ghost towns, common to mining regions around the world, are gradually being reclaimed by the forests which surrendered to them in a more optimistic and expansive age. Complaining about the ubiquitous coal dust and apparent apathy of the people, a new minister fresh from seminary was upbraided by a parishioner: "If you take time to look and listen with an open mind, you'll find beauty here in both the people and the place."

If ever there was a people challenged by Shakespeare's *Coriolanus*, it is the folks of Ms. Davis' home: "Adversity is the trier of spirits. Common chances common men can bear. When the sea is calm, all boats alike show mastership in floating." Or as Lucinda repeated her grandpa's advice: "You have to stand whatever comes along, Cindy, but it's up to you how you want to stand it." Job had nothing on Davis' heroine.

If anyone is qualified to tell the story of this place and the wrenching changes it has undergone, it is Adda Leah Davis. I suspect that a considerable part of this story is autobiographical, especially the dreams of a country girl to get a college education and escape from the "box" that she thought shut her off from the world and its great but yet unrevealed promises.

Davis herself is a native of McDowell County. Hers is an admirable story of a woman who earned a degree at Concord College when she was 40 years old, taught school on a provisional certificate, attended summer school and extension classes, and raised four children.

She founded the first oral history theatre in the county and recruited performers ages 18 through 79. After writing for the Welch Daily and the Industrial News of Iaeger, she served for six years as Director of Economic Development for the county. She now lives in Rosedale, Virginia where she helps raise a grandson and writes books for elementary school children.

Lucinda's Mountain, written from the perspective of a local, is the first of a planned trilogy to be followed by a portrait of the area drawn by a young outsider doctor and the final volume, a synthesis of the two points of view.

Jerry Beasley
President, Concord University
Athens, West Virginia
October 2006

Chapter I

"What is wrong with you? Are you stupid or just don't know how to drive? You almost ran over me!" shouted Lucinda as she pulled herself up from the mud hole. Still clutching her bag of groceries, she looked down in horror at her new blue dress. It was the prettiest dress she'd ever had. Now it was covered with muddy water and splotches of dirty brown mud.

Lucinda's eyes focused on the once shiny but now mud-speckled Chevrolet car and the tall, glaring, young man standing beside it.

"What the devil were you doing walking in the middle of the road on a curve?" he yelled. "If I had hit you it would serve you right."

She stared in hurt amazement as he suddenly began laughing.

"You look like you've been mud wrestling. Here, let me wipe some of that off your face," he said, starting toward her with a large white handkerchief.

Having difficulty breathing, Lucinda hadn't said a word after recognizing him. This was the man who had offered her a ride two weeks ago and had lived in her daydreams since then. Now he was laughing and making fun of her. Anger took over just as he stretched out his hand with the handkerchief. She slapped his hand away.

"Don't do me any favors, mister! That won't ease your guilty conscience. Just look at my dress. It's ruined!"

She looked down and gasped in red-faced embarrassment because now the dress clung like a wet, muddy sheath, blatantly revealing every curve in her body. Lucinda looked up and in angry humiliation shrieked,

"What are you doing on this road anyway?"

"Trying to meet pretty girls," teased the man, while his eyes lingered on her clinging dress. Seeing where his eyes were directed, Lucinda dropped her head. Muddy water ran down her face and dripped from her hair. She tried to control her urge to cry as her now wet grocery bag began to fall apart.

The driver, who had been boldly looking at her body, pulled his attention back to the problem and said,

"I'm sorry. I'll get you another dress."

"Get me another dress!" blurted Lucinda raising her head to glare in astonishment, "No, you won't. I don't know you."

"Well, I can fix that. I'm the new doctor for Bradshaw - Jason McCall," he replied with a smile. "Now, can you tell me the young lady's name that needs the new dress?"

Seeing her dream man standing there smiling, she decided that she might as well tell him. She wouldn't have a chance with him anyway, but at least he would know her name. He was a doctor, probably from some big city, and she was a backward little hillbilly who had just finished high school. Some hidden desire urged her to smile brilliantly from a rosy face speckled with mud.

"I'm Lucinda Harmon. I'm sorry I was in the road, but everybody walks through the middle when nothing is coming. I just didn't hear your car."

Jason offered the handkerchief again, "Here Lucinda Harmon, wipe your face, doctor's orders. I'm afraid you may get that muck into those beautiful blue eyes."

Lucinda was standing rigidly, still on the edge of the mud hole, her dress heavy with mud. She reached for the handkerchief at the very moment that the grocery bag finally gave way. In her desperate attempt to snatch some of the items, she lost her balance and fell again. More embarrassed than ever, she began scrambling up from the dirt and lingering muck, but as she put her weight on her right foot she immediately crumpled to the ground yelping in pain.

"Sit still, you clumsy girl, before you break something," said the doctor in exasperation. He grimaced in disgust but stepped into the mud, bent down, and began to work each foot.

When he moved her right foot, Lucinda winced. "Ouch, don't be so rough," she grumbled in an attempt to keep from crying. She gulped and tried to smile as the doctor finished his examination and rose to his feet.

"Well, it isn't broken but badly sprained. I'm sorry if I hurt you. I guess I'll have to carry you to the car."

"No you won't," Lucinda protested as she was scooped up and carried toward the car. "I can't ride in your car."

"Well, I don't see why not. I'm not about to make passionate love to a crippled mud wrestler," he replied, grinning broadly.

Nobody had ever mentioned passion or love to Lucinda before and she didn't know what to say. She decided to ignore it and questioned, "What about my groceries? I can't leave them and I don't have another bag."

"First things first," said the doctor as he opened the passenger door and placed her on the seat. After easing her legs around without causing too much pain, the doctor proceeded to gather up all her groceries, which he placed in the trunk.

Getting back in the car Jason sat looking at her, "You're a very pretty girl, mud and all. How old are you? I first thought about twelve until I saw all those curves and changed my mind." Not waiting for her answer, he continued, "You're not very big. Let's see, about five-foot-two, 110 pounds, blue eyes, blonde hair, and dimples." He said all this as his eyes traveled leisurely over her body. "Yes, you are definitely a very pretty girl."

Lucinda sat shocked and staring in amazement. Here was a grown man, a good looking man, talking to her of passion and love plus telling her she was curvy and pretty. *"I'd better get out of this car. I'll bet he's the kind of man Mommy warned us about,"* she thought. She grasped the handle and opened the door.

"Here, what are you doing? You can't walk on that foot. Shut that door so I can take you home." Jason reached across her to close the door, making her quake in terror. When he heard her frightened squeak, he stared in unbelief. "Don't look at me like I'm an axe murderer. I'm not going to hurt you, you silly girl. I'm just going to take you home." Seeing her visibly relax, he smiled, "All set. I need directions, please. I assume somewhere at the bottom of this hill."

"Go left at the bottom of the hill, the second farm," mumbled a very subdued and embarrassed Lucinda.

Lucinda arrived home in a car driven by the man who had lived in her dreams for over two weeks, but what a fiasco reality was. A muddy bedraggled girl with a sprained ankle hadn't impressed this big city doctor with his once shiny new car. By the time they pulled up in the front of the house, Lucinda had resigned herself to the adage of "all dreams have to end" and this was the end of her dream.

Lucinda's mother, Nancy Harmon, came onto the porch to see who had arrived. Not many of their guests came in cars. Seeing Lucinda being carried from a fancy car, Nancy hastened out to hold open the gate as the doctor, black bag and all, walked through and up the walk. He climbed the steps onto the porch with Lucinda held firmly in his arms. Even though Lucinda had protested about being carried, she was secretly thrilled to be carried by this handsome city doctor.

"What's wrong," queried Nancy? "Is her leg broke?"

"No, but it is badly sprained. She can't walk without a lot of pain," answered the doctor. He placed Lucinda in an old ladder-backed chair on the front porch, set his bag down, and then turned to Nancy. "If you could clean that mud off, I'll treat and bandage her leg," he said, grinning down at Lucinda.

At the request of this stranger, Nancy hurried away to get the water, soap, and towels. Straightening as if to get up, Lucinda sputtered, "I'm not a baby. I can do it myself." She immediately fell back from the gentle push of the doctor's hands on her shoulders and the excruciating pain that sliced through her foot.

"No you don't, blue eyes," cautioned the doctor. "You don't want to really break it, do you?"

With ashen face and large pain-filled eyes, Lucinda shook her head, whispering, "I think you may be right," and went limp. The doctor pushed her head down below her knees and told Nancy to bring some water.

When she had recovered from her momentary weakness, Lucinda had her legs and feet cleaned and swallowed two aspirin. With the injured foot bandaged to Jason's satisfaction, he rose to leave.

"Oh! I forgot to introduce myself," he said, offering his hand to Nancy. "I'm Doctor Jason McCall, newly arrived doctor for Bradshaw. I'm on my way to see a Mrs. Artemis Lester on this road, I think. This is only my second visit and the first was after dark."

"I figgered you must be a doctor since you was ordering me around right smart like and had that black bag," Nancy said with a grin. "Aunt Sarie has been poorly, but I didn't know she was worse. You're on the wrong road though. She lives on the other fork of the ridge. Didn't Lucy tell you?"

"Lucy? Oh! You mean Lucinda," said Jason. "What's your real name, Miss Harmon?" he asked Lucinda.

Lucinda looked up from a rosy red face as Nancy interrupted, "It's Lucinda, but most of us call her Lucy. It's just easier I guess. She don't like it though, since she got grown."

"I think Lucinda is a pretty name," Jason said smiling at Lucinda. "I didn't ask how to get to Mrs. Lester's though. I was more interested in getting Lucinda home at the time," said Jason, never taking his eyes from her mud-spattered face. "Will I have to go back to the highway to get to Mrs. Lester's house?"

"No," said Nancy. "Aunt Sarie lives on the right hand fork of this ridge. You know where the road sort of makes a forked Y, with the middle part going up a hill?"

He nodded and shifted his bag to his other hand. Searching his pocket for his keys as he stepped off the porch, Jason turned suddenly. "Mrs. Harmon, you have some groceries in the trunk of my car. I almost forgot them. Do you have a bag or something? The one they were in fell apart."

"Pokes are scarce as hen's teeth around here. I'll just go out and bring them to the porch in my apron. You don't need to bother. You've already done enough," said Nancy, smiling apologetically as she hurried down the walk behind him.

Jason lifted the trunk lid and placed several items into Nancy's waiting apron before he gathered the rest in his arms and strode back up onto the porch. He waited patiently, looking at Lucinda, until Nancy had disposed of her load and relieved him. She repeatedly thanked him and apologized because he had gotten dirt on his clothes.

Jason smiled and waved her thanks aside. "A little dirt never hurt anybody, Mrs. Harmon. Don't let that bother you. Just look at Lucinda's pretty blue dress. I ruined it and I'm truly sorry, but it did help me to meet your family. A doctor needs to know as many of the people in his area as he can, so maybe this was all good luck. Well, it was good except for Lucinda's sprained ankle." Jason looked at Lucinda and smiled again before asking for further directions to the Lester home.

"Well, like I said, you go up that hill and about halfway down the other side; there's this narrow little old road that goes twixt two gate posts, course there ain't no gate. Uncle Jeb never took care of his place much," reflected Nancy. "Anyhow, go twixt them posts and that leads you right to the house. You'd better call out 'fore you get out of your car, though. Uncle Jeb's got a passel of the meanest biting hound dogs you ever seen. I wouldn't want you to get bit," Nancy firmly stated.

"The boys must have had the dogs out hunting the first time you wus there or they'd have eat you alive 'fore anybody got to you. Everybody is real careful about visiting Uncle Jeb's especially at night, so I guess you wus lucky cause his hounds has bit several people," explained Nancy. "All of us mountain folks keep dogs, but they ain't all biting dogs unless they're hissed, of course. Folks have so many dogs on this ridge that it's been nicknamed Hungry Hound Ridge," continued Nancy with a laugh.

"Thanks for the warning, Mrs. Harmon," said Jason. "I wouldn't want to be attacked by biting dogs." Turning to Lucinda who sat quietly, numb from her experience and the dulling sleepiness brought on by her first ever aspirins, Jason reached down and gently squeezed her hand. "Sorry about the mishap. Perhaps we'll meet again under more favorable circumstances. Stay off that foot for four or five days."

Seeing a pair of crutches leaning against the wall in the corner, he walked over and brought them to her. "Here, use these when you have to get up. Who else is crippled in this family?"

Lucinda's eyes clouded and brimmed with tears as she mumbled, "They're Papa John's. He died two months ago." The still painful memory of seeing her Dad's grief when he lost his own father, added to today's trauma, was suddenly just too much. Tears drenched her cheeks as she dropped her head. She didn't want this man's pity, though; she wanted something, a nebulous thought in a befuddled mind.

"Mrs. Harmon, I think Lucinda needs to lie down for a spell. She's been through a very traumatic experience. Do you need my help?" Jason questioned.

"No, I can get her to her bed. Thank you anyway for all your help. I spect it's caused you to be late on your house call, ain't it?" queried Nancy.

Jason, who had again walked down to the gate, turned to explain the situation, "No, I won't really be late. I told them I'd be there sometime today. Mrs. Lester is not a well woman at all."

"Yeah, she's had that bad stomach complaint for purt nigh two years now. Old Doc Harrison was treating her 'fore he died," explained Nancy, following him down to the gate. "Poor old soul, she's had sech a hard life. Uncle Jeb ain't been very good to her. The younguns caught Uncle Jeb gone and took her plum to that hospital in Welch for some tests. When he come back, Uncle Jeb throwed a pure fit, and wouldn't let her have them x-rays Doc Harrison wanted her to have. That was nigh onto a year ago. It don't make no sense for him to be so mean. If'n it hadn't been for Aunt Sarie, he wouldn't a had nothing but his hind end and elbows." Suddenly realizing she was speaking to a stranger, Nancy clamped her hand over her mouth and turned red. Seeing Jason's smile, Nancy grinned sheepishly. "Well, it is the truth. Uncle Jeb ort to carry her around on a pillow after all she's done for him."

Shaking his head, Jason stuck out his hand to Nancy, who grasped it gratefully.

"There's no accounting for human actions, Mrs. Harmon. They'll fool you every time. If you folks need me, I'll be around for a while."

Nancy, who had given his hand a hearty shake, backed away with, "Thank ye' again, Doctor, I guess you'll probably see some of this family 'fore too long."

CHAPTER 2

Nancy stayed on the porch watching Jason's car stir the dust as it made a u-turn below the house. It went around the tall Lombardy poplar and a silver maple tree that stood in the center of a rustic circle of hollyhocks, bleeding hearts, and rough hewn grass. Then the dust spiraled up in a cloud as the doctor revved the engine to rush up the small hill above the house. Nancy thought he was driving awfully slow as he passed the house, but then realized he was really looking things over. Nancy laughed as she told Lucinda, "I'll bet he never does figger out what my wash place is. Burb didn't even know what I's fixin' till I got it done. That big flat board twixt them two locusts saves my back from bending so low over my washtub when I'm scrubbing on the scrub board."

Nancy nodded thoughtfully and said, "I reckon he must think my three piles of rock are for roasting something. They could be used for that I reckon, but I've just been heating my lye water on them. It just made good sense to put it all out there beside the fence where I can spread things out to dry."

Looking back at Lucinda who was still in her chair, Nancy said, "Let me grab the rest of my clothes off the line and I'll help you to lay down. I've still got the overalls to do 'cause I couldn't wash them Monday with Burb working the mules. Them ornery things would kick dirt all over my clothes on their way to the barn."

Burb had built the barn last year when Nancy had been begging him to make her a walk and a new gate to the front yard. The barn was built instead and Nancy built her gate and a board walk up to the house. Before Nancy turned to help Lucinda in the house, she watched the car go around the curve above the barn and out of sight. "He may not think it's much of a place but it suits me just fine," Nancy said assuredly as she turned toward Lucinda.

The weathered hewn log house stood on the left facing the road. Not being able to afford a spring to pull the gate closed, Nancy had filled a gallon lard bucket with old broken tools and slipped the chain that pulled the gate closed through the bail of the bucket. "It don't look too good," Nancy complained when she had it centered on the chain. "It keeps the gate closed though. I can't stand them chickens pooping all over my yard," quipped Nancy with a satisfied smirk.

To a carpenter, the plank walk from the gate to the porch would be thought of as a cobbled up mess, but Nancy had planted rose moss, sweet Williams, and marigolds along the edges on both sides and thought it looked really pretty. "It may have a higgledy-piggledy look but it matches the house," said Nancy, smiling as she looked at the sparkling checkerboard-paned windows beaming a welcome. Purple morning glories twirled up the porch posts and chased a clothesline the length of the porch to grow in profusion around the stone chimney at the end.

"I don't care what nobody else thinks about my place and my plank walk," Nancy stated firmly. "I like it. It's clean and it smells good," she added with an appreciative sniff as she reached down and lifted Lucinda to her feet.

"In the morning, I'm going to sweep out in front of the gate if it don't rain," pronounced Nancy as she carefully guided a hopping Lucinda toward the middle room.

After getting Lucinda settled, Nancy came back to the porch on her way to the kitchen. She stopped to get a zinc bucket from a shelf nailed to the side of the kitchen wall. Carefully taking the long handled dipper from the bucket, she laid it to the side as she made her way to the well. Nancy looked all around her sniffing the air. A pleasant aroma came from inside the tall, homemade picket fence, which made a square around the house, and sheltered roses in bloom along with other flowers. "That city doctor can turn up his nose if he wants to but I wouldn't trade this place for all his fancy cars and city ways," stated Nancy with satisfaction.

Nancy hoped he could do something to help Aunt Sarie. Everybody on the mountain knew and loved her but they didn't think much of Uncle Jeb since he was considered lazy and also mean to Aunt Sarie. Everybody heard what a fit he threw when he returned from a visit to his brother. The children had gotten Aunt Sarie to have a set of tests while he was away. Old Doc Harrison said she had something bad wrong with her stomach and she needed some more tests but Uncle Jeb wouldn't hear of it. His contention was that Aunt Sarie would live every day the Lord put her here to live whether she had any tests or not, and he didn't have money to spend on tests anyway. Aunt Sarie seemed to go along with him, and old Doc Harrison couldn't do anything since then, except help with the pain.

While Nancy was drawing the water from the well, she thought about the trips Doc Harrison had made all over the tops of these mountains. She hoped this young feller would be as good. "He'll probably be scared of these roads, 'specially in the winter time," thought Nancy as the water came to the top of the well in its long slender container. This doctor was probably used to wide paved roads; not like here where roads staggered drunkenly up, down, and around the steep hillsides like bridle paths through a forest. Burb often said that people never thought that one day there would be cars and trucks, and the roads were just fine for wagons, carts, and sleds pulled by horses.

The coal company had got the railroad to come into McDowell County with depots in places like Bradshaw. Anybody that wanted to go far off, like to War or Welch, always went to Bradshaw and caught the train. The trains were brought in to haul coal but they also put some passenger cars on and some people had ridden as far away as Beckley, according to Burb. Mountain people didn't have much to do with the coal companies except to sell them prop timbers and produce from their gardens but when they needed to get somewhere they did like the railroad.

Many of Burb's friends often stopped to visit and they had long discussions about the coal companies, the unions, politics, or anything else touching on life as they knew it. Uncle Albert Wyatt always said that the priority of the coal companies was the profits to be made from coal and the miners were not half as important as the almighty dollar.

Depending on whom one talked to, you got several opinions. If you talked to a mine owner or one of their bosses, you would hear it said that the area would never have been developed without the coal companies. According to a company man, the railroads were here because the companies had gotten them to come in and the people should really appreciate that service. In one sense, most people realized that the railroad had exposed these mountain areas to a broader world. It was sort of like a box which had never been opened and the railroad caused a crack in the box; some people hated the crack and others wanted to see it widen.

The first unraveling of the security blanket for the people of the mountain was when the coal companies began to send men in to buy up the mineral rights. With no outside interference or influences, they had lived secure, independent, and peaceful lives. There was a code of honor in the mountains respected by everyone. A man's handshake was a sacred trust but the land buyers insisted on written contracts and deeds which still had little relevance at first. It was only when a mine was opened and suddenly a farmer's well went dry, or people were awakened in the night with their house shaking from a mountain bump, that people began to notice that something was different, but without questioning why.

Mostly however, the mountain tops were still the same as when the early Scotch-Irish settlers first moved in. The tops of these high mountain ridges had been their homes for a long, long time. Neither Burb nor old man Jim Horn would sell an acre of land or access to the mineral rights, regardless of the price offered. Burb's answer was, "This piece of hillside is mine, on the top and under it, and no fast talking city feller is going to cheat me out of it. We've made out fine here on this mountain before we even knowed what mineral rights was and no coal company is getting a foot of mine," he stated firmly when one of his neighbors sold his mineral rights to Berwind Land Company.

Agents for both Berwind and Pocahontas Land Companies practically lived on the mountains until many of the people had succumbed to the offers of money to buy an automobile, build a house, or maybe get a needed operation. These stalwart mountain people were fiercely independent; willing to help their neighbor but refusing a handout. Lucinda's civics teacher often said that independence cost them their mineral rights since it helped them pay for things they needed. Like Burb Harmon, they all paid for whatever they wanted or needed but never failed to share their bounty with neighbors.

Nancy took her water into the kitchen to begin supper. Burb would be home soon and expected food to be on the table. As Nancy looked out the window, she thought that Burb's big old logging truck didn't help the rutted roads any. She knew she would probably hear the truck before it ever came into view. The truck cut ruts so deep in the road that a car had a hard time staying out of them. The state hadn't built the road to their house. Neighbors had traded work so Burb would haul their produce off to Bradshaw to be peddled and also to get winter coal for their stoves hauled.

Without the benefit of an engineer, most of the ridge roads were just rutted, narrow lanes, barely wide enough for two cars to pass, and very little thought to elevation. They were all mostly horseshoe curves, one after the other, up, down, and around the hills on the easiest route possible.

Harvey Wagner, an injured logger, had complained bitterly about how the companies only wanted to provide for the people in their camps since they needed workers and had no consideration for anyone else. "All these coal camp folks has got good houses, better than mine anyhow, 'cause the coal company needed workers. These companies ain't dumb. They know that without houses, doctors, and some way in and out, their workers will go someplace where they can get those things. That's only fair to the miners but just 'cause they're living in town don't give them no right to act like they are so much better than we are. I wouldn't go down in a mine for two or three of their fine houses."

There were many discussions in Harvey Morgan's civic classes about coal mines and their owners. Lucinda had known since she started high school that the bosses lived in the bigger houses on the hills above the coal camps. She thought that the bosses made more money and could therefore build bigger houses. However, Mr. Morgan had said that the companies built all the houses and opined that keeping the classes separated seemed to be a top priority from the company perspective. Lucinda had never been there but learned that other towns in McDowell County like Gary and Coalwood had a golf course and a country club to be utilized by the 'big' people.

Jack Perkins, one of Lucinda's classmates said, "Island Creek will have a picnic or dinner at the country club once a year to show their thoughtfulness of their workers, but they certainly don't make friends or invite us to dine. They don't dirty their hands with the actual work in the mines or in the maintenance of the camps either."

Mr. Morgan interrupted with, "Now, let's be fair. The companies pay workers to do that. That is how jobs come about. A company or a person wants something done and they create a job and pay somebody to do it. It's called the Law of Supply and Demand. The coal companies want people to dig the coal and the workers want the pay for doing it. What do you think of that?" The bell rang before another discussion was started.

The companies had not only built the houses, but the company store, the doctor's office, and supplied the doctor. According to Burb, the coal companies had a deal with West Virginia University to give young doctors free training or something in a kind of coalfields doctoring program in order to get doctors to come to coal fields, like McDowell County.

Lucinda was fascinated by her history and civics classes in which she studied the economy. Coal was booming and counties like McDowell were really prospering. In the West Virginia Blue Book, Lucinda had found that 93,000 people made their homes here in McDowell County. Even the small town of Bradshaw had two theaters, a taxi stand, a drugstore, two department stores, two grocery stores, a bus terminal, two restaurants, and five beer joints or bars. Going through town on the school bus, Lucinda saw that people thronged the streets and spent money freely on the good things of life. Watching these people, it seemed as if they thought the mines would be here forever and all they needed to do was work and enjoy the benefits. They all seemed prosperous and happy.

Lucinda wondered what would happen if the mines closed. These people would probably have a rough time feeding their families, especially in the coal camps or towns. Lucinda knew that her folks and the other people on the mountains wouldn't have that problem. They didn't have much but it was theirs and they sure didn't owe the company store. She knew they didn't believe in buying on credit. Mountain people didn't even go to the town churches since the townspeople paid their preachers a salary.

Lucinda's cousin Bea had said that the Methodist preacher at Jolo was sent in by the church conference but that Island Creek certainly contributed. Mr. Lawson, from the top of Three Forks Mountain, had told Bea that "Mountain people wouldn't be caught dead in one of them 'man-made' churches." Lucinda knew this was true since none of the big church buildings were to be found on the tops of the mountains. Lucinda didn't know what Mr. Lawson meant by 'man-made' but the established churches were certainly not on the mountain ridges. Mountain churches were sometimes log buildings or sometimes made of rough boards painted white and were usually secluded in shady glades.

These churches were not advertised and unless you lived on a particular ridge you wouldn't know a church building was there. The little building on the top of Crane Ridge above the town of Raysal was a small whitewashed building with Mount Zion Primitive Baptist Church written above the door. It was almost hidden in a grove of maples, oaks, and locust trees. Without the map, on the back of their church bulletin (called a Minute), people would have a difficult time locating the church. These mountain churches had no seminary trained preachers, no musical instruments, at least none of the Baptist churches did, and nothing fancy as to stained glass windows or pews. The only music heard was the perfectly blended congregational voices raised in praise.

John Henry Addair, the principal of Iaeger High School was supposed to have said, "Give me a school full of these mountain children. They appreciate the chance to learn." Lucinda did not know if that was true or not but Mr. Addair had always spoken to her, although gruffly.

Lucinda had gradually come to realize that her way of life on the mountain was far different from even her cousin Bea's who lived at Jolo. Bea attended Sunday school, went to movies, dated boys, wore store bought dresses, and even wore make-up. Bea's dad was a carpenter for Island Creek Coal Company and they bought things at the company store. Lucinda really thought her cousin's family was very well off since they had a couch in the front room instead of a bed and dresser like Nancy had. Lucinda knew that many mountain people were very intelligent but it puzzled her when she realized that they seemed backward and naïve. Grandpa always said, "They hide their light under a bushel," and Lucinda wondered why. She thought it might be because some of them had very little formal education. Burb had finished the eighth grade and one aunt had gone to high school for a while and she supposed that others had also. People came to Burb all the time for help with matters involving the law. Lucinda thought he must be really intelligent but Nancy told her it was because Burb had been a county deputy for several years.

CHAPTER 3

While Lucinda was cooped up in the house with her sprained ankle she had lots of time to think. She went over and over the events leading to her meeting with Doctor Jason McCall. Lucinda wondered if this meeting was meant to be, like the saying often expressed by some of her dad's friends. Her dad always disagreed with them, saying, "Now boys, the Lord didn't make no robots. He set this earth in motion and put everything here that man would need. Man has some choosing to do. He gives a man a brain and it's up to him whether he uses it or not. Things happen to some and don't to others but I never have believed our natural walks are ordered of the Lord."

Still, Lucinda sometimes wondered about this concept when certain things happened. First she saw Jason on the highway and he had stopped to ask if she wanted a ride. She had day dreamed about him for the next two weeks and then he almost ran her down. She wondered if that was meant to happen. She would really like to believe that Jason was chosen for her.

Lucinda felt sorry about her dress. It would never look the same again even though Nancy had washed and ironed it. Nancy had made the dress from a blue feed sack printed with tiny pink and yellow flowers. Lucinda had gotten her claim in first on last month's hog middlins sack. "This time I'll have a new dress instead of Ellen. She always gets first choice of everything," Lucinda told Nancy when she asked for the sack.

Nancy, a genius at dressmaking, had made an exact copy of a dress Lucinda liked in the Sears Roebuck catalog. Nancy measured Lucinda across the shoulders, around the bust, waist, and hips, and also the length from her waist to mid-calf of her leg. She then laid out the cloth, looked at the catalog, and snipped away until all the pieces were there. Then she drew up the old ladder-backed chair with the woven birch bark seat and sat like the maid in Rumpelstiltskin, turning those old feed sacks into gold.

Lucinda had proudly preened as she looked at herself in the faded mirror. "That blue background makes your eyes look bluer than they already are, Lucy, but now that waistband, I don't know. Is your waist that small or are you just holdin' in?" Nancy questioned, as she walked around to look it over for flaws. Lucinda had puffed out her chest and tried to do the same to her stomach, giggling with the effort.

The first chance she had to wear the new dress was the hottest day in 1950. It was August 5th, three days ago and what a disappointment that turned out to be. That morning she had taken her usual sponge bath and donned her beautiful new dress. She was being sent to Vencill's Grocery on Route 83. She relived every detail of that day, even to the heavy weight of her waist length honey blond hair, tied back in a pony tail. She had been walking down the long, dusty road above the Jess Compton hill with a large brown bag of groceries when disaster struck.

Lucinda smiled sadly as she reminisced. The ridge road had been scraped, but it hadn't rained in a while and the dust was thick, especially when a car passed. Convict laborers had been used to build Route 83 in 1938, and it was black topped in 1939 but none of the ridge roads had gravel on them and were either dust, ruts, or mud. Cars and trucks wearing chains dug deep ruts in the clay soil in winter. These ruts got wider and deeper as the winter progressed and were only smoothed out with the first road scraping in the spring. Most of the road seemed almost level after the scraping, but vehicles still splashed through the mud holes that seemed to form everywhere.

Lucinda, like everyone else, unconsciously walked the edges, or in dry weather, right through the middle of the mud holes where there was dry higher ground. That day, she had only the dust to contend with for most of the way, since the road had received its second scraping for the year.

She recalled her favorite daydream of a tall handsome man who appeared and swept her off her feet. He then married her and took her away from the kind of life Mama and her older sisters were living. Odell, her oldest sister, had five children and a husband who gambled, drank whiskey, and made babies. Oprey, the next oldest, whose husband was crippled in a slate fall in the No. 1 Bartley mine, had three children. Faye had two children and moved from one coal camp to another living in dread of a layoff, a mine strike, and having more babies. Ellen wasn't yet married but was engaged to Benny Pruitt, a boy from another fork of the same mountain ridge. Her mother and sisters were shackled and chained to Bradshaw Mountain and its rigorous demands on the lives of women. Lucinda thought it might be different in the towns or some other place and she wanted to find out.

It made her so sad to think of the wonderful life she had lived on this mountain, until she got grown. Bradshaw Mountain was a safe, happy childhood cradle which nurtured every aspect of her early years. When her beloved, silver- haired Grandpa talked about 'a city set on a hill' she thought he was speaking about their mountain. Now Grandpa was gone and she wanted to get away. If she stayed here she'd end up with the same kind of life as her mother and sisters, and she couldn't imagine a worse fate.

Lucinda remembered Granny Jane, the midwife who delivered Oprey's and Odell's children. Lucinda considered the horror which Granny Jane called "deliverin'." She didn't really do any "deliverin'" or anything else except eat and drink coffee. She almost let Odell die when her first baby was born. Burb Harmon threw a fit and went racing for the doctor when he happened to come home from work early. But unless someone complained, Granny Jane gave doses of castor oil and then whiled away the time eating and drinking until each child came screaming into the world from their mother's tortured and bleeding body.

Constantly, Lucinda thought about ways of getting away from the top of the mountain. No midwife would ever deliver a child for her. If she couldn't have a doctor, she just wouldn't have any children. She didn't know how women could keep from having babies but surely there was some way. She would have liked to talk to her mother or somebody about things like that but Nancy never ever talked about anything personal with her. Lucinda was not even allowed around the cow when she was calving, and therefore knew nothing about that part of life.

She shuddered and switched her mind back to the day she actually met her dream man. She recalled how tired her arms had gotten and her struggles to relieve the pressure by shifting her bag of groceries from one arm to the other as she trudged down the road. It was amazing how many little things she remembered about that day but they were shadowed by the way she felt when she had been held close in strong, muscular arms. She remembered thinking her Mama would be upset, which she was, because Lucinda couldn't get the vanilla flavoring, even though she had a bag full of baking soda, baking powder, oatmeal, rice, coffee, salt, sugar, and a slab of bacon.

This load wasn't any bigger or heavier than other loads she had carried, but it hadn't been packed very well in the bag. The contents shifted unevenly, first one way and then the other, as she walked. Sam Vencill didn't care how he packed your bag as long as he got his money, but his wife Minnie always packed bags to balance. She did not know him before, but Lucinda had not liked Sam Vencill since she and Ellen first started in high school. They had been buying a loaf of bread, a jar of peanut butter, and ten nickel cakes each week for their lunch and charging it to Burb. Then one day Sam Vencill refused to let her have a loaf of bread in front of a store full of people. She didn't care if her dad had put a stop order on any more charges to his account; Sam Vencill didn't have to tell the world about her family's private business. Minnie wouldn't have done that.

When Minnie was there, she would often sneak in a candy bar or once even a soda pop. Burb, always said that if Sam didn't have Minnie he'd soon be out of business, but Lucinda doubted that. All mountain folks went there even though they felt that Sam Vencill had gotten above his raisin' since he moved out to a house on the highway and was running the store. Most folks claimed that he'd never been out of the wilds of Panther Creek, until he met and married Minnie. The talk was that if Minnie hadn't married him he'd still be down on Panther Creek selling moonshine whiskey. She'd heard Adam Henson and some other men who visited Burb saying that maybe Sam Vencill was still selling moonshine.

"I don't believe all them men go under that floor jest for feed for their hosses and mules. Charles Brewster ain't got no animals a-tall and he goes under there purt nigh ever day," said Adam, spitting an amber stream at the

34

big Dominecker rooster whose head had poked through a crack in the picket fence.

"How come you know so much about who goes under that floor Adam? You ain't been buying feed too, have you?" asked Burb looking over his glasses.

"Burb Harmon, you know Millie would pull every lick of my hair out if I's to come home with likker. Now, I ain't blind and I've seen a heap of men around here going under that floor after closing time."

However, Lucinda knew there was only one store on the highway that ran along the top of Bradshaw Mountain and people had to buy from Sam Vencill. They couldn't walk all the way into Bradshaw every time they needed something, even if it was only ten miles. Not knowing Lucinda was out on the back porch and could hear their talk, Mr. Hensen said, "Wouldn't surprise me if some night Vencill's store caught fire. A lot of mothers are talking about their boys getting moonshine from somers' close. I wouldn't be a bit surprised if that new Deputy-what's his name-uh, Stevens, don't get word if Hallie Burton's boys keep getting likkered up." Lucinda didn't think it would bother her much whatever happened to Sam Vencill, but she liked Minnie and didn't want her to suffer.

"I'd say he keeps it a secret from Minnie if that's going on. Minnie likes younguns too good to do anything to hurt one," said Burb with certainty.

The big bags of corn meal and flour were always left for her dad to bring home as he came from work, along with the 25 pound tub of lard which was bought each month. Her mother always tried to sneak in the "little grub" as she called it, to keep her dad from throwing one of his fits about buying foolishness. He sure liked Mommy's cakes which were made with that foolishness.

Two weeks before that day, Lucinda had also been walking along the newly paved Route 83 when a really nice looking man passed in his fancy car. He stopped the car, backed up, and flashing beautiful white teeth, said, "It's awfully hot to be walking. Would you like to ride?" He had raven black hair, worn a little long on the neck, or at least longer than Lucinda was used to. His black brows arched over sparkling brown eyes. He had high cheekbones and what mama would call a ruddy complexion. Though seated in the car he seemed to be tall and broad shouldered but slender. Not like her brother Gordon, who was tall but husky. Lucinda was fascinated by his gentlemanly appearance. It only took one look and Lucinda realized this was her dream man.

She was tempted to accept a ride, but Mommy had warned her to never ride with strangers, handsome or not. Nancy scared her girls half to death with her tales of rape and mayhem without giving any of the details. The only thing Lucinda really knew was that, according to Nancy, filthy, nasty things were done to girls by strange men if they got the chance. With that thought in mind, Lucinda pointed down the road and automatically answered, "No, thank you. I'm just going to the store."

He drove on then, but Lucinda still kept his image in her mind. From that time on, her daydreams revolved around the man who had almost run her down.

Lucinda hadn't complained about walking to the store on the day she sprained her ankle because it gave her a chance to meet her dream man again. It also gave her the time alone that she needed to plan her escape. She had often heard old people say, "Nothing ventured, nothing gained" and "The Lord helps them that help themselves." She intended to take a chance and beg the Lord to help her. There just had to be more to life than marrying and having one baby after another, not to mention all the back breaking drudgery of a woman's life in these mountains.

Also, always in the back of Lucinda's mind was this longing to know; a hunger to learn, to see, to understand everything that books had revealed there to know. Her first source of learning came from her mother's father who made his home with them and was Lucinda's constant companion and tutor. Her Grandpa had taken a flour 'poke', torn it apart and printed her name on the unfolded purple sheet, and Lucinda was hooked on learning.

Back then, and still yet, there were no books in the Harmon household except the Bible. So Grandpa used the Bible and taught her to read. Lucinda didn't recall actually reading any of the stories but she knew them because Grandpa had told them to her. When she went to school, reading was so easy and she went from first grade to third grade in one year. From that time on, she read everything she could get her hands on; even borrowing books.

That wasn't enough to fill that aching hunger that left her empty and longing to know. She knew that reading books was good but felt that she was woefully lacking if she could never experience what she had read was out there. The more schooling she got the hungrier she seemed to be. Once she had tried to talk to Ellen about this unfulfilled longing, but Ellen thought she was being silly.

"Everybody wants something, Lucy. We just can't have everything we want. I just wanted a husband and a home of my own. I've been trying hard to get it, and I reckon I'm going to. I guess you're just going to have to be hungry for something that ain't so hard to come by. Junior Clayton has always liked you, but you won't give him the time of day. I think you're too particular. You don't really know what you want."

Lucinda recoiled at the thought of Junior Clayton's cold groping hands and eyes that seemed to see right through her clothes. He seemed to be under the impression that since Odell and Faye had married Claytons she would too. She knew that even Burb thought a lot of Junior Clayton since he worked in the woods with him. "Best man with a team I've ever worked and he ain't bad at skiddin either. In fact he could just about run the whole loggin job if I's sick or something," bragged Burb.

Lucinda shivered in revulsion and thereafter kept her dreams to herself. Ellen just did not understand nor did anyone else, it seemed.

"It can't hurt to meet a good looking man while I'm waiting for my chance. They can't all be like Junior Clayton," she pondered aloud. She didn't want a man who would live and die either working in timbering jobs or down in a coal mine. Both of those jobs tied a man and his family right here and they could never move up in the world. She was tired of being thought of as backward and ignorant.

Lucinda's mind then settled on the fiasco that led to her actually meeting Jason McCall. She had been a mile from the paved road, and just around the next curve was a mud hole. Not hearing any cars, Lucinda started walking the high place in the center of the mud hole to save teetering along the narrow edge of the road. Cars coming down the road ran right through the middle and splashed anyone unfortunate enough to be on the side of the road. Lucinda was almost through the mud hole when the car came barreling around the curve. The driver gave a mighty blast on the horn, swung the car almost over the edge of the road and passed her before he came to a stop. Lucinda had jumped towards the side but had fallen in the edge of the mud hole. This was how Lucinda Harmon met Jason McCall. Looking back later, she often wished to the Lord she hadn't met him, and yet knew she would never forget him as long as she had breath in her body.

CHAPTER 4

Since May 24, 1950, the day she graduated, Lucinda had begged to go to Welch and get a job. Her dad had been adamant at first, but when she continued to pester him he said he'd see about it. This to Lucinda was another refusal, but she knew she would have to wait.

Much to her surprise, her dad came home one evening in September saying he had found her a job. Lucinda was ecstatic. This was the chance she had hoped for. She would have taken any kind of job just to get away. If she stayed here on the mountain nothing would change and she did not relish that thought. According to Grandpa and all the old folks who came to visit, Bradshaw Mountain had been the same for hundreds of years. The only thing that had changed was the use of cars and trucks by some people instead of the mules and horses used when Grandpa was a boy. People were born, grew up, married, raised their families, and died right here on the mountain; never venturing farther than Bradshaw or occasionally to Welch.

Like their mother, her sisters seemed to be repeating the pattern and Lucinda couldn't bear the thought of such a fate. Until now, she had loved the top of the mountain more than any place on earth. She recalled the fresh, clean breezes that blew through the sage grass on the tops of the hills and the howling winter blasts that moaned around the eaves of their old log house. She remembered the sweet smell of wild honeysuckle, the taste of mountain tea, and the huckleberries found all through the woods. She was entranced by the startled deer and rabbits she met on the woodland path to school and the birds which sang along the way. She loved the loneliness and also the sense of safety she felt on this mountain. But now that she was grown, the mountain seemed to epitomize all the hardships of women's lives and the isolation from the modern world. When her brother Nathan returned from World War II, he told of things she had only read about. He had been exposed to a broader world and it wasn't long before he left their mountain and McDowell County, never to return. He had gone into the Navy from a job at No. 1 Bartley mine. The job was waiting on him when he returned. Burb even had a letter from the superintendent of the coal company offering Nathan his old job but Nathan refused. Burb became upset and told Nathan how foolish he was to leave a good paying job, but it didn't deter Nathan's ambitions for a better way of life.

This only made the longing worse for Lucinda. Here was positive proof that there was a better way. There was so much she wanted to see and know and she ached to escape. It was like being caged in a box but Nathan had cut a hole in the box and she meant to get out.

Burb had been cutting timber for Jackson Wilson, a civil engineer, with an office in Welch. He had inquired about work in Welch for his daughter, describing her skills and how well she had done in school. Mr. Wilson had immediately said he needed some secretarial work and someone to answer the phone in his office. The following Monday morning Burb took Lucinda to Welch for her interview. Mr. Wilson shared an office with two other engineers, Joe Dalton and James Howery. The office was on the ground floor of the Richie Building on Bank Street. Lucinda was hired on the spot, with miniscule determination of her qualifications by Mr. Wilson.

Accompanied by her dad, Lucinda traversed the town seeking affordable rooms to rent. Through information obtained at the Flat Iron Drug Store, she found a room on the fifth floor of a building on Elkhorn Street at a right angle to Main Street.

A Mr. & Mrs. Hartley had an apartment with an extra room they were willing to rent to a nice, neat, and decent girl. "You can't bring any boyfriends up here," Mrs. Hartley said decisively. Lucinda assured her that she did not have any boyfriends.

"She'd best not get any either," stated Burb, "not unless she wants to find herself right back on the farm where she started."

All the way home Lucinda hummed with the truck engine, "Free at last, tum-tee-tum, free at last." She was still on Cloud Nine as she darted here and there helping put supper on the table until Nancy cautioned her, "Steady yursef, Lucy. You're goin to break something." A heartbroken Nancy tried to smile and act happy for Lucinda, who just couldn't be still. She even interrupted Burb's explanation of how he had gotten her a really good job. She surprised everyone even more by breaking her usually quiet manner with talk. She talked excitedly about the things she would buy for everybody, and lots of books.

After supper Lucinda went to the room she shared with Ellen, who was to be married shortly. She had borrowed a cardboard suitcase from Odell, her oldest sister. It wasn't very big but Lucinda only had the suit she graduated in, one pink dress, the fateful blue flowered dress, two skirts, two blouses, one slip, one bra, and five pairs of panties. She had some more made from bleached feed sacks, but she never intended to wear those again. She did not have a coat, but she had a heavy cardigan sweater that someone had given Ellen. Lucinda stood in her bare feet as she polished her loafers and carefully stored them in the suitcase.

She had gotten the loafers just before she graduated. She'd wanted a pair from ninth grade on, but there was just no money to buy shoes when she could have shoes that one of the older girls had given her. In her senior year she had gone to work in Ammar's Department Store in Iaeger during the Christmas holidays. She saved enough to buy the longed for loafers, and inserted shiny new pennies in their slots.

Even though she was elated, Lucinda found tears streaming down her face as she climbed into the truck the next morning. "Bye, Mommy, I'll see you this weekend. Now you don't have to worry. I won't be out nowhere at night. No, Mommy I won't talk to strange men. I'll be careful. I love you Mommy." This last was yelled out the window as the truck swung past the front gate and started up the hill.

Burb didn't talk much in the almost three-hour drive. This didn't bother Lucinda because she felt honored to be riding in the cab of the truck. Other than getting to ride in the cab when Burb now and then took her to the bus stop on his way to work, she had always ridden in the back. As she and Ellen had gotten older, they had been ashamed to ride to church in the back of the truck. They had to hold down their dresses and leave their hair to blow into a tangled mess. That put a stop to church going unless they walked.

Lucinda thought she was going to be sick going over Coalwood Mountain. She had always been plagued with motion sickness. Now she wondered how she survived the twenty-two miles each morning and evening to get through high school. The long ten miles of horseshoe bends down Bradshaw Mountain made her stomach queasy before she was halfway down. But from Stringtown to Bradshaw the road was fairly straight and her stomach would settle back to normal. The torture wasn't over, however, because she still had to travel the road between Bradshaw and Iaeger, where the high school was. This road was twelve miles of nothing but curves, bends, and dips and wound in and out around the side of the mountain above the Dry Fork River.

Lucinda remembered sitting on the front seat with her eyes glued to the road straight ahead the entire four years. After two disgusting and embarrassing mishaps, Lucinda was assured of the front seat the full time. Even then the trip was an ordeal. The curves were scary enough but mostly she was afraid of not making it to Iaeger before she lost her breakfast. She made it into Iaeger after those first two episodes, sometimes barely hitting the ground before disaster struck.

When Burb pulled to a stop below the apartment, he sat with the engine idling. "Cindy, girl you're awfully young to be out here on your own. Men are strange critters and they like pretty girls, so you have to be real careful. Men will offer you gifts and lots of stuff, but you get away from men like that and stay away from them. Don't you be nowhere with no boys or men by yourself. Do you understand what I'm talking about?"

"Daddy, I don't know a soul over here and I certainly won't go nowhere with strangers," replied Lucy. "You don't have to worry. I won't go out after dark and I won't be in none of these beer joints, and I won't be flirting with any boys, I promise."

"Honey, I hate to say this but boys ain't no worse than grown men, even married men," cautioned Burb with a grimace. "You just don't be too friendly with none of them, you hear?" Burb reached over and gathered her close and gave her a big hug. "After all, I ain't got but one Cindy and I don't want nothing to happen to her."

Lucinda hugged her dad tightly, opened the door and jumped from the running board to the street. Quickly she ran to the back for her suitcase which gave her time to force back the threatening tears. Then she climbed up on the running board, leaned through the window to hug her dad once more before she turned and ran up the stairs. If her dad saw the tears running down her cheeks, he might not let her stay.

Lucinda had mixed emotions that night; both fear and excitement, which kept her awake. So many new things were happening at once. She had never spent a night away from home except with her cousins in Jolo. Even then Ellen was there to tell how to act. Now, she was afraid of doing something that would make her feel more ignorant than she already felt.

What if she did something and Mrs. Hartley wouldn't let her stay with her? Also, she had no idea what she might encounter on this new job. This was a whole new world she was entering and she wanted to do well. Living with eight brothers and sisters who were so much older and wiser had left Lucinda with a feeling of inadequacy and very low self-esteem.

She felt good about learning however, because there is where she had gotten praise. Therefore, she liked to try new things when none of her family was present to tell her how silly and stupid she was. Trying to think of this as another learning experience Lucinda eagerly stepped out the next morning.

Stopping at the bus terminal, she bought a doughnut and milk which caused her stomach to cramp. She trashed the doughnut but hurriedly drank her milk before the final walk up Bank Street to the office.

What if she couldn't learn the job, or what if she didn't like Mr. Wilson? He had seemed nice enough when she and her dad came for the interview. Lucinda had been excellent in shorthand and typing before she graduated. She had a four point average in every subject but she did not know much about life, especially about life in the work world.

Mr. Wilson was already there when she arrived and greeted her with a brilliant toothy smile, which Lucinda thought unusual for an old man. Most people she knew had either lost some of their teeth or all of them by the time they were his age. This morning she noticed that his eyes watered even when he smiled. Lucinda felt uncomfortable and wondered why, but assumed it was because he was her boss.

He arose from his desk and started toward her saying, "Well, you certainly are a beautiful addition to this dreary office," just as the door opened. A short, slightly built man with a white hard hat and thick glasses came in with a roll of drafting paper under his arm.

"Morning Jim," said Mr. Wilson. "I've hired us a secretary. You know, you, Joe, and I, talked about it."

"Yeah, it was mentioned, but don't you think you should have let us in on the interview," replied Mr. Howery. "Well, introduce me. I'm at least getting to meet her. How old are you, young lady?"

Coming around the desk and putting an arm around Lucinda's shoulders, Mr. Wilson beamed at Mr.

Howery. "This is Lucinda Harmon. You know, Burb Harmon that is clearing that tract of land at Davy. Lucinda is his daughter. It's her first job but she knows typing and shorthand."

Sensing Lucinda's anxiety, Mr. Howery's hand came out as he smiled, "Welcome aboard, Lucinda Harmon." Lucinda shook his hand with relief. She still had a job. She gradually moved from the heavy arm around her shoulder. Mr. Wilson went out later and Lucinda spent the day answering the phone and typing letters, written in longhand, by both men. Typing was no problem, but she had never used a telephone except for one time and it was a party line. Lucinda prayed that she would not be asked to make any long distance calls until she became better acquainted with the instrument.

She learned that Mr. Howery lived on Summers Street and had two daughters, one the same age as she was herself. Sensing that Mr. Howery loved his family gave her a sense of trust, and made her feel easier about the job. Later, when Mr. Dalton came in and they were introduced, she found that same sense of comfort. She wondered why she felt this way with both Mr. Howery and Mr. Dalton, but so ill at ease with the older Mr. Wilson. She learned from her landlady that Mr. Wilson was married with a grown-up family and that he and his wife were pillars of the Presbyterian Church in town. Lucinda had always trusted church members and therefore thought she was just being silly.

During that first month, Mr. Wilson went away with his family for two weeks. This allowed Lucinda to get better acquainted with Mr. Howery and Mr. Dalton who laughed and joked as they did their work. They taught her about the telephone after her honest but embarrassed admission that she had never used a telephone. They were very helpful by telling her about places to go and places she should avoid. Their caring concern and advice reminded her of her dad, and she truly appreciated their help.

The following week Mr. Wilson was back and tried to get closer and even friendlier. He was either brushing against her as he passed or patting her on the shoulder or commenting on how nice she looked in her clothes. Lucinda was getting more and more wary, even fearful. Each weekend came with Lucinda wanting to tell her dad. But she dared not tell since she knew that Burb would make her quit and come home and she did not want to go home. Lucinda had already bought a winter coat, a nice pair of leather pumps and a pair of ankle boots but she still needed other things. She had now turned seventeen and in her short time here she had learned more about how to dress and what kinds of clothing to buy. The cold days of January, 1951 had arrived and the coat and boots were a must. She had to walk to work and also walk from the highway down Brushy Ridge when she went home.

The first time she came home from Welch, she almost panicked when the bus didn't turn down 83 at Yukon towards Bradshaw, but went right past the intersection towards War. She had bought a ticket to Bradshaw, and didn't have enough money to buy another ticket, plus pay the fare back on Sunday. When the bus pulled into the station at War, however, the driver said, "There's the bus to Bradshaw so you folks going that way better hustle." Lucinda did and it didn't cost her anymore. Also on this trip, she was one of the first passengers to get on, so she got the front seat, deciding this would be her method of making sure she avoided the embarrassing mishaps that motion sickness caused. It was bad enough to have that happen on a school bus, but to have it happen on a passenger bus was unthinkable.

Lucinda had been avoiding Mr. Wilson as much as possible but she was always on edge. Once when she had come in a little early to finish some letters, Mr. Wilson came in early and almost scared her to death. She had typed her letters and one letter needed a copy of a deed inserted. She made the stencil and was at the mimeograph machine when she felt arms go around her and a large hand cover her breast. She jerked back and screamed, shoving the machine against the window with a crash. When she turned, she realized that the arms and hand belonged to Mr. Wilson. When he saw the terror in her blanched face, he began to profusely apologize, saying he was just intending to give her a morning hug. Lucinda stood quaking with fear but Mr. Wilson acted so humble and kept apologizing until she finally calmed down enough to accept his apology. Now, however, she shivered every time she thought of him and quaked with fear when he came in the office when the others were not there. She had thought, since he seemed so sincere when he apologized, that he would never try hugging her again and he hadn't. However it did not stop his pats, smiles, and brushing against her at every opportunity. She became so edgy that any comments about her body or looks made her wary. She constantly looked for another job, but she wasn't yet eighteen and most people would not hire her. Mr. Wilson's actions were making her life miserable.

Even though January was cold, she made the trip home, as usual. She got off at Brushy Ridge and began the two mile walk to her home, pondering all the way about how to handle her situation. Again she took the high road in the middle of the mud hole, which now almost covered the entire road except the high spot in the middle. In winter the mud holes turned to soft gushy mud that clung like glue. There were some dry spots on the left side of the road which saved her from another spill. Again a car's horn blasted as it came speeding up the hill. This time Lucinda jumped to the side of the road and the car came to a jarring halt just past the mud hole. The door opened and Lucinda Harmon and Jason McCall looked at each other with bated breath. Jason interrupted the silence with, "Lord, girl we're going to have to stop meeting like this."

He got out of the car and came around the hood. "Still walking in the middle of the road, aren't you?" queried Jason with a smile. "Where have you been, anyway? I haven't seen you in months." He was surprised by his delight in seeing her.

Lucinda was almost speechless. She had told no one, but she had daydreamed about Jason from the day he had offered her a ride almost a year ago. She often re-lived the disaster of the day they actually met, and the joy of being held in his arms. Now, here he was again and she was too embarrassed to look up. Jason reached over and lifted her chin, "Hey, I didn't scare you that bad, did I? I've been watching for you, you know. Aunt Sarie told me you had gone to work in some town. What kind of work are you doing?"

Getting control of her emotions Lucinda smiled, "I have a job in a civil engineering office in Welch. I take dictation, type, and answer the phone. Why were you watching for me? Did you want to see me make a fool of myself again? I have learned a few things since I've been away, you know." She moved from her precarious spot on the edge to more level ground and then did a bold sashaying step towards him saying, "Besides, why would a big city doctor be asking about a hillbilly like me?" She rolled her eyes in question.

Jason grinned at her attempt at flirtation, "You didn't make a fool of yourself. It was just an unfortunate accident. You looked real cute - even almost beautiful, especially in your wet dress," he teased.

Lucinda cringed at the same blatant admiration she had been warding off from Mr. Wilson. She shivered at the thought of Mr. Wilson and now here was her dream man saying some of the same things. This 'city slicker' probably thought she was dumb enough to believe him. She had learned the hard way that some men tried to use flattery to take advantage of naïve young girls. Therefore, she straightened her shoulders and glared at Jason, "I don't like to be made a fool of Dr. McCall. If you'll excuse me, I'm on my way home and I don't want to be late. Goodbye, Doctor." Lucinda marched off down the road.

Lucinda didn't look back but she clearly heard, "Well, I'll be damned. Stupid hillbilly, what do I care?" before a door slammed and the car roared past her flinging mud in all directions.

Lucinda wanted to find someplace and bawl her eyes out but no telling who may come along. Gossip was the 'spice of life' on Bradshaw Mountain and night wouldn't fall before Nancy would be asking why she had been crying. Of course she could blame the mud spattered all over her first new coat.

Lucinda slowly wiped her eyes, squared her shoulders, and walked faster muttering aloud, "I'm not going to waste any more time dreaming about you." However, the ever present image of Jason stayed in her head as well as the memory of how it felt to be held close in his arms.

CHAPTER 5

Back in the office Lucinda spent more time avoiding Mr. Wilson than she did typing letters. Never before had anyone touched Lucinda inappropriately and he had scared her half to death. Anytime she was alone in the office, she watched the door warily; fearing a repeat of that hug and groping hand from the back. Such constant vigilance was wearing her nerves thin as well as her body. She didn't have a scale but knew she had lost weight, since most of her skirts and dresses were bigger in the waist. Nancy had noticed it the last time she was home and asked if she was sick.

Nancy was not the only one who asked the same question. She had gone with Nancy to a bean stringing at Aunt Rhoda Wagner's. While Lucinda was threading the big needles used to pull the string thread through the beans before they were hung to dry, several of the women had commented on her weight loss. Some of them thought she might be homesick and others thought it was due to not getting good farm cooking. However, Sir Marget had slyly hinted that maybe she was keeping late hours. Nancy put a stop to her tongue, "Sir Marget, if you kept your hands as busy as you do your tongue, you'd be better off. Lucy ain't that kind of girl and you know it."

Lucinda went back to Welch determined that she was going to stop worrying and beg the Lord to help her. She told herself that Mr. Wilson couldn't really harm her in broad daylight right there in the office. But since the office had no windows opening on the street, Lucinda was still uneasy.

Finally, in early March, she came back from lunch and found a note from Mr. Howery. He wanted the letters

on his desk finished and also stated that he would be out
the rest of the day. At one o'clock Mr. Wilson had not
returned from lunch and Lucinda hoped he didn't. Most of
the time the other engineers were only out for a few
minutes at a time. The fourth week of working, Mr. Wilson
had offered to take Lucinda with him to the job site to see
her dad. She went, but after that one time, Lucinda had
always declined with the excuse of too much work. She
had also declined an offer of a weekend trip to Huntington
where she would be taken to a play.

She had gotten so frightened on that one occasion
of going to see her dad that she didn't dare repeat it. She
had been offered new clothes, a driver's license, and free
access to Mr. Wilson's car all due to Mr. Wilson's wish to
help a pretty girl better herself. Lucinda hadn't known how
to handle this kind of talk and finally said, "Do you think
your wife would mind helping me shop? She'd be afraid of
riding with me since I am just learning to drive." Mr.
Wilson acted astonished for a second before saying his
wife seldom went out. "I like helping young people and
my wife is sick a lot. I get awfully lonely having to go
everywhere by myself. You would enjoy a trip to
Huntington, wouldn't you?"

Lucinda told him that her dad would not want her
to go and besides she couldn't afford to do things like that.
Mr. Wilson reached over and patted her arm smiling, "It's
free, Lucinda. I don't want a thing except you could be a
little friendlier and nicer to a lonely man." All this was said
as her arms were rubbed and her hand squeezed and
patted and with the admonition that if she sat so close to
the outside door it might come open and she could fall out
and get injured. Still, Lucinda had clung to the door. If Mr.
Wilson had taken an off road or pulled over to stop she
knew it would be easier to jump out and run.

After that, all of Mr. Wilson's offers and pleas fell on deaf ears. Lucinda still stayed in a dread and couldn't wait to turn eighteen, upon which she had been promised another job. She had gone to Appalachian Power Company saying she was eighteen and was hired but she had to have a physical and bring in a birth certificate. She had already lied about her age and now she lied again, saying she didn't have a birth certificate, but they told her it would be filed at the courthouse in the clerk's office. Then she had to confess to her fabrication, "I really need a job. I can't help it because I graduated so early, can't you take me now?" The manager was very sorry but said that was a hard and fast rule and they could take her on as a trainee at eighteen but not before. She had several months to wait and dreaded every day.

On a fairly warm day for early March she was typing and dreaming about another job when the door opened ushering in Mr. Wilson. Under his arm was a large box of candy, which he deposited on her desk as he went to hang his coat on the hall tree. "I felt you should have a reward for all the fine work you're doing," said Mr. Wilson as he came to stand behind her chair. "You do like chocolates, don't you, Lucinda?" he inquired as he ran his hand down the length of her hair. "You have such beautiful hair. The color is like sunshine on honey. Do any of your boy friends tell you that?"

Terrified, Lucinda pushed back her chair and jumped up, almost knocking the chair over. Mr. Wilson said "oomph" as the chair landed on his protruding stomach. But Lucinda didn't even notice in her panic to get out of reach. She turned from the far side of the room near the mimeograph machine and saw his look of surprise. "Oh! Did that chair hurt you Mr. Wilson? I'm sorry but I have a lot of letters to get out for Mr. Howery. He wants them finished this evening so I have to hurry."

Mr. Wilson started towards her again smiling, "Yes, I saw the note Jim left for you. He will be away all evening. It will give us a chance to get better acquainted and have a little talk. You'll have plenty of time to finish those letters. Here, sit down and open your chocolates. I'd like to know your plans about the future. Do you want to go to college? I talked to your dad yesterday and he said you had always wanted to go." Smiling benevolently, Mr. Wilson came closer and patted her arm. "I had no idea you were so ambitious. I just might be able to help you go to college. What do you think of that?"

Lucinda moved away, quaking inside. She couldn't stand for that old man to touch her. "I do want to go to college, Mr. Wilson, but I need to work until I'm eighteen in order to get the money."

Following close, on her heels Mr. Wilson reached to touch Lucinda's shoulder. She jerked away and turned for the door but tripped on the leg of a desk and landed full against his chest. Of course, she then found herself engulfed in a bone crushing hug and a kiss, which only missed her lips because she quickly turned her head. Giving a frantic shove, Lucinda jerked free and ran out the door. A misty rain was falling but that didn't hinder her flight as she sped up the street away from the office, leaving her coat behind. From there she walked up one street and down the other until she was too chilled, damp, and tired to think, and then dragged herself up to her room. She shut the door and cried herself into an exhausted sleep. She awoke the next morning at her usual time, more tired than when she lay down. In the bathroom she felt that she just couldn't go on as she was, and earnestly tried to pray. It had been a long time since she had sought help from the Lord. She did not know whether to go back to the office. She didn't even know if she had a job. So, like Grandpa had always told her, "When you don't know what to do or how to handle some problem, just remember that the good Lord always hears." She hoped the good Lord had heard her cries from the floor of the bathroom. When she rose from her knees she felt that she needed to go back and talk to Mr. Howery and Mr. Dalton. She may have lost her job, especially if Mr. Wilson told them a different story. She never wanted to see Mr. Wilson again, but if she wanted another job she would need references. If Mr. Howery and Mr. Dalton knew the true story she felt that they would both write letters for her. Finally she sought the advice of Mrs. Hartley, her landlady.

After listening, Mrs. Hartley gave her a reassuring hug and told her to go straight to Mr. Howery and tell him exactly what had happened.

Dreading every step that brought her closer, Lucinda made her way to the engineers' office. When she pushed open the door, she almost wept for joy to find Mr. Howery alone at his desk. Quickly, before her nerve failed her, Lucinda walked up to his desk and asked if he had time to talk with her. Mr. Howery, seeing her puffy eyes and trembling lips, pushed back his papers and asked her to be seated. When Lucinda had finished with her tale, Mr. Howery sat swinging his glasses back and forth for a few seconds. "Lucinda, you come on to work just as you have been and either Joe or I will be present at all times. In the meantime, why don't you look around for another job and then we will see what Mr. Jackson Wilson has to say for himself."

Lucinda, taking Mr. Howery's advice, found it very difficult to even look at Mr. Wilson, who entered the office about 10 o'clock. His smiling, "Good Morning All," seemed to be forced as he looked first at Mr. Howery and Mr. Dalton. When he turned to Lucinda, she realized he was uneasy and wanted to make sure that she hadn't told anyone about the incident. "Why did you run out yesterday? I think of you like a daughter. I didn't mean any harm. I'm sorry if I frightened you," said Mr. Wilson, beaming a smile to everyone in the office. "Lucinda has done such good work that I bought her a box of chocolates yesterday. She was trying so hard to get all those letters out and had to make some stencils for the mimeograph machine. She tripped as she started back to her desk and landed against my chest and I kept her from falling. I guess she hasn't been around many men because it scared her nearly to death when I kept her from falling," he explained. "You have no need to fear me, Lucinda. I wouldn't hurt you," he entreated.

"I guess you are right, Mr. Wilson. I haven't been around many men," stammered Lucinda. "Let's just forget it ever happened," she begged.

Mr. Wilson smiled benevolently, "Of course, my dear. We'll go on as if it never happened."

Mr. Howery and Mr. Dalton were as good as their word, for they never left Lucinda alone in the office again. They even began to help Lucinda look for work in another office in town.

Through a friendship of Mr. Howery's, Lucinda was able to go to work for Bascom Fidelity Insurance on Court Street. Mr. Howery had written a letter of reference, plus called Mr. Bascom on Lucinda's behalf. Lucinda did not know how much Mr. Howery had told Mr. Bascom about the situation. She was afraid that people would blame her for Mr. Wilson's actions, and hoped he wasn't told. Nancy had always said, "If a girl acts nice and decent, men won't say things to her or get out of the way." Lucinda knew she had acted the same with Mr. Howery and Mr. Dalton and they certainly hadn't acted like Mr. Wilson.

When she went for the interview and was hired, Lucinda walked hurriedly back to her room occasionally wiping the tears from her face. When she reached her room and went into the bathroom, she wept aloud since she felt she could not be seen or heard.

Since nothing was said at the insurance office about the incident with Mr. Wilson, Lucinda assumed that Mr. Bascom did not know anything about it. She decided she would put it behind her and only remember that some men paid compliments and bought gifts expecting something in return. Lucinda knew she would probably be wary of compliments and trusting men for a long time to come.

She still had to go back to the Engineers office, and all the way she breathed a silent "Thank you Lord, thank you so very much." She also thanked Mr. Howery and Mr. Dalton for all their kindnesses to her. Mr. Wilson was out and she was very glad she did not even have to say goodbye. She questioned Mr. Howery about whether it was wise to not say anything to Mr. Wilson and was reassured by his answer. "Just go on and don't worry about Mr. Wilson, Lucinda. Joe and I will concoct some kind of story. He'll be afraid to say anything. He knows that we were not taken in by his story about what he did that day."

So, Lucinda walked out of the first real job she had ever had a wiser girl in the ways of the world. She was again going into a new situation and work that she knew nothing about. It made her nervous and afraid but her grandpa had always said, "If you want something bad enough, you can get it. But you have to be willing to work hard, take chances, and pray," and Lucinda felt like she had done all three. After a restless night of worry and anxiety, she went silently into the bathroom. It was a small windowless room with sound proof walls, or so Lucinda thought. Feeling that the Lord had heard her with the fiasco of Mr. Wilson, she again knelt to pray. She didn't even know why she knelt; it just seemed like something she should do. "Lord, please forgive me if I did anything to cause Mr. Wilson to act like he did. Now Lord, I am to start a new job and I ask that you please help me to learn what is expected. I'm so afraid Lord. Everything that happens is something new. Please protect me Lord, and help me to see danger. Hold my hand please and guide me," freely begged Lucinda aloud. Mrs. Hartley sat with her coffee cup suspended in the air as she heard the earnest plea, then slowly wiped her eyes.

Lucinda finally arose from her knees feeling much better about this new endeavor. "Well, I'm not so sure about praying but I sure have tried," thought Lucinda as she showered and dressed in preparation for her new job. Stepping out of her bedroom later, she suddenly grinned, "I've learned about showers, inside toilets, riding buses, telephones, Dictaphones, mimeograph machines, and I've also learned a lot about men since I came over here, especially feely, touchy old men." She winced, shook her head knowingly, squared her shoulders and went humming out the door and down the stairs.

CHAPTER 6

Lucinda began her new job in the last week of March and Mr. Bascom, his wife Ellen, and Mary Lou, the other girl that worked in the agency, were very kind, patient, and helpful. Before a month was out, Lucinda was able to wait on customers and type most of the forms used in applying for insurance. Her pay wasn't as much as she had made working in the engineering office. Also in the first month of her new job, Mr. Hartley became ill and had to have a separate bedroom. Since Lucinda's was the only extra room in the Hartley apartment, she had to move. Mrs. Hartley apologized and hated to see her leave but Lucinda assured her that she understood. In April, she found a new place to live on lower McDowell Street but a month's rent in advance was required. So, on that weekend Lucinda was stuck in Welch with very little money. She didn't even have the bus fare to go home. Her new landlady, Mrs. Sparks, seemed very nice and had offered to cook supper for Lucinda, when she was home. Had Mrs. Sparks been there that weekend, she would have let her have a sandwich and coffee, but she and her husband were away for the weekend.

After counting her money carefully, Lucinda decided she would get a doughnut for breakfast, not eat lunch, and buy a hamburger and soda for dinner on Saturday. That left Sunday to get through and she could have one meal which would keep her from starving. Lucinda walked the streets looking in the shop windows, going into Woolworth's and looking at so much in every aisle that the clerks began to watch her very closely. She was so hungry that when the clock in the courthouse struck six o'clock Lucinda felt it was time to eat. She hurried quickly to Franklin's Dairy Bar and ordered her hamburger and a 7-Up soda. Someone had ordered fries but hadn't waited for them. Marie, one of the waitresses who knew Lucinda, asked if she would like to have them with her hamburger. Lucinda thanked her and took her order to a booth in front of the window through which she would be able to watch the people on the street. She sat happily savoring every bite when someone stopped in front of the window and looked straight at her. Dr. Jason McCall smiled and walked around the corner to the entrance, came in, and made his way to her booth.

"May I sit down, Miss Harmon?" asked Jason.

Lucinda's eyes were large in her face and forgetting that he thought of her as a dumb hillbilly, she smiled brightly as she nodded and said, "Sure. What are you doing here?"

Jason eased himself into the seat across from her and sat studying her closely. "Why have you lost weight?" he questioned. "Don't you earn enough to buy food?"

Lucinda, expecting him to tell her how pleased he was to see her, was astonished. "What a thing to say," she sputtered. "Every time I see you, you either tell me I'm dirty, or stupid, and now I'm skinny," she raged angrily as she swallowed to control the threatening tears.

"I'm sorry, Lucinda," said a contrite Jason. He reached over and picked up the trembling hand as she put down her soda. He gave her hand a reassuring squeeze while looking at her very kindly. "I didn't mean that you were skinny. Honestly, I didn't. But you have lost weight since I last saw you. I only asked out of concern," he smiled and rubbed his thumb across the top of her hand in a comforting fashion.

Feeling better and now miraculously not so lonesome, Lucinda smiled. "It's okay Doctor. I was feeling a little lonely. You see, I usually go home on the weekends."

"So, I guess you stayed over for a big date tonight," queried Jason.

"No, I didn't - didn't have - ," catching herself in time from telling him about her lack of funds, "I didn't want to go home this weekend. I have to learn to be away more than a week at a time, you know."

"Good. So, now you're free to show me some of the town, aren't you?" smiled Jason.

"There's not that much to see, really. There's only the ball park, the golf course, and the Sportsman's Club at Gary. That's all there is to see. I haven't really been to any of them except the ball park. Mary Lou, from work, says the Sportsman's Club is really nice. You may have to be a member to get in, though," replied Lucinda.

"I have several hours to kill tonight and I'm lonesome myself. Why don't we spend them together? Then we'll both have someone to talk to," smiled Jason, still holding her hand.

Pulling her hand free, Lucinda looked at Jason warily, "I don't know why you are doing this. You must have numerous girlfriends, prettier and smarter than I am."

"But, my dear girl, I am a stranger in this part of the country. I haven't met many girls yet," replied Jason. Getting to his feet after glancing to make sure she was finished, Jason reached for her hand again and pulled her gently to her feet. "Come on, let's go see the sights."

So, once again Lucinda found herself in the doctor's car but this time she was clean, and didn't have a sprained ankle.

That night lying in her bed, Lucinda went over the evening, savoring every word, every look, and every touch and storing them away to be cherished forever. They had first gone up through the narrow two-lane road past the

Gary No. 9 Coal Tipple with its towering smoke stack shooting clouds of white puffy steam into the sky. Lucinda found Jason so easy to talk to. They talked about the coal industry and how it created dependency in its workers. Lucinda told Jason how she had always thought people living in the coal towns or coal camps lived well. "Really, I thought they were rich. They always had the latest fashions and were in everything at school. Their parents didn't seem to mind what they bought as long as the mines were working. Even when the mines were on strike, it didn't seem to make much difference. But, my brother Gordon says that they owe the company store so much that they will never break even."

Jason was puzzled, "Don't your parents go to the company store?"

"We don't buy much but what we do buy, we pay cash for. My dad wouldn't go in debt. I can just hear him saying, 'If you don't have the money to pay for something, you'd better learn to do without it.' Besides, none of us, except Gordon I guess, has ever been in the company store to buy anything. We go to Jones and Spry or to L & R department stores," answered Lucinda.

They talked about education and Lucinda told him about her dream of going to college. Jason told her what Aunt Sarie had said about her wanting to go to college. "I just could not understand your dad not wanting you to go to Berea College. Doesn't he know that it would not cost him anything? I know it's in Kentucky but it's the only school I know of that will allow you to work to pay for your education. After all, there are trains and buses and you wouldn't be stranded with no way home. I just don't understand since he must have known how much you wanted to go. There would have been no question from my parents if I had a sister," stated Jason. He sympathized

with her and told her to keep trying and perhaps she
would find a way to go.

"You don't understand," said Lucinda. "Girls on the
mountain don't go off to work or to school. Ellen and I
graduated from high school, but I'm the first girl in our
family to move away from home to work. People on the
mountain don't like, or are afraid of anything new, and
girls leaving home before they marry, is a new thing. I
don't really know why, but I do know they are afraid. I feel
very lucky to be working over here. I guess I'll never get to
go to college. I don't see a way of doing it, and even if I
did, Dad wouldn't let me."

"Do you think it's a religious thing?" asked Jason.

Lucinda thoughtfully said, "I don't think so. Of
course the Bible does say that women are to remain silent
in the church, and if they need to know anything they are
to ask their husbands, doesn't it? That has to mean
something different from that though, since some women
have drunks for husbands. Surely they're not expected to
ask a drunk for answers, are they?"

"Lord, I don't know. I've only read what the Sunday
school teachers made us read and didn't remember that,"
grinned Jason. "How do you know so much about the
Bible? Do you go to Sunday School?"

"We don't have Sunday school or any of that stuff,"
said Lucinda smugly. "Grandpa always said it was man-
made teaching and we need to be taught by the Lord."

"He may have been right," laughed Jason. "I sure
didn't learn much from my Sunday school teachers. I'm
glad I went though. It probably kept me out of a lot of
trouble."

Jason asked her why none of the established
churches were to be found on the tops of the mountains...
Lucinda had never thought about it but she knew that in

towns the companies built the churches and maybe helped pay the preachers. She wasn't sure about that but she would ask her cousins who lived in Jolo. That time she had gone to church with them everybody put money in a plate that was passed around. At the time she hadn't thought about it but now she realized that the preachers would have to have more than the small amount on the plate just to buy groceries. She knew that their preacher didn't hold down a job like Preacher Hiram did, because her cousin told her he didn't. So, he got an income from somewhere and she knew her parents as well as other mountain people didn't believe in paying preachers. She had often heard Preacher Sam Addair say that the gift was its own payday.

"The gifts and callings to preach are gifts of God and we don't believe they need any other rewards. All of our preachers hold down jobs just like everybody else," stated Lucinda proudly.

Jason came back with, "How do they have time to write their sermons and visit the sick then?"

"Write their sermons" snorted Lucinda. "That's man-made stuff. The preacher is just the instrument through which the Lord sends his messages to his people and the preachers don't write it down. They couldn't anyway. They don't know whether the Lord will bless them with a message or not. They have to depend on the Lord. Besides, we pay our own way and we don't want some organization sending us somebody to save our souls, which aren't lost anyway," stated Lucinda firmly.

Jason laughed, thoroughly enjoying her seriousness and homespun philosophy. She looked like a little kid explaining something of dire importance, and he realized that she was completely sincere. "Lucinda, I don't know about your faith but I know you are convinced. I might even consider attending one of your church services. Does Aunt Sarie believe the way you do?"

"I'm not a church member," mumbled Lucinda "but I believe just like my Grandpa did, and Dad and Mom also. Aunt Sarie is the oldest member, and one of the best in the church where Dad and Mom have their membership."

They had laughing arguments and agreements as they climbed on up along the tree lined road to the gates of the Sportsman's Club. Sure enough a big sign stated, For Members Only.

Reluctantly, they turned and started back down the mountain. The car windows were down and the moonlight flickered in and out through the trees making eerie patterns on the roadway. Lucinda had never been in a car alone with a man at night before and here she was not only alone but in a stretch of road which ran right through the woods. This moonlit night will be another one of my treasured memories thought Lucinda, feeling so happy she could almost fly right away. She plummeted to earth, however, when Jason pulled to the side of the road and stopped. Lucinda turned in fright, "Why are you stopping? I want to go back to Welch." She had suddenly remembered her mother telling her what happened to girls who went off with strangers and Lucinda was beginning to panic. Jason looked at her and realized she was scared, "Lucinda, I'm not going to rape you. I wanted to just stop and talk." Seeing that Lucinda was as scared as ever, he said, "I don't guess we need to talk here." He started the car and drove on down the mountain until they came out of the woods into the town of Filbert. Lights were still on in all the houses and Lucinda breathed easier. They had talked about mining, timbering, schools, and

Lucinda's job, but Jason had told her nothing really about himself.

"Do you have brothers or sisters?" asked Lucinda.

"One brother," said Jason.

"Are there only two children in your family?" asked Lucinda in amazement. "Is your mother sick? I mean, most women have more than two children, don't they?"

Jason let out a roar of laughter, "My mother would be sick if she had more than two, I think," he said, still laughing. "Lucinda, where I come from, there are many families with only one or two children. They feel it is too expensive to raise a big family."

Lucinda sat very still, mulling this idea over. She had been raised to believe that a woman had every child the Lord intended her to have. Now, Jason was saying that women could have only what they wanted. He was a doctor and surely he would know. She wondered how his mother kept from it since she had to sleep with her husband and do that- nasty business- that made babies. Her mother, her sisters, and other women who Lucinda had heard talk, acted like having babies couldn't be helped. *"Gosh, I hope he never finds out how dumb I am or he'll never want to see me again,"* thought Lucinda.

She sat quietly pondering until Jason said, "What's wrong? Do you want the windows up? If you'll slide over this way a little, the wind won't blow your hair."

By this time they were back in Welch and Jason drove straight on to the Welch-Pineville road instead of making the left to Lucinda's place. She sat up really straight and demanded, "Where are you going? This is not the way to McDowell Street."

"There's a drive-in restaurant on this road and I thought we could go there and get a sundae or a sandwich. I'm hungry," replied Jason. Lucinda relaxed. She was hungry too, but she wouldn't have said anything for the world. She could get a sandwich and not eat all of it, then take it back to her room and have it tomorrow.

They pulled into the Sterling Drive-In and a waitress came out to take their order. Jason turned to inquire what Lucinda wanted. She was unsure since she may be expected to pay. So, she said, "You go ahead and order. I'm not really hungry."

Jason shook his head in disbelief, "We'll have two double cheeseburgers, fries, and two vanilla milkshakes to go, unless this lady says otherwise," he said with authority, while looking at Lucinda.

"That- that will be fine" stammered Lucinda. What if she didn't like milkshakes? She had always been afraid to order one, even though she had wanted to, but they were more expensive than a coke or lemonade.

Jason turned the radio on and "Too Young" sung by Nat King Cole poured out into the night air. Lucinda felt like some magical spell had been cast on her. Here she was with the man she had dreamed about for months and months, on a moonlit night and listening to beautiful music. Jason sat looking at her for a long time and Lucinda couldn't have looked away if her life depended on it. The waitress came with two bags and two milkshakes and Jason put them down in the seat between them. He paid the girl and then turned again to look at Lucinda, who was sitting spellbound. He revved the engine and in a slightly gruff voice whispered, "Let's get out of here."

From then until the evening was over, Lucinda was caught up in a magic world. They drove to the little park up Browns' Creek and taking their food to one of the stone tables, sat side by side in the moonlight eating and talking. Lucinda didn't eat but she did drink the milkshake. It must have been good but Lucinda really couldn't remember because an owl up in the woods let out his night call and made her jump. Jason automatically put his arm around her and even when she realized what it was, she didn't move away. They lost track of time until Lucinda realized there wasn't much traffic anymore and asked Jason the time. When he said two o'clock she jumped up in fright.

"It's too late. What if my landlady won't let me in?" she cried.

Jason got up and took her hand. "Come on, I'll take you back. Don't you have a key to your own door? You don't have to go through her house do you?"

"No, but she said I couldn't have boy friends in," said Lucinda.

"Were you planning to invite me in?" Jason asked with a smile.

"No, I wasn't going to invite you in. I only have one room, but she might hear me come in and tell Dad," Lucinda fretted.

Jason just shook his head and drew her to the car still clutching her bag with the sandwich and fries. Neither of them said anything until he pulled the car to the side of the street before the house. He got out and came around to open her door, which she already had open and was halfway out. "Lucinda, couldn't you wait, you won't let a fellow be a gentleman, will you?" questioned Jason as he walked with her across the street and started up the stairs. Lucinda knew she should have waited to let him open her door but men around here didn't do things like that, or at least, the men she knew didn't.

"Stop right here! You can't go in here. What will people think?" blurted Lucinda.

"I hope they'll think that I'm bringing home a very beautiful, but confused young lady," murmured Jason.

"Well, you can't go any farther. Thank you for a nice evening." She didn't get any farther for Jason had pulled her swiftly into his arms and kissed her soundly. Then he turned back down the stairs and went whistling out the door.

Lucinda stood transfixed and touched her lips with trembling fingers. So, that's how a kiss made a girl feel.

CHAPTER 7

In the weeks that followed, Lucinda futilely looked along the streets in hopes of seeing Jason again. He hadn't exactly said that he would be back but while they were eating he had said, "I'll have to make a way to see you again. You're too pretty for your own good." Lucinda had smiled and told him she would be glad to see him again. She made two trips home and even went into Bradshaw once but still did not see Jason. She was afraid to ask about him because that would cause questions and if Burb knew she had seen Jason that would be the end of her stay in Welch.

She knew that Jason was treating Aunt Sarie, and thought she might learn something by asking about her. When she asked, however, Nancy said, "They've been settin' up with her for two weeks now, poor soul. I don't figure it will be long now, but you never can tell. The Lord may have some purpose to keep her here a little longer. I stayed night afore last. Me and Oprey stayed together. It makes it hard for either one of us with Burb getting up so early to go to work and Oprey's man crippled. I allus worry with that old pot bellied stove they got in the front room. If the house wus to catch on fire, what in the world he'd do about getting the younguns out, I don't know." Lucinda still did not know anything about Jason since no mention was made of him.

Now it was the first of May and when Lucinda went back to Welch, she decided to erase any thought of Jason from her mind. Ralph Baxter, who was the town postman, and delivered mail on McDowell Street, always stopped and talked to her when they passed. He had often asked her to go to the movies. Just last week he had asked again but of course, she had said no. On the bus ride over the mountains she thought that dating Ralph might help her forget Jason.

On Tuesday, she saw Ralph coming up the street as she was on her way to work and she waited.

"My! You look chipper this morning," greeted Ralph.

"I am chipper, if that means happy," smiled Lucinda.

"Are you happy enough to go to a movie with me tonight? *South Pacific* is playing at the Paramount and I know you like musicals." Once when they were waiting in line at Franklin's Dairy Bar, Lucinda had told him how much she had enjoyed, *Singing in the Rain*, with Debbie Reynolds and Gene Kelly.

Lucinda smiled as she said, "You know, I believe I am."

His face wreathed in a broad grin. Ralph did a two-step, bowed, and then said, "I'm happy, too. Is six o'clock too early? The feature starts at seven but sometimes the cartoons and previews are nice."

"Sure, six will be fine with me," smiled Lucinda.

She started on and Ralph said, "What's the hurry? I may want to take you to Franklin's Dairy Bar for a sandwich."

"All right, that sounds good. Right now though, I have to go or I'll be late for work. See you at six," said Lucinda as she hurried down the street and turned left up Court Street where she worked.

Maybe if I date Ralph, he will take me to the Starland Drive-In Theater at Big Four, thought Lucinda. She was like a sponge soaking up every new thing she could experience. If she heard about it she wanted to try it except when it involved intimacy with the opposite sex. If a man wanted to do more than kiss her she quickly cut the date short and never saw him again. A drive-in movie and a carnival were two things she wanted to attend and now maybe she could. A carnival was coming to Vivian Bottom above Kimball and she couldn't wait. Also, Mary Lou had said it was fun to go to Blakeley Field and see a baseball game. The way Mary Lou described it made Lucinda want to go even though she knew nothing about ball games, or really any sports. She hadn't taken physical education in high school because Burb wouldn't allow her to wear shorts or pants and she couldn't go on the gym floor without tennis shoes which she didn't have.

Lucinda planned where she would ask Ralph to take her first and began looking forward to the evening. She really hadn't been having much fun except for the time Jason took her out, which she would never forget.

"This should get Dr. Jason McCall right out of my head," Lucinda said aloud as she dashed in the office door on the eight o'clock chime of the courthouse clock. She hurried upstairs to her desk, put her purse in a drawer, slipped the headphones on, placed a cylinder in the Dictaphone, uncovered her typewriter and went to work. In an hour she had finished the letters on the Dictaphone but still had some shorthand to transcribe before lunch. She was typing rapidly when she was interrupted by a request on the intercom.

Thinking Mr. Bascom wanted her to take dictation; she gathered her pad and pencils and hurried into his office. To her surprise, when she opened the door, there were three strangers in Mr. Bascom's office. Feeling she had been mistaken, she turned to leave but was stopped by Mr. Bascom. "Come in, Lucinda. There's somebody here I want you to meet."

"Lucinda, this is Dr. Charles Stewart, President of Concord College," stated Mr. Bascom, putting his hand on the shoulder of a man standing beside his desk. "Dr. Stewart, this is Lucinda Harmon, the girl we were discussing." Dr. Stewart arose extending his hand and Lucinda shook his hand while looking very puzzled. Mr. Bascom turned to go behind his desk and then stopped apologetically, "Oh! I'm sorry. Lucinda, this is Mr. Rogers, the College Dean, and Mr. Hatfield, the man who has all the money," said Mr. Bascom in introduction.

After shaking hands with each man, Lucinda took the chair Mr. Bascom indicated. "Dr. Stewart is an old friend of mine. In fact, we went to college together. Of course, he's moved up in the world and I'm still climbing the ladder," quipped Mr. Bascom. "Anyway, Dr. Stewart is here in the county visiting all the high schools to promote Concord College. Luckily, he stopped by to see me. We started talking and I thought about you, Lucinda. I've heard you talking to Ellen and Mary Lou about how you'd love to go to college. You would like to go, wouldn't you?"

Lucinda's mouth dropped open in speechless amazement. Right out of the blue Mr. Bascom was asking her if she wanted the moon, the stars, and everything. "Oh yes, Mr. Bascom, more than anything," breathed Lucinda. Then reality set in and she said, "But I can't go, Mr. Bascom. I don't have the money and Dad won't let me go to Berea or someplace where I could work my way through."

"What if you could work your way through at Concord?" questioned Dr. Stewart.

"I'd love that, sir, but Concord doesn't have that kind of program, does it?" asked Lucinda.

"No, we actually don't have a program like Berea's but we do have work study. It's a new program, and you could make enough to pay for your tuition, room, and meals. You would still have to pay for transportation and buy your own books and other expenses. How does that sound to you?" asked Dr. Stewart with a smile.

"Oh! Dr. Stewart, it sounds wonderful," beamed Lucinda, but then sobered. "I don't have any money at all though and no way to get any except from my work here. I had given up the idea of going to college and spent my money on clothes," murmured Lucinda.

"That will be one less expense, then," stated Mr. Bascom. "Lucinda, I feel that you should try this. You are smart and a hard worker and I just don't think you should pass up an opportunity like this. Ellen and I have talked about it and even if Charles hadn't stopped by we were going to suggest it."

"What would I have to do to get started and how much money would I have to have?" Lucinda asked Dr. Stewart.

"You'd need to fill out an application, which I have here, have Mr. Addair mail your high school transcript to us, then come to Concord and register for summer classes. I think it would be easier for you to get introduced to college life in the summer when there are not so many students. As to money," he turned to Mr. Rogers, "What do you think, Theron? Could she get by on $300 for this summer?" asked Dr. Stewart.

Mr. Rogers studied a moment, "If she can find all used books and live frugally I think that would do it."

Lucinda stood quietly thinking and the men waited patiently, "How soon would I have to get all this done?"

"This is the first of May and everything should be done by the last week in May because classes start the first of June for the first session," replied Dr. Stewart.

"I'll have to go home and talk this over with Dad and maybe he will take me to Iaeger to ask Mr. Addair to mail my transcript." Lucinda told Mr. Bascom and Dr.

Stewart about how difficult it was to travel anywhere. Burb only had the big old logging truck and he was always working. It was just especially hard to get to any place when one lived on Bradshaw Mountain.

Picking up the phone, Mr. Bascom smiled, "Well, we can take care of that right now." He dialed a number and waited, then said, "Hello, John Henry, how are you, old buddy? Fine, fine, more work than I can handle and yes, your policy is still safe. Listen, John Henry, what I called you about, I need a transcript. You remember a Lucinda Marie Harmon-Yeah, Bradshaw Mountain-Yeah she is. No, I did not know she had a 4.0. Good! Good! Well, we're going to send her off to college. No, Charles Stewart is here in my office and they have a new program at Concord called Work Study and she's going to go on that. Sure, she deserves a scholarship. You need to talk to my buddy, Ch- Dr. Stewart about that," finished Mr. Bascom as he passed the phone to Dr. Stewart.

They talked pleasantries for a few minutes and then, placing his hand over the mouthpiece, Dr. Stewart motioned that he wanted to speak privately. They all stepped out, closing the door behind them. Mr. Bascom told Ellen and Mary Lou what was going on and assured Lucinda that those two men were trying to work out something to help her.

Soon Dr. Stewart opened the door and motioned them back in, Lucinda was very hesitant but also eager to know what happened. Dr. Stewart waited until they were settled and then turned to Mr. Bascom, "John Henry Addair is something else, isn't he? He's got more ideas than a dog has fleas," surmised Dr. Stewart as he gave Lucinda an intent look. "Can you take shorthand and write business letters and is your spelling good?" he abruptly asked.

"I can type eighty words a minute. I can take dictation, and I'm a good speller, but maybe you should ask Mr. Bascom. I've taken dictation from him and typed his letters," stated Lucinda solemnly.

Mr. Bascom walked to his desk, picked up the letter tray, and offered the contents for Dr. Stewart's inspection. "Does a scholarship depend on that?" inquired Mr. Bascom.

"No, but to work in my office would. Lucinda, how would you like a job in my office? My secretary needs some extra help since she is now in charge of grant procurement. I'd forgotten about it until John Henry mentioned us being able to procure grant money. But, if you had a job in my office, you could go to school half a day and work half a day. You would make enough money to pay for almost everything you need. Then after the first semester you would be eligible to apply for a scholarship," informed Dr. Stewart.

Lucinda stood transfixed, stunned at this marvelous offer. She knew she could do the typing, shorthand, and the other office jobs. But to be offered a job working for the president of Concord College was just like a fairy tale. She had a hard time believing all this was happening to her.

She was definitely moving up in the world. How many seventeen year olds from a mountain top in McDowell County had the opportunity to date a big city doctor and now go to college? For a moment Lucinda felt she must be special and then remembered Grandpa saying, "Pride goeth before a fall," and felt ashamed.

Lucinda was so overwhelmed by these acts of kindness that she was almost speechless. Her eyes filled with tears, she compressed her lips, and blinked to keep from crying, "I don't have the words to tell all of you how much this means to me. I thank each of you with all my heart and I promise I will work very hard to live up to your expectations."

Lucinda would be going home this weekend with a lot of news but she was worried about how Burb and Nancy would take it. She would have to convince them some way, that this was an opportunity of a lifetime. After the reaction Nathan had gotten, Lucinda felt sure that Burb wouldn't even listen. In Burb's mind women should stay at home and didn't need to know much. "Girls just want to go to school to meet boys and they can do that without schoolin'," was his reply when Odell had wanted to go to high school.

On that Thursday evening before she would go home on Friday, she was eager for Ralph Baxter to come. She wanted to tell somebody about her chance to go to college. Ralph, however, didn't give her a chance until he bragged about being allowed to drive his Dad's brand new Packard sedan. Lucinda politely listened as he told her of all the attributes of this wonderful machine, not caring about any of it. She was thinking of how much she would like to tell Jason about this opportunity.

Jason would have been so surprised but pleased if she could have told him. Now, she could meet him as a college girl and the gulf between them wouldn't seem so wide. But, she couldn't tell him because she hadn't heard from him in over two months. The last time she went home she had asked if the doctor from Bradshaw was still treating Aunt Sarie. "More than likely is, or else I'd a heerd something about it," said Nancy.

Lucinda had been so sure he would come back to see her but was mistaken. "*He's just like all the other men I've met who want to take advantage of an ignorant hillbilly,*" grumbled Lucinda to herself.

Money to go to college was one of her worries as she tried to save. Her Dad was the greatest worry, however. He would not approve of her quitting her job much less going farther away from home. She'd cross that bridge on Friday night when she went home. There was only one thing that gave her a little hope. She thought her dad would be proud if she became a teacher. Burb Harmon had always respected teachers. If one of his children got a whipping or spanking at school, they got another one when they came home. Ernie, her youngest brother, had found that Burb made no idle threats when it came to discipline. Twice, Ernie had been switched two times in one day. Once he had asked to go to the toilet and on the way had let the air out of the back tires of the teacher's car. "Little snot-nose Dora Campbell caught me and broke her neck to tell Mr. Kennedy. I'll fix her neck in the morning," threatened Ernie when questioned. Burb warned him about bothering Dora but the next day Dora Campbell got a bloodied nose, and Ernie was switched twice again.

Finally Ralph finished his gloating and became a ready listener. Actually he gave her some good points to use in her argument. Also, Ralph bought her supper and that saved some money so she readily accepted another date for the following Monday night.

CHAPTER 8

On Friday evening after supper Lucinda walked into the front room and sat in the corner of the couch near Burb's chair. When a commercial came on, she said, "Daddy I need to talk to you and Mommy. I wish you would turn off the radio and just hear me out."

Nancy was sitting near the fireplace darning socks but stopped in the middle of her stitching when she saw Lucinda's face. "What is it, Lucy? Are you in some kind of trouble? God in heaven, don't tell me you been out with some boy."

"No, Mommy, no-you know me better than that. I wouldn't do something like that." Seeing Burb's glare, Lucinda got up and walked to the window then turned back to her dad, "Can I turn off the radio?"

"Go ahead, just turn it off. This must be awful important, so just spit it out. What have you done, girl?" Burb's ferocious glare over the top of his glasses made Lucinda tremble inside. She took a deep breath and walked back to the couch and took her seat.

"Daddy, you and Mommy know that I always wanted to go to college, don't you? I have a chance to go. I just found out this week and if you'll agree I can get everything worked out and start the first of June," pled Lucinda.

"You've got a lot of nerve girl. You're shore proof that 'if you give a girl an inch she'll take a mile.' It wasn't enough that I got you a good job and let you leave home when you was only sixteen years old. No, you have to keep pushin.' Now, you want to go way off somers where I couldn't find out what you are into. No, my answer is no. Absolutely not! You ain't goin, and if I hear any more about it you'll leave that job and come home where you ort to be. Shouldn't a let you go in the first place. The other girls didn't and they made out just fine." Burb abruptly got up and walked out of the room and Lucinda rose with tears streaming down her face, and turned to Nancy.

"Mommy, I want to go so bad. The president of Concord College offered me a job in his office and I can work my way through. Oh! Mommy, I want to be a teacher. I'm not wanting to do anything wrong. I just want to learn how to teach little kids." Lucinda sank to the floor in front of her mother and buried her head in her mother's lap, crying miserably.

Nancy sat stiff as a board for a few minutes and then tentatively put her hand on Lucinda's head. She began a gentle stroking, "Here, Lucy honey, don't take on so. It plum breaks my heart but, child this is so brand new for yer pap. It is for me too, but I think I'd be right proud to tell people my baby was a school teacher. Why don't you jest dry up yer cryin and go wash yer face? I believe we need to all sleep on this tonight." Nancy stood up and pulled Lucinda to her feet, "Go on now. Do like I told ye. Tomorrer is a new day and folks just can't see thangs clear in the dark."

Lucinda didn't feel it would be any different in the morning but what else could she do, so she hugged her mother and went to the kitchen to wash her face. Then making her way around the hill to the outhouse, she thought, I'll go down to grandpa's grave, well not really his grave but at least where his blood was buried when he was embalmed. Lucinda shuddered as she remembered seeing Nathan carrying that huge bucket, which Ernie said held Grandpa's blood. Big John Pat Fanning had embalmed Grandpa there at the house and all the waste had to be disposed of. Nathan was crying so hard he could barely see the path. He thought nobody saw him but Lucinda did. She watched him dig the hole and pour the contents of the bucket into the hole and then cover it with rocks and dirt. Nathan hadn't seen her, because a five year old can hide in a small place. The family always commented about the lilies and roses they found stuck in the ground behind the outhouse. They had never asked her about it but they had questioned Ernie, Gordon, and Ellen who vehemently denied any connection.

Lucinda made her way behind the outhouse and sat on the ground close to the sacred spot. She whispered, "Grandpa, I know this is foolish and I know you aren't there. I can't go to the graveyard though, it's too far, but I need to talk. I wish you were here. You'd know what to tell me. I wish you could talk to me now. Seems like the older I get, the more I need you."

Lucinda sat there for a few minutes feeling foolish. That's what she had always done when she was a child but she was grown now. Suddenly it was as if Grandpa had spoken, "Remember to pray, Cindy. There's your help." Lucinda rose and walked back to the house wondering if she really heard that message or was it just her imagination.

Lucinda had been fearful and yet eager to go home that weekend to plead her case with her dad. Even if she convinced her dad, she still needed $300. She was so close, if she could only get her foot in the door.

When Lucinda awoke on Saturday morning, after Burb's adamant refusal on Friday night, she dreaded getting up. She lay thinking about what could be done. She had tried to pray last night until she went to sleep and had fitful dreams all through the night. Finally she got up, donned her newly bought robe, and ventured into the kitchen. Nancy was putting a bowl of gravy on the table, but turned, "Morning, Lucy. Ain't it a purty morning? Jest look at that sunshine a streaming through the winder. Makes a body glad all over, don't it?"

Lucinda walked over and hugged Nancy furiously, "Is Daddy up?" Burb came through the back door slamming the screen as he entered and went to the wash pan to splash his hands and face. Then, not saying a word, he went to his usual place at the head of the long, oilcloth-covered table.

"Nan, you know I forgot, but that feller from Welch is sposed to be here around eleven. Do you reckon you could fix one of them rhubarb pies like you made last Sunday? I'd say he'd take a likin' to it," said Burb, as Nancy placed a plate of biscuits by his place.

Nancy agreed to make the pie but urged him to hurry and eat so she could ready things up. Lucinda and Burb didn't speak a word although Lucinda sneaked furtive glances in his direction. Burb soon left the table and Lucinda gloomily plodded around helping Nancy clear the table and do the dishes. Then from habit she took a pan of water from the water tank on the end of the stove and went to her room to bathe. When she came out she saw a basket of laundry which had been dampened and rolled to be ironed. She went to look for the irons, telling Nancy she would do the ironing. She went to the little storage room on the back porch, but couldn't find the irons. When she came back in, there stood Nancy beside a new ironing board, and an electric iron hooked into a receptacle in the drop socket of the overhead light. Lucinda was amazed, "Where'd you get that iron and ironing board? I know Daddy didn't buy it." Electricity had been brought in a year ago and Burb complained about the electric bill all the time.

"Why, Odell and Gordon brung them both to me
last week, Lucy. Ain't they jest the finest thangs? Why, I
can stand right in here and iron, and not burn plum up
from having that old hot stove stoked up. Them younguns
is the best thangs to me that ever wus. I know Odell done
without to give em to me but she swore she didn't." Nancy
gave a delighted smile as she spit on the iron surface,
"Here she is Lucy—hot as a fire cracker. Now, don't scorch
yer pap's shirts."

Lucinda ironed for about an hour and had only four
more pieces left when a car pulled into the parking place
below the house. Lucinda looked out the window. She
didn't know the man who got out of the passenger side
but the man driving was Colonel Ballard. Lucinda had
talked to him several times when he had come into Mr.
Bascom's office. In fact, Mr. Bascom had bragged to him,
just this week about Lucinda's good luck in getting to go to
college.

Burb met the men on the porch and brought them
into the kitchen. Lucinda had continued ironing but
stopped when Burb said, "Nancy, I want you to meet Joe
Hankins and Colonel Ballard, old friends of mine." Nancy
started across the room to shake hands but stopped as
Colonel Ballard said, "Lucinda Harmon! Well doggone! I
should have made the connection but I didn't. Burb
Harmon, you have a really sharp daughter. Is she the first
one of your children to go to college? Mr. Bascom said it
was pure luck that President Stewart stopped by his office
last week."

Colonel Ballard turned to see a stunned Burb, who
recovered quickly, "Yep Colonel, she's the first. She wants
to be a school teacher. She just told us about it last night
and I didn't get all the details. I jest know she has to begin
the last of May."

The Colonel turned to Lucinda, "I thought school started the first week in June. I may have been mistaken though."

Lucinda smiled hesitantly, "No Sir, you're right, but Dr. Stewart told me to have everything ready by the last of May and come a day or so early to learn my way around before the other students come."

"Oh, I see. Well, I know Burb is so proud that he'll help you get everything ready. After all Burb, how many girls from this mountain have gone off to college to become a teacher?" The Colonel smiled all around as if he had bestowed a blessing on the entire house, and Burb looked as if he had been the recipient. Lucinda breathed a sigh of relief, smiled at the Colonel, and folded the ironing board while thinking, *"God moves in mysterious ways."*

From then on Burb acted as if he had initiated the entire thing and was eager to help in any way Lucinda suggested. Even though she couldn't save but $100, her dad said, "Don't worry Cindy. I've got friends that can spare a little money." He had then gone with her to Uncle Jim Hardin and she had signed a note for $200 to be paid back in installments. So, now she could go to college but she was also in debt. People in her family did not go into debt and it was scary but Burb had assured her that her case was different. She could pay $200 back in no time.

Lucinda realized that her dad had really been the means of her going to college even though he didn't know it. He had allowed her to go to work, even getting her job, and his friendship with Colonel Ballard was the clincher. "He just didn't know that if I saw a crack I would make an opening," mused Lucinda happily.

On the following Monday night, Lucinda asked Ralph to take her to the Starland Drive-in Theater, located at Big Four, north of Welch. Ralph eagerly agreed and

Lucinda thought it must be good since he seemed so eager. Before the movie was half over she learned why Ralph liked the drive-in. She had been kissed, had moved hands, slapped, shoved, and finally threatened to get out of the car.

Ralph apologized, "I didn't do anything more than every other guy does at a drive-in. If you didn't want to smooch, why did you ask to come? Just look around you, Lucinda."

Lucinda looked all around and saw many kissing couples, some she couldn't see at all, and in some cars it seemed as if a wrestling match was taking place. She was shocked. "Ralph, I didn't know. I've never been to a drive-in before, and I'll never ask to come again. Please believe me. I don't do things like that." She was almost in tears and Ralph quickly replaced the window speaker in its stationary holder in their car space and drove back to Welch.

He looked repentant as he patted her on the shoulder, "It's okay Lucinda. I'm kinda glad you're not like that but you can't blame a guy for trying." They had left the movie knowing more about the each other than they had before. Also, Lucinda left a much wiser girl than she had been an hour before visiting the drive-in theater.

They had two or three dates in the next two weeks and Ralph began to ask why she wanted to go to college anyway. "I like you just like you are. If you go away to college you will be too smart for me," complained Ralph.

"You don't understand, Ralph. I am so tired of feeling like a little old backwoods hillbilly who knows nothing about the world," explained Lucinda. "When I was in high school, the town kids acted as if I wasn't there and even some of the teachers treated the mountain kids like they were dummies. The kids from the coal camps were not one bit smarter than we mountain kids. I always thought that the teachers treated town kids special because they dressed nice and could be in all kinds of activities. It was unfair and I hated it. Most of the mountain kids made better grades but it didn't seem to matter unless you were a cheerleader or on the ball teams. I just want to show people that I'm just as smart as the next person. All I need is a chance and getting to go to college is the best chance I'll ever get."

"Didn't you have any friends in high school?" asked Ralph, in amazement.

"Sure I had some friends- but not many," replied Lucinda. "Most of them were from the mountain or from Jolo. One or two from Iaeger were nice in my last two years, but I still didn't fit in. I guess part of it was because I was younger than most of the other students in my grade and too shy to put myself forward, and I certainly didn't have the right kind of clothes," confessed Lucinda.

"I would be your friend if you'd stick around. I thought you liked me," stated Ralph. "You know that when you leave here, you won't be back in Welch."

"No, I probably won't for four years at least," explained Lucinda. "Ralph, we are both young and you'll find somebody else. Remember that girl we saw last night that kept looking at you? I'll bet she would go out with you. I know she looked daggers at me," Lucinda said, smiling. "She knows you. I'll bet you used to date her. Did you date her, Ralph?"

Turning beet red, Ralph grinned, "I was going with her when I met you. That's why she looked at you like that. She doesn't like you much."

Lucinda's eyes opened wide in shock, "Ralph, why didn't you tell me? I don't want her to not like me. You go back and make up with her. Please! She's a really pretty girl."

"You really want me to go back to her, don't you?" sniffed Ralph. "You've not been really interested in me at all. I guess I will go back to her if she will have me."

"Ralph, I really like you as a friend and I don't want you to be mad at me either. Please let's still be friends. I'll go and talk to her if you want," plead Lucinda.

"No, don't do that. She's bigger than you and she's awfully mad right now." Ralph put out his hand "Well, let's part friends then, but I'll always remember you."

"I, too, Ralph. You've been a good friend and I'll always treasure these past weeks. We've had some good times, haven't we?" Lucinda smiled, "After all, who could forget getting stuck in the Silver Bullet high up in the sky, upside down, in a thunder storm? I'll remember Vivian Bottom as long as I live."

They laughed and talked like old friends recalling memories until they came to Lucinda's place and then shook hands again before spontaneously giving each other a hug of farewell.

Lucinda felt that she had learned how to spend time with a boy without feeling like an ignorant fool. She now felt she had gained some social graces and would fit in better than she would have before she met Ralph Baxter. She still did not know how to dance and she was still easily embarrassed and turned beet red at compliments but she was getting better.

Nobody at college would know anything about her background and she wasn't going to tell them. It wasn't that she was ashamed of her people or where she was from but people always made assumptions when you told them you were from Bradshaw or Bradshaw Mountain. She always heard, "Bradshaw! I hear they have a killing there every Saturday night," and, "How many beer joints did you say Bradshaw had?"

Going to college marked the end of Lucinda's sojourn in Welch, but it was only the beginning of her new life. From there, her struggles increased to make or do something with her life, different than all the women before her had done with theirs.

Even at an early age Lucinda wondered why she hungered to know so much. Odell, Oprey, Faye and Ellen never talked about books, school, or wanting to know. It wasn't that they couldn't read or were not smart because they were. They had wisdom about life that seemed to elude Lucinda. They knew how to sew, cook, clean, raise a garden, and all the other things they had been taught. Everybody on the mountain talked about what fine wives and mothers Nancy and Burb's girls were. It always made Lucinda feel proud when she heard good things about her sisters and her parents, but she still wanted more than to be a good wife and mother. She couldn't do anything like her sisters, and felt so inadequate. She wondered if that childhood feeling of inadequacy had led to this feeling of never being able to measure up or be as good as her sisters when she grew up.

When they started talking curtain material and what kind of furniture they would like to have, it seemed foolish to Lucinda. To her, one needed a stove to cook on, a table to eat on, and a bed to sleep in. Like her dad, she saw no sense in putting in windows to get light inside and then covering those same windows with curtains. Her sisters thought she was weird and she felt as if she must have something wrong with her because she had no interest in the things they knew. Often she thought she would have been better off if she didn't like to read or crave to know the meaning of unanswerable things, but she always had from the time that Grandpa had taught her to read.

Odell, Oprey, and Faye used to read "True Romance" stories aloud as the family sat around the fire at night, but after the first time, Lucinda lost interest. It wasn't that she didn't like love stories but she was more interested in stories of people doing great things to help others. She was especially fond of books that gave her heroes or heroines who reached their goals despite seemingly immovable obstacles. She loved history and particularly liked to read about Abraham Lincoln reading by the light from the fireplace. She borrowed books from her Aunt Margie and read every book she could get from the school library. It seemed as if there was a great hunger inside of her for knowing.

John Henry Addair, the principal of Iaeger High School, had referred in a graduation speech to Gene Stratton Porter's "Girl of the Limberlost" and her struggle for an education. This fired Lucinda's imagination and desire to go to college even more after she had read the book.

CHAPTER 9

Lucinda's introduction to Concord College was hard but wonderful. The studying was trying but she gloried in the knowledge. It was then that she began to really think about McDowell County and its people. All her history and civil government classes and especially West Virginia history whetted her appetite to learn more. Lucinda had no idea then why she felt the need to know so much about her county, except that she loved it, especially Welch, War, Iaeger, Bradshaw, and Bradshaw Mountain.

Everything would have been fine if she could have gotten Jason out of her mind. She had come home at the breaks, and not once, in those first months at Concord College had she seen Jason McCall. During the breaks she took every opportunity to go to Bradshaw, even thinking she'd like to get sick, so she could see the doctor; Jason being the doctor. She learned from Maggie Barker, that Jason was so busy he rarely had time for a decent meal.

In 1951 she came home for Thanksgiving and found that Aunt Sarie Lester had died. Having always loved Aunt Sarie, Lucinda felt really sad at this news. The wake was in the home and Lucinda attended with her parents, and two sisters. She and her sisters rode in the back of the logging truck, like many mountain families.

Lucinda knew that town funerals were held either at churches or at funeral parlors but mountain people kept their loved ones at home. Most of the time family members were not embalmed but recently a law had been passed requiring embalming so Aunt Sarie had been embalmed. Once on the mountain, an Estep girl had died, or so they thought, and she had not been embalmed. On the way to the cemetery they heard a noise coming from the casket and when they opened the casket the girl was

91

alive. Still, some people were dead set against embalming even after the example they had witnessed. However, a few became staunch supporters. Jess Clayton, Junior's dad, had said to his family, "You'uns better take me to a funeral parlor and let a doctor check to see for sure I'm dead fore you nail me into a coffin. Cause if you'uns don't I'll come back and haint every one of you till the day you die."

Burb parked at the end of the road and they all walked to the house. It was warm for November and children played in the yard and lane leading to the house. Men stood outside leaning against fences, yard palings, and corn cribs, chewing, smoking, and talking. A few young girls were hanging around outside the house in hopes of catching the eye of their favorite young man.

Funerals on the mountain were as much a part of life as being born. Like in James Still's *River of Earth,* these people seemed to know their path and accepted where their river of earth was heading. They believed the Almighty Creator was the best guide anybody could have. At an early age children saw death, illness, good times and bad times, thus keeping at bay the trauma that is often associated with death.

Only once, in all the funerals here on the mountain that Lucinda had attended, had she seen children bothered by being present. This had happened several years ago when Lucinda was too young to be allowed to race around with the other children. When a neighbor, Will Cousins, had been missing for an entire day, a search party had been formed and his body was found in the woods down near the creek. He must have died early that morning for rigor mortis had set in before he was found. As a result, the family could not get his mouth closed. Old man Will was a dark man who always had a black stubble beard and his teeth were large. The casket was placed in a bedroom which opened off onto a porch. People could go from that same porch in through the front room door, through that room into a kitchen, circle around through one bedroom, then on into the other bedroom where the casket was, before going back onto the same porch.

When people first arrived for the wake service, it was around eight o'clock and the moon hadn't risen. Children, as usual, were weaving in and out through the crowd, making a circle through the rooms as described, completely ignoring the casket. The moon arose around nine o'clock and cast an almost daytime light on everything it touched. It cast its full glow on the face of Will Cousins just as Jeffrey Clayton and Lucinda's brother Ernie were going to make a mad dash from the porch into that bedroom to hide from Jessie, Jeffrey Clayton's older brother.

Looking back as they ran, they stumbled headlong and were almost flung atop the body. Jeffrey Clayton slumped to the floor in a dead faint and Ernie let out a scream that no banshee could have uttered as he made a flying leap backward, going off the high end of the porch.

People were running and Jeffrey's mother let out a long low wail when she saw her son lying as if dead. Nancy Harmon found Ernie lying at an angle below the porch. He had knocked the breath out of himself but had come around. However, when Nancy reached down to lift him up; he was trembling from head to foot as if he had the ague. Burb came from inside the house and, seeing the condition Ernie was in, picked him up and carried him to his truck and the Harmon family went home.

This was an unusual occurrence, however, and most mountain children found funerals more of a social gathering unless the dead person was an immediate family member.

However, Ernie would not go to funerals after that until he was completely grown and still preferred not to, according to his wife, Birdie.

When they arrived the first person Lucinda saw was Junior Clayton, who was headed her way. She smiled at everyone present, except Junior, acting as if she hadn't seen him, and hurried to the house, walking between Oprey and Ellen. I'm going to stay inside if they have ten preachers tonight, thought Lucinda.

Aunt Sarie's casket was set up in the front room. All the furniture had been moved out and Fanning Funeral Home who was taking care of the funeral had lent chairs which were set in rows. They filled the room except for about a two- foot space in front of the casket. This was where the preachers would stand after the viewers had filed by and spoken to the family. Mary Lizzie, Aunt Sarie's daughter from Ohio, was the only family member present when they went in. After Nancy and her daughters had spoken to Mary Lizzie and looked at Aunt Sarie, they ambled around the room speaking to the many acquaintances and friends whom Lucinda hadn't seen for a long time.

Everyone was curious about Lucinda since she had been away. They wanted to see if she had "put on airs" after living in Welch for over a year and then going on past Bluefield to college. Sarah Margaret whom everyone called "Sir Marget" took her to task about going off and worrying her poor mother half to death. "Ain't you going to ever marry, Lucy?" she questioned. To this Lucinda had replied that she might someday and only drew more attention to herself when Sir Marget said, "Don't make no sense then to go off and spend a lot of money when you can learn all you need to know right here at home. Most of the time when girls get that fer away from home, they get into trouble." Lucinda didn't like all this attention and the avenue Sir Marget was embarked on, and was almost ready to get up and go outside when Preacher Hiram started a song and everybody fell silent.

Nancy and her daughters had found three empty chairs on the fourth row which was two rows back from Sir Marget and for that Lucinda was thankful.

There were four preachers to take part in the service and Lucinda settled down for a two hour service. A young preacher named McClanahan got up first and talked a few minutes, led the congregation in a song, and knelt to pray. Lucinda felt that Aunt Sarie would have liked what he had said and was glad she had come tonight. The next preacher she didn't know and sat drowsily watching moths fly in through the door and flitter around the globe of the oil lamp glowing on a table beside the casket. She would have gone to sleep if Preacher Gillespie, the third to get up, hadn't had such a loud voice which he often raised even louder. I wonder if he's trying to wake the dead, thought Lucinda mischievously.

Then Preacher Hiram arose and everyone set up straighter and moved forward in their chairs. He was a small man with kind eyes showing laugh wrinkles. His white hair seemed to glow in the pale light and even though his voice was soft, it was clear and full of authority. Lucinda thought, If God calls preachers then he surely called Preacher Hiram.

With the fingers of both hands touching, Preacher Hiram stood quietly before he said, "Brothers and Sisters, Sister Sarie Lester is at rest here tonight. This is the easiest bed she has ever laid on. No more will she worry over her children, her neighbors, her church - she has escaped the bonds of time. She has met her last enemy and her spirit has gone back to the God who gave it and her body will return to the dust from which it came. But, my friends I tell you that this is not the last we will see Aunt Sarie, 'For the Lord himself shall descend from heaven with a shout, with the voice of the archangel, and with the trump of God' and declare that time shall be no more, then those that live and remain shall not hinder those that sleep but we will all be caught up together in the air to meet with our Lord and Savior, Jesus Christ. He gave himself a ransom for all. Now friends, one all is just as big as another. The scriptures declare that the cattle on a thousand hills are his, and the gold of Ophir is his, but best of all is that all souls are his. Now, if that is so, and the Bible says it is, then the devil doesn't own anything, does he? Jesus was the sacrifice that redeemed us and since eternal heaven has never been tore up and it was seen in Wisdom, from and before the foundation of the world, then can anyone tell me how anybody can escape going to Heaven since the Lord said 'Where were you Job, when the morning stars sang together and all the sons of God shouted for joy?' Now some will say they are not all the sons of God. Well, if they are not, then tell me how did they get here? Didn't God create all things and don't it all belong to him?"

By this time some people were shouting, two or three men had gotten up to shake Preacher Hiram's hand, and Mary Lizzie got up and hugged him. Lucinda felt like it herself and then wondered why, since she wasn't a church member. Then the congregation was all on their feet in the final song and the service was over. The funeral would be the next day at eleven o'clock.

Children had come in with their parents and looked at Aunt Sarie, some of the grandchildren were crying and even Uncle Jeb was quietly shedding tears. Lucinda thought, I hope I leave that kind of legacy when I go. Everybody had something good to say about Aunt Sarie.

Lucinda attended the funeral at the cemetery the next day but was not moved as she had been the night before. Like all Primitive Baptist funerals they had three preachers and Lucinda was glad of it. She had been to funerals where they had four or five preachers and the funeral would last all day. She didn't know much about any other churches, however, except the old regular Baptists, which were also prevalent in the mountains. They believed if you weren't baptized that you'd "split Hell wide open" when you died, according to Burb. Lucinda had thought about that and wondered how a God of Love like Preacher Hiram talked about could send somebody to a place to burn for ever and ever.

Several times when she was younger Lucinda had gone down to Jolo to visit her cousins and had attended Sunday school in the Methodist church with them. She liked the crafts and stories even though she didn't believe some of the things the teacher said. Grandpa had always said, "Child, you'll hear all kinds of things in this life, and see all kinds of things but you don't have to believe it or be a part of it." So, Lucinda kept quiet but believed what she wanted to.

Too many things were going through her mind to pay much attention to the service that day. Then too, she had kept a weathered eye on Junior Clayton to make sure she didn't get near enough for him to try to put his arm around her or to ask her for a date. She didn't want to date anybody. Well, anybody but Jason McCall, and that didn't seem likely after all these months.

On the Christmas break she had seen Jason pass in his car as she went down Bradshaw Mountain. She was in the back seat of her brother's car and of course he didn't see her. Then two days later Nancy came down with influenza and Lucinda went with her to the doctor. When she walked into the office with her mother, Jason almost dropped his stethoscope but did not say anything except hello. He examined Nancy and gave her some pills and cough syrup and then turned to Lucinda. He winked and said, "I hear you are working in Welch?"

"Not anymore. I'm attending college," Lucinda said, smiling proudly.

"You're in college! Where?" queried Jason.

"She met the president of Concord College and he gave her a job and she borrowed the rest. Now she'll be the only one of my children to go to college," boasted Nancy hoarsely.

"Well, well, things do happen when I'm away, it seems," said Jason.

"Away! Where have you been?" asked Lucinda.

"A new requirement was added and I had to go back to medical school for some extra training and then I stopped off to visit the family. It caused me to lose touch with the people I cared about back here," said Jason as he looked intently at Lucinda.

A bright dimpled smile glowed from Lucinda's face and eyes, as she realized that he hadn't forgotten her after all.

Just as they were ready to leave Jason said, "Lucinda, would you like to go to a movie with me tonight?"

Lucinda turned bright hopeful eyes toward Nancy, "May I, Mommy?" she begged.

Nancy thought for a minute, "Well, I don't care if Burb don't. I guess you've been out enough to know how to behave yourself." Turning to Jason, "Burb's in the car. You'll have to ask him," said Nancy. Jason walked out behind Lucinda, not even looking at the patients in his waiting room, as he closed the door. At the truck he opened the door for Nancy and Lucinda before hurrying to the window on the other side.

"Mr. Harmon, may I take Lucinda to a movie here in town tonight?" asked Jason.

Burb looked shocked for a minute. "You don't know Lucinda. What do you want to take her to a movie for?" demanded Burb.

"Yes, I do know Lucinda, Mr. Harmon. She was the first girl I met when I came here. It was before Aunt Sarah Lester died. I almost ran over her and she fell in a mud puddle. I just never did forget her and that's why I want to take her to a movie," explained Jason. Upon Burb's grudging consent, Jason went whistling back into his office.

CHAPTER 10

Jason arrived at six o'clock and Burb turned the porch light on saying, "I'd better give him some light fore he falls on that walk. I forgot to put another plank where that uns' broke."

Nancy looked up in amazement, "You forgot! Pears to me like you forget a lot of things then, Burb Harmon, seeing as how me and Ellen had to fix the fence tuther day to keep the cow in. You forgot to fix it for nigh on to two weeks."

By this time Jason had gotten out and made his way to the front door. Lucinda was ready for his knock and quickly opened the door. Jason was invited in but he declined saying, "We don't have much time. The movie starts at seven o'clock." They left with an admonition from Burb, "Have my girl back here by eleven o'clock. I think she's too young to be flirtin anyway." Jason assured Burb that they would be back by that time, and taking Lucinda's arm, walked quickly to the car.

Lucinda's face was beet red, "Jason, I'm sorry. Dad's not very trusting."

Jason told her he understood, but laughed, "Your dad would have a hemorrhage if he knew about us meeting in Welch, wouldn't he?"

They drove down the winding curves of Bradshaw Mountain discussing what a pretty road it would be without the ugly coal chutes stuck out over the road on several curves. Jason, like Lucinda loved country roads but these eyesores destroyed the landscape. Jason explained that coal was mined in Pennsylvania also, but companies were not allowed as much freedom there. Coal companies owned all of McDowell County from Jason's perspective. "They're bent on getting every ounce of coal in these mountains aren't they? I don't know why they are allowed to destroy the landscape in the process. Seems to me that your elected representatives aren't minding the store," said Jason, assuming Lucinda understood his meaning.

Lucinda, however, didn't have much understanding, but was beginning to question things that happened. "Why shouldn't they be allowed to get the coal out if they own the mineral rights?" she asked.

"Do you think it's right for coal companies to change the course of the river to make a coal processing plant, which will be near the railroad?" asked Jason in answer.

Lucinda's eyes opened wide in sudden understanding, "No, but they did. I heard Dad and Gordon talking about Island Creek moving the river over next to Route 80 in order to build No. 6 tipple near the rail line," replied Lucinda thoughtfully. "Every time there's a flood the river undercuts the road and then the state has to repair the road."

Jason smiled knowingly, "See there. Now, are your elected representatives minding the store?"

They reached Bradshaw at a quarter past six and decided to drive up Route 83 towards Bartley since the feature did not start until seven o'clock. Jason drew an unresisting Lucinda to his side, and with one arm around her, drove slowly back to Bradshaw.

Later, Lucinda could not remember the movie, but she would never forget the drive back up Bradshaw Mountain. Again there was a moon, but about halfway up the mountain big soft flakes of snow began to fall. They drifted slowly down, making lacy patterns on the windshield, until the wipers swept them away to be replaced by more. The car was warm, and the radio softly hummed *Hello, Young Lovers, wherever you are,* as Jason held her close and finally pulled over on the last curve before the top. When he kissed her, Lucinda knew this moment would be etched in her memory forever. Perhaps Jason remembered her fright when he had stopped on the way down from the Gary Sportsman's Club, for he was very careful to not get out of line, and Lucinda was thankful. She doubted if she would have had the courage to stop him if he had.

"Lucinda, do you know what you're doing to me?" whispered Jason. "I have thought of you, and tried to get you out of my mind, for months, with no luck. Lucinda, I believe I've fallen in love. But, I don't know about you, Lucinda? How do you feel?" questioned Jason, now feeling unsure.

"Oh! Jason, I know I love you. I have from the first time when you stopped and asked me to ride. You remember that?" asked Lucinda snuggling closer. Reluctant to break this magical spell that had her bemused, Lucinda sat silently content.

"What are we going to do, Lucinda? I know you are young and need some time but we do need to date and get to know each other."

"Jason, I have to finish school and you won't stay here. You'll want to go away after your time is up, won't you?" questioned Lucinda.

Jason sat very still for a few minutes. "I haven't really thought about it, but I think I could live in Welch, could you?" replied Jason.

"I don't know," whispered Lucinda. "Ever since I started high school and realized that there was a better life away from these mountains, I've wanted to leave. All I could think of was how to get away and not end up like Mommy and my sisters, but now I realize that I really love this place. I've learned that there are all kinds of mountains- not just Bradshaw Mountain. There has to be more to life than staying right here on the mountain and having a baby every year. But the place, it's home and I feel safe here with all the people I love. It's kind of like the hills are a shelter or a calm place where you know what is going to happen next. When I first went to Welch I had so many decisions to make, and I felt so unsure, and afraid. Am I making any sense, Jason?"

"Sure you are. This has been a known place and way of life and any change is scary. It takes a lot of courage to brave the unknown, but there is a better way Lucinda. It isn't good for people to lock themselves away from new ways of thinking and looking at things. You see, Lucinda without any outside influences, people get stuck into a pattern. I'm glad you want to be different. As to the place, I feel the same way about where I was raised. But, if we should decide later to marry then we will build a life together, and it won't matter where we live, will it?" asked Jason. Seeing Lucinda's startled, wide-eyed expression, he quickly added, "We don't have to decide tonight though. I'd better get you home before Burb Harmon comes with his shotgun," said Jason after another quick kiss.

Lucinda spent four more evenings with Jason. They went to War, saw a movie and ate at the War Drive-In. On the next evening, they drove to Iaeger and ate at the bus terminal. On the other evenings they just drove around until they found a quiet place and parked. Lucinda was not afraid or embarrassed with Jason now, and allowed more intimate caressing, but when his hand covered her breast she jerked away in outrage. "Jason McCall, what kind of girl do you think I am? That's not nice. You take me home," stormed Lucinda, with tears running down her face.

"Lucinda, I'm sorry but most men take more liberties than that. You don't know one thing about natural human tendencies do you?" asked Jason in amazement.

Lucinda muttered, "Mommy said men would do anything that a girl would let them. She said nice girls didn't let men feel all over them and I'm a nice girl, so you take me home".

"All right," said Jason in exasperation as he started the car. He didn't pull out but turned to Lucinda, "Will you read a book if I bring you one?"

"What kind of book?" Lucinda questioned doubtfully.

"It's about human reactions and sexuality." Seeing the startled wary expression in her eyes, Jason quickly added, "Lucinda, you need to learn a few things. Will you read it?"

Lucinda dropped her head but agreed to read the book and Jason pulled her close and drove into Bradshaw. After that, they just drove around, stopping once at the skating rink in Stringtown, but mostly just driving and talking. Each evening had seemed better to Lucinda than the one before. On their last night, they each promised to write once each week and Lucinda promised to come home on the spring break.

Letters were exchanged, but Jason always complained in his letters about not having access to a telephone so they could talk. He wrote things in his letters that he couldn't have talked to Lucinda about in person, but still they got to know each other better in that way. Jason wrote that he had always been allowed more freedoms than Lucinda would allow which made Lucinda uneasy. He said that he had been very careful because she was so young and innocent and Lucinda wondered what he meant but feared to ask.

However, Lucinda wasn't really bothered by anything except not getting to see Jason. As long as she received Jason's letters she was on cloud nine. She read each letter over every day until the next one came, and then tied all the letters together in a bundle for safe keeping. She could hardly wait until spring break, in March, when they could be together again.

Jason wrote that he had planned to surprise her one weekend in February with a visit, but a blizzard cancelled his plans. Lucinda was set to go home for a weekend on the first of March riding with a Mullins boy, but he changed his mind at the last minute.

Spring break finally arrived, but Lucinda did not go home. There was a collegiate scholarship contest to be held in Huntington, and Lucinda had been chosen to participate. It was the hardest decision she'd ever had to make, but she just couldn't turn that kind of opportunity down. She was sure that Jason would understand. She wrote him a long letter explaining the situation and left it for her roommate to mail. That scholarship would take care of her last two years of college, and she wouldn't have to borrow any more money.

Lucinda arrived in Huntington full of anxiety about the contest and her lack of social skills. Dr. Hurst, the scholarship sponsor, had said there would be dinner and dancing at the awards presentation and all participants had to attend regardless of who won. She was to share a dormitory room with two other entrants, Alice Mercer from Alderson-Broaddus and Janice Waverly from West Virginia Technical Institute. She liked both girls but was in awe of them since they seemed so worldly and sure of themselves. When she met the male entrants, Jerome Petry from West Virginia University and Henry Boone from Marshall College there in Huntington, she was even more uneasy. But Jerome Petry was such a happy, caring person that he soon had her feeling much better and enjoying his company.

When she and Jerome were chosen as finalists and then eventually won first and second places, she was ecstatic even though Jerome was the first place winner.

They had the big dinner, and seated beside Jerome she found herself enjoying the meal but refusing the wine offered with dinner. The other participants kidded her about being a Puritan but she didn't relent. Lucinda had seen too many drunks to not realize the effects of alcohol.

When the dancing started, Lucinda refused, and everybody but Jerome thought it was because of her religion. For some reason, Jerome wasn't dancing but sitting beside her. He sat quietly, a few minutes and then asked, "Lucinda, have you ever danced?"

"No, I don't know how to dance," confessed Lucinda without any embarrassment. Jerome had that effect on people and Lucinda found herself telling him that she would like to dance, but was afraid of making a fool of herself.

Many times since she had come to college, she had come downstairs to find someone playing a dance tune on the piano, and she found her feet wanting to move. Sometimes it was so beautiful she just wanted to listen, such as the time someone was playing Leroy Anderson's *Blue Tango*. That would be her favorite instrumental for the rest of her life. Lucinda thought it amazing that she loved classical and contemporary music so much when she had been brought up on Uncle Dave Macon, Ernest Tubb, and Lefty Frizzel. She didn't tell Jerome all of this, however, and soon he had her on the floor doing a slow waltz.

The news media was there snapping pictures of the winners and doing interviews. Lucinda did not realize the story and pictures would be carried in the local papers. They did a picture of Lucinda and Jerome hugging each other as their names were called as winners and gave each of them a copy which Lucinda really appreciated. Jerome had told her about his engagement to a girl in Montgomery and Lucinda told him about Jason McCall. They were happy for each other.

So Lucinda came back to college with the assurance of enough money for another two years at Concord College. She wrote Jason another letter even though he hadn't replied to the first one. When she asked Amy Jordan, her roommate about the other letter, she said, "I left it in the office mailbox. Mrs.Bodkins takes the mail to the post office, so, I know it went out." Amy said she would take this letter to the post office herself to insure it was mailed. Lucinda waited and waited and still no answer came.

She wrote again but it was returned with a scrawled note on the envelope, saying, "NO LONGER HERE." Then, she received a letter from Ellen saying that Jason had left Bradshaw. Ellen didn't know any more than that, and Lucinda did not know how to find out. She didn't have the address of Jason's parents or she would have written to them.

She threw herself more deeply into her studies and her work in Dr. Stewart's office. Always before, walking through the long row of pines from the library to Sarvay Hall, her dormitory, gave her such pleasure and peace but now it meant nothing. After a month the sharp edge of her grief was blunted but she was still unable to sleep, and still cried into her pillow. She lost weight and her appetite. Even the sight of food made her nauseous. Finally Mrs.

Bodkins, the house mother, sent her to the infirmary, where she was given Pepto Bismol, and told to see her family doctor. Having no family doctor, she said she would, and left. That night Lucinda dreamed that Jason was calling her name, but she couldn't find him. She awoke with a start, and cried the rest of the night.

When she felt too bad to work, she realized that she needed help. That evening, Lucinda made her way to the ball park, behind the science building. The place was deserted and she went behind the dugout where she could be neither seen nor heard. Once again, she knelt, to pray. She arose, not feeling any better, but felt she had tried. Grandpa had always said, "People ask the Lord for help and expect an answer right then. Sometimes He wants us to figure things out on our own. If we can't, He is always there to help us. He does answer our prayers. However, sometimes we may not like the answer. The Lord always knows best. We just have to trust him." Lucinda walked slowly back, wondering if she could really trust the Lord and wait on his mercy. The last time she had gone to the Lord was while she was in Welch and the Lord heard her that time. After that was when she got the opportunity to go to college.

When morning came, she felt hungry for the first time in over a month. Amy and Lucinda walked down the stairs, to the basement dining hall. Twelve people sat at each table and food was put on the table in platters and bowls. When Amy kept passing bowls to her Lucinda took some scrambled eggs, a piece of sausage, and a piece of toast, which pleased Amy. She had been worried about Lucinda. She thought Lucinda may have gotten pregnant but was hesitant to ask her. She knew Lucinda was crazy about this Jason. She hadn't seen him since Christmas though and that was over three months ago. What if she is pregnant and doesn't know what to do, Amy thought to herself?" Lucinda, when you went out with Jason during Christmas did you all- ah- you know- get real familiar?" Seeing Lucinda's lack of understanding, she decided to be bold, "Lucinda, did you and Jason have sex?"

Lucinda's eyes were enormous in her pale face. "Did I what? You mean, you think I would do something nasty like that? Amy, you know I wouldn't do that with nobody- not unless I was married. I don't know if I even could then."

Amy grinned and hugged her, "Lucinda, I know you're eighteen, but you know about as much about life as my baby sister and she's only eleven. Starting today, I'm going to teach you about the birds and the bees."

That evening Amy came into the room, closed the book Lucinda was studying, and sat down on the bed facing Lucinda." Lucinda, you do know how babies get here, don't you?" Seeing Lucinda's red faced nod she continued with, "Do you also know that sex, not only can be, but is enjoyable?" Lucinda jumped up and ran out the door, slamming it behind her. Amy ran after her and finally caught her walking through the pines towards the library.

"Lucinda, please wait. I didn't mean to scare you. I was just going to tell you that even if you'd had sex with Jason I would still be your friend." Lucinda stopped and stood looking dumbly as Amy talked her into going over to the ball field. Once there Amy gave her some very eye opening information without being too graphic. She learned that women did not have to have a baby unless they wanted to. She didn't believe some of the things Amy said, especially that part about that stuff married people did being enjoyable. She wondered how Amy would know about something like that being enjoyable. Lucinda thought that many of the things Amy told her were made up to shock her. Amy told Lucinda that sometimes couples undressed each other and would have told her more but Lucinda turned and ran.

CHAPTER 11

Lucinda decided she had moped around long enough. Wondering why Jason did not answer her letters didn't help any. She had always wondered why Jason should have fallen for a dirt poor hillbilly such as herself, anyway. Finally, she decided that he had changed his mind and she had to forget him. So in the following months she tried really hard to do just that. She dated two or three of her college classmates even though she didn't enjoy herself at all. Jason may not love her but Lucinda was having a hard time forgetting him. She decided to join the Thespian Club because one of her friends said acting helped people learn to cope. It did help because one could pretend to be someone else whose life was the way they wanted it to be. She was given a starring role in the spring drama festival but in that part the heroine won her true love. "Truth is nothing like fiction," Lucinda said, with a sad smile.

In June, Nancy had written that they had a new doctor in Bradshaw. "That doctor feller, who acted like he liked you so much, went back to Pennsylvania or somewhere. It's better to stick to your own kind, just like I always said," wrote Nancy. After that, Lucinda had tried harder than ever to forget him. She dated Bill Springer from Oakhill, who was as different from Jason as daylight and dark. He taught her more about dancing and they dated off and on for a few months. She liked him but he wasn't Jason and they finally drifted apart. Now she was back home and she had a job.

Lucinda didn't have her degree yet but her dad had injured his eyes in a logging accident and couldn't work. The hospital bills would be enormous and since Burb was a private contractor, he had no medical insurance. Nancy had written to Lucinda worriedly, wondering how they were going to manage. Odell had given them $100 outright and Lucinda wondered how in the world she could afford to be so generous. Odell had five children, all in school. Lucinda knew that Odell had been working in a restaurant in Iaeger for about six months, but didn't make much.

One day George Bryson, Superintendent of McDowell County Schools, was visiting Concord College. When he came into President Stewart's office, an idea like a bolt from the blue, flashed into Lucinda's mind. She had been worrying about her parents and how she could help and here was a chance. She would ask him about teaching.

She went into President Stewart's office to tell him of Mr. Bryson's arrival, and while there, told President Stewart what she wanted to do and why. Although President Stewart regretted that she would be leaving, before she had her degree, he still promised that he would mention it to Mr. Bryson.

The two men left the office at lunch time and Lucinda waited impatiently for their return. She had not planned to go to work until she had her degree but she couldn't allow her parents to be in need if she could help it. She knew that it would be really hard on Burb if he had to go into debt and couldn't pay. Her family just did not get into debt, for the Bible said "Owe no man" and they lived by that.

When Mr. Bryson returned, he stopped by her desk and asked if they could talk. Lucinda smiled and offered him a chair. "Dr. Stewart tells me that you want to teach," said Mr. Bryson.

"Yes Sir, I would really like a school," answered Lucinda.

"What makes you think you could teach?" questioned Mr. Bryson.

"I don't know that I can, Sir, but I know the people in the mountains and I'm willing to work and study, or whatever it takes, if you will give me a chance."

"Well, Miss Harmon, I have a vacancy at Estep School. Do you know where that is?" asked Mr. Bryson.

"I've never been there, but I know it's on the Panther Fork Road," said Lucinda.

So, Lucinda was hired and told to come to the school board office in Welch by the 13th of August. It was now the 6th of July and the second term of summer school would be over on August 10th. Lucinda would just have time to go home, go to Welch, and find a way to get to work each day.

Now Lucinda was a school teacher but only provisionally. Since she had not gotten a degree, she would have to go to summer school and take extension classes to finish. She would still need more classes in college to earn her degree. Lucinda would have had the money, since she had gotten that scholarship in Huntington, but her dad was more important. "Besides," thought Lucinda, "extension classes and summer school won't be so bad if I can get the classes I need." Lucinda knew that her parents would object to her leaving college, but she refused to let that deter her from doing what she felt was right.

Estep School was a two-room school about eight miles down on one fork of Panther Creek, but only one of the rooms was in use for classes. The other room was used to play in on rainy and cold days. When Lucinda asked Mr. Bryson about this, he said that it was due to another slump in the coal industry. This had caused many people to leave the area to find work. Also families were not as large as they once were and many of the county schools were being closed.

Lucinda would have sixty students in grades one through eight. She did not know their ages or any of their parents but these were country people and she felt sure of a welcome.

Burb and Nancy were tickled to have their baby girl home again but hated that she had left school early. Yet, they both made it clear that they were so proud of their daughter, the teacher.

The house seemed lonely with only Burb, Nancy, and herself. Lucinda was used to a dormitory full of girls laughing and calling back and forth. Her sister Ellen had married and lived near so she would be able to see her, which would be some help.

Eight miles, morning and evening, was too far to walk every day, so Lucinda would have to board with someone near the school. She would earn $130 a month which would not leave much for room and board. Burb said he would help and he did. When old man Jake Kannard came to visit, while Nancy and Lucinda had gone to the post office, Burb had inquired about places to stay on Estep Ridge. Mr. Kannard had told him that Lucinda could stay with him and his daughter, Dora Mullins. They decided it would be fair to charge $30 a month for a room including meals and lunch for school.

School started on September 3rd that year and Lucinda's brother, Gordon, and his wife Emily took her to Mrs. Mullins' house on Sunday evening. Dora Mullins was a big, rawboned, blonde woman, tanned from outside work. Her firm calloused hand engulfed Lucinda's warmly as her wide gray eyes twinkled in smiling welcome. "Burb's been telling us about his daughter, the teacher. I think he's told everybody on Bradshaw Mountain about you. Let's set a spell and then I'll show you your room. It ain't the Waldorf Astoria but it's clean."

They visited with Gordon and Emily until they left and then Dora said, "Come on up and have a look. You can put your things away whilst I cook supper." Lucinda was taken upstairs to a room under the eaves with a slanted roof. It was pretty with starched curtains at the small window and a half bed with matching spread. A broomstick had been nailed across one corner to hang her clothes on. Beside the bed was a small chest with three drawers in which she put her other things. When her make-up and clock were placed on the top of the chest, Lucinda was ready to go down and meet Mrs. Mullins' father.

He came out of a room off from the living room and shook her hand, saying, "You can call me Uncle Jake. Your daddy and everybody else does, 'cept them as don't like me and I don't want them to call me nothing anyhow." She had heard her dad talk about "old man Jake Kannard" and this was the man in person. So, he became Uncle Jake and Mrs. Mullins became Dora. They were to be her closest friends for a whole year.

She liked them both immediately. They made her feel so welcome and treated her as if she was a family member. Supper was fried pork tenderloin, wild greens, cornbread, and soup beans, the same fare she had always had at home except that Nancy always had a cake or some kind of dessert to finish the meal. *"I'll just have to get used to no dessert, I guess,"* thought Lucinda.

Lucinda helped do the dishes and then went to the living room with Dora who switched on the television set. It was a black and white, 17 inch Motorola and resided in a place of honor on a table that took up the entire wall near the front door. Under the television was a snow white

115

starched table cloth which had intricate lace edging. Lucinda, having never seen much television since Burb and Nancy did not have one, was thrilled. She laughed hilariously at the antics of Sid Caesar and Imogene Coca and then sobered while becoming absorbed in the trials of The Virginian.

Precisely at nine o'clock the television was turned off by Uncle Jake and everyone was told "good night" which Lucinda learned was the signal for lights to be turned out every night. Uncle Jake watched the electric meter on the outside wall as if he could slow its movement by staring at it. Lucinda learned that he often ran in the house to see what was being used if the meter hand was moving very fast, and demanded that short work be made of whatever it was.

Lucinda soon learned that Uncle Jake was an unusual character. He was a short rotund man, with small twinkling eyes and a moustache, who said what he thought and acted however he wanted to. "It ain't nobody's business what I do. They don't feed me and they don't buy my shoes," was his come back when Dora fussed at him about his actions. Lucinda got the shock of her life one morning when Uncle Jake was late getting up. Dora told her to go open his door to see if he was all right. When she opened the door, the first thing she saw was a bright, polished casket open on the floor with Uncle Jake in it. She stood gaping until Uncle Jake raised his head and looked at her, "I wus just wonderin if it still fit. I've got fat here lately."

Lucinda was so shocked that she just stood there, until Uncle Jake said, "What's the matter, Lucy? Ain't you never seed a casket afore?"

She finally mumbled, "I've never seen one kept in somebody's room before. You nearly scared me to death. I thought you were dead." Then she turned and went back to the kitchen to tell Dora. But before she could tell her, Uncle Jake came in, "Dory, why'd you send Lucy in there and not tell her about my casket? I thought she was going to keel over."

Dora cackled, "Pa, you done that for meanness, didn't you? You heard me telling her you had overslept and figgered I'd send her. I swear, Pa, you just won't do."

CHAPTER 12

That first morning Lucinda awoke at six o'clock to the smell of bacon frying and the voice of Dave Garroway and his little chimpanzee, J. Fred Muggs, waking America on the Today show. This doesn't seem much different from home, thought Lucinda. She grew up during World War II and every morning she was awakened to Lowell Thomas giving the war news on the radio. "If I can save some money, I'm going to buy Daddy a television," Lucinda promised herself.

She jumped out of bed and slipped into the chenille robe at the foot of her bed. She made her way downstairs and out the kitchen door to the outhouse. She had to go through the chicken yard to get there and going in was no trouble but the big Rhode Island Red rooster took exception to her invading his territory on her way back. She escaped with only one or two pecks which didn't quite make it through her thick robe. Dora laughingly told her that once he got used to her, she wouldn't have any trouble. Lucinda must have been hard to get used to because the rooster continued to be aggressive. This warranted hurried trips through the chicken yard each morning and night. Soon she devised a plan of throwing kernels of corn to the farthest reaches of the chicken lot and making a dash while the rooster ate. When she packed her bags each Sunday, three or four ears of unshelled corn were always included. She made no comment when her dad later said that his corn didn't seem to last this year.

Lucinda ate her breakfast of egg, biscuit, and bacon washed down with milk and then packed a peanut butter and jelly sandwich and an apple, which came from the Mullins' trees, before going to get dressed.

She took her usual sponge bath since no houses on the mountain had indoor plumbing. Then she donned a pleated navy blue skirt, a white cotton blouse, a lighter blue cardigan sweater, blue socks, and black and white saddle oxfords and was ready for school.

Lucinda hurried down the stairs and as she entered the kitchen to get her lunch, Dora turned from the stove. She looked Lucinda over and then burst out in a loud guffaw, "I'd like to see some of them boys' faces when you walk in. They'll think they've died and gone to heaven."

Lucinda stopped with a puzzled look, "What do you mean? Don't I look right or something?"

"You look all right for a fourteen year old but a lot of your students are boys sixteen and seventeen years old," Dora chuckled.

"But I'm eighteen years old and I'm the teacher," stated Lucinda with conviction.

"Well, girl, you know you're eighteen and you're the teacher but you look fourteen and purty to boot and that's how the boys are going to see you," Dora stated matter-of-factly. "I'll bet you'll be getting a lot of apples and hazelnuts this fall, especially from your male students."

"Maybe I should go back up and put on my blue corduroy outfit that I showed you last night. What do you think, Dora?"

"It won't make a bit of difference. You're not big as a piss ant and them blue eyes are going to shine no matter what you wear. Just go on girl, and act tough," Dora said smiling wisely. Seeing Lucinda's crestfallen look, Dora was immediately contrite. "Me and my big mouth," said Dora shaking her head. "Just go on, you won't have no trouble. Just don't pay no mind if the boys ask a lot of questions and leap to do your bidding. They're all harmless. One thing about it, I'll bet the attendance will be the best this year that it has ever been. Go on now. Just march right in there as if you was as big as a mountain, like me," instructed Dora.

All the way to the schoolhouse Lucinda repeated Dora's advice but actually following it was another matter. As she reached the top of the knoll that hid the schoolhouse from the main ridge, Lucinda heard children's voices filled with laughter. Also mingled in were rough masculine voices talking and laughing uproariously. Her heart sank, "What have I gotten myself into? I don't know how to teach little kids. But to teach grown men- boys- I don't even know how to act with them. Lord, please help me," breathed Lucinda as she started down the knoll. Her head was bowed until she heard, "Look, I guess that's the teacher."

Lucinda raised her head, squared her shoulders, and marched down the hill, smiling and saying, "Good Morning," as she went. When she reached the porch of the schoolhouse, she was completely encircled with small children, middle-sized children, big children, and grown men with beards.

"Some of these people must be parents," thought Lucinda looking up at a bearded young man who towered over her. "Which child is yours, sir?" asked Lucinda with a smile.

"Ain't none mine. I'm in the 8th grade," blurted the red-faced giant as the other students roared with laughter.

Seeing his discomfort, Lucinda reached out and touched his shoulder, "I'm sorry. It's just that you are so tall. What is your name?"

"James Estep," mumbled the giant and began to clear the way so Lucinda could enter the school. Thus her first day began and set the stage for most of the days of that year.

A small round woman with coal black hair plaited into one thick braid didn't take a seat with the other students. When Lucinda looked up, she said, "I'm a parent." The woman looked about 18 years old and Lucinda was amazed when she said three of the children were hers. Finding that her name was Nellie Blevins, Lucinda said, "Mrs. Blevins, you don't look old enough to be a mother."

"I'm twenty one but I got married when I was almost 15. I had the twins and a new baby just about every year, but if I could help it I wouldn't have any more," stated Nellie decisively.

Lucinda stood looking at her for a second and then mumbled, "You and I must have a talk, Mrs. Blevins. That is, if you want to."

"If you know some way to keep from having babies, I shore do want to know" blurted Nellie loudly.

That, of course, got the attention of all of the older students who perked right up anxious to hear more. A very embarrassed Lucinda moved quickly into the hall. Mrs. Blevins followed Lucinda out, just as Lucinda hoped she would. "We'll have to talk some evening after school," said Lucinda quietly, as she waved goodbye to Mrs. Blevins. Lucinda did not know much but she had Jason's book and remembered the things her roommate had told her about birth control.

Lucinda had been stunned when she came home and began telling Faye and Ellen what her roommate had revealed to her and they fell over laughing. *"They knew all the time but they still had babies,"* thought Lucinda and wondered why. When her sisters kept laughing, she ran outside feeling very foolish. It was much later before she realized that her sisters had really wanted their first children. But the others came because her sisters often had no access to the needed items. Odell's husband and maybe some of the others did not want to use contraceptives.

Lucinda planned to tell Nellie Blevins what she had learned from her girlfriends. She knew there were contraceptives, diaphragms, and the rhythm cycle touted by most Catholics. Surely Mrs. Blevins would be able to use one of them, or at least try. She could get her husband to buy the contraceptives since Amy had told her that a person had to go to the pharmacist and ask for them. It just wasn't right for a young person like Nellie to wear her body out having one baby after the other. Nellie was a pretty girl and just a little older than Lucinda but looked much older, which made Lucinda more concerned.

Lucinda thought of all this as she went back inside and began to seat all her students according to grades. She really did have 60 students, in grades 1st through the 8th. "Lord, give me wisdom and courage," breathed Lucinda silently as she stood looking at row after row of faces. She squared her shoulders, smiled bravely and said, "My name is Miss Harmon." She wrote her name on the board then printed it just beneath. Then in the notebook she had brought with her, she began on row one taking the name of each student, having to ask some to spell their names. She found that just like everyone she had been raised with, Louise was pronounced Lou-e-zy, Lester was Lus-ter, Panther was Pant-er, and Edgar was Egg-er.

In her record book she recorded four first grade students, eight second graders, eight third graders, ten fourth graders, eight fifth graders, ten sixth graders, six seventh graders, and six eighth graders. She assigned seats and handed out books, or at least what books she found in the metal cabinet at the back of the room. She was so engrossed in what she was doing that she did not see the three or four hands held high in the air until this rough male voice said, "Teacher, these younguns wants their recess. Are you goin to have one?" Lucinda gave a red faced glance at her watch and stood, "Children, I'm sorry. You are released for 15 minutes."

Lucinda walked onto the porch to keep a watchful eye over the playground. She was instantly surrounded; mostly by the first graders. She stood hesitantly in the center of the group for a few minutes and then taking a child's hand said, "Let's go play 'Drop the Handkerchief.' Do any of you know the game?" She was joined immediately by a laughing mob of girls. She looked at the boys and said, "Aren't you fellows going to play?"

"We ain't playing no sissy game like that," came from several directions until suddenly the small hand she was holding on her left was jerked from her to be replaced by the calloused palm of James Estep. She looked around in surprise and protest at the treatment of little Agnes Beavers, who was now crying. She started to reprimand James until Mary, Agnes's sister, pulled her into the place beside her in the circle. Then one or two at a time, most of the other boys joined in. By the time the 15 minutes was up, Lucinda had been the recipient of the handkerchief 10 times. She didn't have to make long runs, however, since all of the older boys always left a place for her to get back in the ring, beside of them of course.

When the noon recess arrived, Lucinda did not offer to play with the children. She feared the treatment received at recess. Putting her empty lunch bag on the porch steps, to protect her clothes, Lucinda sat to watch the activities. Soon she had to make room for all the little girls and some of the younger boys, who wanted to sit with her. She sat happy and content until a high pitched wail from the lower end of the playground sent her on a run to investigate. As she arrived on the scene, James Estep had already pulled Billy Puckett to his feet and was in the process of helping Garson Lester off the ground. Garson had a bleeding nose and Billy had scratch marks down his face. "Boys, why are you fighting?" questioned Lucinda angrily.

"He tripped me sos I couldn't catch the ball," accused Billy, pointing at Garson.

"No, I didn't, Teacher. I swear to God I didn't. He was running past me and tripped over my shoe," sobbed Garson. When Lucinda looked down she believed him. Garson was wearing a man's high topped work boots which were much too big for him. Lucinda almost wept as she really looked at this pitiful child. He wore a girl's blouse under bib overalls that only reached to just below his knees, no socks, and those huge shoes that made his thin spindly legs look like match sticks. "Were you trying to catch the ball too, Garson?" asked Lucinda.

"No, he don't play. He just gets in the way," sneered Billy. Looking at her watch, Lucinda grasped Garson's hand and said, "Well, lunch is over. We'll settle this on the inside. Come on. Let's go in now."

Inside Lucinda settled everyone down and then decided that she would try to turn this into a lesson of fairness and compassion. "We are going to have a trial and let you decide who is right or wrong. Now, we need a lawyer for each of these boys. Who wants to be Billy's lawyer?" When she got no volunteers, she was frustrated and wondered what to do. "Why don't any of you want to be a lawyer? This is just a way to learn about court trials. Wouldn't you like to know about things like that?" questioned Lucinda.

"We don't know what a lawyer is sposed to do," blurted J.D. Click.

"We ain't never seed a trial before," stated another boy. Then Lucinda realized she was going too fast and would have to just use a judge for this first time.

"I'm sorry. You're right and I'm wrong. I shouldn't have asked you to act as something you know nothing about. So, for this case, I will act as the judge and we won't have any lawyers today."

Lucinda proceeded to let each child who had witnessed the fight tell what they had seen happen. Not one child had seen Garson stick out his foot. In exasperation James Estep cut in, "Aw, these little old mean younguns are wastin time. We all know that Billy got mad cause he missed the ball and took it out on Garson. He does Garson like that cause Garson can't run and play on account of he has to wear his Pap's shoes. If I had got down there first, they wouldn't a been no fight. Billy knows I won't let him pick on Garson," finished James with a hard look at Billy. "Yeah," said many voices around the room and from that agreement, Lucinda said her verdict was that Billy should apologize to Garson and lose his recesses for two days. She asked if the students felt this was fair and they all agreed but some said he should be paddled. After saying he was sorry, Billy sat dejected either at the verdict or for fear of what James Estep would do to him. For whatever reason, he was quiet and the first discipline case was over for Lucinda.

This was a presidential election year and all the children were wearing buttons and arguing, and even coming to blows at times. They seemed to be enjoying it very much but Lucinda dreaded elections just as she always had. General Dwight David Eisenhower, the Republican, was running against Adlai Stephenson, the

Democrat, and Burb Harmon, since his eyes had gotten better, had been campaigning. Burb was the Republican committeeman for Sandy River District and Jim Puckett was the Democratic committeeman and even though they were friendly the rest of the time, they certainly were not during a campaign. The "big shots," as Nancy called them, were constantly coming from Welch to plan strategy with Burb. Nancy dreaded it almost as much as Lucinda.

Lucinda shuddered as she remembered the time, during the election in which Franklin Delano Roosevelt was challenged by Wendell Wilkie, that Burb went to the polling place with his pistol in his pocket. He also had a man there with jars of Noah Stewart's best moonshine whiskey, paid for by the men from Welch. The children had asked Nancy why their dad had taken a gun and who he was going to shoot? Nancy had explained that it was only to keep the peace. People still looked to Burb as they did when he was a county deputy and they would listen to him. Still, it was that same election when a man had gotten his ear bit off in a fight on the election grounds. It was also that same night when three men on horses had come down the road and Burb had gone out to meet them with the gun. Nancy always dreaded election time because she knew Burb would spend the last dime they had to get his candidate elected. They all remembered the time he sold their only cow to have money to spend in the election.

Lucinda was not old enough to vote the first time she remembered going to the polling place with Nancy. She was shocked at the language she heard, the number of drunks on the grounds, and the money changing hands before many people went inside to vote. Nancy only went to vote to keep Burb from yelling, "You don't care nothing about your country, woman. When we quit voting we'll lose our freedom." Lucinda knew, as did the rest of the family that Nancy could only vote for the Republican candidates if there was to be any peace at home. Lucinda decided early in life that when she was old enough to vote, nobody would know how she voted.

Even though Lucinda had a perfect opportunity to really create good lessons using the election, she just could not bring herself to do much. Some of the children wore badges and had stickers on their tablets and Lucinda did have a spelling lesson using election terms. She knew that the arguments were a reflection of what they heard at home and therefore ignored it all unless it came to fights. She also knew that anything she said would be carried home by the children. Since she was Burb Harmon's daughter they might be suspicious if she mentioned the Republican candidate more than once. She therefore tried to keep the children calm and steer clear of anything to do with elections.

This was the second major happening during the school year and had come right after they had held their "box supper" at the school. Lucinda and the parents had worked and planned and it had turned out well. They didn't want to wait until it was really cold and so had decided on the second Saturday night in October and hoped they didn't get a big snow. They knew that if it was set for the last Saturday night in October it would be Halloween and that would have been a bad time to have it. On Halloween local boys felled trees, blocked roads, scared people, and played all kinds of tricks.

CHAPTER 13

Box suppers were big social events for mountain people and everybody wanted to help. Dora Mullins and Nellie Blevins had asked people to bake cakes for the cake walks and asked stores to donate prizes for the pretty girl and ugly man contests.

Billy Puckett's brother Jessie had promised to get a local band to provide music and James Estep's dad volunteered to call the square dances and to auction off the boxes which the girls had brought.

Two of the Lester women made signs announcing the box supper and put them up in prominent places. Dora laughed and said, "I guess you know there'll be a lot of campaigning at the box supper, don't you? It'll be all right though. They'll spend big trying to get the votes, until they get drunk and get mad."

Lucinda told her that Gordon had asked the new deputy in Bradshaw to put in an appearance that night. He told Gordon he would but didn't know when nor how long he could stay. Dora seemed relieved and said, "I'm glad because the last time we had a box supper down here there was a pure free-for-all, but I think you've got it covered. So, I'm just going to have me a good time."

After that Dora was really excited and laughingly said, "We might even get us a feller. God knows I ain't going to meet none staying down on this ridge with Pa." Lucinda thought about that as she walked to school, wondering why Dora had never married again. Lucinda knew that Dora's husband had been killed six years before, and she had not dated since. Dora was a pretty woman, but a little on the big side, according to Burb. Gordon and Burb always laughed and said a man didn't want a woman so big he couldn't whip her. Lucinda doubted if Dora would stand still for a whipping from any man. She, herself, thought it might be nice to meet some decent man to take her to movies or skating, once in a while. But the idea of dating only made her think of Jason. She knew she would never love anyone else like she did him....she just couldn't. Now, that she hadn't seen Jason for so long, Lucinda wished a thousand times she had known more and hadn't been so silly. She thought her actions were due to her having so much trouble from that old lecher, Mr. Wilson. Of course, Jason had talked about wanting to marry her, silly or not, but now she explored every avenue imaginable trying to understand why he had never answered her letters. Deep inside she felt that something had happened, but now she was left with this deep longing like an open sore that would not heal.

As the date for the box supper drew closer, Lucinda was a nervous wreck, but she felt that everything was as near ready as she could make it. Her brother Gordon had the deputy sheriff from Bradshaw promise to show up sometime before ten o'clock and stay as long as he could. Burb said it would be safer even though mountain people were usually well behaved. "Well now, some of those boys on the ridge get kinda rowdy with moonshine in them," cautioned Gordon.

Lucinda had fixed her own box with great care, filling it with two of everything, including chicken, biscuits, apples, bananas, and cake. She had chosen lilac crepe paper to cover her box and tied it up with deep purple ribbons and bows. She hadn't planned to fix a box, but Dora had told her it was expected of the teacher.

Neither Burb, nor Gordon, was allowed to see Lucinda's box. They might describe it and if Junior Clayton found out he would be sure to buy it. Gordon laughed hilariously when he told Lucinda how much Junior Clayton was looking forward to eating with her at the box supper. So, she hid her box in a much larger box with crepe paper all around it and put it on the back of Burb's truck with the jars of Kool-Aid, the cake that Nancy had made, and the two door prizes she had bought.

Burb said he wouldn't be going, but Gordon would go to be with her. He seemed apologetic but Lucinda was silently pleased. After what Dora had said about campaigning, she had been dreading Burb's attendance. If Burb Harmon found himself in a crowd around election time, he would campaign, and often made people angry. "That's all right, Daddy. I know you don't like being out at night. I'll be fine with Gordon and Emily," said Lucinda.

Emily, Gordon's wife, had been a real sister to Lucinda and had helped her on many occasions. Lucinda could talk to Emily and tell her things she wouldn't tell her sisters. Emily didn't think she was silly and she always kept the secrets Lucinda shared with her. When some of the family put her down or hurt her feelings, Emily always understood but sometimes said, "You let people walk all over you. When are you going to learn to stand up for yourself? You shouldn't care to make them mad; they sure don't care to hurt you." Gordon was the kind of brother who tried to help all of his family. Lucinda couldn't talk to him like she did Emily but she trusted his judgment and knew she could depend on him if she needed him. Lucinda wished they lived on the mountain so she wouldn't be so lonesome.

The night of the box supper was warm, with big round harvest moon lighting up the school house and grounds. The entire school yard was now filled with cars, trucks, and many horses tied to the trees bordering the grounds. Lucinda was amazed at the number of people crowded into those two rooms. Even though it was October, the rooms were stifling hot and all the windows had to be raised. Everything was moving like clockwork and Lucinda began to relax and really enjoy herself. The only cloud on her horizon was the attempt to stay so busy that she couldn't be stopped by Junior Clayton.

Mr. Estep was a great emcee, the musicians played well, and best of all, she had heard no arguments. Ten cakes had been walked off before the pretty girl contest was begun. When the nominations began, Junior Clayton piped up with Lucinda Harmon. There was much clapping and shouting but, with a very red face, Lucinda declined since she was the teacher. There was much grumbling and complaining especially from Junior Clayton but her decision was accepted. Several other girls were nominated and a really pretty Lester girl won, bringing in $50.

When the Ugly Man contest was announced, Dora nominated Uncle Jake and several others were nominated. Uncle Jake ran neck and neck with Nellie Blevins' dad, Harvey Baker. When it seemed as if Mr. Baker would win, Uncle Jake climbed up on a chair, took out his false teeth, and made a truly horrible face. He immediately won, mostly because everyone was afraid he would fall off the chair and get hurt. "Pa, you get down off that chair, you old coot. You'll break your fool neck. You're seventy-five years old and trying to act sixteen again," shouted Dora, hurrying to help him down.

"Dory, you got a big mouth, girl. You didn't have to holler out my age," yelled Uncle Jake as she helped him to a chair.

Lucinda looked around warily, fearing that someone would be there with moonshine and ruin it for everyone. She also told Gordon to circulate. She wondered whether the deputy was going to show up. If her dad was any example, drinking a little moonshine would only loosen the billfolds of the men, but too much would lead to fights. *"What in the world will I do if fights break out,"* worried Lucinda.

Bidding off the boxes was the next thing on the program and Mr. Estep was very good at tantalizing the bidders with all the delicious food in each box. When each box reached $4.00, the girl who prepared the box had to come forth so bidders could get a look at her. This sometimes spurred the bidders on and sometimes the bidding stopped dead. When a really heavy Justus girl's box was up for bids, Lucinda heard somebody whisper, "I ain't spending my money to eat with that."

Lucinda had put her box near the end of the table, hoping the excitement would build on the others and hers would not draw much attention. It didn't work that way, however, for Mr. Estep picked boxes randomly from each end of the table. Suddenly Lucinda saw her box being held up in the air and she hoped nobody saw her look, or at least what she felt she looked like.

Mr. Estep turned the box around until all sides could be seen and said, "Now just look at this box. It's almost too purty to look at and it's heavy too. I'll bet some real purty gal has fixed this box. Who's going to start the bidding?"

From somewhere in the back came a loud fifty cents, then seventy-five cents, then $1.00 but then the bidding stopped. "Now come on. I know you fellers just got paid cause it's Saturday night. You can't see whose box this is unless it goes to $4.00," Mr. Estep stated. "Well, H-- uh, Heck, I'll bid $4.00," said James Estep, Lucinda's 8th grade student.

Mr. Estep lifted the box up and looking on the bottom said, "Well, what about this? My boy is going to get to eat with the teacher. Come on up here Miss Harmon, and let us look at you."

Lucinda walked dejectedly through the crowd until she stood beside Mr. Estep who immediately said, "Okay now, I'll bet there'll be some bidding cause she's purtier than her box, ain't she?"

"That she is and I'll bid $5.00," yelled out Junior Clayton and Lucinda's heart fell to be perked right up when another voice yelled $5.50. From there the bidding ran up to $10 and James Estep was heard to say, "Pap, will you let me have some more money?"

"Sorry son," replied Mr. Estep. "I may work in the coal mines but I've got a family who eats it all up faster than I can bring it in. I ain't like these single fellers. I guess you'll have to bow out of this one."

The $10 bid must not have been Junior Clayton's since he immediately bid $11 and from there it was run up to $20 and everybody was getting really interested. Lucinda was interested only in hoping that Junior Clayton did not get her box. The bidding went on to $25 and everybody had about quit. Junior Clayton started to get out his wallet and come up to get the box when another voice from the doorway said, "Thirty dollars."

Lucinda looked back and saw a tall, handsome stranger standing beside the deputy sheriff. Lucinda's heart caught in her throat for a moment. In the darkness she had thought it was Jason. He had Jason's build and until he came into the brighter light, his auburn hair looked dark. Everybody looked around, as did Junior Clayton, who immediately stiffened and yelled, "$35."

"Fifty dollars," yelled the stranger and Junior Clayton turned red and gave the man an angry look but made no further bid. The man who had won the box wore a brown leather bomber jacket with a fur collar, with a white turtleneck shirt underneath, and brown dress slacks. Lucinda realized he was taller than Jason but maybe heavier and more muscular. He walked with an easy assured gait and smiled, showing beautiful white teeth, as he made his way to the front and into Lucinda's life.

CHAPTER 14

Lucinda gazed in amazement at this tall auburn haired man who had spent $50 to eat with her. He had sparkling hazel eyes, or so Lucinda thought, but couldn't be sure. Whatever color they were, Lucinda felt warm from the way they seemed to devour her. His hair was cut short and lay in waves. He had a cap that looked like a part of an army officer's uniform which he carried under his arm. He placed his hat on the table and pulled a wallet from his back pocket and proceeded to extract a bill of money from a fold of many other bills. Mr. Estep said with a grin, "Well now, since you seem to have a lot more than $50 do you want to pay a little more to know her name?"

"I know her name is Lucinda Harmon. I know she is Burb Harmon's daughter. I know she's the teacher, and the prettiest girl I've ever seen," said the stranger with a smile, still gazing intently at Lucinda.

"What's your name?" asked Mr. Estep grinning. "I don't want to send our teacher off to eat with a feller when I don't even know his name."

The stranger stuck out his hand, "I'm Jeff Marshall. I came with Deputy Stevens, and I'm sure glad I did." He stood with the box in his hand for a few minutes, then looking at Lucinda, he smiled, "You do talk, I assume, since you teach school."

Lucinda flushed in embarrassment and said, "Of course I talk, but I'm amazed that you'd pay $50 for somebody's box that you've never seen before."

"Let's go find someplace to sit down and eat and then I'll explain myself," smiled Jeff. He put his cap back under his arm, held the box with the same hand and with his free hand grasped Lucinda's elbow and walked with her to the back of the room, passing Junior Clayton on the way. Junior gave Jeff Marshall a glowering frown and then snarled, "You had more money than I did tonight, Mister, but don't get any ideas about my girl."

"Junior Clayton, I am not your girl," sputtered Lucinda angrily.

The man looked down at Junior and smilingly said, "Seems like you're mistaken man. Better luck next time." Then he shoved two seats together with his foot and turning to Lucinda said, "Your seat, Miss Harmon," pointing to the chair on the left. Squeezing into the other seat, which was much bigger, he gave a sigh of relief and turned to Lucinda smiling. "I wasn't sure I could fit into these seats since they are for school kids."

"Some of my students are almost as big as you are," stated Lucinda as she adjusted her skirt.

Jeff motioned at Junior Clayton who was giving him a malevolent stare, "Well, it seems I have some competition. He isn't one of your students is he?"

"No, he is certainly not one of my students. What do you mean competition? Competition in what?" asked Lucinda puzzled.

"He seems to think you are his girl and you're going to be somebody's girl, aren't you?" asked Jeff.

Realizing he was probably just flirting, Lucinda changed the subject. "You were going to tell me why you paid $50 to eat with a stranger, remember?" queried Lucinda in expectation.

Jeff proceeded to untie the ribbons, unwrap the box, and lift the lid as he said, "When Jack Stevens asked me to come down here with him, I only came to kill some time. However, when I stepped up on that porch and looked inside I was certainly glad I came. I saw the prettiest girl I've ever seen and I'd have paid a $100 to get to meet you."

"Oh Lord, what should I say to that?" Lucinda nervously thought and quickly said, "You're way ahead of me, Mr. Marshall. I don't know you and you don't know me and I'm really not interested in being anyone's girl."

Jeff Marshall looked steadily at her before saying, "Well, let's eat and maybe you'll change your mind. I might be a really nice guy. What kind of men do you like?"

Lucinda was dumbfounded, "What kind of men? I don't like any kind of men. I mean, I'm not interested in any man," stated Lucinda flatly while thinking of Jason. By this time Jeff had divided the chicken, the fruit, and the cake on two napkins.

"Are you dating somebody, engaged, waiting for someone?" queried Jeff anxiously, holding a piece of chicken halfway to his mouth.

Lucinda, who had lost all desire to eat and only wanted this to hurry and be over with, answered, "Something like that."

"Something like what- engaged, dating, or what. Is it that man who is giving me those death looks? If it is, he's going to get a run for his money."

"Junior Clayton- Lord no. I wouldn't date him. It's...well there's somebody I care about," mumbled Lucinda, hoping that he would stop this line of questioning.

Jeff Marshall sat thinking and then said, "Does he care about you, and if he does, where is he tonight? I wouldn't send you out where all these men are by yourself if you were my girl. He must be crazy or blind."

"He's not here, I mean he doesn't live here," stated Lucinda defensively and took a bite of chicken which almost choked her. When she coughed and gasped for breath, Jeff reached over and slapped her back and then handed her an opened bottle of Nehi soda. When she regained her composure, she said, "Sorry, I guess I'm a little nervous."

"This is the first time I've had that kind of reaction from a girl, and I haven't even kissed you yet," said Jeff with a wolfish grin...

Lucinda's eyes blared in alarm as she stated, "You're not apt to get the chance either. Mr. Marshall, I appreciate you buying my box and helping the school but I don't appreciate your attitude." She rose quickly to her feet, saying, "I've spent too much time away from my duties. Excuse me please, and I- it was nice meeting you. Goodbye Mr. Marshall." She moved the hindering seats, and made her way back to the front of the room, where the last of the boxes were being offered. She busied herself with the cake walks, the gathering of loose paper, boxes, and food scraps, trying to get her thoughts in order and plan a way to handle this situation.

Mr. Marshall was good looking, seemed nice but was a fast talking flirt. He undoubtedly had money, and he was watching every move she made. She admitted that she found him attractive but that's all she knew, and then there was Jason. She knew she would never forget Jason but she didn't even know where he was. Last week, Ellen had learned from Maggie Barker that Jason was in the army. Lucinda didn't know if that was true or not and had no way to find out. He had said that he loved her and then wouldn't answer her letters. She had not heard a word from him since before she went to Huntington on that scholarship tryout. She had explained it all to him in her letter and then she wrote him again when she got back and got no reply from either letter. Then Nancy had written that he had left Bradshaw, but she didn't know where he had gone.

"Maybe he's in the army. What if he is in Korea," worried Lucinda. *"I'll never see him again,"* was her constant gloomy thought. *"Get him out of your mind. It's just not meant to be,"* she scolded herself.

Finally, the box supper was all over, and Lucinda began to pack up everything with the help of Dora, Nellie Blevins, the Esteps, Emily and Gordon. She went out to the truck carrying a crate of empty pop bottles to be returned to the store. As she stepped off the porch, Jeff Marshall reached out, taking the crate from her. "That's too heavy for you, little girl. You must have big muscles," he teased.

Thinking he had left after she had told him off, Lucinda was startled. "Thanks, but I am pretty strong. I was raised on a farm," explained Lucinda, as she flexed her muscles. "Where are you from, Mr. Marshall? You're not from Bradshaw, are you?" asked Lucinda.

"No, I'm from Gilbert, but I just got hired to work for Island Creek Coal Company. Right now, I'm living with an aunt over at Coalwood. Do you know where that is?" asked Jeff.

"Sure, I used to work in Welch, many moons ago, and rode the bus through Coalwood almost every weekend"

"It couldn't have been many moons. You don't look to be more than 14 now. I know you'd have to be older than that to teach, but I swear you don't look it," stated Jeff." I guess you'd have to be about 22 to have gone to college and now to be teaching."

"No, I'm only eighteen, but I don't have my degree. My Dad damaged his eyes in an accident in the woods and I quit college and came home to teach so I could help out," explained Lucinda. "I'm going to finish up in extension and summer school, though."

"Not many girls would do that," stated Jeff. "You must love your Dad very much. Didn't he have any medical insurance?"

"No, Dad's a private timber contractor," replied Lucinda. She thanked Jeff again for helping her with the bottles and started back to the building, but he stopped her.

"Lucinda, may I call you Lucinda? It seems so formal to call a girl your age Miss Harmon. Besides, I hate to say, Miss Harmon, may I see you again?" Jeff smiled expectantly.

"I don't really know that much about you, Mr. Marshall. You may be married or be anything since nobody around here knows you. Besides, you're too flirty," stated Lucinda bluntly.

"Jack, Jack," yelled Jeff. "Come over here and tell this young lady that I'm single, not a murderer, and that I don't flirt with everybody," commanded Jeff to the approaching deputy sheriff.

"Do you really want me to tell her about you?" asked the deputy smiling as he stood in front of Lucinda.

"Now, Jack, the truth. This is very important. Lucinda won't agree to date me just on my word, so tell her man, and none of your crazy stunts either," demanded Jeff.

Jack Stevens looked at Lucinda grinning, started to speak and then took another look at Jeff before saying, "He's telling the truth, Miss Harmon. I lived right beside him from the time I was three until I was thirteen. We were best friends and he's not married. He has broken a few hearts along the way, I guess, but I can't arrest him for that. The only bad thing about him is that he's got a better job than me and won't share his money," teased Deputy Stevens. Just at that moment the quiet was shattered by

140

the radio in the police car. Deputy Stevens ran to the car and answered the call. Turning to Jeff he said, "I've got to go Jeff. Sorry to break up your romance, but if you want to get back to Bradshaw tonight you need to get in this car." The Deputy started the car and began backing to turn.

Grabbing Lucinda's hand and giving it a squeeze Jeff said, "I'll be back down here about three o'clock next Wednesday evening. Is that all right with you? Please?" pleaded Jeff.

"Sure, you can come back but I'm not promising anything," stated Lucinda and Jeff mouthed, "Thanks," as he ran for the car.

Lucinda spent Sunday alone, not going to meeting with Nancy and Burb. She liked to be alone to think. Jason was still the only man she wanted to date but she would probably never see him again. It was really lonely here with no young people to talk to and nothing to do. Now she could watch television, since she had bought Burb a set with her last pay check.

She washed her hair and put it up on curlers then put together a meat loaf to have for Nancy and Burb's dinner when they returned. They would be surprised because they didn't know she could cook. Lucinda's sisters had run the house before they married and they had never allowed Lucinda to do much in the kitchen. During her growing up years it didn't matter to Lucinda whether she could cook or not. She had roamed the woods, hunted the cows, fed the pigs, dug potatoes, and chopped wood while building her dreams of getting away and doing great things.

Dora Mullins thought it was scandalous for an eighteen year old girl to be unable to cook, and had begun to remedy that situation. About once each week, Dora sat at the kitchen table and coached Lucinda as she cooked the evening meal. On other evenings she taught her how to fix special dishes and to bake cakes and pies. Last week Lucinda had mastered the meatloaf and since Nancy had all the ingredients, she would give them a treat. Lucinda smiled happily visualizing the expression on Faye and Ellen's faces when Nancy told them.

Burb and Nancy were surprised and grateful since they were both tired. They had taken Aunt Armindy to her daughter's house which was up a hollow in Stringtown. Burb had to put chains on the truck to get over the rutted road. Then he had to take them off when he got back to the highway to keep from wearing them out.

Lucinda hadn't been worried since Primitive Baptists and Old Regular Baptist meetings were always two hours and sometimes more, depending on the number of Elders present who got up to preach. Lucinda, who had gone with a friend to several Old Regular Baptist meetings, thought their meetings were longer than the Primitive Baptist where she went. Primitive Baptist preachers didn't get up and sing entire songs all by themselves. The congregation always sang with the preacher and he or some other Elder often lined, or called out the words, to the songs. Still, the Old Regulars seemed to have more preachers getting in the pulpit and then, with each one or almost each one singing a solo, plus the congregation singing some songs, their services lasted longer.

Burb took a nap after dinner while Lucinda and Nancy talked about her cooking and Lucinda told Nancy about Jeff Marshall and asked Nancy's advice.

"Well Lucy, I don't see as it would hurt anything just to maybe go to a movie or something with him. He must be a decent feller or the deputy wouldn't have said so, I don't think," advised Nancy.

142

Burb drove Lucinda back to Dora's around six
o'clock which gave her time to discuss Jeff Marshall with
Dora.

"Don't you be crazy, girl, and turn that good
looking feller down. I guess he's got a car else he couldn't
get down here, so get while the getting is good, I say,"
laughed Dora.

Lucinda had told Dora about Jason and now she
said, "But Dora, I love Jason and I don't care anything
about another man."

"You'll get over him, Lucy and besides he ain't
going to be back here. It's been almost a year, ain't it?
Don't you think he would have got in touch some way if he
loved you? Besides, you may find out you like Jeff much
better. I think you ort to give yourself a chance. It can't
hurt nothing," stated Dora with a laugh. "Shore wish I'd
get a chance like that. I tell you what- ask him if he's got an
uncle, older brother, friend, or jest an acquaintance and
we can double date," grinned Dora mischievously.

Lucinda made up her mind before she went to bed
to date Jeff, but awoke in the night crying over Jason.

CHAPTER 15

Lucinda awoke to a three inch snow on Wednesday morning. Always loving the first snow, Lucinda was even happier today since the snow would keep Jeff Marshall away. The burdened trees bowed in silent salute to the glistening snow as the sun rose high over the hills, streaking the surrounding community with a rosy glow. "A picture postcard," breathed Lucinda in appreciation. She pitched a snow ball at the Blevins' dog that always came to the gate barking as she passed. This morning the dog was accompanied by the Blevins children, bundled and ready to walk proudly beside the teacher.

The children played a game of walking in the teacher's tracks all the way to school, often falling and rolling in the soft white flakes. Lucinda hurried along before the children became wet and much colder.

The Justus children met them at the door with big smiles. "What's happened to make you Justus children so happy this morning?" asked Lucinda.

"My Daddy is coming home from the army," trilled a smiling Mindy Justus.

"Yeah, he's been over in Korea and he didn't get crippled," chirped her brother, Billy.

"That's wonderful," smiled Lucinda. "When is he coming?"

"He's in the hospital, but he'll be out in two or three weeks. Then he's coming home," stated Mindy proudly.

"He'll be home for Christmas, won't he, Teacher?" asked her brother doubtfully.

Leaning down to hug little Billy, Lucinda reassured him, saying, "Sure, Billy, if he gets out in two or three weeks that will be before Christmas."

This morning the students hurried through their lessons in order to begin on the decorations. Christmas was going to be special this year for Estep School. The box supper brought in $350 and every child was to get a present and a bag of edible treats. Dora and Nellie Blevins had volunteered to do the shopping after each child made a wish list. Dora said, "If they make a list, every youngun will get something it's been wantin and never hoped to get." She grinned happily, "Ain't that the best kind of gift to get? You know, always dreamin; but figgerin it will never be real, and then get surprised."

"Dora probably hasn't had many good surprises in her life," thought Lucinda as she listened. If men around here would take the time to see what a wonderful person Dora really is she'd be remarried in no time. But most men were attracted to a nice shape and a pretty face even if the woman was as dumb as a coal bucket.

Lucinda and the children spent the time after lunch decorating, and practicing the songs and poems for the Christmas play to be performed on December 20th.

With all the singing, Lucinda failed to hear the car pull into the school yard and when there was a knock on the door she jumped in surprise. She looked at her watch and saw that it was three o'clock. She feared that Jeff Marshall had made it after all.

She cracked the door, peeped out, and saw that it was Jeff Marshall. He had been trying to knock the snow from his boots and wore a frown at the results. The frown was replaced by a smile when he saw her. He looked at his watch, "It's three o'clock, Teacher. When do you let out school?"

"It's time right now, so if you will just go wait in your car," said Lucinda and Jeff went back off the school house porch.

"What's he doing here?" snarled James Estep, rising from his seat. What James did, the other children did, so they all stood up.

Frustrated, Lucinda said, "Well, since I've kept you late and everybody is already standing, just get your coats and lunch pails and go on home. We'll practice again tomorrow."

There was much scuffling and scrambling as the children donned their coats, boots, and hats. Finally they all left, except Garson Lester and James Estep, who dawdled along trying to be last. Hearing the final, "Bye, Miss Harmon. See you tomorrow," she turned to James, "Will you help Garson, James?" she asked. "His feet will be frozen trying to wade the snow in those shoes," she explained as she looked pleadingly at James.

"You know I will, Miss Harmon. Ain't I always done anything you asked?" questioned James under his breath as he left the building.

"Oh Lord, What else is going to happen this year? All I need is for that big giant to have a crush on me," groaned Lucinda. As she heard the last child go out the main door, she began straightening the desks, erasing the blackboard, and picking up dropped paper.

The door opened bringing in a blast of cold air and Jeff stood staring at her. "Do you also do the janitor work, Lucinda?" asked Jeff as he walked into the room.

"No, but Mrs. Blevins has enough to do without us leaving so much clutter," stated Lucinda. Jeff came to stand at her desk as she put it in order, "I'm surprised to see you. When it snows, people don't get out on the mountain roads unless they have to."

"And you were hoping I wouldn't come, weren't you, Lucinda?" asked Jeff as if reading her mind.

"Well, I- No, I wasn't hoping- I just don't know," stammered Lucinda awkwardly, not knowing how to be truthful without being rude.

Jeff unzipped his jacket, put his hands in his pockets, and walked over to peer out the window. He stood watching it snow for a few minutes, then turned, "Lucinda, you said this man you like is not here. When did you see him last, anyway?"

"It will be a year this Christmas" replied Lucinda sadly.

"Hell, the man must be a paragon to leave that impression," blurted Jeff. "Listen, I don't want to try to compete with this saint or whatever he is, but don't you think that in a year he would have gotten in touch if he cared?"

Lucinda dropped her head, "You may be right. Everybody says the same thing, so I guess I'm just being young and silly," said Lucinda trying to smile.

Jeff came around the desk and took her arm saying, "Come on woman, get your coat on and we'll go see the sights- wherever they are," as he helped her on with her coat.

Outside, Lucinda saw the new blue Ford pick-up truck and thought that no sights would be seen in it tonight. He'll never get it out of this ridge. It's too light in the rear end. As Jeff opened the door and helped her in, she said, "I hope you have chains for this truck."

"I shouldn't have any trouble. I didn't getting down here," said Jeff as he turned to Lucinda questioningly, "Do you want to go to the Sunset Drive-in on the highway or into Bradshaw?"

"I think I'd better not go any farther than the drive-in tonight. I'll have to go tell Dora, my landlady, first and I have to be back before nine o'clock," replied Lucinda.

Jeff had gotten his key in the ignition but turned in amazement, "Nine o'clock! Do you mean to tell me that you pay rent and still have a curfew?"

"No, not a curfew but nine o'clock is Uncle Jake's bedtime. That's when he turns the lights out and that means everybody goes to bed and I don't want to break his rules. Dad told him to watch out for his little girl, so, no, I don't intend to be out past nine," stated Lucinda firmly.

Shaking his head in wonder, Jeff started the engine and said, "Okay, where does this monster live?"

Lucinda directed him to Dora's house where he went in to be introduced. She told Dora and Uncle Jake where they were going and said she would be back before nine o'clock.

"Young man, if you think you can bring a pick-up truck down here and get back up Tom Wyatt hill without chains and some weight in the back end you're not as smart as you look like you are," stated Uncle Jake loudly.

"I have chains, but I don't have any weights. You just mean something heavy to hold the back end down, right?" asked Jeff.

Dora asked, "Pa, could he put about three of them cinder blocks piled up by the woodpile in there tonight?"

"Well, I reckon he could, especially since Burb Harmon said to take care of his girl. At least that way, he can get her back here in one piece," grinned Uncle Jake.

After thanking them both, Jeff held the door open and Lucinda preceded him out to the truck. She pointed out the cinderblocks on the way and Jeff knocked the snow off of three blocks and heaved them into the truck bed over the tailgate. Lucinda thought he must be very strong since those were large blocks. She watched him being so careful about damaging the paint on his truck as

148

he positioned the blocks just right, one at a time. "They'll slide all over the bed of his truck as he goes up Tom Wyatt hill no matter how he loads them," Lucinda said aloud, chuckling softly. *"When he gets his truck all scratched up he'll not come down this ridge again,"* thought Lucinda.

Jeff pulled out into the road and then turned on the radio. Ralph and Carter Stanley came on loud and clear, making Lucinda wince. Jeff immediately turned off the radio saying, "I play the radio all the time when I'm by myself, but I don't need it now."

"It's okay if you want to play it. It won't bother me," said Lucinda, even though Bluegrass was not her favorite music. She had been raised on the music of Uncle Dave Macon, Bill Monroe, and Ernest Tubb, and hadn't liked it then and liked it less now. Until she went to high school, Lucinda had only heard the music which the older girls played on the radio. They listened to "Farm and Fun Time" with Lester Flatt and Earl Scruggs, and "the Grand Ole Opry" on Saturday night when Burb would allow it. Most of the time he wouldn't let them sit up and play the radio, saying it ran the battery down.

In high school Lucinda was in the school choir and she loved it. She had learned not to practice at home though. One time she was singing *Love's Old Sweet Song,* as she drove the cows up through the field and Ernie heard her. When she got home he was telling about hearing a ghost moaning down in the Rachel field. They all laughed and had a really good time at her expense.

Later when she went to work in Welch, her landlady played the piano and had lots of classical records, and Lucinda fell in love with music. She also found that she loved musicals in the movies. Then when she went to college and heard Leroy Anderson's "Blue Tango" and

Tommy Dorsey's Big Band music, she found her kind of music for life.

All these thoughts flickered through her mind as the truck labored and spun through all the snow, now churned into mud and slush, on the way out of Estep Ridge. They didn't talk much since Jeff had to concentrate on keeping the truck going and out of the deepest ruts. In the long level place through Murphy's Flat, Jeff said, "Why in the world would people want to live in a place like this?"

"It's their home. They've lived here all their lives and made out fine. I live on a ridge myself. We are all used to putting chains on and off at the highway," defended Lucinda.

"What about the kids who go to high school? Or do any of them go to high school? School buses don't come down in here, do they?" questioned Jeff.

"No, buses don't run on any of these ridge roads. Some kids walk to the highway, like I did but Sarah Lester, a widow lady on this ridge, really intends that her girls go to high school. She made some kind of arrangement so that her oldest daughter stays with the postmistress and goes to school. I'm sure that the three in my school will do the same," Lucinda stated in admiration.

"How far did you walk to catch the bus?" asked Jeff.

"Dad said it was two miles but in the winter it seemed like four," laughed Lucinda. "If I hadn't wanted to learn so badly it would have been tempting to just stay at home."

Jeff looked at her solemnly, "Most girls would have, you know. Why didn't your Dad take you to the bus stop? He has a truck, doesn't he?" asked Jeff.

By now they had reached Tom Wyatt hill and Jeff shifted into second gear and went roaring and spinning up the hill and made it almost to the top before the truck slid first one way, with Jeff fighting the wheel, and then it went the other way, before going into the ditch line. The back left wheel was down in the ditch and the right front was lifted off the ground. There they were and Jeff couldn't get out of his door.

Pounding the wheel, Jeff shouted, "Hell- what a damn mess." Then turning to Lucinda, he said, "I'm sorry, Lucinda. I guess you'll have to get out and let me out that side. I'll get us out of this mess some way."

Lucinda pushed but could not get the door open. Jeff levered himself over with great difficulty since the truck was slanted. Finally, almost in Lucinda's lap, he gave a tremendous shove, and crushing Lucinda in the process, got the door open. He had to climb over Lucinda and tumble out. He reached up his arms for Lucinda but the door slammed shut and he had to wrestle it open again. After three tries, Lucinda lurched forward and fell into Jeff's waiting arms almost causing both of them to fall.

Jeff righted himself, stood Lucinda in the snow, avoiding the sticky mud, and then turned to the truck. He went to the back and Lucinda heard a thump and another curse. She walked back to the rear end of the truck and saw how deep the ditch line was. "I think you'll need to get a pole or something to lift up on the rear end, and then maybe I can push," she started, but didn't get to finish.

"You push! That would be like an ant trying to move an elephant," grumbled Jeff as he angrily strode down the hill, to return with a fence rail.

"If you took that off Tom Wyatt's fence you'd better not break it or he'll have you arrested," stated Lucinda.

"Let him- then he can get this truck out," replied Jeff in exasperation. He put the rail under the back of the truck, stood on the bank above the ditch line, and tried to pry the wheel out of the rut. It moved slightly, but not enough to help. Swearing, he shoved the rail under the wheel again, but only succeeded in sliding off the bank, into the ditch himself. He climbed out, and gave the truck a mighty kick, before wiping the mud from his face.

"You're acting like a child throwing a tantrum," blurted Lucinda. "It isn't the truck's fault that we went into the ditch."

Jeff gave her a look of exasperation, "I know it, but I'm so mad. I just needed to get rid of some of my anger. I don't know how in the hell to get this damn truck out."

Luckily, Mr. Estep and his son James, who had been to the store, were returning home. They stopped, got out, and seeing the expression on Jeff's face, Mr. Estep said, "You ain't used to these roads, are you son?" He looked over the situation, then got back in his jeep, turned it around, and backed up as close to the truck as he could. Getting a logging chain from the jeep, he hooked one end to a trailer hitch on the back of his jeep, and the other end to the front bumper of Jeff's truck. This done, he told James to get in the jeep and Jeff to get back in his truck. Then, going behind the truck, he put the fence rail under the axle, and told James to put the jeep in first gear, and pull out. He told Jeff to be ready to hit the gas as his truck got traction. After much spinning and slinging mud, the truck came out and up onto solid ground. As the truck moved up the road, Lucinda looked at poor Mr. Estep. The mud from the ditch had been flung in his face and on his clothes, and yet he smiled as if that was a normal occurrence.

Lucinda walked up the edge of the road, keeping out of the mud, to where the truck was and was helped back in the truck by James. "Looks like a fool would know to put on chains in the winter," smirked James.

"James, hush your mouth," stormed Mr. Estep as he walked up the hill behind the truck. He looked apologetically at Jeff.

Jeff frowned but said, "He isn't far wrong. Mr. Kinnard told me I'd better put chains on, but with the cinder blocks in the back, I thought I could make it. I should have listened to him," stated Jeff, grinning from a muddy face. Mr. Estep was worse since he looked like he had fallen in a large muddy pool. He had wiped his eyes and mouth and, thankfully, his cap kept his hair free of mud.

Jeff looked at Mr. Estep contritely, "I'm so sorry Mr. Estep. I wouldn't have had this to happen for anything. But, I honestly don't know what I would have done if you hadn't come along. I thank you so much. How much do I owe you?"

"Nothing. I'm glad to help you young fellers learn. I'll bet you'll know next time," said Mr. Estep, grinning as he helped Jeff put on the chains.

He left them, going to his jeep with a hearty laugh at Jeff's mud-spattered clothes, but still refused the money Jeff offered.

Lucinda sat happily thinking, *"I'll not be bothered with Jeff Marshall after this. He sure is mad, and I can tell it is killing him to have mud all over him, and his truck too. It will be better if he doesn't come back since he's got such a bad temper and cusses like a sailor."* She was more convinced when Jeff opened the door and raked his once shiny boots against the edge of the running board, trying to rake off some of the sticky clay. He swore again, but softly this time, as he climbed in the truck anyway, bringing great chunks of mud with him.

Turning to Lucinda, he said, "I'm sorry Lucinda. What a mess! I wanted it to be so perfect but I promise you I'll come more prepared next time."

CHAPTER 16

Lucinda realized, then, that Jeff Marshall was very serious in wanting to date her. She admitted that it felt good to have a handsome man act like he was crazy about her. He also seemed nice except when he was angry. So she made up her mind that she would date him for a while. It was lonely at home, and if she dated Jeff, she would at least have something to look forward to.

When they reached the highway Jeff did not bother to take off the chains. It was only two miles to the Drive-In, and he would need the chains again to take her back to Dora's. Every time he heard a clink, however, as the chains banged against the fender of his truck, he winced in agony.

At the Drive-In, Jeff got out saying, "Do you mind if I find the rest room and get some of this muck off? I hate mud and dirt!" Lucinda nodded her assent, recognizing that being muddy was making him very uncomfortable. He returned, mostly mud free, except for his boots and pants. He grinned, "I tried to clean myself up. I hope you know that I'm usually not this messy."

The waitress soon came out to take their order. While waiting for their food, they talked easily, getting to know each other. Lucinda learned that Jeff had two sisters, one older than him and the other younger, and two younger brothers. Margie, his oldest sister, was married and lived in Logan, and Jill, the younger sister, was engaged to the coach at Pineville High School. His brothers, Bob and Jimmy, both attended Gilbert High School. His father was a disabled railroad engineer. His parents lived in a coal company house which they had been allowed to purchase.

Jeff had finished high school but didn't go to college. His Dad had gotten hurt in a train wreck, just before Jeff graduated from high school. Jeff had gone to work to help out. He became a miner, since the only kind of work he could get was in the coal mines. His uncle, who lived at Panther, got him a job at Cub Creek for the Walter Day Coal Company. He was seventeen years old when he went to work loading coal in 24 inch coal buckets. "I had to hold my lunch pail in my teeth, crawl back to where the coal was, and lay on my belly sometimes. But, if the roof was a little higher, I could double my legs up under me, and shovel coal. Later, I had the lofty name of brakeman, but first, I loaded coal on a pan line which was little pans that moved on a chain out to the cars, which were loaded with coal." At Lucinda's shocked gasp, he continued, "Needless to say, I looked for another job right fast. I only worked there for two months, but I would get terrible headaches from the fumes and smoke when a dynamite blast was set off. I had to go back to the face to load the coal, before the smoke had cleared. On that job I worked the day shift and then doubled back and did the night shift, and still only made $16." Seeing Lucinda's amazement and yet impressed expression he continued, "Then at Mill Creek Coal and Coke Company, at English, I graduated to a real brakeman. I had to go in with a string of cars, get them loaded, and bring them back out, while laying flat down in the coal," laughed Jeff.

"Where did you go to work then? I would have left here and gotten a job somewhere else," stated Lucinda.

"I needed to stay close to help Dad so I went to Mill Creek and then to No.1 Bartley, where I am now. There weren't many jobs when I started but now there's plenty of work for a miner. The pay is good, and you can't get fired for nothing, now that we have the union. A miner makes more money than any other work around here, and I like money," said Jeff smiling.

Lucinda made no comment because she knew her dad and brothers did not like unions. Burb always said that unions had too much control over the workers' lives, and he also said it made it hard on the companies. The company couldn't fire a man, even if he 'wasn't worth the powder and lead to blow his brains out,' as long as he belonged to the union, according to Burb. Lucinda didn't know what to think, but her dad was a pretty wise man, and he sure wouldn't work for a company that forced him to join a union. Lucinda's brother Gordon worked for Island Creek Coal Company, but he was on salary, and didn't belong to the union.

Lucinda's other brothers had married and moved away to Michigan and Virginia, and were working in other industries. Nathan, her oldest brother, owned his own construction business, near Radford, Virginia, and Ernie was an insurance salesman for Horace Mann Insurance Company, in Monroe, Michigan.

By the time they returned to the Mullins household it was eight o'clock. Lucinda turned to say thanks as she opened the truck door, but Jeff stopped her, saying, "Wait, not so fast Lucinda. It's only eight o'clock anyway. Now, when can I see you again? What about a movie Saturday night? There's a movie called *Shane* playing at the Hatfield Theater in Bradshaw. Alan Ladd stars in it, and he's good- or don't you like Westerns?"

"I like some Westerns. I guess Saturday night will be okay, if Dad and Mom don't care." Lucinda thought that she would have someone her own age to talk to, and the weekends wouldn't be so long, if she dated Jeff.

"Brushy Ridge isn't as long as this one is it?" asked Jeff. When Lucinda told him it was only two miles to her home, he smiled with relief. "Good. I'll be there about five o'clock, since the movie starts at 7 o'clock, and we'll want to get something to eat first. Does that sound good to you?" asked Jeff smiling.

"Sure, I think that will be fine. I mean, I don't guess Dad will care," stated Lucinda hesitantly.

Jeff reached over and picked up Lucinda's hand lying in her lap, and rubbed the back as he said, "I've really enjoyed myself this evening, even with getting in the ditch and having muddy clothes. God, it will take me a week to get this mud out of my truck- but it's still been worth it. The next time I come down here though, I'll borrow Jack Stevens' jeep. He's looking for me a place to live in Bradshaw, which will be closer to my work, and closer to you. It's a long way to Coalwood, and somebody else may try to snatch you up. If I'm his neighbor, he'll be more willing to loan me his jeep," quipped Jeff with a grin.

"If you have a good place where you are, hadn't you better stay there? If you're staying with your aunt, I'm sure it is much better than you could find in Bradshaw," said Lucinda, not wanting him to move, if it meant that he thought they would be going steady.

Jeff sat looking at her as he held her hand, and Lucinda sat very still, but did not pull her hand away. "Lucinda, I want to be closer, so I can see you as often as you will allow me to. I enjoy being with you," said Jeff rubbing the back of her hand.

Lucinda had enjoyed herself, or at least enjoyed doing something different, and Jeff was nice. Suddenly she smiled, "I enjoyed myself too, Jeff. Thanks for all the trouble." She patted the hand holding hers, and said, "But, now I have to go in because I have a set of papers to grade tonight."

When she patted Jeff's hand, he grasped both her hands between his, and smiling said, "It wasn't too bad, was it Lucinda? See, I told you we only needed a chance. I know one thing, I'd never walk off from you without a word, and that's a promise." Then, he started to move across the seat toward her, but Lucinda pulled her hands away, and quickly opened the truck door.

"I'll see you Saturday evening, Jeff. Be careful going back out of the ridge," cautioned Lucinda, as she slammed the door. She didn't remember Uncle Jake's cinder blocks, until she got in the house.

Lucinda changed her mind several times before Saturday, but Ellen and Nancy told her how foolish she was, to 'moon around over a lost cause,' according to Nancy. When five o'clock came, Lucinda was dressed in a blue corduroy jumper with a white blouse underneath, saddle oxfords, and white socks. She thought she looked fairly nice, and Nancy said, "Burb, don't our little girl look pretty?" Burb looked up from his paper, and studied her, then said, "Yeah, she looks like a pretty little girl. I swear Cindy; you ain't big as a pissant. You need to grow some. Are you eating enough?" Lucinda vowed that she ate too much at Dora's, and they knew how much she ate at home.

Lucinda thought that she looked good, but changed her mind when Jeff told her, "I almost feel like I'm taking a kid out tonight. Every time I see you, I swear, you look younger."

"Well, I'm not a kid, but I'm getting older by the minute," Lucinda said with a smile, deciding to never wear this outfit again. "Maybe I should put my hair up in a bun. I'll bet that would make me look older."

"Don't you dare? That hair is too beautiful to hide. I like you just as you are, even if people will think I've kidnapped somebody's kid," laughed Jeff.

They laughed and talked all the way down Bradshaw Mountain. Lucinda soon realized that Jeff was deliberately swinging the truck around the steep curves, in an attempt to make her slide closer to him. She hung on though, and didn't move an inch. Jeff laughed triumphantly, as he made a wide, quick swing on the last curve, and she slid over before she could catch herself. His arm quickly encircled her waist, and pulled her more snugly to his side. Lucinda tried to pull away, but he held her, saying, "I swear, I don't pinch or bite, but I am cold. So be still woman, before we both freeze to death."

They rode into Bradshaw, and stopped at the bus terminal, where Jeff said they could get a good meal. "I almost went on to Bartley, while I had you this close to me," said Jeff as he released her to get out. "But, if I had started on through Bradshaw though, you would have tried to jump out, and I would have wrecked," laughed Jeff as he got out.

They went into the bus terminal where numerous people knew Jeff. Soon several young men came over to their table and started talking to Jeff, but kept ogling Lucinda. She was beginning to feel uncomfortable, and Jeff was getting upset and angry. From clinched jaws, he abruptly said, "Sorry fellas. She's my girl, and I think you need to go ogle somebody else. Besides, we need to eat before the movie starts, so please excuse us." The men frowned sourly, but slowly moved away, without being introduced.

They ate fried chicken, green beans, creamed potatoes, biscuits and peach pie with ice cream for dessert. Lucinda only ate half of the food on her plate and Jeff said, "Lucinda, no wonder you're so small, you eat like a bird."

"There's enough food on that plate to feed a logger. You've been telling me how little I am, and then want me to eat like a horse," said Lucinda, laughing.

They finished their meal and went to the theater, with Jeff holding her hand as they crossed the street. Once seated, he put his arm around the back of the seat, and Lucinda didn't move away. They sat this way, drinking Pepsi and eating popcorn, until the movie was almost over. She did get upset, however, when Jeff asked her something, and when she turned to respond, was soundly kissed. Lucinda angrily jerked away, "What's the matter with you? This is a public place and besides I don't want you to do that. I want to go home," she demanded, as she rose from her seat.

The movie was just ending, and Jeff rose without a word, and walked out behind her. At the truck, Jeff unlocked the door, and opened it for her. Lucinda climbed in, and sat almost in tears, not understanding why. It really wasn't awful- the kiss was rather nice in fact, but it wasn't Jason who kissed her.

Jeff slowly got in, closed the door, started the engine, but didn't pull out. He turned to Lucinda, "You sure know how to deflate a man's ego. I've never had a girl to act as if I was repulsive," stated Jeff.

Lucinda recognized she had hurt him, and didn't really mean to. She also realized that she had acted pretty awful. She turned towards Jeff, and put out her hand, "I'm sorry. I acted awful and the kiss wasn't bad at all. It was- well, unexpected - and all those people saw us," stammered Lucinda.

Jeff grasped her hands, giving her a sober look, "You do beat all, Lucinda. You're making a pure yo-yo out of my emotions. I'll have ulcers before I really get to know you," smiled Jeff. "After we get on the road, will you sit over here beside me please?" begged Jeff.

Lucinda moved over, as they left the middle of the town, and in this way, they rode all the way to Lucinda's house. When they stopped at the gate, Jeff said, "I want to kiss you again, but I'd hate the same reaction?"

"I told you I was sorry, Jeff, but I don't..." but suddenly she was in his arms being kissed. She realized that Jeff knew a lot about kissing.

"Oh Lucinda, I just knew I'd love kissing you, but I wondered if I was going to ever get to find out," whispered Jeff before he kissed her again.

Lucinda pulled away, dazed, and opened the truck door, but Jeff stopped her, "What about tomorrow? Can we go somewhere or do something tomorrow? Is there any place you'd like to go or anything you'd like to do?"

"I'll be gone all day tomorrow, and I have to go back to Dora's tomorrow evening," said Lucinda.

"Where are you going tomorrow, and who with?" asked Jeff jealously.

"I'm going with Mom and Dad over in Virginia, to church. They always have dinner, so we'll be gone most of the day," Lucinda said wondering why he seemed so upset.

"Oh! Well, I guess that's okay, but what if I come and take you back to Dora's?" questioned Jeff eagerly.

"Sure, that's fine, if you want to. It will save Dad from having to take me. It won't save you any, though," smiled Lucinda.

It was settled that he would come at 5:30, and they would go to the Sunset Drive-In to eat, before they went back to Dora's. Jeff wanted to kiss her again, but Lucinda got quickly out of the truck, and went through the gate, before she turned and said, "See you tomorrow evening, then. Goodnight, Jeff."

CHAPTER 17

Jeff was there promptly at 5:30 on Sunday, but he was in a jeep. When he entered the front room, Nancy offered him a seat by the stove after he had shaken hands with Burb.

"Would you like a piece of cake and some coffee?" asked Nancy.

Jeff looked up, smiling, "Thanks Mrs. Harmon, but I guess I'd better not. Lucinda and I are going to eat at Sunset Drive-In," he explained.

Lucinda came in, pulling on her gloves, and carrying her suitcase and purse. "I'm ready, Jeff, whenever you are," she said, as she bent to change into her boots.

"I'm ready, too. Did you notice that I drove a jeep? I guess your parents know the story about the ditch line, don't they?" questioned Jeff.

"Yeah, she told us" laughed Burb. "You must have lived in the coal camps all your life or you would have knowed what a mess these roads get in, in the winter."

"You're right. I was raised in a coal camp, and Wednesday was an experience I won't forget for a good while. I thought I'd never get that mud off my boots, and out of my truck. I've not even tried to wash my pants yet," laughed Jeff.

"Do you do your own washing?" asked Nancy. "Most boys take their clothes home for their mama to do."

Jeff grinned in amusement, "I'm a little old for a boy. I'm 28 years old and have been on my own for a few years. I was living with an aunt at Coalwood, but I have a room in Bradshaw now." Then seeing that Lucinda was ready, Jeff said, "I guess we'd better go. It was nice meeting you, Mr. and Mrs. Harmon."

"Lucy, if you get sick or need us, get Dora's brother to leave word at the store. They'll tell Burb or Gordon." This was said as Nancy came over and hugged Lucinda good-bye.

The jeep was harder to get into, but with Jeff's help, Lucinda was soon seated and ready to go. Since the jeep had bucket seats, there was no snuggling close and Jeff looked over and said, "You are a mile away, but there's nothing for it, unless you want to sit on my lap," smiled Jeff with raised eyebrows.

"I don't think so, Mr. Marshall. I'm quite comfortable where I am," teased Lucinda playfully.

"Well, don't blame me, if we both freeze to death, with all that air space between us," teased Jeff.

Thus they spent the trip out to the Sunset Drive-In, where they had bacon, lettuce, and tomato sandwiches, fries, and sodas. Lucinda had refused a milkshake, saying it was too much with all the other food. Still, Lucinda left part of her food on the tray.

They drove slowly back down Estep Ridge. Jeff pulled over at Murphy's Flat and Lucinda looked puzzled.

"Why are we stopping here? It's getting late, and we need to go on."

Jeff leaned over just as Lucinda turned back from looking out the window and kissed her quickly, and started to pull her over. Lucinda jerked away, "Jeff Marshall, if you have any idea that I'm in any way indecent, just get it out of your head right now. Take me on to Dora's, or I'll get out and walk the rest of the way."

Jeff looked astonished, "A man can kiss a girl without thinking she's indecent. Sure, I'm a man, and I'd like more than a kiss, but I don't go any farther than I'm allowed to go. I wasn't going to do anything but kiss you though, honest. Don't look so shocked. You're in no danger from me. Lucinda, I know we haven't known each other long, but I feel something very special about you." Seeing that Lucinda was still unsure, Jeff smiled, "All right, I promise - no more stops on lonely roads." He shifted into gear and pulled out, and drove slowly on to Dora's house, where the porch light was on. Jeff got out, took Lucinda's suitcase, and started walking her to the house. As they passed the wood shed, which cast a shadow hiding them from the house, Jeff said, "Just a minute, you have something in your hair." Lucinda turned and was pulled gently into his arms, and thoroughly kissed. Lifting his head, he then kissed her face, saying "something here and here" as he showered kisses on her face, and then returned to her lips, just as they heard the house door open. Lucinda pulled away, and started on, and Jeff grabbed the suitcase from where he had dropped it, and moved on behind her.

Uncle Jake spoke from the porch, "It's a good thing you showed up. I was coming out to turn off the light. You ort to watch that meter hand run when this porch light is on. Hurry on in, before we all freeze to death."

Jeff yelled, "I'm not coming in Mr. Kinnard, but I've brought your cinder blocks back. Do you want them put back in the same place?" Uncle Jake told him to put them beside the shed, waved off his offer of payment, but accepted his thanks, before he pulled on the chain that turned off the porch light, and went inside.

Thus the pattern was set for Lucinda's courtship which would prove to be much briefer than Lucinda had intended.

Lucinda's weeks were taken up with trying to impart knowledge and kindness to her students, and her Wednesday evenings and weekends were spent with Jeff. She was growing to like him very much. Yet a song, a word, a train whistle, and many other things, would make her think of Jason, and she'd feel unbelievably sad. She tried desperately to put that part of her life behind her, since she had no other choice.

When little Mindy Justus' dad came home, she came to school, talking proudly about her Dad, but Billy was upset. "My Daddy ain't crippled but he can't hardly see. He has to wear them old dark glasses all the time and he falls into things," complained Billy.

"But, he's getting better, Billy. He says a doctor over in Korea worked on his eyes, and now he has to go to Welch every week. He thinks he will get to see better after a while," stated Mindy.

Lucinda assured them both that doctors knew a lot more now than they once did, and there was a good chance that he would get better. They seemed to feel better before they went home, but the next week, on Thursday, they came with their mother and said they were moving to Iaeger. Mrs. Justus said they had to move, since there was no way they could get to the doctor every week from down on the ridge. Before she left, she told Lucinda that the doctor that used to be in Bradshaw was the one that treated her husband in Korea.

Lucinda trembled inside as she asked, "Do you mean Dr. McCall?"

"I don't know. That was before we moved here. Carl just said he used to be in Bradshaw, and what a good doctor he was," replied Mrs. Justus.

Lucinda just knew that it was Jason. That's why he hadn't written. Maybe he hadn't gotten her letters, but Lucinda couldn't see how, since Amy Jordan had taken them to the post office to mail, or at least she said she had. Lucinda wondered if he was still in Korea. What if he had gotten hurt or killed? Lucinda shivered at the thought.

That night she told Dora about what Mrs. Justus had said, and Dora thought it wasn't likely, since that doctor had operated on Carl Justus' eyes. "Your Jason wasn't no eye doctor was he? I thought he was just a family physician," stated Dora.

"That's right, he was, because he told me that if he wanted to specialize, he would have to go back to school, for at least two years," said Lucinda.

She felt somewhat reassured, but it started her dreaming about Jason again, and that Saturday night she went shopping in Richlands, Virginia, with Gordon and Emily, and didn't wait for Jeff. She told Nancy to tell him that she felt like they were getting too serious, and she had decided she didn't want to date anyone, for a while. Nancy didn't want to give him that message, since she had gotten to like Jeff, and thought Lucinda was making a mistake. Lucinda went on with Gordon, but she was miserable the whole time, and Emily finally said, "Lucinda, are you certain that you don't like him? Jeff Marshall is crazy about you. He's got a good job, and he's good to you. I believe he would get you anything you asked for. What do you want, anyway?"

"I know - I know," said Lucinda. "It's just that- well, I can't forget Jason McCall. I know I'll probably never see him again, but I just can't help it. I was doing well until Carl Justus came back from Korea and mentioned a doctor from Bradshaw. Then it started all over again," sighed Lucinda.

Gordon had been quietly driving but now spoke up, "Sis, do you think you're being fair to Jeff? After all, you have been seeing him on a regular basis, and I know for a fact that he has you a Christmas present."

"Oh no," moaned Lucinda. "I don't want to hurt Jeff. I really like him, and he is so good to me. I don't know what to do. What should I do, Gordon?"

"I think you should forget about that doctor. He ain't our kind. You ask anybody, and they'll tell you that a person is better off to marry someone like themselves. I mean, somebody that don't feel like they are better than we are," stated Gordon firmly.

"But Gordon, Jason wasn't like that. I know he was from a big city, and yes, our ways puzzled him, but he didn't feel like he was better than us. We loved each other - it was real," explained Lucinda.

"Sis, that was the first man you ever thought you loved, and you were young. Don't you think the relationship was colored by all the excitement of living away from home, meeting a man from a big city, and the 'being swept off your feet' kind of thing?" questioned Gordon.

"I don't know. I just don't know," groaned Lucinda and remained quietly miserable all the way home.

When they got home, Nancy and Burb were still up, and the first thing Nancy said was, "Don't ever ask me to do a thing like that again, Lucy. That boy was tore all to pieces. He turned so white, I thought he was going to faint. He went out of this ridge flying. I was afraid he'd wreck. It wouldn't surprise me if he gets drunk tonight."

"Mommy, I'm sorry. I shouldn't have asked you to do that. I hope Jeff doesn't do anything foolish. Now, I'll worry all night. Gordon, you see Jeff at work don't you?" asked Lucinda.

"I see him most days, but you don't care, remember. He's not that fancy doctor," sneered Gordon.

As the rest of the family told Lucinda how awful she was to do Jeff that way, she had trouble not crying.

Finally, she said, "I guess all of you think I should marry Jeff, don't you?"

"I don't think you'll find anybody that loves you more, or will provide for you better than Jeff," said Emily.

"I don't think you should have led him on, like you have, if you were going to drop him when that –that doctor is mentioned," sputtered Gordon.

"Jeff is one of us, Honey. He's our kind of people," said Nancy.

"Now, I ain't wantin' my baby girl to marry and leave me," put in Burb "but if you're going to marry, you'd probably be getting a good man," he finished.

Lucinda was crying by this time, "But, I'm not ready to marry, and you all don't really know Jeff. You should have heard him curse when we went into the ditch line that time. He was so mad," sobbed Lucinda.

"Hell, I'd cuss too, in a situation like that. Besides he didn't cuss you. He was just embarrassed because he wanted to impress you," explained Gordon.

All her life, there had been all of these older and wiser brothers and sisters, who seemed to know everything, and Lucinda had gotten in the habit of doing what they said, and thinking it was right. Now her Mom and Dad had joined them, as well as Dora and Uncle Jake. "All these people are telling me the same thing. They must be right," thought Lucinda sadly.

"Okay, Okay, I'll date him again, if he still wants to, then maybe all of my family won't be against me," exploded Lucinda.

Nancy went over and put her arms around Lucinda saying, "Honey, we ain't agin you. We all love you. We just hate to see you eating your heart out for that doctor. We all know, and you ort to know, you'll never see him again."

After that, they all sat around the fire and discussed the family gathering at Christmas. All the family was to be home, and it was very exciting. Lucinda got involved in the plans, and felt better, until she went to bed. Then she rolled and tumbled, and finally tried to pray.

'Maybe that's the cause of all my anxiety about dating Jeff. Could it be, that the Lord is working with me, and wants me to join the church?' wondered Lucinda. She knew that Preacher Hiram had thought she wanted to join at Aunt Sarie's funeral, because he had asked Nancy if she had a problem with Lucinda uniting with the church. Nancy had come home and asked her if she had wanted to join the church, and Lucinda said, "Why no, Mommy, I was just hurt about Aunt Sarie. I do like to hear Preacher Hiram preach, though. Sometimes, I feel so full of love, it makes me want to hug everybody, but that don't mean I want to join the church."

She knew that, even though she felt good at times in church, she didn't feel like she was ready. That was a lifetime commitment, and she just wasn't sure that she had been called. Lucinda knew that unless she was called of God she could be baptized a dozen times, and still not be a true church member. She went off to sleep deeply troubled.

She dreamed that she was getting married, and somewhere in the background someone was crying brokenly. When she awoke, she was more troubled than ever.

CHAPTER 18

Gordon took Lucinda back to Dora's on Sunday evening, and they talked all the way about Lucinda's situation.

"Gordon, when you married Emily, did you feel that she was the only girl in the world for you?" asked Lucinda.

"I knew I loved her, Sis, but I had been out and around, and had dated dozens of girls. That doctor was the first man you ever dated, and I could tell you had stars in your eyes. I even told Mam that she should talk to you. I was afraid you were going to get hurt - and you did, but not in the way I was afraid you would," explained Gordon.

"You don't mean you thought I might - well, you know. I'll never do that, Gordon. You don't have to worry about that, but I did love him. I know it was true love," stated Lucinda firmly. She sat thinking that she didn't know whether she could have refused Jason anything. Now, she was so thankful that she hadn't been put to the test.

"What if - say, I'd marry Jeff, and then Jason would come back. What would I do then?" questioned Lucinda.

"If Jeff is the kind of man I think he is, he'll make you forget all about that doctor," grinned Gordon.

"I've been dating him since the middle of October, and I still haven't forgotten Jason. Well, maybe a little bit," confessed Lucinda.

Gordon grinned and said, "Well now, Sis, marriage has a few extras that are powerful incentives."

Lucinda turned beet red and began talking about how bad the road was. They talked about the snow and Christmas until suddenly Lucinda said, "Did you know that Jeff is a big union man?"

"Yea, I already know that, but as smart as that man is, and the way he is moving up in the company, I'll bet it won't be long before he is on salary. Mr. Jenkins was talking to me about him yesterday."

"Gordon - if you see Jeff - and you want to, you can explain to him some of what I'm going through," said Lucinda hesitantly.

"Are you saying you'll make it up with him, and forget all about that damn doctor?" asked Gordon.

"I like Jeff and he is fun - I just — well, tell him I said I was sorry about Saturday," said Lucinda.

By this time they had arrived at Dora's, Lucinda got out of his truck, and turned to say, "Gordon, maybe it would be best if we leave it alone. He won't come back, anyway."

Gordon shrugged, "Whatever you say, Sis. It's your life, and you can make it miserable if you want to." He carried Lucinda's suitcase to the porch and hugged her as he said good-bye.

Dora was putting the finishing touches to supper as Lucinda went in.

"Something smells good. Is that turkey I smell?" sniffed Lucinda.

"It shore is, and you're just in time to get the wishbone," laughed Dora.

Lucinda grinned as she ran up the stairs to put away her things, and hurried back down saying, "I need some kind of luck. Maybe the wish bone will help."

"What do you need luck for? You got more luck than me. You got a fine looking man crazy over you and..."

"I've not now" said Lucinda firmly.

Uncle Jake came in from the back porch, where he had a bird feeder, shivering and blowing on his hands.

"It's cold enough to freeze a well digger's ass. Uh, oh, didn't know you was here, Lucy," said Uncle Jake grinning mischievously. "It is mighty cold out though."

"How come your feller didn't bring you back? That wuzn't him I know, cause I didn't see that red hair," supplied Uncle Jake.

"Pa, that man's hair ain't red, its auburn," laughed Dora.

"Well, you could have fooled me. His hair shore ain't black, but whatever color it is, he didn't bring you back, did he?" asked Uncle Jake.

"No, he didn't bring me back this time," answered Lucinda hesitantly. "In fact we broke up, and I don't guess he'll be coming anymore."

"What's the matter with him? Don't he make enough money?" asked Uncle Jake laughing.

Dora stopped on the way to the table, with a bowl of green beans in her hands. "Yeah, I want to know why. I'll bet it was you done the breaking up, but why?" questioned Dora.

"I- well- I just felt we were getting too serious, and I'm not ready for that," answered Lucinda.

"Well, gol darn, I thought you'uns was dead serious. He's been here one night every week, and seen you on Saturday, too. Then he's brung you back down here on every Sunday for purt near three months. Married folks don't see much more'n that of each other," declared Uncle Jake.

"Yes I know, but he has begun talking about what kind of house I want and I'm ---well, it's just too soon, I think," returned Lucinda.

"Dora, did you ever hear the beat of that? I swear you young fellers don't appear to have no sense a tall. That's the reason people spark, Lucy. They want to see if

173

they like each other, before they tie the knot, and all of them want a place to live once the knot is tied, don't they?" questioned Uncle Jake.

By now, they were all seated at the table and began filling their plates before Dora broke the silence,

"Lucy, I know you're young, but I think you'd better start living in the real world, honey. That doctor ain't coming back. You know it, and everybody else knows it. So, why don't you just accept it, and get on with your life?" demanded Dora.

"What's this about a doctor? First time I've heerd about a doctor," barked Uncle Jake.

Realizing she wasn't supposed to have said anything, Dora covered it by saying, "Aw, Pa, a boy she met in college, who was studying to be a doctor."

"Aw, that old stuff is just puppy love. That's fer younguns. You're grown now, Lucy, and teaching school, so plant your feet on solid ground, girl. You can't live on air dreams," grunted Uncle Jake.

When Dora noticed that Lucinda was on the verge of tears, she said, "Pa, did I tell you that Nellie Blevins' old man got his leg broke?"

This led to a long discussion of the carelessness of loggers, and the way they were ruining the mountains.

"They fall trees into the forks of young saplings and plumb ruin that young tree," grumbled Uncle Jake, as he complained about the waste of good timber. "When it's gone, I'll bet a lot of people will be real sorry they wus so wasteful. There ain't many big boundaries of virgin timber left, or so Burb tells me. He'd found a big boundary of virgin timber in the head of Crane Ridge, just before he got his eyes messed up, hadn't he?"

Lucinda agreed that her dad had found a lot of virgin timber about the time he was injured, because

Gordon had walked through it with him. Uncle Jake started to say something else, but Dora interrupted.

She didn't want Uncle Jake to get started on one of his harangues about people not taking care of the land, and piped up with, "Pa, there's a John Wayne movie on television tonight, and it's about time for it to start." This abruptly ended any discussion as Uncle Jake made a hasty removal to the living room.

After helping do the dishes, Lucinda claimed a headache and went to her room. *"I must be wrong,"* she thought. "Everybody thinks I'm doing Jeff wrong. They all say that Jason will never come back. But, why is something still telling me to wait," groaned Lucinda soundlessly.

This was the last week of school before the Christmas break, and Lucinda had a full work load. She and Dora would have to wrap all the Christmas gifts and pack the treats themselves since Nellie Blevins wouldn't be able to help now. She'd have to be home to care for her husband. Being so busy helped Lucinda keep Jeff off her mind during the day. Her nights, however, were filled with troubled dreams full of haunting images of Jason and then an angry Jeff took a heavy toll on Lucinda's energy level.

By Wednesday, she was worn out and was glad when three o'clock rolled around. She eagerly donned her coat and boots to go back to Dora's. That wasn't to be though, for just as she stepped out onto the porch, a jeep came barreling into the school yard and Jeff got out. The usually neat Jeff had been replaced by a much thinner man, with a shrunken bearded face, wrinkled clothes, and tousled hair. Lucinda gaped in a stunned, round- eyed stare, wondering what he was going to say.

"Hello, Lucinda," spoke Jeff quietly as he walked to the porch.

"Hello, Jeff. Did you just get off from work?" asked Lucinda.

"No, I got home at ten o'clock this morning and I've - I saw Gordon this morning. He told me about - Can we go back inside, so we can talk?" asked Jeff.

Lucinda opened the door and walked back in with Jeff behind her. When he closed the door, he grabbed her shoulder and spun her around, "Lucinda, you've put me through hell----do you know that? I've been going crazy because of some damn fairytale - some son-of-a-bitch doctor. I'd like to meet him face to face, and when I was through with him, your daydreams would be over, that's for sure," stormed Jeff.

"Jeff, I'm sorry if I hurt you. I just wanted to be sure. I mean if we go on, and then one of us changes our minds, it would be worse," pleaded Lucinda earnestly.

"One of us, hell! I'm not going to change my mind. All this time I've wondered why you keep me at arm's length. I know you like my kisses but then you freeze up like an iceberg. All because some damn big city doctor comes down here and tells a pack of damn lies to get the attention of a little hillbilly. I'll bet he's somewhere laughing right now. Don't you think he would have kept in contact, if he cared for you? That damn man just wanted to see how far he could get with you," sputtered Jeff angrily as he started toward her and staggered.

Lucinda backed away in fright, "Jeff, you've been drinking. You're drunk," accused Lucinda.

"Yes, I'm drunk, and I've been drunk every day this week, and it's your fault. I don't drink, or I didn't drink, until you came along and made a pure idiot out of me," blazed Jeff. "Gordon said you would see me again. Did you say that?" asked Jeff.

"Yes, I told Gordon that as we came down the ridge, but before he left I told him that maybe it would be best to just let it alone. You're all wrong about that doctor, as you call him. He didn't try to get out of line at all. He was a gentleman," said Lucinda.

"Hell, I've tried to be a gentleman, too. What have I done that turned you off? I guess I just don't measure up to that gentleman doctor, do I? We've been dating for three months and I've never even touched you except for a few kisses. I've tried to do everything that I thought would please you, and then you send word that we need to call it off. I guess he came back, or wrote you a letter, didn't he?" blazed Jeff.

Lucinda had stood listening in stunned silence, then said, "No, Jeff. He hasn't come back, and I haven't heard from him. It isn't that."

Jeff lurched over and sat down in one of the large seats, then sat waiting and looking at her. "I want us to date again. You know that, don't you, Lucinda?"

"I'm going to sit right here until you make up your mind. You know I love you, and you know I'll be here. Do you want to throw that away because you hope that damn doctor will come back? You're going to have to make up your mind. I just can't stand any more of this," stated Jeff adamantly.

Lucinda walked back and forth a few turns, before saying, "Do you always drink when something doesn't go your way, Jeff? I don't need someone that can't handle problems any better than that," said Lucinda.

"If you would just straighten up and act your age, I'd never take another drink. I'm not a drunk. In fact I never drink more than one beer, now and then, but Lucinda, I've been about to go crazy," mumbled Jeff.

"You must not have slept, or washed your clothes, or even combed your hair all week," stated Lucinda.

"I've not- well, not often. When a person drinks from the time they get off work until they fall asleep, they don't have time to do many of the nice things. I had already started drinking when Gordon ran into me in Gus' place in Bradshaw. He told me all about your famous doctor. I got so mad I drank some more, and then I decided to just come down here, and here I am. I want you to look me in the eye, and tell me you don't care anything for me," said Jeff who had lurched to his feet and grabbed Lucinda by the shoulders spinning her to face him.

"Phew, you smell like a moonshine still," said Lucinda, trying to pull away.

"No you don't, Miss Harmon. Smelly or not, I need you to look me in the face, and tell me that you hate the sight of me, and I'll go. It will kill me, but I'll go, and never bother you again," said Jeff in a wobbly voice.

Lucinda crumbled, "Oh Jeff, I don't hate you; you know that," cried Lucinda miserably. "I just wanted to be sure and I- I really do like you a lot, Jeff," said Lucinda as big tears filled her eyes and ran down her cheeks.

Suddenly she was crushed against a rock hard chest, and enclosed in bands of steel as Jeff hugged her so hard she feared her ribs would crack. "Lucinda, please, please don't ever do this to me again, please," begged Jeff brokenly.

Lucinda locked her arms around his back and said, "Okay Jeff, I guess I have been a little girl, long enough."

Disheveled or not, Jeff kissed her hungrily but when his hands and caresses became more personal than Lucinda wanted, she pushed him away saying, "No, Jeff, that's enough."

"No, it will never be enough; besides, we're going to get married aren't we? At least I want you to marry me. I've wanted to marry you since I stepped upon this porch in October, and saw you for the first time. You will marry me, won't you, Lucinda?" begged Jeff.

All the advice from the family, Dora, and Uncle Jake came swirling to the forefront of her mind as Lucinda looked up at Jeff. His face was etched in anguish, and she saw so much love in his eyes, that she hesitantly mumbled, "I- I guess."

Lucinda found herself being twirled around until Jeff stumbled. He then lowered her to the floor, to be kissed again. "Now Jeff, I said I guess, but if you don't stop, I may change my mind," laughed Lucinda. "Besides, you won't remember any of this when you are sober," accused Lucinda.

Still holding her close, Jeff said, "I'm sober now, Honey. Boy, am I sober. Let's get married Christmas," beamed Jeff.

"Why that's next week. I want a summer wedding," said Lucinda

"A summer wedding! Good Lord, that's months away. I don't think I can stand to wait that long," argued Jeff, but seeing the stubborn gleam in Lucinda's eyes he quickly relented.

"Okay, but I'd rather get married next week. But since it will be the only wedding you'll ever have, I'll wait until June, if I have to," said Jeff.

"Well, now how about you taking me back to Dora's. It's suppertime and I'm starved. I haven't been eating much lately," quipped Lucinda.

Jeff looked at her closely, "You do look a bit hollow eyed and you've lost weight. So, it was hard on you too, huh," grinned Jeff.

"I guess so. I've not had a good night's sleep in a week, and Dora and Mommy have been pushing food on me," smiled Lucinda.

"I guess we've both got it bad. Are you sure you want to wait until June? Couldn't we marry sooner than that?" quizzed Jeff as he gathered up her coat, which she had taken off, and put it around her shoulders.

"No, no we can't any sooner than that, for sure," stated Lucinda adamantly. As she walked out, she thought about summer school, and said, "Really, I think it will have to be the last of August."

CHAPTER 19

"The last of August! Why?" demanded Jeff in alarm.

Lucinda was amazed that she wanted to delay this rush to marry. I shouldn't want to delay it if I really love him, she thought. Seeing his crestfallen expression she tried to explain. "Remember me telling you I didn't have my degree, and would have to finish up in extension classes and summer school- well, this summer, I have to go to school," reminded Lucinda.

"You don't need to finish now. I will provide for you," grinned Jeff.

"I know you will Jeff, but I want to get my degree, so I'm going to summer school," stated Lucinda firmly. She had worked too hard and nobody was going to stand in the way of her getting her degree.

Hearing the determination in her voice, Jeff cautiously said, "Couldn't we get married the last of May, before you go to school? After you're mine, I won't have to worry about somebody else snatching you up," said Jeff, trying to grin as if he was kidding.

By this time, they were almost at Dora's and Lucinda said, "We can discuss this on Saturday. That is, if you're coming up on Saturday, we can," said Lucinda inquiringly.

Stopping the jeep at the gate, he leaned over to kiss her, and said, "I'll be there- I'll be asking Mr. Harmon for your hand in marriage," beamed Jeff.

They got out of the jeep and Jeff started walking in with her. Lucinda asked puzzled, "Are you going in? You never do ...."

"I'm about to burst, Honey. I have to tell somebody our good news," laughed Jeff.

"No, no don't do that, Jeff. I want Mommy and Dad to be the first ones we tell," cautioned Lucinda. By this time they were at the porch and Uncle Jake had already opened the door.

"Well, well, now maybe we won't have to listen to that sniveling all night," laughed Uncle Jake, holding open the door and booming, "Come in, come right on in."

Dora came in from the kitchen grinning broadly, "You look a sight better this evening than you did when you left here this morning, Lucy," she said gleefully, and then looking at Jeff she said, "But you don't look too good. A little more of this break-up would about do you in, I believe."

"You're right there, Ma'am, that's for sure. If she ever tries a stunt like this again, I'm going to take a stick to her," grinned Jeff.

"Best thing to do is marry her and get her pregnant. Women ain't apt to run off in that kind of condition," guffawed Uncle Jake.

Seeing Lucinda's beet red color, Dora turned on Uncle Jake with, "Pa, watch your mouth, you old coot. You've embarrassed Lucy to death."

Puzzled Uncle Jake retorted, "Why, I didn't say nothing. I was jest giving this boy some advice."

"Sounded good to me, Sir, and I'm working on it," said Jeff, but hearing Lucinda's embarrassed gasp, quickly said, "I mean I'm working on the marrying bit."

Lucinda was so embarrassed, but knew that this was the kind of kidding most mountain people used on romantic couples. She just wanted it stopped, so she said, "Jeff, if you're going to work tonight, don't you think you'd better go."

Jeff looked at his watch and said, "Yea, I guess I had since I do need to shave and it's a good distance back to

Bradshaw." He turned to go, shaking hands with Uncle Jake and, lifting his hand to Dora, said, "Take care of my girl for me. I just wanted to come in and ...," noticing Lucinda's malevolent glare he grinned and continued with, "to let you all know that everything is okay again." Knowing of Lucinda's inhibitions, Jeff grabbed her hand, pulled her to the door, and out on the porch, where he grasped her chin and deliberately kissed her lips, saying "I'm not ashamed to let people know how I feel about you, so get used to being kissed, sweetheart," and went quickly down the steps.

Lucinda was embarrassed to go back in since they had been in front of the glass door, but nothing was said. Dora walked back into the kitchen and Lucinda climbed the stairs to her room. She dropped down on the bed dejectedly, thinking, "Now I guess everybody will be satisfied," and didn't know why she felt sad.

She dreaded going home, on Friday. She knew Gordon would have told the family about talking to Jeff and maybe seeing Jeff since Wednesday. She hoped not, but then thought it may be easier if he had. On Friday, Burb came to take her home, eager to tell her that Ellen, who had married Benny Pruitt the year before, was expecting a baby. All the Harmons loved babies and there hadn't been a little one around for a long time. The youngest children were Odell's. But she and her husband were now talking of moving to Monroe, Michigan taking her young children away. Nathan and Ernie had moved away and so had Faye. Ellen's baby would certainly be spoiled by everyone, especially Burb and Nancy.

Nancy said "Looks like coal mining is going to separate my family whether they work in the mines or not. Most families move away because the mines are on strike, but my family is all moving away to keep from working in the mines."

Burb had always said he certainly didn't blame his children for moving away, for if they stayed here they would have to work in the mines or in timber. If they worked in the mines they would have to join the union. "It's one thing to want to join something, but it's something else when you're forced to," was Burb's favorite adage.

Gordon, of course, depended on the mines for his living, but his salary was there, strike or not. However, he often had to work when the regular miners had holidays, and, of course, he worked when they were on strike. He would get so angry when the men would strike every hunting season. "Some of those men don't have two pennies to rub together, and yet they are the first ones to clamor for a strike. If they were striking over a grievance, I maybe could understand it, but to strike just to go hunting," he'd fume.

Gordon and Emily were there when Burb and Lucinda arrived, which surprised Lucinda since he usually didn't get off from work until 4:30 each day.

"What are you doing here at this time of day?" asked Lucinda wonderingly.

"He got sick and had to go to the doctor," spoke up Emily. "When he drove his truck into the yard at half past one, I almost fainted. I went running to the truck, but when he got out and didn't look hurt, I was ready to pounce on him," smiled Emily. "You know all that belching and burping he's been doing- well, he's got an ulcer. Looks the picture of health too, don't he?" asked Emily.

"It's this sister of mine that caused it," said Gordon as he hugged Lucinda fondly.

"Me! What have I worried you about? Oh- well, you can stop worrying; we made up," said Lucinda smiling.

"It's a good thing you did. That man was going off the deep end and fast, too. I bet he lost 10 pounds in a week's time. Did you notice how much he had lost?" questioned Gordon.

"Yes, I did but it serves him right. Did you know he had been drinking? Really, I think he stayed drunk the whole time," frowned Lucinda. She grimaced and looked at Nancy saying, "Would you want a man that gets drunk every time some problem comes up? Remember, this is the man who you, and all the rest, want me to marry," said Lucinda.

"Now, wait a minute, Sis. Be fair. Jeff never drank, or so I'm told by Deputy Stevens, no less. He's known Jeff all his life and he's never seen him act like he has this past week. By the way, you're not getting any brownie points from the police in Bradshaw either. However, that may change now," grinned Gordon.

Burb, who had been quietly listening to all this, said, "He seemed to have more sense than that. It didn't do him a bit of good. I'm kinda surprised."

"Wait now, Pap, have you forgot that time when Mam took a notion to go over in Wyoming County for a spell. Seems to me I remember being told that you got drunk, went over there, loaded her up, and brought her home," Gordon teased, mischievously.

"She had my younguns with her," Burb blustered, as he remembered.

Emily came in from the kitchen and said, "If you men want any supper tonight, go get washed. If you don't wash, you don't eat at Nancy's table."

In this way, the embarrassment and the questioning that Lucinda expected was diffused.

Everything was back to normal, or so she hoped. She still dreaded the evening, since Jeff had said he was coming to ask Burb for permission to marry her.

Lucinda dreaded the idea of marriage even though she wanted a home of her own. There were so many things she didn't know about relationships between men and women and was too inhibited to talk to anyone about them. What little she knew came from her girl friend at Concord College, and the few pages she had read in the book that Jason had brought her. She was so shocked by the pictures on the first few pages that she had hidden it away and hadn't looked again. She had kept the book, though, because Jason had given it to her.

Jeff came at half past four on Saturday which was an hour earlier than usual. Lucinda had just gotten back from visiting Ellen. She was surprised and wondered if anything was wrong, but Jeff said in a teasing voice, "I have two special reasons for coming early. You already know one, but you'll have to wait on the other one."

He grasped her hand and they walked into the living room where Burb was very involved in a wrestling match on television. Lucinda always laughed to herself at her dad's actions when watching wrestling. He jerked, punched, and wriggled almost out of his chair if he thought he wasn't being watched. Jeff broke Burb's concentration or they would have gotten a free show.

"Hello, Mr. Harmon, how are you today?" asked Jeff, coming into the room. Startled, Burb jerked upright from his crouched position and turned a glaring eye at the intruder, but when he saw it was Jeff, he immediately changed.

He stood, saying, "How are you son? You been doing all right?" He slowly went over and turned off the television, but not before his man had pinned the other one.

Jeff shifted uncomfortably and looked uneasy but answered, "I'm fine, I guess."

"Well, set down - set down, you don't need to grow no taller," said Burb as he indicated the couch. Jeff went with Lucinda to the couch and sat down.

He took a big breath and then began, "Mr. Harmon, uh – well, I don't know how to say this except just coming right out. Mr. Harmon, Lucinda and I would like to get married, if you have no objections."

Burb shifted in his chair and looked at Lucinda first. His gaze made her uncomfortable, but she didn't look away. "Well, this is shore a change in your mind since last week, Cindy. Are you sure this is what you want to do?" questioned Burb, probingly.

Lucinda squirmed in her chair but knew she had to answer him, so taking a deep breath she said, "Well, Daddy, everybody I talked to seemed to think I was just being silly. I do care for Jeff, and I decided to take everyone's advice. We thought about maybe August. I have to go to summer school if I want to teach next year, and I wanted to get that over with first."

"You'll keep going and finish school then. That's good. I don't want you to quit before you graduate. You've worked too hard, and then you never can tell what might happen," said Burb, speaking his thoughts aloud. "I didn't hear you say you loved him, though. Do you love him enough to spend the rest of your life with him, Cindy?" questioned Burb bluntly.

Lucinda sat very still for a minute, while the question raced through her mind. Did she love Jeff enough to stay with him the rest of her life? She looked at Jeff with his white anxious face, silently pleading, and thought, 'Yes, if Jason had never been, I would rather be with Jeff than anyone else I've ever met.'

Resolutely, she looked at Burb and smiled, "Well, Dad, I love him enough to stay a life time with him, if he can stand me that long."

Burb sighed and nodded his head before turning to Jeff, "I heard that you threw a big drunk last week. Do you make a habit of that? Cindy is my youngest, and she has been a good girl. I'd want her treated right," stated Burb bluntly.

Jeff was red in the face but he spoke up bravely, "I did get drunk last week, Mr. Harmon, and I'm ashamed I did. I know it wasn't a very mature way to act, but I'd never had anything to hurt like that before. It's not my normal reaction to problems, I assure you. I've never drunk much in my life. I promise you, Mr. Harmon, that I'll be good to Lucinda. I love her, and I'll work to see that she has a good life."

For some reason, Lucinda wanted to cry, and would have run from the room, but Jeff still clung tightly to her hand. She sat still, as if waiting for a miracle or something.

No miracle occurred however, it only got worse. Jeff said, "I came early this evening, because I hoped you would agree we could marry, and if you do, I want to take Lucinda over to Gilbert tonight. I want her to meet my parents. They have asked us to supper. Is that all right with you, Mr. Harmon? We could be back by half past ten or eleven o'clock at the latest," stated Jeff.

"Since you're going to marry him, I think you need to meet his folks, Cindy, so if your Mam don't care, it's okay with me," ceded Burb soberly.

CHAPTER 20

Lucinda dreaded going to Gilbert but knew it was expected. She went back to her room, and changed into her blue suit, hoping to look more mature.

In the jeep, Jeff said, "In Bradshaw, we'll drop this jeep off and get my truck. It's more comfortable, and you won't be so far away." He rolled his eyes, imitating Red Skelton's "Clem Kadiddlehopper" and his funny expressions, and had Lucinda giggling as they went out of the ridge.

"You're so silly, Jeff," laughed Lucinda and then sobered as she thought about meeting his family. "What if they don't like me, Jeff? I feel like I'll be on trial, and I'm scared to death," she groaned.

Jeff slowed to a stop, and clasping her hands, said, "You don't need to worry. They will love you. If they don't it won't make a bit of difference to me."

"Well, I certainly don't want to separate you from your family, so I'll try to get them to like me," teased Lucinda.

Jeff started the jeep moving again as he said, "Lucinda, I mean this with all my heart. You'll be my wife, and everybody had better be good to you, and leave you alone, and that means family, too."

Lucinda looked at Jeff curiously. He was looking almost angry about something. "Jeff, you bother me. Do you expect someone to try to hurt me?" asked Lucinda.

Jeff's face cleared and he turned toward her, smiling, and said, "No. Who'd want to hurt you? I just want to make sure you know that I will take care of you."

In Bradshaw, he left her in the jeep while he started the truck to let it warm up. Deputy Stevens came over just as he returned to the jeep and opened the door. "Do you mean to tell me that my jeep will be free tonight," grinned the Deputy.

"It will be until around a quarter past ten tonight. I'm taking my fiancée to the folks," Jeff stated proudly.

"Your fiancée! You're getting married! Well hell, I thought we'd be burying you, and here you are engaged. When did this all happen? This ain't one of your gags, is it?" asked Deputy Stevens.

Grinning from ear to ear Jeff said, "Nope, it ain't no joke. I asked her Dad tonight and he approves. I'd marry her tomorrow but she wants to wait until August."

The Deputy looked at Lucinda, "Any special reason for August, Lucinda? I know Jeff don't want to wait," mumbled the Deputy knowingly.

"I have to go to summer school, and I want to have that behind me. If I don't go to school, I may not get a school to teach next year," stated Lucinda.

"Oh! Do you plan to work after you marry? I didn't figure Jeff would want you to," said Deputy Stevens.

Lucinda was astonished and turned questioning eyes to Jeff, "You wouldn't try to keep me from teaching, would you? I love teaching," stated Lucinda firmly.

Jeff looked as if he didn't know what to say. He looked at the Deputy angrily, "Jack, will you please keep your mouth shut. We've not had a chance to talk about things yet. I'll not stop her from doing something she has her heart set on," said Jeff, turning to Lucinda and nodding in assurance.

"I'm sorry, Jeff," said the Deputy, stepping back as Jeff opened the door.

"I guess the truck is warm, by now. We'd better go if we want to get there by 6:30," said Jeff as he went around the jeep to help Lucinda out.

As Lucinda went ahead and got into the truck, she left Jeff and the deputy talking. Jeff soon joined her, laughing. "That Jack is a scamp. He once heard me say that no wife of mine would work, and now he's making a big deal out of it."

"Why would you say a thing like that? I have lots of friends who work, especially teachers. If women didn't teach, how would children learn?" demanded Lucinda.

Jeff pulled her to his side, kissed her cheek, and said, "Okay Honey! Okay. Don't get all steamed up about it. We can settle all of that later." He swung around in the parking lot, and pulled onto the highway before Lucinda said anything, but almost stopped at her next comment.

"No we won't, Jeff. If you're going to try to stop me from teaching, we may as well call it off right now," said Lucinda rebelliously.

"Now, now Lucinda, I didn't say anything about trying to stop you from teaching. It's just that I was raised to believe that a man wasn't worth much, if he couldn't support his wife. In my family, men who allowed their wives to work were talked about and considered to be a lazy, no- good person. This is just a whole new concept for me," said Jeff reasonably.

"Well, sure, I know Daddy wouldn't have let Mommy have a job outside of the home, but that was a different time. Besides, women really work hard at home; they just don't get paid for it. I like to have my own money, and pay my own way. I'm used to doing that, and I'm going to keep on working," Lucinda stated firmly.

By this time they were going through the straight stretch of highway at Lex, and Jeff had not replied, but Lucinda could see that he was upset. His jaw muscles clenched and unclenched, and when he found a place where it was safe to pull over, he did just that, leaving the engine to idle.

Turning to Lucinda, he pulled her into his arms, kissing her hungrily, and mumbled furiously, "Lucinda, I'm crazy about you. I can't live without you, and if it takes being laughed at or whatever, that's the way it will be. But you'd better never even look at anyone else."

Lucinda looked up at him questioningly, "If I'm going to marry you, why would I want to look at anyone else?"

With his chin resting on the top of her head, he said, "Yea, I know but that's why I don't want to wait. I won't worry so much once you're mine."

Lucinda pushed away from him, "We're going to be late and then what will your parents think? Probably they will think I'm corrupting their son. So, let's go."

Jeff gave her a quick kiss and then pulled out, smiling. They drove on to Iaeger talking cheerfully and sometimes lulling into companionable silences, which was also comfortable. Lucinda relaxed and rested her head against his shoulder, but when he dropped his hand to her knee, she sat up and shoved it off, saying, "Don't."

Jeff looked shocked, "Don't? I didn't do nothing but put my hand on your knee, for God's sake. What's wrong with that?" demanded Jeff.

Lucinda sat silent for a few minutes and then said, "I just don't want you to."

Jeff shook his head grimacing, "Thank God you allow me to kiss you, because I sure as hell can't touch you anywhere else. We are planning to get married Lucinda, and that entails a little more touching than that, you know."

Lucinda dropped her head. She was embarrassed. She'd heard her sisters talk and they said men sometimes did things that led to other stuff and, things she didn't know about. God, I'm so ignorant. The Bible says if you sow to the flesh then of the flesh you reap corruption. Does that mean that- stuff- that's in that book? But, men and women do that, and that's what makes babies, so it must not be wrong. The Bible also says to marry, multiply, and replenish the earth, but I don't believe I can do that. It must not be too bad though, for Mom and all my sisters seem happy, mused Lucinda silently.

Jeff slowed down, tightened the arm around her waist, and when she looked up, he said, "Honey, you are really innocent, aren't you?"

Tears sprang to her eyes, and not looking up, she mumbled, "Jeff, I don't know much about men. I've not dated much."

"Lucinda, look at me, please" begged Jeff.

She raised tear-filled eyes and Jeff swung off the road, saying, "Oh Honey, what am I going to do with you? When you look like that, I can't stand it. Please don't cry. I'm glad, well, part of me is glad you are so innocent, but I believe it's going to be rough going, and it scares me to death. I will promise you this, Lucinda, I'll be patient and kind, and I swear that I'll never hurt you. Now, just relax and let's forget all about this, and I'll be very careful where I put my hands, at least for right now," promised Jeff as he grinned mischievously.

They drove on into Gilbert, which was all lit up with Christmas lights. Lucinda's delighted gaze lingered on each display. Until Jeff stopped the truck, she had forgotten her fear of meeting his family, but now it came flooding back, and she shivered in dread.

As they got out of the truck, Jeff said, "Now remember, you are more important to me than anybody. Now, come on. I'll be right beside you."

Lucinda looked at the house and thought, *"Gosh, this is a lot different than our old log house. I wonder if Jeff has told them what kind of house I live in?"* The big two-story house was decorated with colored lights and wreaths in the windows, and on the glass front door. Nancy always wanted to have lights, but Burb said it would run the juice bill up, and besides, they wouldn't be safe. They always had a tree with green and red crepe paper decorations, but no lights. *"They must be well off,"* thought Lucinda as she and Jeff walked onto the porch.

When the door opened, Jeff squeezed her hand and stepped inside with Lucinda beside him saying, "Here we are folks. Meet the future Mrs. Jeff Marshall."

A tall smiling man with graying auburn hair met them at the door and right behind him was a slender woman with merry blue eyes and black hair. They both engulfed Lucinda and Jeff in a shared hug saying, "You're late and we thought you'd changed your mind. Come on in."

They entered the living room, which had a high ceiling with a spangled light dropping from the center. There was a mixture of muted pale greens, mauves, and grays in the sofas, chairs, and drapes which made the room beautiful. Lucinda sniffed at the wonderful smell of cedar and spices either coming from the kitchen or from the large Christmas tree in the corner.

Mrs. Marshall said, "Here, Lucinda let me take your coat. Is Lucinda what you're called or do you have a nickname," she inquired as she took the coat.

"I'm called lots of things, Mrs. Marshall, but I prefer Lucinda," said Lucinda, with a timid smile as Mrs. Marshall hung her coat on a coat tree in the entrance foyer.

Jeff's jacket was tossed down on a chair next to the wide fireplace, where a fire burned cheerfully. He patted the sofa on the other side, motioning Lucinda to sit beside him. He turned to his Dad, "Where's Margie and the others? Aren't they coming?"

Just then laughing voices were heard on the porch as the door opened, and a beautiful young girl, about Lucinda's age, came into the entrance. "I said you had beaten us here, Jeff. I knew that must be your new truck. But I saw some mud on it and I almost thought it couldn't be yours. Mud on your-r-r truck, I don't believe it," teased Jill, his youngest sister.

Behind Jill was a heavy set blond man, who Mr. Marshall introduced as Sam Duncan, Jill's intended. "We've got two of our children here with their future spouses tonight, Mom," said Mr. Marshall. "Let's hope they hurry and get hitched so you and I can go on a second honeymoon." Mr. Marshall grinned and wiggled his eyebrows amorously at his wife.

Mrs. Marshall snuggled up to her husband saying, "Sure, Handsome, I just can't wait. Which cane do you plan to take," then laughed gaily at her husband's pseudo shocked expression.

"I could get married the first of the year if that would help you any, folks," said Jill. "What about you, Jeff? Couldn't you help these two old folks out before they kick the bucket?" asked Jill playfully.

Jeff looked at Lucinda and said, "One should be enough right now. But they can still go because I will be living over at Bradshaw."

Mrs. Marshall had noticed the glance Jeff had given Lucinda and quickly said, "Let's get ready to eat. Another car has just pulled up and by the time I get the food on the table, everybody will be in."

Margie and her husband came with their two children, Howie and Penny, as well as Jeff's brothers,

Bobby and Jimmy, who had been spending the day with them. They all trooped in together and introductions were made all around. Lucinda went in to dinner with Jeff and was seated beside him. Soon she began to relax. She thought it was strange when Mr. Marshall told everyone to join hands. Then he asked Penny, Margie's daughter, to say the blessing. Lucinda knew that some people did things like that, but she had never been a part of it. It was all right, but she felt prayer should be from the heart, and not just words. Then she thought she shouldn't judge since she didn't know what was in Penny's heart.

The food was very good, and everyone praised Mrs. Marshall on the wonderful lemon meringue pie offered for dessert. Lucinda had taken a little of everything passed to her, lest Mrs. Marshall would think she didn't like her cooking. Soon she felt really full and didn't take any pie, saying, "It looks delicious but I honestly can't eat anymore right now. I'm too full to eat another bite. I just ate too much of everything else."

"Too full, why you haven't eaten a teacup full," boomed Mr. Marshall smiling.

"She's not going to be expensive to feed," laughed Jeff as he related how she only ate about half of anything that they ordered in restaurants.

"Well, she's not big enough to hold tons of food, like this family." said Margie, grinning.

They all arose from the table and Lucinda offered to help with the dishes but Margie said, "No, not this time, Lucinda. You just go on in the living room with Mom so you two can get acquainted. Jill and I will do the dishes after you and Jeff leave. Right now we're only planning to put the leftover food away. The next time you come though, we'll have some dishes saved back, so you can really help," she twinkled merrily.

CHAPTER 21

Back in the living room, Mr. Marshall asked Jeff to go with him to the garage. He grinned at Mrs. Marshall and said, "And don't you come poking your nose out there."

As they left, Mrs. Marshall invited Lucinda to sit beside her on the sofa. When they were comfortably seated, Mrs. Marshall said, "When did you and Jeff decide to marry? I know it's been since Monday, for I talked to Jeff that evening, and he didn't say anything about it. He did sound strange though."

"We didn't decide until Wednesday evening. Well, really we didn't know for sure until this evening, because Jeff hadn't asked Dad's permission. We didn't know what Dad would say. My dad has to know his future sons-in-law are good men, before he will give his blessing. I'm the last one, and he has always been very concerned for my welfare."

"You couldn't have found a better man, even if he is mine. Jeff has never smoked, drank, gambled or anything that is considered bad. I don't see how any parent could object to him," stated Mrs. Marshall smugly.

Lucinda sat thinking what she would say if she knew that Jeff had not only been drinking, but drunk for several days. She said, "Yes Ma'am, I agree and so do my parents now, but they don't know him like you do."

"Of course, I know that, but knowing Jeff as I do, you are really making a good match. You'll never have to work or want for anything. Jeff may not be making a lot of money right now, but he is moving up with this company, and he doesn't waste his money," bragged Mrs. Marshall.

"I'm sure that helped with Dad's decision, but it didn't matter to me, Mrs. Marshall. Besides, I'll be teaching, and that will be extra income for us," stated Lucinda, before she realized that Mrs. Marshall probably had the same feelings as Jeff about wives working.

"You're planning to work after you marry!" gasped Mrs. Marshall in astonishment.

"Yes Ma'am, I plan to teach," said Lucinda, wishing that she had kept quiet.

"I feel sure that Jeff won't allow that. It's a matter of pride, you know. All the Marshall men are like that," Mrs. Marshall said proudly, as if that made it right.

"I'm sorry if he feels like that but I do plan to work," said Lucinda firmly, as the men came back in, shivering from the cold. She was sitting very still in white-faced silence.

Jeff stopped dead when he saw Lucinda's face. Turning to his Mother, he saw that she also wore a stormy expression. He walked over to Lucinda and took her hand, "What's the matter, Honey? Are you not feeling well? "

Lucinda kept her eyes down, since she was on the verge of tears, but mumbled, "I'm okay, maybe a little tired. We probably need to leave. We told Dad we'd be back early."

Jeff looked puzzled, but realized that something had gone wrong while he was out. He looked at his watch and said, "Yea, you're right, it's time to go. I'll get our coats."

As Jeff left the room, Lucinda looked at Mrs. Marshall and said, "I'm sorry if you are disturbed but Jeff and I will work it out."

Mrs. Marshall rose to her feet as Jeff came in with the coats, and Lucinda rose to put hers on. She came over and hugged Jeff, then patted Lucinda on the shoulder and said, "I'm sure you will. You come back and see us."

Mr. Marshall came over and shook Jeff's hand, and grinned as he gave Lucinda a hug, saying, "Since you're going to be our new daughter, I may as well start, just like I'm going to continue."

Lucinda looked up at him and smiled, "Thank you, Sir. I appreciate that very much," as she slipped her arms in the coat Jeff was holding, and then turning, said, "I'm glad I met all of you." Turning towards Mrs. Marshall, she said, "Thank you for inviting me. The food was delicious." Margie and Jill came in from the kitchen where they had made themselves scarce. Lucinda wondered if Mrs. Marshall had told them to give her a chance to see what kind of girl Jeff was getting. She smiled, saying, "Thanks girls, for not making me do dishes."

"Like I told you, we'll save up some for you the next time," laughed Margie as she and Jill came over and hugged her, before saying, "Welcome to the family, Lucinda."

Then she and Jeff went out and down the steps to the truck, but were stopped by snowballs coming from two directions. "Cut it out, boys" yelled Jeff as he grabbed Lucinda's hand, and ran to the truck laughing.

Lucinda stopped, and grabbing a handful of snow, aimed a snowball that landed in the center of Jimmy's chest as he stepped out from behind the truck. The ensuing snowball fight had both Jeff and Lucinda covered before Jeff yelled, "Uncle - stop, boys. We're going to be wet, and we have a long way to go."

Both Bob and Jimmy came over, gave Jeff a hug, stood for a moment, and then hugged Lucinda also, before saying, "The next time you come, bring your gloves and some warm clothes and we'll have a good fight."

Lucinda laughingly promised that if she ever came again, she would do just that, as she climbed in the truck and shut the door.

Jeff started the truck, turned on the lights, and looked over at Lucinda, "Come over here woman so you won't freeze before the truck warms up," said Jeff as he pulled her close.

Lucinda sat quietly contemplating whether she should tell Jeff about what had happened. They rode for a few miles, and then Jeff asked, "What happened between you and Mom while I was outside?"

Lucinda wondered how much she should tell him, before saying, "Well, she was telling me what a good match I was making in getting a man like you."

"Oh Lord! She would. I thought she said something to upset you. She did, didn't she? What else did she say," questioned Jeff quietly.

"Aw Jeff, I guess she was just being a mother. She wanted to make sure that her boy was getting a good wife. That was all right," said Lucinda evasively.

"No, it was more than that. She didn't even hug you when we left. There was something else. What was it," pried Jeff.

Lucinda hesitated and then said, "Okay. She told me in no uncertain terms, that you would not allow me to work, and I told her that I intended to work. I think she feels you are getting a bad wife," stated Lucinda.

"How in the hell did that get started? Do you mean she asked you right out if you planned to work?" questioned Jeff.

"No, she didn't ask me right out, but she went on and on about what a paragon you were, and how you would always take care of me, and provide well for me. Thinking she was worried that it would be too hard on you,

200

I told her that was okay, since I intended to teach anyway," confessed Lucinda, still feeling the hurt of being attacked on her first visit.

"God, I wish you hadn't told her that yet," said Jeff quietly.

"Why Jeff, did you want me to lie to her? I hadn't planned to tell her. It just slipped out and besides, you told me you would be right there with me. Margie and Jill stayed in the kitchen, just to give her a chance to grill me. What was I supposed to do? I am going to teach, and if that is something you can't live with, then it's better to find it out now," said Lucinda, sliding to the other side of the truck seat.

They were back in Iaeger by this time and Jeff pulled in at the bus terminal and put the truck in park, but left the motor running. He switched off the lights, and turned with a heavy sigh, "Why is it, that every time you and I go anywhere anymore, some damn controversy comes up? I had it planned to have you meet my parents, and they would be pleased and happy like I am, and then this happens," groaned Jeff.

"Well, don't blame me. I didn't ask her how she and your father lived, or how well he provided for her. She was the one with the third degree," said Lucinda in a trembling voice. "Just take me home, Jeff. We'll just call it off. We're too different."

Suddenly she was crushed in his arms, "No! No, Lucinda, don't even think about breaking up. We're not that different. It's just that, all these little things will crop up, but we can work them out. Mom shouldn't have said anything. I wish to God she hadn't, but I'll talk to her, and it won't happen again. I promise," begged Jeff.

Lucinda pushed out of his arms and said, "Now Jeff, I don't want you going over there hurting your mother's feelings. If you do, she will never like me, no matter how hard I'd try. Maybe, if I hadn't been so nervous I wouldn't have reacted like that. I don't know. I do know this though, I am going to school and I am going to teach. Teaching is not sinful, nor is it dangerous, and neither is going to school. I intend to do both and I'm not ashamed of doing either of them. I would have thought you would be proud that I want to better myself. I'd want you to. Don't you want to be proud of me?" questioned Lucinda.

"I'm proud of you already, Honey. I couldn't be any prouder if you were Queen of England. It is just a new way of thinking. I'll get used to it, and it's okay. To prove it, I'll take you to Concord every Monday, and be back to get you on Friday," smiled Jeff.

Lucinda's whole face lit up, "You'd do that, Jeff, when you feel the way you do?"

Jeff pulled her back into his arms, "Lucinda, I'd do anything for you. That's anything but sharing you with someone else, and there I draw the line. I don't know what I might do if you wanted somebody else," said Jeff threateningly.

"Jeff, you're jealous. That's the silliest thing I ever heard of. You don't have anything to be jealous of. Grandpa always said that 'jealousy was crueler than the grave' and I think he's right. You can make yourself miserable, and if you keep that up, I will be miserable, too," complained Lucinda.

Jeff sat looking as if he was absorbing her into himself, and then hugging her close, he said, "I didn't think I was jealous. In fact, I don't recall ever being like this before, but I've never been in love before. I thought I was, when I was in high school, but I soon realized I could live without her, and I wasn't jealous of her. I think it's that damn doctor. I'd like to beat the hell out of him," snarled

Jeff and then crushed her to him again and gave her a bruising kiss.

Lucinda jerked away, "Jeff, there's a side to you that I don't like. I think you'd better take me home," demanded Lucinda.

"No- now listen, I'm just disappointed because you and Mom didn't hit it off, and then you talking about calling off our engagement. I'm sorry, Lucinda, I think I'm a bundle of nerves, too. Please forgive me, and I promise I'll control my jealousy. You're right. I know that you are honest, and you wouldn't have agreed to marry me if you thought you would be interested in someone else. I'd have been better off if Gordon had never told me about that doctor," stated Jeff quietly.

"I think maybe you should thank the doctor, Jeff. If he had come back, we may have married, and you and I would never have met," said Lucinda hesitantly.

Suddenly Jeff grinned, "You've got a point there, but anyway, I'm glad he's gone and is never coming back." Then he turned to Lucinda, "Honey, can we start over and make a deal tonight that when we have differences, we will talk them out and not get all upset and break up?" asked Jeff with his heart in his eyes.

Lucinda looked at him and suddenly smiled as she reached up and patted his cheek, "You're like a little boy, but you can learn, I think."

"Thanks, Sweetheart," breathed Jeff as he kissed her gently then shifted into gear and turned up Route 80 towards Bradshaw.

CHAPTER 22

It was nearing Christmas and there had been no more visits to the Marshalls. Jeff still visited on Wednesday evening, Saturday, and took her back to Dora's on Sunday. He begged Lucinda to move up the wedding date, on each visit, to the last of May, but Lucinda was adamant. "I can't concentrate on my studies with a home and husband to think about," argued Lucinda.

On the last day of school before Christmas, all the parents came. Lucinda was overwhelmed by her many gifts, knowing the parents who provided them were not well off.

The play went well with most children knowing their parts. They sang the carols with gusto, even if off key. Nothing, however, touched Lucinda so much as little Garson Lester. With pennies, nickels, dimes, and Lucinda's help, the school bought a pair of knee high lace-up shoes, and a pair of socks, as a special present for Garson. On Dora's suggestion, the entire school had contributed for one month on this project.

Garson's gift was labeled "The Special Gift" and the children were so excited. In fact, Lucinda thought they were more excited about the special gift than about what they hoped to get.

James' father, Mr. Estep, was Santa Claus. Each child got a gift and a bag of treats, and then Santa gave Garson his special gift. All the children clapped and gathered around to watch Garson open his gift. When they saw his face as he pulled out those shoes, most of the children had tears in their eyes, and many of the parents.

Little Garson, lovingly, rubbed his shoes, felt the socks, and then asked if he could put them on. He soon had them on, with Lucinda's help with lacing, and then he went to each person in the room saying, "I thank you," with great solemn eyes brimming with tears. Lucinda knew she would never forget this Christmas as long as she lived.

Lucinda wished that Jeff could have witnessed the whole scene. Maybe it would help him understand why I want to teach, thought Lucinda, as she gathered up the loose paper and set the place to rights. "My neck will probably be bruised from being hugged so many times," said Lucinda to the now empty seats. James Estep was the only student who hadn't hugged her, even though Lucinda knew he wanted to, but she was glad he didn't.

Lucinda was surprised when Jeff showed up in Deputy Stevens' jeep to take her home. She thought Burb would come for her, since Jeff was working. All her gifts were put in the back of the jeep, as well as report cards she planned to work on, during Christmas break. Then they drove back to Dora's to get her suitcase.

Jeff laughed, "Do you think you'll be able to do any of that when you'll be invited everywhere?"

"What do you mean? We don't get invited places at Christmas. All the family comes home," said Lucinda.

"Well, Mrs. Marshall to be, we have been invited to the country club in Gilbert for a Christmas dance. We've been invited to a Christmas Cantata at the Methodist Church in Pineville. Margie and Howard have invited us to dinner this Saturday night and then the folks want us to come to their house Christmas Eve or Christmas Day. So, there are that many invitations. Do you think it's enough?" asked Jeff as he shifted into low gear to go up Tom Wyatt hill.

Lucinda was amazed. All these invitations were unexpected and certainly different from the Harmon Christmases. What did one do at a country club, and what

205

was a cantata? She didn't mind going to Margie's but she sure dreaded meeting his mother again. "When was all this decided? Don't you think you should have asked me first?" demanded Lucinda dejectedly.

"Lucinda, I didn't say I had accepted. I said we had been invited. We can go, can't we?" asked Jeff. "After all, there isn't much to do here on Bradshaw Mountain and Christmas is a special time."

"I guess you think we're hicks because we don't go out to parties, don't you?" questioned Lucinda.

"No, now I didn't say that. But Lucinda, you know that there isn't much to do. We've only eaten at the Sunset Drive-In, or gone to Bradshaw to a movie, since October. I'm pretty sick of both, to be honest. I thought you'd be happy to do something different. Your dad wouldn't let you until we became engaged, and I didn't expect it, but now we can, if you'll just go, please," begged Jeff.

Lucinda knew he was right. When she first came back from college, she was often lonely and bored but she had gotten used to it again. She gave out a long, drawn out sigh, and said, "When do this country club dance and this Cantata take place? They may both be on the same day."

Jeff grinned as they pulled out onto the highway, "I'd hug you if I could but you know how it is with the air space in this jeep. God, I'll be glad to get back to paved roads for good. Wouldn't you like to see the last of these mud holes, ruts, and potholes?" asked Jeff.

"Nobody's making you come down to Estep and Brushy Ridge. In fact, I tried to discourage it if you remember," snapped Lucinda.

Jeff pulled over in front of Sam Vencill's store and shut off the engine, before he turned. "Now, now Lucinda, temper, temper. Remember, we promised we would talk out our differences," reminded Jeff. Seeing Lucinda was still upset, he said, "Lucinda, I'd be a liar if I said I liked mud, ruts, coal stoves, outside toilets, and a lot of things that you are used to. But that doesn't mean that I feel better than you. I was just raised differently, and frankly, I'm glad I was. Really now, wouldn't you like to go to a bathroom inside the house instead of going a mile around a hill, and then have to plop your butt down on that cold, cold seat," Jeff said, with a laugh, and then shivered in remembrance.

Lucinda laughed as she remembered him asking the location of their bathroom right after he had asked Burb for her hand in marriage. When the path around the hill was pointed out, his eyes opened wide in disbelief, but he didn't say anything. However, she stood at the window, watching him try to avoid the mud and yet hurry, since he didn't take his coat. He sure traveled much faster on his way back.

"You didn't say a word when you went to our outside toilet that time," smiled Lucinda.

Jeff raised his eyebrows quizzically, "But, have you noticed I've had much better bladder control since then?" he laughed.

Lucinda gurgled with laughter, "I think maybe I could get used to indoor plumbing."

Jeff laughed as he leaned across and gave her a quick kiss. "Now, isn't this a better way to settle things," he questioned.

Lucinda smiled and nodded in agreement as he pulled out from the store and started down Brushy Ridge. Suddenly she thought about what women wore to a country club, realizing she didn't know. She hated for Jeff to know how backward she was but knew that he'd find out anyway, if she married him.

She turned in her seat, "Jeff, what do the women wear to a country club dance?"

"Oh, they really deck themselves out; you know, evening dresses, and all that," said Jeff carelessly.

"No, I don't know, Jeff. I've never been to a country club for any reason. I didn't even get to go to my senior prom. I don't have an evening dress, so I guess you'd better go alone," stated Lucinda.

Jeff stopped right in the middle of the road, "No, I'm not going alone. You are going with me. We'll go to Welch or Bluefield this weekend and buy you an evening dress. How does that sound?" offered Jeff.

Lucinda thought about her finances and knew she would have about $50 left over this month, but she had planned to buy her mother a coat for Christmas. She would love an evening dress, but Nancy had never had a new coat, and Lucinda wanted to buy her one. "No, we can't, Jeff. I won't have enough money. There's a present I want to buy Mommy, and I'd rather do that than buy myself an evening dress," replied Lucinda.

"I didn't mean you would have to buy it, Mrs. Lucinda Harmon Marshall. I want to buy it myself," Jeff said, smiling possessively.

"I couldn't let you do that. I mean, a girl doesn't take expensive gifts from men. Mommy wouldn't let me take it," stated Lucinda firmly.

Jeff shook his head in exasperation, "You mean to tell me that your mother won't allow me to buy you a Christmas present. I never heard of a man being engaged to marry a girl, and can't be out with her after dark, can't buy her gifts, and is not allowed to touch her anywhere below the neck. That's just pure damn silly," barked Jeff angrily.

"My family is not silly, Jeff Marshall. You can think what you want to. My parents raised five decent girls, and they're proud of it," shouted Lucinda.

"Well, I'm surprised that every damn one of them are not old maids or frozen up old prunes. Don't do this. Don't do that, because it isn't nice. Nice, hell! What your Mom has done is scare the life out of you and all the others. No wonder Odell's husband is a drunk. It is not indecent for your fiancé to touch your knee, for God's sake," blasted Jeff in frustration.

Lucinda looked at Jeff keenly, "You just take me home. Asking Daddy if you could marry me does not give you license to do whatever you want. All my sisters are married and happy, so don't tell me that junk about frozen prunes," growled Lucinda angrily.

Jeff let out on the clutch and went speeding around the road. When he came upon the curve below the Wilson barn, he was going too fast and his back left wheel slid over the edge of the road. He turned, giving a sheepish grin, "See how frustrated I am. Couldn't we get married before August?" Reaching over and grasping her hand, Jeff said, "Aw, Lucinda, I'm sorry. I shouldn't have said all that stuff, but Honey, you have no idea how a man feels. Listen, if I ask Mrs. Harmon about buying you an evening dress, will you let me buy it? I want us to go to that dance. I want to show you off," mumbled Jeff contritely.

Lucinda really wanted to go dancing but more than that, she would love to have an evening dress. She could just see herself whirling around the dance floor in a lovely blue dress with yards and yards of skirt. It had to be blue. She looked at Jeff and smiled as she said, "Well, get this jeep back on the road and let's go ask her."

CHAPTER 23

That Saturday, an excited Lucinda found herself sitting beside Jeff as they rolled into Bluefield. She had ridden a bus through this town, but had never stopped. Carillons were chiming from a big fancy church right off Main Street, and all the shop windows and store fronts were decked in Christmas array. Lucinda was almost dizzy from staring, first right and then left, as they drove through town. She just couldn't wait to walk down the streets adorned for Christmas. Jeff stared with pleasure at her glowing face and shining eyes. She was like a child turned loose in a toy store, and Jeff was exhilarated just watching her.

Linking her hand with his, he started marching hurriedly down the street. She wouldn't march though. She wanted to linger in front of every display, and sometimes just stop in the middle of the pavement, listening spellbound to the carols. Everybody they met smiled and some said, "Merry Christmas." Jeff realized that seeing the expression on Lucinda's face was enough to make anyone wish her joy.

As they walked, Lucinda suddenly stopped in front of a store window which displayed evening dresses. Right in the center of the window, was a blue evening dress. It had short puffed sleeves, a rounded neckline, and yards of billowing skirt, which seemed to be encrusted with sparkling gems. Lucinda gazed in wonder, "Oooh! Isn't it beautiful," breathed Lucinda reverently.

Jeff didn't hesitate, but pulled her with him, as he opened the door and went inside. A sales girl came immediately to their aid, and Jeff asked about the blue dress in the window. Lucinda was so excited she hadn't said a word, but when the sales girl said the price was $300, she gasped aloud and turned to go. Jeff held her fast by his side, as he asked if she could try it on. The sales girl went immediately to ask the manager, and Lucinda turned to Jeff with anguished eyes, "Jeff, I don't have enough money, and I can't let you spend that much on one dress. You work too hard for your money."

"Shh! Let me worry about that," said Jeff putting his arm around her waist, and pulling her close to his side. The manager, a tall stately woman in a black suit and red high-necked blouse, came over with a smile, "Sir, that dress is the only one we have like that right now, but I can order you one."

"We can't wait. She needs it next Saturday, and we can't get back up here before then. If you can get another, why not let us try that one? It may not fit but it looks like it will," said Jeff.

The manager stood hesitantly, with her mouth twisted awry in thought, "To tell you the truth, Sir, the dress has a torn place in it, and we haven't had the time to get it repaired. It doesn't show in the window, and it makes for a good display."

"Can the dress be fixed? I mean, is it something that can't be repaired?" questioned Jeff.

"No, but it will take a professional seamstress. Do you still want to look at it?" asked the manager.

When Jeff nodded affirmatively, she told the sales girl to go up into the window and bring out the dress. Upon inspection, both Lucinda and Jeff saw the large rip in the seam on the left side, under the arm, and a tear in the tail of the skirt. It looked as if someone had tried to fit into the dress, but was too fat, and caused the seam to give. They couldn't understand how the rent got in the tail of the dress, unless the fat girl did it deliberately. Lucinda looked so bewildered, as if she had been offered a present, and then had it taken away. Jeff insisted that she try the dress on, and let him see how it looked. She was led away to a fitting room and helped into the dress. It was a perfect fit, and made her look like a fairy princess, or so Lucinda thought. The sales girl must have thought the same thing for she said, "My, you look like royalty in that dress."

When Lucinda was brought out for Jeff's inspection, he walked around the dress nodding and shaking his head. He lifted her arm and looked at the torn place which had been carefully pinned. He picked up the tail of the skirt and inspected the torn place there. Lucinda stood in muted embarrassment. Then Jeff turned to the manager, who was standing slightly to the side, and started to bargain but the manager interrupted, "It is very becoming on her. It looks as if it was made for her," she smiled.

Jeff still stood silently looking at the dress, then stated that they would take it, but for $50 less than the ticket price, since it would cost at least that much to have it repaired. Lucinda thought Jeff didn't even like the dress, but she liked it, and if they could get it for $250 that would be a big savings. Lucinda knew that her mother could repair the damage, and nobody would ever know. The manager said she'd have to go and ask her partner.

"You don't think the dress looks good on me, do you, Jeff?" asked Lucinda.

"God, yes, Honey. You look good enough to eat, but I was putting on an act to get the price down," said Jeff in a whisper, as he grasped her hand and laced his fingers through hers. He began to notice the other customers looking at Lucinda, and stepped back to give them a better view, and to hear the awed sighs from many of the women. Lucinda saw that these women were acting like she was beautiful, and she felt beautiful for the first time in her life.

The manager came back, saying that they had agreed to let them have the dress. Turning Lucinda around to take her back to the fitting room, she suddenly stopped, "This dress needs a tiara to wear with it, and I have one that is just right for it. Would you like to see it, Sir," she addressed Jeff.

Jeff shrugged, "Sure, we can look at it, but I really don't think that dress needs anything except my fiancée to wear it." Many of the shoppers, gathered around, nodded in agreement, but one or two said she should look at the tiara, anyway. The manager went away and soon returned with the tiara, wrapped in tissue paper. She unfolded the paper to reveal a sparkling rhinestone crown, which she immediately placed on Lucinda's head. She stepped back to view the result. She then turned Lucinda toward a mirror against a wall. Lucinda looked at the tiara, but it just did not make any difference to her; she only wanted the dress. She turned to Jeff, shaking her head, and then said to the manager, "No, Ma'am, I'm not the tiara type I don't think." Jeff didn't say anything and the manager agreed reluctantly.

Lucinda was helped off with the dress, and it was placed in a large box, as Jeff paid the sales girl. They went out of the store, with less money, but very happy. When they succeeded in getting the cumbersome box inside the truck, there wasn't much room left for Lucinda. Due to her delight and appreciation for her first evening gown, Lucinda impulsively kissed Jeff on the lips, for the first time. Soon, she had doubts if that was a wise thing to do. She had to forcefully shove Jeff away, "My God, Jeff, you can't eat me, you know. I didn't know a kiss would get that kind of reaction."

Jeff grinned, trying to look sorry but not quite making it. "Well, that's the first time you've volunteered any kind of affection. I can't afford to miss any chances. Anyway, you're safe over here now that I'm over my momentary madness. I'll be good, I promise."

Lucinda snuggled closer to his side and they left Bluefield singing Christmas carols. They sang all the way to Northfork, where they stopped at a restaurant and went in. When Jeff heard the music playing and saw bottles of beer being carried on trays, he took Lucinda's arm and propelled her back outside. "I'm sorry Lucinda; I didn't know that was a Honky-tonk". They decided to drive on into Welch to get something to eat.

When they got to Welch, Jeff said, "I've heard people talk about the Sterling Drive-In. Do you want to go out there?"

Lucinda knew she turned pale, but it was dark in the truck and Jeff couldn't see her. The last time she had eaten at the Sterling Drive-In was with Jason, and she didn't want to go back there. "No, that's too far out of town. Let's go down to the Mountaineer Grill at the lower end of town. They have good food."

"Okay, whatever you say, Ma'am," Jeff drawled like a cowboy as he turned right on Wyoming Street. The manager of the grill remembered Lucinda and came over to their table. "Hello there, pretty girl. Where did you slip away to? I've not seen you in a long time."

Lucinda smiled with pleasure, "Thanks for remembering me, Gus. I didn't think you would."

"Honey, not many men would forget a pretty girl like you," said Gus, smiling broadly, until he saw the scowl on Jeff's face. "Oh Ho, who's this scowling, young Lochinvar? He's ready to belt me, I think."

Jeff looked up into the smiling face of this white-haired Greek and said, "She's my fiancée and I'm quite protective of her."

"Sure, sure, tis good, but remember, you can hold a butterfly in your palm but if you close your hand on it, you will kill it," Gus said, nodding his head wisely.

Jeff looked dumbfounded. Was this old man trying to tell him something? He wasn't trying to smother Lucinda, but it did make him angry when men admired her so blatantly.

Lucinda saw Jeff's troubled look and put her hand over his. "He's just being nice, Jeff. I ate here almost every morning when I lived in Welch, and Gus always waited on me, didn't you, Gus?" smiled Lucinda as she looked at her old friend.

"She had scrambled egg, toast, slice of tomato, and milk. Same every day and never gained an ounce" said Gus seriously.

Jeff relaxed and smiled as he told Gus how he tried to get her to eat more, but wasn't having any luck. He even told Gus how hard he was trying to get Lucinda to move up the date for their wedding. Gus stood looking at him for a moment, "Marriage is a lifetime commitment and our Lucinda just wants to make sure, don't you, pretty girl," he said shaking his head for emphasis.

Lucinda smiled and explained why she wanted to wait until August, and Gus nodded in understanding. "Well, we may as well order since I'm not going to get any help from you," said Jeff with a polite smile.

"Take the spaghetti. It is very good. I make it myself," bragged Gus, writing swiftly when they agreed. Then he left to soon return with water and a beaming smile, as he also put two goblets on the table, and poured wine into each glass. "To celebrate for my pretty girl" offered Gus, saying it was free.

Lucinda looked at Jeff and he looked at her. Never having tasted wine, Lucinda was afraid it would make her drunk, but Gus said, "Wait until the spaghetti comes then have the wine with your dinner. It is good for you, pretty girl. It won't hurt you, I promise." Jeff smiled, nodding in agreement and Lucinda decided she would try it.

She had the wine with her dinner and it seemed to have no effect, which surprised her. They thanked Gus, and were very surprised when he pressed the bagged bottle of wine into Jeff's hands, as they left. "To celebrate with and remember Gus," he chuckled as they went out the door.

Lucinda had been to Bluefield, let a man buy her a dress, kissed a man on the lips, and drank wine with her dinner. This had been a day filled with new experiences and Lucinda was happy.

CHAPTER 24

Lucinda relived the country club dance in her mind for weeks. Most of it was wonderful. Jeff had given her a beautiful diamond engagement ring for Christmas. It was a half carat in a 14 karat gold marquis setting that winked and flickered in every light. Lucinda saw her sisters looking in envy, and was sorry they hadn't gotten an engagement ring. At the same time, she knew that the really important things in life were not rings or any material things. It was funny, but after she had promised to marry Jeff, the lessons and values which grandpa had talked about, had begun to be more on her mind. She had even started reading the Bible some. She really didn't know why, she just seemed to want to.

The night of the dance, Lucinda had dressed and come into the front room to wait on Jeff. Burb and Nancy went on and on about how pretty their baby looked. When Jeff came, bearing a corsage of little pink rosebuds, Burb immediately offered him a seat. Lucinda thought this was unusual, until she realized that Burb wanted to lay down the law, about how he was to conduct himself toward her. He didn't blurt anything right out, but he kept saying things like, "I know it is tempting to get a little carried away when a girl is a pretty as our Cindy" and "Any boy that treats my Cindy wrong, will have to answer to me."

When they left, Jeff laughed halfway out of the ridge, "If I'd had any ideas of taking advantage of you, Mr. Harmon sure put a damper on them. He's sharp though. I'll bet he was a lady's man in his day. But, come on over here. I'll try my best to control my baser urges," said Jeff still laughing.

The dance was scheduled for seven o'clock and they arrived a little early, which gave Lucinda time to look at the other girls as they came in. She was satisfied that she looked as good as any of the others. That gave her ego a big boost. She began to relax and enjoy herself.

Jeff's family raved about her beautiful dress and Lucinda got many admiring glances from the men. Jeff was so proud he almost strutted, unless some man became too obvious in his admiration. He stayed close by her side, avoiding introductions as much as possible.

She and Jeff danced well together and his mother came over and whispered, "You two should win a prize for the best looking couple on the floor."

Lucinda thanked her warmly, and the uneasy feelings she had about Jeff's mother, seemed to be changing. She still felt that Mrs. Marshall did not exactly approve of her, but it seemed she was trying.

Mr. Marshall was a different story altogether. After Lucinda had danced twice with Jeff, he came over saying, "It isn't fair for you to dance the entire night with the prettiest girl here," as he waltzed her away.

They were laughing and talking when a tall sandy haired young man tapped Mr. Marshall on the shoulder and said, "How about it, Pop? I'd like to dance with this fairy princess."

Mr. Marshall released her reluctantly, looking around for Jeff. Lucinda saw his reluctance, but did not know the usual practice, so she moved onto the floor with the stranger. He danced well enough, but constantly tried to draw her closer than she wanted to be. It was closer than Jeff wanted her to be also, if the looks he was giving them from the sidelines was any indication. The music soon stopped and Lucinda was glad. She smiled at his thanks and turned to go back to Jeff, but the man still held her hand. She tugged her hand from his saying, "Excuse me, my fiancé is waiting for me," and walked back to Jeff who stood glowering.

He had been very upset with his dad for releasing her to some strange man, but Mr. Marshall chided him with, "Son, people cut in all the time. We can see everything that happens out there, so don't get upset."

When Lucinda reached him, he immediately wanted to know who that fellow was. Lucinda confessed that she didn't know his name, and she hadn't asked. When she saw the sour look on Jeff's face, she linked her arm through his, "I didn't want to dance with him Jeff, but I didn't know what I was supposed to do. Your dad just turned me over to him. I told him I wanted to go back to my fiancé."

Jeff looked down at her with relief, tilted her chin and kissed her swiftly, "That's my girl. I guess he didn't know you were engaged." Smiling, they went holding hands to the refreshment table.

The different finger foods offered were like foods from a foreign country to Lucinda, since she had no idea what most of them were. Being daring, she took a little of everything that looked good, before joining Jeff's family at a corner table. Jill, Margie, and even Mrs. Marshall just couldn't get over how she looked in her beautiful dress. Lucinda told them the story behind the purchase of the dress, and they all thought Jeff had been a shrewd shopper. Mrs. Marshall had been eyeing her ring for some time. She hadn't said anything, but when Jill asked how much they eventually gave for the dress and was told $250 Mrs. Marshall said, "Land sakes Jeff, you're going to spend all you make down in that hole for Lucinda's Christmas, what with that dress and that big diamond."

Jeff looked at her sharply, "Mom, Lucinda is my future wife and I'll spend much more on her if it will make her happy."

His look wasn't lost on Mrs. Marshall, who smiled saying, "I know son, and I didn't mean anything. I was just saying how expensive things are these days."

Jeff got to his feet, drawing Lucinda up, and circling her waist, he waltzed her out on the dance floor. As they passed the glass doors to the outside, Lucinda saw the blond stranger who had danced with her with a bottle turned up to his mouth. She didn't say anything because she didn't want Jeff to get angry again, but she wondered if others were slipping out to drink. As the dance ended, Jeff said, "Gosh, the time has flown. Guess what time it is." Lucinda tried to grab his arm to look at his watch but he held his arm too high for her to reach.

She playfully reached up, putting her arms around his neck and he quickly lowered his arms pulling her close. She immediately twisted around and looked at his watch, laughing all the time. When she saw that it was midnight, she gasped, "Don't you think it's time for Cinderella's coach?"

Before Jeff could answer, the blond man came strolling up and said, "Are you being offensive to this princess in distress?"

"I beg your pardon, were you addressing me, Mister?" Jeff bristled.

"Well, I don't see anyone else mauling her, do you?" snarled the man from whiskey fumed breath.

Jeff pushed Lucinda behind him and gave the man a shove, sending him staggering into a table. When he straightened up and came charging like a bull, Jeff was waiting, but before he got there, two of his friends propelled him towards the outside. Jeff started to follow,

220

but Lucinda grabbed his arm, just as Mr. Marshall arrived"
"Now Jeff, cool off. The man was drunk. You don't want to
have any trouble here," said Mr. Marshall patting Jeff's
shoulder.

After that, the evening palled. Everyone soon
began to gather their wraps in preparation for home.
Lucinda hadn't said a word, but when she looked at Mrs.
Marshall, she realized that she was being blamed for the
incident. Mrs. Marshall hadn't really said anything, but her
lips were set in a grim line, and she gave Lucinda baleful
looks.

She was really glad when their good-byes had been
said, and they were back in Jeff's truck. Jeff wrapped her
heavy cape snugly around her, drawing her close, as he
turned the heater to high. "I'm sorry, Lucinda. I hope that
didn't ruin your evening. I know that fellow was drunk, but
he had already pushed himself on you for a dance. That
was just a little more than I wanted to put up with. You
didn't want to dance with a drunk, did you?"

"Jeff, you know I didn't want to dance with
anybody but you. I was having such a good time until that
happened. There must be something wrong with me. I
know your mother thinks I'm causing you trouble, but Jeff,
I don't know what I'm doing wrong," wailed Lucinda.

Jeff nestled her closer to him, kissing the top of her
head, then her eyes, then her mouth, "Honey, you didn't
do anything. You don't do anything. It's just that you're so
pretty, that every guy that sees you wants to meet you. Of
course, that goon did a little more than that. But you're
wrong about Mom, she was just upset. Really, she just
didn't want her family to look bad. Mom's into this social
etiquette thing. She's afraid some of her friends will frown
on the conduct of her family," laughed Jeff.

He asked if she would like to hear some music and turned on the radio when she nodded. George Jones and Tammy Wynette were singing 'Hold On' and Jeff let it play, asking if she liked it. She said she did and it really wasn't bad, so he just left it tuned to that station as they rode along. They didn't talk much, each caught up in their own thoughts. Jeff turned down the radio and said, "Lucinda, will you please just think about getting married in May? Now, I know you don't want to, but just think, since you lost the scholarship when you started teaching you will have to borrow money to go on. But, if you will agree to marry in May you won't have to borrow any money to go back to school. I'll give you the money, and I'll take you to Concord, and come back and get you. I may even come over on Wednesday nights," said Jeff, grinning like Red Skelton.

Lucinda sat, not saying a word, until Jeff jostled her arm, "Say something."

"You told me to think. I'm thinking, I'm thinking - and I can't," stated Lucinda.

"I don't see why not. Just give me one good reason. I won't expect you to keep house, do laundry, or anything while you are in school. That way you would have time to work on your lessons," argued Jeff.

"Now Jeff, you agreed that we'd get married in August and now you are constantly nagging me to move up the date. That's not fair. I agreed to marry you, but only if you would wait until August," declared Lucinda huffily.

"Okay, okay. Don't get upset. You must not love me as much as I love you. I'd get married tonight, but you want to wait months and months. I don't see what the difference is, if you're going to marry me, whether it's now or a few months later," argued Jeff.

Lucinda frowned as she moved back so she could look at him, "Jeff Marshall, I don't want to argue about this every time we're together. I said August, and if you don't stop pestering me I may move it to next December," said Lucinda adamantly.

Jeff clamped his jaws together, and drove in silence until they reached Bradshaw. Patsy Cline was now on the radio belting out 'Crazy' and Jeff pounded the dash saying, "That's it. I'm crazy, just plain crazy for loving you the way I do. I can't help it though, and you know it. That's why you're doing me this way." Glancing sideways at her, he said, "Don't worry, I'm not going to start again. Just keep on loving me, will you Lucinda?"

Lucinda slid close and leaned her head on his shoulder, "I'm not trying to be hateful, Jeff. I just want to be sure, and August gives us plenty of time. This is a lifetime commitment and I don't want to wake up some morning, ten years down the road, and regret it."

Jeff stopped in the parking lot of Moore's store in Stringtown. He drew Lucinda into his arms and kissed her passionately. Looking down into her face, he said, "I know you enjoy my kisses, but you are so reserved or inhibited that you won't let me get close. I'll never hurt you and I'll make sure you never regret marrying me. I love you to distraction, and I hope that one day you will feel the same way."

Lucinda looked around guiltily and Jeff laughingly told her that the store was closed and everybody was in bed. "Someday, you're going to realize that kissing and hugging, and a lot of other things are not something to be ashamed of or sinful. I know you don't believe me now, but you will, my girl, you will."

CHAPTER 25

Christmas was wonderful with all the family gathered around Nancy's loaded table. Everybody laughed and told funny things that had happened in the past year. Lucinda, however, became quieter than usual when the time came to leave for the Marshall's. As soon as she had helped clear the kitchen, Jeff came in and said, "I guess we'd better leave or we'll be late."

So, Lucinda climbed into Jeff's truck, wishing with all her heart there was some way out of it. She had gone to the Cantata with Jeff and everything was fine. She enjoyed the music and songs and the fellowship afterwards. Jeff's sisters were really nice and she enjoyed being with them, but Mrs. Marshall was a different story. Lucinda wondered if she was doing something wrong, but if so, she honestly didn't know what it was.

When they arrived, Mrs. Marshall met them at the door smiling a welcome and giving each of them a hug. Lucinda relaxed a little, thinking it was going to be better. It was all through supper with everyone laughing and kidding each other. Later as they sat in the living room, Mr. Marshall asked Jeff if he was still investing part of his pay in company stocks. That's when things went awry.

This was a surprise to Lucinda, but she thought Jeff must be a smart business man. But when she saw Jeff turn red and look at her, she was puzzled. Jeff smiled at her and said, "Not for the last few months. I've wanted to make sure I had enough money to go see my girl and buy her a few things."

It was then Mrs. Marshall quickly spoke up, "Jeff, I'm sure Lucinda wouldn't want you to buy her so much when you have been saving for your future, would you Lucinda?"

Lucinda turned red and, looking puzzled, said, "I didn't know Jeff had been saving and I didn't ask him to buy me anything. In fact, I've told him not to buy me things."

Feeling Lucinda tense up beside him, Jeff picked up her hand, lacing their fingers together, "Don't blame Lucinda. If it was left to her, we wouldn't do anything but go back and forth to that school where she teaches and eat at a drive-in."

Mrs. Marshall's mouth had taken on that thin line that Lucinda was beginning to recognize, and she started to say something else but Mr. Marshall interrupted, "Well, son, it's none of our business anyway. I shouldn't have asked but I was wondering if their stock is as reasonable as it was last summer."

"Actually, it's gone up a little but not enough to hinder me buying some more, probably this month, unless I can talk Lucinda into moving our wedding up," grinned Jeff, looking hopefully at Lucinda.

"I wish she would," said Jill. "Why don't you, Lucinda? Then you and I would be young brides together."

Trying to change the subject, Lucinda said, "When are you getting married?"

"We have to wait until Sam's school is out, which is May 28th this year. Yours will be out too, Lucinda, so we could be married at the same time, if you would, please," begged Jill.

Lucinda could feel Mrs. Marshall's eyes on her and she was getting very uncomfortable again, "I have to wait until I go to summer school and get that behind me. If I was already married, I'd be thinking of things at home and couldn't do as well on my lessons."

"I think she's right. She and Jeff haven't known each other very long and it just makes sense to give themselves some time," smiled Mrs. Marshall.

"You're sure a lot of help, Mom," growled Jeff, but didn't say anymore after taking a look at Lucinda's face.

Suddenly Lucinda thought she understood. Mrs. Marshall did not want Jeff to marry at all, but she certainly did not want him to marry Lucinda Harmon.

They left about 8:30 since Jeff had to work the next day. Mrs. Marshall had mentioned at 8:00 that even though she loved their company, they really should get back, since Jeff had a day's work ahead of him. Lucinda thought that if she knew how late he'd been staying out on Saturday nights, she would have a fit. He always stayed until 9:00 on Wednesday nights and at least until 11:30 on Saturday nights. He would have stayed longer on Wednesday nights, but Uncle Jake's fetish about turning out the lights put a stop to that.

Since Mrs. Marshall did not want Jeff to marry her, Lucinda felt she had an ace in the hole. It would help to stop Jeff's nagging to move up the wedding date. Still yet, it hurt to know Mrs. Marshall didn't like her, especially since she didn't know why. Maybe Margie would tell her if she could approach her in just the right way.

Lucinda didn't have to wait very long to find out why Mrs. Marshall did not like her, and she didn't have to find out from Margie. Three weeks later, she discovered the reason herself. A man working with Jeff went to sleep on the job and the boss fired him. Lucinda heard this from Gordon. According to Gordon, the man had been caught sleeping twice already and so the foreman was certainly within his rights. That did not keep the men from striking.

When Jeff came down on Wednesday night, he told Lucinda that there was talk of a strike. When Lucinda

226

questioned why, Jeff said it was because a man was fired unfairly. He proceeded to tell how the man had a sick wife and had been losing a lot of sleep taking care of her, so he had gone to sleep on the job. The foreman had caught him sleeping and fired him without going through a grievance procedure or some such. Lucinda felt sorry for the man, but felt that people could not go to sleep on the job, without getting fired. His negligence could have caused a bad accident and the loss of lives. She understood the foreman's position also.

When she went home that weekend, and asked Gordon more about it, he had another story to tell. He said that if the man had told the foreman about his wife's sickness, he could have stayed off from work for a few days. He couldn't afford to have someone asleep on the job. This kind of conduct could cause the foreman to lose his job as well as jeopardize the lives of all the men.

These two conflicting stories, or really two different ways of looking at the same story, gave Lucinda an idea of the vast difference in the way her family thought about unions, and the way Jeff thought about unions. Now the entire mine was shut down. Gordon said some of the men were complaining because they wanted to work. Miners, however, knew how dangerous it was to cross a picket line and very few tried it. Those that did were taunted and called "Scabs" and worse, threatened with violence. Lucinda remembered a few years earlier when a miner from Bradshaw had crossed the picket line and that night he was "waylaid" and beaten up badly. Lucinda felt that was awful because the miner had six children at home to feed and he needed that payday.

Before Jeff came on Saturday night, Lucinda had made up her mind not to mention anything about the strike or the union. She didn't have to though, because

Burb brought it up as soon as Jeff walked in. "I guess this strike will put "paid" to your marriage plans won't it, young feller?"

"No, Sir, it won't hurt me. I've been saving my money. Of course, I hope they go back in soon. I could use a little more," smiled Jeff.

"How long you reckon they'll be out this time?" questioned Burb.

"We've got a good union steward and I think he'll get it settled pretty quickly," Jeff stated as he came to the kitchen door, asking for Lucinda. Lucinda came in from her bedroom, off from the kitchen, and stopped dead. By the look on Jeff's face, she guessed Burb had been questioning him about the strike.

"Lucinda, Mom has asked us to supper tonight. Can you go?" asked Jeff looking hopeful.

Lucinda looked at Nancy who was seated behind the table peeling apples, "Is it okay with you, Mommy? We'll come back early," promised Lucinda.

Nancy agreed after confirming it with Burb. Jeff and Lucinda escaped before a big argument was started about the unions. As the truck pulled up the hill above the house, Jeff let out a loud sigh as he laughingly said, "Whew, you came in just in time. Your Dad was raring to go about this strike. Why is he so against unions?"

Lucinda felt almost like her dad and wondered how she should answer without getting into an argument and ruining their evening. "I guess you'll have to ask him, Jeff. He knows more about it than I do. We don't sit around discussing unions at our house."

"No-o-o, I don't think I'll ask him," laughed Jeff as he motioned for Lucinda to move closer. "Anyway, it will be settled soon, and we'll all be back at work. I have to walk the picket line on Sunday, though. So, I can't take you back to Dora's." Jeff said sorrowfully.

Lucinda started to protest, but changed her mind, and fiddled with the dial on the radio instead. Suddenly, Nat King Cole's mellow voice came out loud and clear, *'they try to tell us we're too young.'* Lucinda twisted the dial so vehemently that Jeff said, "Well, I know for sure you don't like that man's singing. That's good though, because I don't like him either." Lucinda found some instrumental music that was soft and pleasant and left it until Jeff said, "You like that elevator music?"

"Elevator music - I don't know what you're talking about. It's just a big band instrumental but I don't have to listen to it," stated Lucinda as she pushed the off button.

Jeff started laughing, "Gosh, you're easily offended tonight. I was only kidding. Bobby and Jimmy started calling that "elevator music" when Margie or Jill played it. It reminds them of music that they had heard in an elevator once when they were really young, and got a good scare. They sneaked away from Mom and hopped on an elevator. Someone had gotten on behind them and pushed a button, and the elevator took the boys to the sixth floor, before it stopped. They were hysterical when Mom found them. After that, they knew if they said it reminded them of the elevator, that Mom would make the girls change the station."

Lucinda laughed as she remembered Jeff's young brothers with fondness. They had been like brothers to her, ever since that first night, when they had thrown snowballs at each other. In fact, every member of Jeff's family acted as if they really liked her except for Mrs. Marshall. Lucinda puzzled over this as they rode along. Jeff took his arm from around her shoulders and turned the radio back on. They rode on into Iaeger in easy companionship. Lucinda loved having someone to be this easy with. She felt sure, at that moment, that marriage to Jeff would be fine. But how was she to get his mother to like her, she wondered.

They talked and laughed all the way over Johnnycake Mountain and on into Gilbert. Mrs. Marshall met them with a smile and this time hugged both of them. She even told Lucinda she looked nice in the blue angora twin set and darker skirt. "Blue's your color, Lucinda; it's very becoming. Does Jeff tell you that?" asked Mrs. Marshall smiling.

"He usually does but he hasn't tonight," grinned Lucinda as she looked hurt. Knowing Jeff was as tense as she was about her relationship with his mother, Lucinda punched him, "Why didn't you tell me what you thought?"

"Because I was trying to get away from your dad as fast as I could," mumbled Jeff.

"Doesn't Mr. Harmon like you, Jeff?" questioned Mrs. Marshall looking almost eager.

"Sure, he likes me, Mom. He just doesn't like unions and since we're on strike, I knew he'd have a lot to say," said Jeff.

By this time Mr. Marshall had joined them and Mrs. Marshall didn't get to delve into this situation. Lucinda could tell by her look that the discussion wasn't finished, however. That worried Lucinda but not as much as what she discovered later that same evening.

CHAPTER 26

When they arrived from basketball practice, Bob and Jimmy were pleased to see Lucinda. After much teasing and hugging, they all trooped into the dining room. Jeff and his brothers set the table and poured drinks. Then Lucinda and Mr. Marshall carried the food to the table. Mrs. Marshall was a good cook and Lucinda praised her baked pork chops. Lucinda was promised the recipe since Mrs. Marshall knew Jeff liked pork chops. "Of course, there's no hurry since the wedding is not until the end of the summer," smiled Mrs. Marshall.

Jeff glared at his mother, fearing she was going to bring up something unpleasant, but she didn't. Lucinda helped her with the dishes, even though she feared being alone with her. Nothing was brought up, and in fact, she and Mrs. Marshall seemed to be getting along fine and Lucinda was silently thankful.

When they went into the living room, the talk suddenly stopped and then Mr. Marshall quickly said, "Here Lucinda, come sit here on the sofa beside Jeff," as he arose and took a chair near the fireplace. Mrs. Marshall took a seat near her husband as she said, "Were you men telling secrets. You stopped suddenly as we came in."

Jeff grinned, "If we told you, it wouldn't be a secret, would it, Mom? Dad and I were talking men talk while you and Lucinda were talking women talk. Weren't we, Dad?"

Mr. Marshall rubbed his chin and rolled his eyes, "Were we ever! I was telling him about the birds and the bees."

Jimmy came down the stairs, and looking at Jeff, said, "Guess who I saw today. I saw Geneva Clary, big as life, walking past the school just as I was heading in for basketball practice. She didn't see me and I was glad."

Jeff didn't say anything but Mrs. Marshall exclaimed, "Ginny's back. That's wonderful. Don't you think so, Jeff?" Looking at Lucinda, "Geneva is the nicest girl. She and Jeff were almost engaged before her parents moved to Huntington over a year ago. Her father is head of the union in this area, and he was interested in helping Jeff become a union representative, wasn't he, Jeff?"

Jeff turned red and looked quickly at Lucinda, "Aw, Mom that was a long time ago. It's over and done with. Geneva and I were just kids. I sure didn't care for her like I do Lucinda- not even close," he said as he linked his fingers with Lucinda's.

Mrs. Marshall went on about how influential Mr. Clary was in the community and about his ties with elected representatives. "He would have been able to get Jeff a job in government. Then he wouldn't have to go down in the mines anymore," said Mrs. Marshall. Lucinda sat listening and suddenly realized that Mrs. Marshall's hopes had been pinned on Geneva Clary as a wife for Jeff. Now Lucinda knew why she was so opposed to her, and also why she was so pleased that they were going to wait until August.

Jeff was very upset and Mr. Marshall was looking daggers at his wife, but Jimmy spoke up, "Well, I don't want Jeff to take up with that snob again. I don't care how much influence her dad has. I don't like her. She's Miss Rich Bitch."

"Jimmy! Watch your mouth, Son," cautioned Mr. Marshall still glowering at his wife. "Zane Clary thinks he's more important than he is, Rita. I could hobnob with the governor, too, if I wanted to play the political game. We'd better leave Jeff's life in his own hands - and Lucinda's too," said Mr. Marshall, smiling at Lucinda.

Lucinda didn't know what to say. His mother may as well have said, "Why don't you go back where you came from? Jeff needs someone more important than you." She shifted away from Jeff and looked at Mrs. Marshall, "Mrs. Marshall, Jeff has a mind of his own. If he wants to get back with this Geneva, the road is free. I'm not holding him."

When Lucinda stood up, Jeff jumped to his feet. His face was almost as deeply red as his hair, "Mom, why is it that every time we come over here, you have to start up something to ruin it? If you keep this up, I won't be back much. You need to get this into your head. It's Lucinda I love, Lucinda I am going to marry, and I don't want anyone else. I don't give a damn about Zane Clary and his influence and you can tell him and his daughter I said so," stormed Jeff as he propelled Lucinda toward the hall tree to get their coats.

Mr. Marshall arose and followed them to the door and once outside he stopped Jeff, "Son, you were pretty rough on your Mom. I know she was out of line but she worries so because you're down in the mines. Try to understand her a little. She almost worships the ground you walk on. She always has."

"Now Dad, how would you feel if you loved somebody and this had happened to her? You wouldn't like it and I sure as hell don't like it. How do you think Lucinda feels? Mom just the same as said she didn't want me to marry Lucinda," blazed Jeff angrily.

"I know, Son, but calm down and remember your mother is going through a difficult time in her life." Turning to Lucinda, Mr. Marshall smiled sadly, "I'm sorry, Lucinda. Rita is going through the change and sometimes she blurts out things she regrets later. I'm sure when she has time to think about it, she'll be really sorry. Please try to understand."

Lucinda reached out and patted his hand, "Don't worry about it, Mr. Marshall. I know she's concerned about Jeff's future. She just doesn't understand that it is Jeff's choice. I haven't tried to entice him or- anything. I don't know, really, what she thinks."

Jeff was still fuming as he looked at his dad, "I'm sorry Dad, but you can explain to her that I love Lucinda and if she isn't welcome, then I won't be back. Also, you can tell her that I don't want Geneva Clary, and besides, Jimmy was right. She is a- well, she's not what Mom thinks she is. I certainly would not have married her." Then taking Lucinda's arm, he walked towards the truck, but turned to say, "I'll keep in touch though Dad, so don't worry."

Jeff helped Lucinda into the truck and sat fuming and muttering under his breath before suddenly pounding the dash with his fist. "Damn, damn, damn. Lucinda, I'm so sorry. Honey, I'm so-o-o sorry. I wouldn't have had this happen for the world. I don't know what's got into Mom. I've never known her to act like this in my life."

Lucinda sat quietly as Jeff started the truck and pulled out, "Well, your mom just doesn't feel like I'm good enough for you. My family is certainly not rich, not even close. But I wouldn't trade my life and my parents for all the politicians and fancy jobs in the world. If that is what she wants, then you need to go back to your Geneva," sobbed Lucinda whose nerves were at the breaking point. Never in her life had she talked back to an older person as she had to Mrs. Marshall and she felt awful. Suddenly it was just all too much. "Just take me home, Jeff. I want to go home."

Lucinda's Mountain

They started up Johnnycake Mountain and Jeff pulled off the road and stopped before turning to face her. "Lucinda, please don't cry. You know that isn't what I want. I don't care if I never lay eyes on that girl again; in fact I hope I never do. Listen, don't you remember the first time we came over here and I told you that you were more important to me than anyone? If Mom doesn't like you, she may as well not like me. I won't have you hurt this way. I promise you I won't be back, and I won't ask you to go either," stated Jeff vehemently as he tried to pull Lucinda into his arms.

Lucinda pushed him away and pulled a tissue from her pocket, blew her nose and wiped her eyes, "No, Jeff, I won't be a partner to breaking up your family. She's your mother and she loves you. I won't go back anymore, but I want you to. Honestly, if I'm in your way about getting a better job, then for goodness sakes, go get the job. I don't want you in the mines either."

Jeff sat looking so sad and crestfallen that Lucinda almost wept anew. Suddenly Jeff put his arms around her so tight that she couldn't move, "Lucinda, don't you even think of breaking up with me. Do you hear! I can't stand it. You said you didn't want me down in the mines, but how would you feel if you were the cause of me going nuts? That's what will happen if you break up with me again." Then he was kissing her again, hungrily and bruising, before she pounded on his chest and shoved him away.

"I think you're already nuts- do you know that? What are you trying to do? You and your mom are driving me crazy and I'm tired of it. Just take me home, Jeff Marshall. I just can't take any more of this," and Lucinda began to cry again.

Now Jeff gently put his arms around her and tenderly lifted her chin, "Oh Honey, I'm sorry. Please forgive me, but I get so scared. Lucinda, I have never even dreamed I could love somebody as much as I love you. If I get possessive at times, it's because I'm so scared. Honey, I may as well be dead if I can't have you. I swear that's the truth. You are all I care about, all I think about. Please say you aren't mad at me. I didn't know Mom was going to act like that. Hell, I didn't even know she felt like that. I believe something is wrong with her. We don't have to see her anymore and I won't ask you to go anymore. Lucinda, I'll do anything you want, but don't tell me you want to break up. Just don't tell me that," begged Jeff contritely and Lucinda's heart melted. She moved over and snuggled into his shoulder.

"Okay, Jeff, I know you didn't want your Mom to say all those things, so let's just forget it. There is one thing I will not allow. Jeff, you can't own me. I won't let you own me. I'm a person and I want to be me. So, if we are going to make a life together, don't tie and bind me with your need. If we marry, I'll be good to you, and I'll be faithful to you, but I want to keep my independence and my identity. I will not be your possession," stated Lucinda firmly as she straightened up and looked soberly into his eyes.

Jeff hugged her close, "It's just that I love you so much and I get afraid. You help me and when you see me stepping over the line, just call my attention to it. I don't want to be like that, honest I don't."

They drove on home talking about the Statler Brothers concert in Charleston which they planned to attend in April. They both liked that group and Margie had gotten tickets for Jill and Sam, Jeff and Lucinda, and she and Howard. They had planned to get a hotel and stay the night in Charleston. Lucinda had a hard time getting Nancy and Burb to agree to let her go. Finally, Jill and Margie came to see them and showed them the room registration for three which would be Lucinda, Jill, and Margie. Thus they were assured that Lucinda would be well chaperoned and they relented.

This would be Lucinda's first concert and she talked excitedly the rest of the way home. "Looking forward to the concert will keep February and March from seeming so cold and long, won't it Jeff," gushed Lucinda happily. Jeff smiled, enjoying her happiness.

Lucinda always told Dora everything and she couldn't wait to talk to Dora about what happened at the Marshall's. She didn't tell Jeff about her talks with Dora. He may not understand, but Dora had helped her so much.

Lucinda felt more comfortable talking to Dora than to anyone else except Emily, Gordon's wife. It always seemed that the rest of the family thought she wasn't very important, and they never listened to her. Gordon's wife, Emily, was different and was a really good friend as well as sister-in-law.

Jeff apologized again because he couldn't take her down to Dora's on Sunday. "I'll be there on Wednesday, though," he promised. Lucinda thought it would be hard to walk a picket line or do anything that she really didn't want to do, but Jeff felt it was his duty. She sure had a lot to learn. Next summer she had to take a class called State and Local Governments and she hoped she'd get a better understanding of labor and management than what she had now. She knew that miners had a terrible life before the advent of the unions. She had seen documentaries about mining wars in places like Thurman, and Matewan, and had read about Mother Jones. She had also heard miners tell of their treatment before the union was organized. She felt the unions really helped the miners, at least back then. Still, this strike now, and the strikes called because miners wanted to go deer hunting, were unfair.

Before he left, Jeff wanted reassurance that everything was all right between them again. Lucinda sat quietly holding his hands before giving him a serious look, "Jeff, I'm willing to try, but you have to trust me and you have to realize that you can't own me."

Jeff hugged her tightly before kissing her gently, "Lucinda, I do trust you and I don't mean to try to own you. Just tell me and I'll work on it."

Lucinda agreed that she would as she kissed him on the cheek and slid out of the truck.

CHAPTER 27

The school year was almost over and Lucinda realized that she loved teaching. To see a child's eyes light up when he or she suddenly understood something they hadn't before was such joy. Almost all of her students, except first graders, knew their multiplication tables and most of her upper grade students knew all the states and capitals, the oceans, the continents, the planets, and understood the water cycle. Lucinda was very proud to know she had a small part in their lives. Garson Lester was her greatest sorrow but she knew that she couldn't change his home life.

February crept by and March came blustering in on a blizzard which closed the school for one entire week. This would push the closing day up one more week and that worried Lucinda. The first summer session at Concord College started the last of May and now she didn't know when school would be out. Her monthly check came with a bulletin stating that May 28th was the closing date. She checked the calendar and realized that she only had five days from the closing of school until June 2nd when she had to be at Concord College.

Dora, practical as always, told her to start in April and she could get everything done before the last week of school. "You did ask to come back down here to teach next year, didn't you?" asked Dora.

Lucinda shook her head, remembering the argument she and Jeff had about that. Lucinda had told Jeff she wanted to teach at Estep School again and he was astonished. "Lucinda, we will be married, and we won't be living on Bradshaw Mountain. How in the world are you going to get down there and out every day?" demanded Jeff.

Bristling with indignation, Lucinda jumped to her feet from her parents' sofa, "Who said we wouldn't be living on Bradshaw Mountain? I didn't know we had a house. I'll not go to a house that you've picked out on your own. This is my life to, Jeff Marshall," blazed Lucinda.

Knowing that Burb and Nancy were only on the back porch, Jeff cautiously tried to calm Lucinda down.

"Now, Honey, stay calm. I don't have a house. I just meant that I work at Bartley and live in Bradshaw, and you may be able to teach in one of the schools in that area. That way we would both be close to our work. Wouldn't that be better?" reasoned Jeff.

Nancy and Burb came in about that time. Burb grinned as he saw their faces, "Are you two having what's called a family squabble? We heard Lucinda sounding upset."

"I was just trying to convince her that it would be foolish to ask to teach back down at Estep Ridge next year, since we only have one vehicle. I also thought that maybe she could get a school around Jolo, Bradshaw, Raysal, or Bartley, which would be closer for us both, if we lived somewhere in that area," explained Jeff.

"Why Cindy, that's just plain old common sense. What wus you wanting to do? They ain't no empty houses on this mountain anyway, and besides, it'ud be a heap easier if you had a place with running water in the house, since you will be working. You'd better listen to your man," advised Burb as he walked over and turned on the television.

This was a signal to stop the discussion or go to some other place to have it and Jeff followed Lucinda into the kitchen. Nancy hadn't said anything in the living room, but now she said, "Lucy, honey, I can't hardly stand the thoughts of you marrying and moving away from me but that's life, I reckon. If we live to be old enough, it happens to us all. Anyway, it would please me mightily to see you in a nice house. I want you to have a bathroom, a kitchen sank, and nice furniture, and you're more apt to find that in town."

Lucinda went over and hugged her mother tightly saying, "I don't know if I can leave you either, Mommy. The closer it gets, the scarier it is. But I did promise Jeff and I reckon I'll have to get used to it, someway," mumbled Lucinda forlornly.

Jeff had stood watching and listening and now jumped in with, "Mrs. Harmon, please tell Lucinda that marriage isn't bad. I'll be good to her, I swear I will," said Jeff pleadingly.

"Why no, Jeff, marriage ain't bad. I can't imagine not being married. I think every woman wants to be married, or at least I wanted to marry, and there ain't many times I've regretted it. The only thing is, it grieves a mother so when her last one moves out for good. But, now I know that's the way life is and I'm sure my mam felt the same. So, you younguns get together and make your own plans cause you'ns is the ones that has to live with them. But Lucy, what Jeff said does make sense. I know you think a lot of Dora and you love them little old younguns you've been teaching but you need to consider Jeff now. Once you marry, you'ns need to be trying to always please each other. So, like I said, you all talk it over and decide together what's the best," advised Nancy firmly.

"Lucinda, what if you and I take a ride out to the Drive-In and bring some burgers back for supper. We can talk as we go and save Nancy from having to cook," offered Jeff.

Lucinda quickly agreed after asking Nancy if they would like hamburgers for supper. She had heard Burb say that he liked a hamburger he had eaten in Welch one time and she didn't know if Nancy had ever had one or not. Nancy agreed so they got their coats and went out to the truck.

Even in March, the ridge roads were still rutted and muddy and Jeff, having learned his lesson, had chains on his truck. They talked all the way out to the highway and all the way back. By the time they reached home again, they had decided to start looking for a place to live somewhere off the mountain. Lucinda had also promised to apply for a school either in Bradshaw or one of the surrounding towns. They agreed to spend the following Saturday looking for houses or an apartment there in the Bradshaw area.

Nancy enjoyed her hamburger, admitting, as she finished, that it was the first one she had ever had. "I like to cook, but I swear that was plumb good. I don't know as I could have made one better. I reckon I might just try it though," she said as she grinned in Burb's direction. He could eat hamburgers and watch his television.

When finished, Burb reckoned that it was pretty good but he'd rather have Nan's chicken and dumplins and her fried taters for regular fare. "A working man needs something that will stick to his ribs," laughed Burb looking down at himself. Nancy laughed and said she thought something had been sticking to more than his ribs.

The rest of the evening was spent talking and laughing and Burb beating Jeff twice in checkers. Lucinda sat thinking how nice it was because they all got along so well together. Her parents didn't say things to hurt Jeff.

She still dreaded going to the Marshall's even though Mrs. Marshall did write her a most apologetic letter. Mrs. Marshall said she had been to the doctor and been given some medicine that helped her mood. She begged Lucinda to visit again. Lucinda and Jeff talked it over and once again made a short visit in February. Mrs. Marshall was very nice and nothing was said to upset anyone.

Lucinda decided that, if she married Jeff, she would treat his mother kindly and try to overlook her if she said something. She did not plan to visit her very often though. It just made her too tense and nervous, kind of like waiting for something to happen and hoping it wouldn't.

Dora regretted that Lucinda would not be applying for Estep School again but said their decision made sense. "I'll miss our talks more than anything. It gets mighty lonely down here, just me and Pa. This year has been the best I've had in a long time, Lucy, and I wish it could last, but nothing lasts. It's being born or dying or changing in some way or other. We just have to learn to fit in to life, cause it goes on," spoke Dora solemnly in a deep study. She abruptly jumped up and started for the kitchen. "I'm about to become some kind of philosopher or something like that. Your book learning has rubbed off on me, I bet," laughed Dora as she set a kettle of soup beans on the stove.

Lucinda impulsively went over and hugged Dora tightly, "You're a really good friend, Dora. I think the best I've ever had and I'm going to miss you, and especially our talks."

Dora pushed her away good naturedly and told her to get busy and put on a pan of corn bread, "It won't do to lose your cooking talents. You're going to find how handy they are in the near future."

On Saturday, Lucinda and Jeff looked and asked but found no houses at all in Jolo or Bradshaw. They planned to try Raysal, Bartley, and other communities on up that way the following Saturday. Lucinda didn't know any of the people in Bradshaw and Jeff only knew a few. On that Saturday, however, they still found nothing, even though they covered a wide area. They finally drove back to Bradshaw, ate at the bus terminal, and went to a movie.

Lucinda was worried but Jeff told her that surely they would be able to find something before August. "Of course, if you'd agree to move the wedding up, I'd buy some land and build a house," offered Jeff.

Since the last strike had been settled, Jeff had worked steadily and had been saving most of his pay after paying his rent, buying gas, and food. Jeff showed Lucinda his pay stubs and showed her the budget he had worked out. He also told her how much stock he had bought in the company, but that didn't mean much to Lucinda. She knew very little about such things but didn't say anything because she intended to learn.

Lucinda had also saved most of her last two checks. In October she had bought a living room suit for Nancy. Then she started saving her money for Christmas presents. She had bought the furniture on credit or mostly on credit. She had paid $300 on the furniture but was left owing $250 which she agreed to pay in installments. She intended to make the final payment from her March pay check. Her family didn't have much but they never bought on credit so Nancy and Burb never knew that Lucinda still owed for their furniture. Lucinda told Jeff that had her dad known, he would have taken the furniture back to the store. She laughed, "But if it was his television, I don't think he would be half as upset. He certainly would not be eager to take it back."

Even though they were saving and making plans, marriage still didn't seem real to Lucinda. It was almost like someone else was going to get married. She kept thinking that something would happen to put a stop to it, before it really happened. She knew she should be certain, but was afraid to talk to anyone about it. She also knew that she should not be remembering Jason and dreaming about him if she was going to marry Jeff, but she did. This troubled her so much that she once again began to try to beg the Lord to give her some kind of answer, or some peace, or just whatever she needed to be at ease.

Part of the time Lucinda thought she was being silly. The Lord didn't work out things that people could do for themselves, did he?

On the following Saturday night, she told Jeff not to come on Sunday until about three o'clock. When he wanted to know why, she told him that she wanted to go to "meeting" or church with Burb and Nancy. Jeff asked why the sudden interest in church and she told him she just had an urge to go. "Is there some man there you want to see?" bristled Jeff.

"There you go, Jeff Marshall. I'd be ashamed of myself if I were you. Why would I want to go to church to meet some man? I can meet all the men I want to meet going to and from school or anywhere else for that matter. I'm going to church because I want to and I may start going on a regular basis. You can go too, if you want to, but I am going," Lucinda stated firmly.

Jeff turned red, "I'm sorry, Lucinda. I shouldn't have said that. I won't go this time but I may go some other time. I'll be here at three and we can eat at the drive-in before you go back to Dora's."

Lucinda agreed, but wondered if every time she did something or wanted something different, Jeff was going to react this way. "Jeff, either you stop acting jealous or suspicious every time I mention anything different or I just can't marry you. My life would be miserable like that."

Jeff was very contrite and apologetic. "Lucinda, I'm trying, and if we were married, I wouldn't be like that, I know I wouldn't. It's just that I'm not sure you really love me and it makes me afraid."

"Jeff, if you don't think I love you why do you want to marry me? I wouldn't want to marry somebody who didn't love me," stated Lucinda.

"I know you like me, maybe even love me a little, but I don't feel like you love me the way I love you. I hope you do, but I feel uneasy all the time. I feel okay when I'm with you but when I get away, I begin to doubt. But, Lucinda, whether you love me or not, I love you enough for both of us," confessed Jeff.

Lucinda put her arms around him and gave him a hug, telling him that she certainly would not have agreed to marry him if she didn't love him. This appeared to satisfy Jeff and they drove on to the Sunset Drive-In.

CHAPTER 28

On Sunday, Lucinda bundled into Burb's Model A Ford car, which had replaced the big old timber truck, and rode in style to the meeting house. Preacher Hiram seemed to be talking directly to her. He talked about faith and believing in the Lord. "Most of the time, children, we pray and if it don't happen that same day, we begin to doubt. Now, the Lord, who loves us, knows what we need but we only know what we think we need. I tell you little children that anything we ask in faith will be granted. It may not be granted in the way we think or want it to be, but the Lord hears his children and he will supply their needs. The scriptures tell us to walk by faith and so I say to you, my children, 'go, doubting not' for God is a present God. He is a God at hand and not a God far away."

On the way home, Lucinda seemed to breathe that message into her soul. She felt that some answer would come to give her some peace about marrying Jeff. "I'll follow whatever the Lord shows me," whispered Lucinda and startled Nancy who had almost dozed off in the warm car.

When Jeff came, Lucinda thought he looked more handsome than usual. He had on a brown corduroy sport coat, a cream striped shirt, and brown dress pants and she told him he really looked nice. He hugged her close, "I should have insisted on you going to church before now," he laughed.

Everything they talked about was fun and even the food at Sunset Drive-In seemed to taste better to Lucinda. They laughed over the times they had been stuck in the mud on Estep and Brushy Ridge. Jeff said that he wouldn't know how to conduct himself if she lived some place where he didn't have to wear chains on his truck. He thought the truck would even appreciate Lucinda not teaching down Estep Ridge next year. Putting on his Kadiddlehopper face, Jeff said "My poor old truck complains all the time. Its constant gripe is about the chain links breaking and almost beating its fenders off. Every time I wash it, the truck almost cries when I find a new dent." Lucinda gurgled with laughter and Jeff joined her even though Lucinda knew he hated every dent his truck received. Jeff kept his truck cleaner than most people kept their houses.

Before he left that evening, they talked again about the concert in Charleston and what fun it was going to be. Lucinda was concerned about it costing so much but Jeff said they could afford it. "But what if another strike comes? I wish you didn't work in the mines. Mining is so dangerous and it certainly isn't dependable, since they strike all the time," grumbled Lucinda.

Jeff assured her that he had enough saved to see them through a strike, but still Lucinda didn't like it. Jeff liked the mines, however, and so Lucinda left it at that.

As he was leaving, Jeff reminded her to keep all the Easter Break days free. She had already promised to spend Wednesday night with Margie and then the following Friday would be the concert. "Don't worry. I really want to go to the concert, so I won't plan anything else," promised Lucinda.

"I know you won't deliberately plan anything else," said Jeff. "But, if your family wants you to do something with or for them, you'll forget about everything else. I thought I'd better remind you, so you'll have a reason to tell them you can't."

Lucinda remembered the times Jeff had wanted to take her places and Ellen, Oprey, Odell, or Faye had asked her to do something for or with them, and she had. Jeff was always disappointed and it caused them to argue, Lucinda smiled. "Thanks for reminding me, Jeff. I'll have a previous engagement this time."

Nothing was asked of her and on Wednesday at noon, Jeff came to drive her to Margie's. He came back to work since he had just been moved to the second shift and had to go in at three o'clock. Margie, and her husband Howard, promised to bring her home the next day. Jeff wanted Howard to meet Burb and Nancy. "Since Howard is older, I thought it would be an extra assurance for Burb Harmon," said Jeff when he asked Howard and Margie to do it. "Her dad don't trust me one little bit, nor her either I guess, since he don't seem to believe me or her," grumbled Jeff.

Lucinda really liked Jeff's sisters and his brothers, Bobby and Jimmy. Those boys were now the young brothers she had never had, and she really enjoyed being with them. Lucinda felt she couldn't have asked for a better family to marry into, if only Mrs. Marshall liked her. That was something Lucinda constantly worried about.

Jeff had Friday, Saturday, and Sunday nights of Easter weekend off from work, and was to pick up Lucinda at one o'clock on Friday. Lucinda was very excited since this would be her first concert. The women in her family hadn't gotten to do much, but nobody on the mountain did either, so they all seemed content. Nancy always said, "You don't miss what you ain't used to, so it's better to not get used to things you can't have."

However, Lucinda soon realized they were not all content, or at least Odell wasn't. Odell had finally left the mountain and lived in Iaeger. She came up one Friday saying that she was going to work and soon did. Burb and Nancy scolded her because she wouldn't be home in the evenings when her children came home from school. "I know for a fact that Bud don't want you to work. I'm surprised he'd agree to it," stated Burb.

"I'll bet he'll be mighty glad to have some more money to gamble and drink with. He's not bringing very much home as it is, and he doesn't worry about his children. Besides they are not left alone. Mary Perkins, from across the road, comes in and stays an hour until I get home," explained Odell.

Even with all these adverse reactions, Odell, had first worked in a restaurant, and was now working at Sayer Brothers Department Store in Iaeger. With a big poker win for Bud, Odell now had a car and had learned to drive. Lucinda was so proud of her and admired her determination. In fact, Odell was an inspiration to Lucinda for she felt that if Odell with five children could improve her life, then she could, too.

When she arrived at Margie's house on Friday, they had a surprise for her. Margie had bought Lucinda a pair of blue jeans, saying that she and Jill were going to wear jeans and thought Lucinda could, too. Lucinda had never worn a pair of slacks or any kind of trousers since she was about eight years old. Nancy said it wasn't proper for girls to wear boyish things and Burb would have had a fit. Lucinda didn't know what to do. She didn't want to stick out like a sore thumb. She didn't feel like it was a sin to wear pants, but she didn't want to displease her parents. There was also the chance of someone she knew in the teaching field being at the concert and teachers did not wear pants. When she told Margie and Jill this, they both laughed, "They don't in the classroom. But Lucinda, teachers wear what they want to away from school. That is no business of the school board," stated Jill.

Hoping they wouldn't fit, Lucinda went in and tried them on. She thought they were too snug and walked back into the living room, not knowing that Jeff was there, and turned around saying, "Jill, these are too tight. I can't wear them. They look awful on me," just as a long wolf whistle startled her. She turned to see Jeff staring in admiration.

"Where's Jill?" stammered Lucinda, turning red and darting glances everywhere but at Jeff.

Jill and Margie came in just then and immediately assured Lucinda that she looked just right. Jill showed her how much extra was in the waist saying, "You'll probably have to wear a belt. I swear you're not big as a minute and curvy to boot. Some people have all the luck."

Jeff, knowing how uncomfortable Lucinda was about mentioning any part of her body, kept his thoughts to himself, but every time Lucinda glanced at him, he seemed to be ogling her. Finally, she decided she would wear them but keep her coat on.

They all piled into Howard's Nash Rambler station wagon and drove down Route 119 to Charleston. Lucinda rode in the middle between Jeff and Jill and was soon very warm in her coat. After Jill insisted, she took off her coat but felt really ill at ease. Sam, Jill's fiancé, was to meet them at the Municipal Auditorium in Charleston and they were to eat dinner at the Daniel Boone Hotel where they had their rooms. Lucinda hoped Jeff ordered something besides steak. She had ordered steak when she had been in Huntington for the award and couldn't eat it. When she had cut into it and saw red, which looked like blood, it almost made her sick.

Jeff knew she liked fish and so ordered fillet of flounder on the advice of Margie who said she loved it. Lucinda decided after the first couple of bites that it would probably always be a favorite of hers as well. The men had

251

ordered strawberry daiquiris and Margie and Jill were helping Howard and Sam drink theirs. Jeff begged Lucinda to at least taste his drink. Finally, she was so enticed by the smell and seeing that Jill and Margie acted no different, she took a small sip then several more sips. When they had finished their meal, she realized that she had probably drunk more than her half of the daiquiri. "I guess I was scared for nothing, Jeff. That drink didn't hurt me. I don't feel a bit different. In fact, I feel good," laughed Lucinda. They all smiled and Lucinda didn't realize she was laughing more but she was really relaxed and was having a grand time.

The feeling of ease stayed with her as they made their way to the concert and she said, "This is the most fun I've ever had in my life."

Jeff kept his arm around her possessively but Lucinda didn't mind at all. Jeff was very handsome and she noticed several girls or women looking at him appreciatively. She snuggled closer to him and laughed up at him as he squeezed her closer still and then sneaked a quick kiss. Even that didn't embarrass her as it might have and she wondered about that later.

The Statler Brothers started out with "Flowers on the Wall" and then went on through "This Bed of Roses That I Lay On," and a whole repertoire of Lucinda's favorite songs. She sat entranced until intermission and then they all went out into the lobby to get something to drink and find a restroom. Margie, Jill, and Lucinda slipped away while the men ordered their drinks. On the way back, some man whistled as they passed and said, "Honey, they ought to put you on a billboard advertising jeans."

Lucinda walked on because lots of people were wearing jeans just like Margie had said they would. When they arrived back where the men were, Margie said, "Jeff, you'd better stick close to Lucinda tonight. Some guy back there thought she looked great in her jeans. He said they ought to put her on a billboard advertising jeans."

"He wasn't talking to me, was he? I mean there are lots of girls in jeans here tonight," stated Lucinda who dreaded Jeff's jealousy.

"Where is he? I'll knock the hell out of him," bristled Jeff.

Margie shook her head in dismay. "Jeff, my goodness, he didn't mean any harm. He just thought she was pretty and you can't blame him for that. You should be pleased that people think your future wife is pretty."

"He can think what he wants to but he'd better keep his mouth shut about Lucinda."

Howard, who had gone to the restroom, came back and they went back in to find their seats. After that, Jeff held Lucinda more possessively and glared at anybody who looked their way. Sensing this, Lucinda didn't enjoy the last part nearly as much as she did the first part. But still, this had been the most enjoyable evening she'd had since Jason had taken her out.

Jason again. Lucinda wondered if she would ever get him completely out of her mind. Then she remembered Preacher Hiram's admonition, to 'go believing' and she resolutely put him out of her mind. She told herself something would surely happen to convince her one way or the other before she made the final step.

Back at the Daniel Boone Hotel they all met in the girls' room and sat talking until about two o'clock in the morning. Lucinda's eyes kept trying to close on her and she got up and went in the bathroom and washed her face. When she came back still yawning, they all decided to call it a night. Lucinda commented later that she wasn't usually that sleepy, and Margie said it might be the effect

253

of the daiquiri. Lucinda was surprised because she hadn't thought it had made any difference at all.

They left the hotel at ten o'clock the next morning but stopped and had breakfast at a truck stop on Route 119.Thus they didn't get back to Margie's until one o'clock, which was a little later than they had planned. Margie had planned that they all would go to their parents' house for lunch, but now they would just visit. Jeff had promised Burb to have Lucinda back home before dark on Sunday, so they couldn't stay long.

Lucinda had changed into her skirt and sweater and left the jeans at Margie's, since she was afraid to take them home. She not only wanted to please Nancy and Burb, but her brothers and sisters as well. She always had, and often wondered why, because either they were sometimes wrong, or she had something wrong with her. Lately it was getting very difficult to take their advice about a lot of things.

Burb would be more than upset if she came in wearing something that he felt was improper and she didn't want that. Lucinda knew she would tell Nancy about the jeans. She always told Nancy what she did and she and Nancy talked about it, except for the sex book Jason had given her. Lucinda did not feel that taking the book was wrong, but wasn't sure what Nancy would think. She wouldn't think she was a bad girl, Lucinda knew that. Nancy wasn't that kind of mother. However, later that night, something happened, and Lucinda was too scared and worried to know what she would think.

CHAPTER 29

It was almost two o'clock before they got to the Marshall's and Jeff said they couldn't stay to visit. They left Margie there, but Howard had to make a trip to Columbus, Ohio and left soon after them. Jeff wanted to hurry since they were already late. Mrs. Marshall hugged them both, and told them to be careful on the road.

Jeff's truck had been left at his dad's and now Jeff and Lucinda climbed into the truck for the final leg of their trip. They had driven down through Gilbert and turned on Route 52 toward Iaeger when the truck began to sputter.

"What's wrong? Why is this truck sounding so funny? Is it going to break down?" asked Lucinda worriedly.

"No, I don't think so. It sounds like there's water in the gas. I bought gas at that little station in Long Bottom and they don't sell much gas. I guess that's it. Don't worry. We're not far from Iaeger and if anything happens, there are garages there that can fix it," Jeff assured her.

The truck sputtered and jerked to the top of Johnny Cake Mountain and then stopped dead. It had taken a long time to get up the mountain and when Lucinda looked at her watch, it was four o'clock.

"It will be dark by 7:30," said Lucinda in agitation, "and we're miles from the top of Bradshaw Mountain."

Jeff told her that Burb would understand, once they explained what happened. "Getting down off this mountain is the first thing we have to worry about. I'm going to hold the door open and try to push it off and let it drift down to the bottom," said Jeff as he got out of the truck and began cutting the steering wheel.

"Can I help? I could push on this side," offered Lucinda, opening the door.

"No, keep that door shut and stay inside. Hurry, it's beginning to move," shouted Jeff, putting all his muscle power behind his stance against the door.

Lucinda shut the door and sat quietly as the truck began to move and Jeff jumped in the truck as it gained momentum. Down the hill they drifted with Jeff steering and tapping the brake when it got too fast until they reached the bottom. Then Jeff didn't touch the brake and let it drift as far as it would go. It stopped near the river on a curve with not a house in sight. "I'll have to walk to Joe Cassidy's Garage and get a tow truck," said Jeff as he opened the door.

Lucinda opened her door and jumped out, "I'm not staying here by myself. I'll walk with you."

Jeff smiled fondly, "Actually, Honey, I'm glad you volunteered because I was going to ask you anyway. It's not safe to leave a woman alone in a place like this, so come on, and let's get started."

They walked hand in hand down the road after locking the truck with their bags inside. The garage was about three miles away but Lucinda was used to walking and it didn't seem far. She could tell that Jeff was worried when he said, "I hope it is something they can fix pretty quickly."

Thinking it was bad gas, Lucinda said, "Can they drain the tank if there is water in the tank?"

"I don't know, Lucinda. It may not be that," said Jeff. "I was just guessing when it first started acting up. I just hope that garage is still open."

The garage was getting ready to close when they walked in but Mr. Cassidy sent his tow truck back with Jeff going along to give directions. Lucinda bought a Nehi grape soda and sat down in one of the chairs to wait. Mr. Cassidy was nice and friendly, wanting to know who she was and who her dad was. When she told him she was Burb Harmon's daughter, he said he'd heard of her dad. "They say that Mr. Harmon can appraise a boundary of timber and tell almost the exact board feet of lumber it would yield. Is that so?" questioned Mr. Cassidy. Lucinda told him yes and was pleased to hear Burb praised so highly, and also pleased that he was known so far from the top of Bradshaw Mountain. She knew that several people in Welch knew her dad since he was always so active in elections and at one time he had been a deputy sheriff for the county. Many people still came to her dad for help on legal matters.

Jeff and the tow truck returned, pulling Jeff's truck. The mechanic, who had come back in on the request of Mr. Cassidy, soon had Jeff's truck pulled into the garage. He raised the hood and began to tinker. In a few minutes, he poked his head from under the hood and said, "You won't be going anywhere in this truck until you get a new fuel pump. Your fuel pump is busted."

"This is a practically new truck. What would cause the fuel pump to burst? Well, no matter - do you have one to put on it?" asked Jeff.

The mechanic went into the stock room and rummaged around but came back empty handed, shaking his head. "We ain't got one and can't get one till in the morning. The best thing for you to do is to go down to the motel and get you'ns a room, unless you got folks you can call. I can have it fixed early in the morning."

Jeff offered to pay the mechanic overtime if he would go get a fuel pump and put it on, but to no avail. Lucinda had sat listening in horror. How was she to get home? What if she had to sit here all night? Nancy and

Burb would be standing on their heads. She had to get home someway. She looked at Jeff in silent appeal.

"Mr. Cassidy, could you or do you know of anyone I could hire to take us up on Bradshaw Mountain tonight? I'll pay them double if you know of someone," offered Jeff.

"Well, normally Charlie here could take you in my car but his wife's been calling for the last hour wanting him home. She said their cow was having trouble calving and she didn't know what to do. I'd take you myself but my daughter is in a beauty pageant and I'd be shot if I missed that. Sorry, Son, I don't know of a soul that would do it, especially on Sunday night," stated Mr. Cassidy.

Lucinda was holding her hand over her mouth and keeping her head lowered to hide her tears and anguish. Jeff came over and pulled her to her feet, "Come on, Honey. Let's go down to that motel and maybe somebody there will take us or let us rent their car."

Lucinda grasped at that idea and gladly went out the door holding onto Jeff's arm. They didn't have any luck at the motel either and now it was dark. Lucinda shivered and Jeff wrapped his arm around her trying to be of comfort. "Listen Lucinda, I think the only thing we can do is to get a room here and try to get some sleep. We can't go on until morning anyway. I'd call Dad but he can't see to drive at night. Howard was leaving tonight for Columbus, Ohio and Sam has baseball camp this week. I don't know anything else to do."

Lucinda was supposed to work the next morning and usually went to Dora's on Sunday night. Nobody on the mountain had a telephone. Gordon had just moved to a new house and they didn't have a phone hooked up yet. Odell lived at Long Bottom but that was a long way and she didn't have a telephone either. Lucinda didn't know what to do, and she was afraid to stay in a room by herself in this shabby looking place. She couldn't stay in a room with Jeff. They were not married. Suddenly, she just couldn't hold back the tears and just bowed her head and sobbed.

Quickly Jeff pulled her close, "Lucinda, don't cry. I can get two rooms and at least we can get some sleep. This place doesn't look like much but it may be cleaner on the inside. Let's just do that, Honey."

"Jeff, I'm afraid to stay in a room by myself and I can't stay with you," sobbed Lucinda.

"Yes you can, Lucinda. I swear I won't touch you. I'll sit up in a chair and let you have the bed. Come on, Honey. We can't sit out in the street all night, and Mr. Cassidy has already locked up and gone home. Come on, let's try it," begged Jeff.

Lucinda reluctantly agreed and Jeff went into the office and came back with the key to Room 7. Seven wasn't a lucky number if it had anything to do with the room. It wasn't very clean, and it looked as if there had been a leak. The ceiling had a large circle and water streaks ran down the side of the wall to the floor. Both Lucinda and Jeff were appalled that people would run a motel in this condition.

At least the lights worked, there was a bathroom, and there was heat, so they decided they had to make the best of it. There was one bed, a dresser, a night stand, and one chair. "I wouldn't sleep in that bed for anything. A person could catch all kinds of diseases," shivered Lucinda.

"Put your coat on the bed with the hood on the pillow and lay down with your clothes on. Your skin won't be touching anything, and you can clean your coat. You can't catch anything that way," reasoned Jeff.

Dejectedly, Lucinda sat down in the chair which sagged in the middle and started crying again. "Jeff, my daddy will kill you and me both and my name will be mud. Everybody on top of Bradshaw Mountain will know because Daddy will get Gordon and they'll be out on the roads all night looking for me. When Sir Marget hears about this, I'll be labeled a 'ho – a bad woman. She is the nosiest woman in the world and loves to carry news. It will be all over the mountain before I can get home, and I'll get fired and can't teach anymore." Lucinda bent down, covering her face and cried louder.

Jeff got down on his knees in front of her and pulled her into his arms, "Please Lucinda, don't cry. I wouldn't have had this to happen for the world. You know that, don't you? Things happen and it won't look so bad in the morning. We can explain to your dad. Mr. Cassidy will verify our story. Please don't cry. It's going to make you sick, Honey." Jeff got up and, picking Lucinda up in his arms, sat down in the chair and cradled her in his lap. Lucinda was so distraught that she didn't resist but snuggled into the comfort of his arms. Jeff sat patting her back and rubbing her hair and finally the tears dried up and Lucinda dozed off.

Jeff sat holding her afraid to move lest she awaken and be upset. When he had first sat down, he knew the chair was uncomfortable but the sagging seat was harder to bear since the frame cut into the backs of his hips and legs. He gritted his teeth determined to not awaken Lucinda. However, when his arms and legs began to cramp he decided to lay her on the bed. He laid her down on top of her coat and folded it around her, insuring that she did not touch the pillow. He stood looking at her thinking how little and innocent she was. He looked back at the chair and rubbed his backside. He couldn't stand the thought of sitting in that again. He went to the bathroom, came back into the room, opened the door, and stepped outside to look around, hoping it would help to keep him awake. Finally, he came back in and took the other pillow from the bed, put it on the chair seat, and sat down once more. He was still so uncomfortable that he pulled the chair close to the bed and tried to sleep with his head lying on the bed but that was worse. Finally, he sat down on the bed beside Lucinda and leaned back against the headboard.

Lucinda awoke with a start. Something was in her bed. Something was holding her down and she abruptly jerked up or tried to. She couldn't because Jeff's arm was around her and he was fast asleep. Lucinda gave him a shove and he almost fell off the bed as he came awake. "What have you done to me? You told me you'd sit up in the chair. You lied to me," accused Lucinda.

Jeff sat up wiping the sleep out of his eyes and looked at Lucinda blurrily, "What do you mean, what did I do to you? I didn't do a thing to you except hold you in my lap until you went to sleep," muttered Jeff rising to his feet. "I got cramps in my arms and legs and laid you down on the bed. That chair is impossible to sit in. Believe me I tried," mumbled Jeff as he rubbed the back of his legs. "I sat down beside you and leaned back to rest my head against the headboard. That's the last I knew until now. Nothing happened, Lucinda. Look in that mirror over the dresser. You are just like you were. You've got all your clothes on and you've not been bothered."

Seeing she was not convinced and was almost hysterical, he grabbed her by the shoulders and turned her towards the mirror, "Look, Lucinda. You are just like you were when we came in here. Good God, Honey, what do you think a man could do with all your clothes on and those tights. See, everything is all right."

Lucinda looked in the mirror and saw that what he said was true. She mumbled, "Sorry," from a reddened face but couldn't look at Jeff. She walked over and sat down in the chair and almost fell through it. "I'm sorry, Jeff. That chair is awful. I don't see how you sat in it until I went to sleep." Seeing how tired and disheveled Jeff looked, she was contrite, "I am sorry Jeff, honestly. I woke up and your arm was around me and it scared me to death."

"Lucinda, as wary as you are, don't you think you would have woken if I had tried anything else? I didn't want to have a black eye this morning so believe me I didn't do a thing. I guess I just slid down when I went to sleep and hugged you instead of that pillow I've been hugging every night," smiled Jeff warily.

"What time is it, Jeff? I think my watch has stopped. I have seven o'clock."

Jeff had five minutes past seven and they immediately began to make plans as to what was the best thing to do. "I think we'd better wash our faces and get out of this dump as fast as we can," said Jeff. He knew that being here in the dark when nobody could see them was one thing, but to be here in the daylight was courting disaster, since he was now suspicious about the motel. Travelers would not be enticed to stop at a place looking like this one, and so it was probably used for a different purpose.

Lucinda hurried into the bathroom and made the best of what was available because she too felt uneasy in this place. Jeff was faster than Lucinda and they had all their belongings and were out the door in fifteen minutes. Lucinda stood beside him as he locked the door and turned to take the key to the office, just as a car passed. Lucinda gasped and covered her mouth, "Jeff, that was Bud Clayton, Odell's husband, and he saw us."

"No, if it had been him he would have stopped. It's been somebody else. Come on, let's get over to the garage before somebody passes that really knows us," murmured Jeff quietly. They hurried to the garage just as Mr. Cassidy opened the door.

"Good Morning! How are you folks this morning? I know you and the Missus weren't too comfortable, but it was better than nothing. At least you had a bed to sleep in."

Lucinda realized that Mr. Cassidy thought they were married and she started to correct him, but Jeff had squeezed her arm. She kept quiet and when Mr. Cassidy offered them coffee, she poured cream in it and drank the first coffee she had ever had.

Charlie, the mechanic, had stopped at another garage in the town of Iaeger and gotten a fuel pump. He had come straight on to the garage and had the truck fixed and ready by 8:30. Jeff gladly paid the $75 they charged. He and Lucinda quickly climbed into the truck and began the trip home.

They rode in silence until Lucinda said, "Jeff, I'm scared to death. You've never seen daddy mad but I have. He won't listen to reason. I just don't know how we'll get through this. I wish I'd never heard of a concert."

Jeff grimaced, "Yea, I'm not looking forward to this, not one little bit. Lucinda, we did nothing wrong. We couldn't help it because the truck broke down. We couldn't stay in the garage all night. We couldn't stay in the truck all night either. It got cold last night. What difference does it make anyway? We did nothing wrong."

They both knew that, but felt sure they would never convince Burb. Lucinda felt as if a death knell had been rung for her.

263

CHAPTER 30

The door opened as they passed Sir Marget Dawson's house. Lucinda shivered as if this were a bad omen. "She knows all about this, Jeff. How did she find out so soon?" Lucinda moaned in misery.

"Lucinda, she may be curious but she doesn't know what has happened. How could she?" questioned Jeff so firmly that Lucinda thought he was probably right. Still her dread increased as they neared her home.

As they rounded the curve above the house, Lucinda's heart sank for both Bud and Gordon's cars were parked out front. Jeff came to a stop in front of the gate and hesitantly Lucinda opened the door and got out. Jeff was already out and took Lucinda's hand as they opened the gate, but they didn't get any farther. Burb Harmon came onto the porch looking like an angry warrior, ready for battle. "You've got a lot of nerve, Mister, to come walking in here big as Pete. You've kept my daughter out all night, and not only that, you took her to a motel that is used by prostitutes," roared Burb walking across the porch. "You acted like you loved her and fooled us all. Looks like you could have had more decency than that. You'd better have a good reason."

Jeff bristled, "Now, you just wait one damn minute, Mr. Harmon. I took Lucinda to a motel on the advice of Joe Cassidy." With his chin jutting angrily, Jeff continued, "The fuel pump went out on my truck and I couldn't get it fixed until this morning. I didn't know one damn thing about that motel," explained Jeff still fuming. "I'll admit it wasn't much but it was all there was, unless we stayed out in the cold all night. I'd like to know what in the hell you would have done, since you seem to have all the answers." Jeff was so angry he was shaking and his voice had gotten louder.

Gordon stepped out of the door bristling, "I thought you were a decent fella, Jeff, but right now I feel like beating the hell out of you. Why didn't you hire a car, call some of your people, or try to get in touch with somebody to bring Lucinda home?"

Jeff's fiery head matched his angry face, "Gordon, do you think I'm a damn stupid idiot? I tried to hire everybody in Iaeger to bring Lucinda home. I couldn't get you or any of Lucinda's family because 'nobody' on this damn mountain has a telephone. My dad can't drive at night and the others were all away. Now, if you still want to beat hell out of me, I can give as good as you can hand out," snarled Jeff as he stepped forward.

"Here- here, you'ns quit that quarreling right now." Nancy rushed down the walk, shooting angry looks right and left, as she put her arms around a stunned Lucinda, and cried softly, "Lucy, honey I'm so glad you're home and safe."

Lucinda fell into Nancy's arms." Mommy, Jeff did try. He tried to hire Mr. Cassidy, the mechanic, the people at the motel, and I don't know who else to bring us home but nobody would," wailed Lucinda in anguish. "It's been the worst experience of my life. I've missed a day's work and cried most of the night. But it wasn't Jeff's fault. He really tried, Mommy, I swear he did," sobbed Lucinda.

Nancy shook her head and looking at Burb pulled Lucinda onto the porch and into the house. Burb looked at Jeff with a grimace, "You'd better come on in. Even if your story is true, something has to be done. You've ruined her name."

Walking with angry stride, Jeff followed Burb inside, still set to do battle. Feeling that he had done all he could, he demanded, "Mr. Harmon, do you think I would have walked in here with Lucinda if I had mistreated her? I'm no fool but more than that - I love Lucinda and you know I do. Hell, the only reason we're not married is because she won't agree to it. Lucinda is as innocent today as she was the day we left here. I've done everything that I could possibly do and frankly I've had about all I can take."

Nancy walked over and patted Jeff's arm, "Son, if Lucy says you treated her right, that's good enough fer me. But, you know how tongues wag and the whole top of this mountain knows that Burb and Gordon wus out most of the night looking for our girl," said Nancy looking thoughtfully at Jeff. "Now, if you'ns didn't do nothing wrong and I don't believe you did, people are still goin' to believe otherwise. Now, that's a fact and that's what we have to work on," she stated decisively. "Seems like the only thing fer you'ns to do is go get married as quick as you can, and act like you'ns sneaked off this past weekend and tied the knot."

An audible gasp was heard from several directions but the loudest from Lucinda. "Mommy, I can't get married yet. We're not ready. We don't have a place to live and - Oh, Mommy no, no, we can't get married now," wailed Lucinda.

Jeff stepped gallantly and eagerly into the breach, "Mrs. Harmon, I'm willing to do whatever you think." He looked warily at Lucinda, "That probably is a good idea, because nobody would know but what we got married on Saturday." He looked directly at Burb who was still red faced and glowering.

Burb snarled with a frown, "That's probably the only thing that can be done now. You're shore awful eager. Maybe you planned this. If you did, young feller, you deserve a thrashing."

266

Jeff jutted his chin out like a ruffled neck Rhode Island Red rooster, "I'll be damned, Mr. Harmon, if you weren't an old ..." Jeff took a long breath before continuing. "You can't give a man breathing room, can you? Hell yes, I'll marry Lucinda and gladly and would have any time since Christmas, but I wouldn't pull a stunt like this to make it happen." He glared at Burb but continued in indignation, "You must really have a low opinion of me. I can't say that I like it either, but you think what you like, Lucinda is the one I'm concerned with."

Gordon, who had been standing beside Burb, looked really relieved, "Well, Lucinda, I guess it's been decided for you. You'll be Mrs. Jeff Marshall by the end of the week."

All eyes had turned on Lucinda who had gone as white as a sheet. Suddenly she made a mad dash outside, gagging as she hurried to the end of the porch.

Jeff leaped past everyone and ran to Lucinda, who was trembling all over. He put his arms around her and Nancy ran to get some water. Jeff looked up angrily, "Just look what you people have done. She's been scared to death. She's cried almost all night, and couldn't eat this morning, and now this. Just leave her alone, you hear me. Leave her alone."

Nancy came back with a wash cloth and washed her face. Lucinda waved her away and wriggled free from Jeff's arms. Still he grasped her elbow as she walked slowly back into the house. He seated her on the couch and sat cradling her in his arms. She lay turned into his chest and cried brokenly. Nancy came over, "Honey, come on with me and I'll fix you something to eat. It'll make you feel better. Everything is all right now, just quit that crying 'fore you make yourself really sick."

Jeff went with her to the kitchen table and took the seat beside her. Nancy soon had breakfast on the table and Lucinda numbly tried to force herself to eat, as her mind ran rampant, trying to find a different answer to this dilemma. "Mommy, I don't care what people will say. The Lord knows we haven't done anything wrong and it's unfair to have to marry just to stop people's tongues."

Burb, Gordon, and Odell all came in and took a seat on the long bench behind the table, facing Jeff and Lucinda. Lucinda looked across the table at Odell, expecting her to understand, but Odell said, "Sis, Bud was the one that saw you, and Sir Marget's nephew Wilfred was with him. You see what that means don't you?" Odell looked around the room and continued, "It will ruin your name but what do you think it does to Dad and Mam? They've always been thought well of and so have their children but if something ain't done, that will change. Also, Dad is planning to run for County Commissioner this year and you know how the Democrats will use that information against him."

"Cindy, there's a lot to be said for your mam's idea. You're planning to get married anyway in August which ain't but a few months away," argued Burb reasonably, since his political career was important to him and they were planning on marrying anyway

Lucinda looked at her gathered family and was getting sicker by the minute. They were deciding her fate again. Then she looked at Nancy, "Mommy, I don't feel like I'm ready to get married, but if you think its best I reckon I - I will," mumbled Lucinda through broken sobs. Jeff put his arm around her protectively and motioned the others to let her alone. But Nancy came around the table and lifted her head, "Lucy, child, you know I wouldn't do or say nothing to hurt you fer my right arm, but Honey, I jest don't see no other way."

Lucinda looked at her mother in resignation, "Can I have the rest of this week to get used to it? I - I just wanted to wait until I'd been to summer school." Turning to Jeff, "I'm going to summer school. Do you hear me, Jeff Marshall? I am going to summer school."

Jeff reached over and patted her arm, "Okay Honey, I'll see that you go to summer school." Lucinda's thoughts were so chaotic. She did not want to get married and didn't see a way out of it. Jeff was thinking that he wouldn't have to wait all summer to marry, even if Burb did think he had planned it this way. Nancy, seeing the bewilderment in her baby's eyes was so sad, but felt that marriage was probably the best way.

With a very intent look, Jeff asked, "Do I have this straight? Mrs. Harmon wants us to tell that Lucinda and I got married Saturday and then really get married by next Saturday? Is that correct?"

Everybody except Lucinda nodded yes and Gordon said, "You all can go after school tomorrow to get your blood tests and license. You should have them back by Friday. Then you'll be free to marry on Saturday. That should work, shouldn't it, Pap?" asked Gordon, looking at Burb.

Burb agreed but said Jeff might have to miss some work. Jeff asked Gordon if he could get someone to switch shifts with him for two weeks. Gordon told him he could work it out, which left getting Lucinda to school and back. Gordon said, "Can you do that Pap?"

Burb thought for a minute, then said, "No, I can't this week," and Lucinda thought she had a reprieve.

"Well, I can take her down real early in the morning and then she can wait at Dora's until I can go get her in the evening," said Jeff before turning to Lucinda, to ask, "Will Dora mind if you come to her house at around six o'clock each morning for a while, and then wait there in the evenings until five o'clock. What do you think?"

Burb spoke up, "If I know old man Jake, he's up and about by five o'clock every morning anyway, so that shouldn't be a problem."

Lucinda sat there and let everyone else plan her life and didn't say another word. What could she say anyway? Burb had always been the voice of authority and everybody in the family listened to him. Lucinda felt that if her mother hadn't agreed to this plan, she could have just walked out and let people think whatever they wanted to. Most of the time, the advice of her brothers and sisters had been right but Nancy was never wrong.

Finally, it was agreed that it would all proceed according to Nancy's plan, and Jeff left, going back to Bradshaw to get some of his things. Nancy prepared Gordon's old room in the back of the house for Jeff's use. Lucinda didn't want to see Jeff or anybody else tonight so she went to bed, but did not go to sleep. She lay there crying quietly in her misery and finally began to beg the Lord to help her get through this. "Please Lord, intervene in some way. Work this out until Mommy and Daddy won't be hurt and I won't be so miserable. Oh! Lord, please have mercy. I can't help how I feel about Jason. If there was just some way that I could know we were not meant to be together. Lord please, please help me. I don't mean to be selfish, Lord, but I- I'm not ready to be married," begged Lucinda softly as tears coursed down her cheeks.

She arose the next morning to find Jeff sitting at the breakfast table eating a hearty breakfast. When he pulled out her chair, she stepped around it and took her usual place behind the table. Jeff picked up his plate and sat beside her. "Lucinda, would you mind riding out of the ridge with Mr. Estep each evening? He switched shifts with me and said you could ride out with him, and I could pick you up at Vencill's Grocery. If you will do that, we'll have more time in the evening to get the things done that we have to do. I could be at the grocery by 3:30 and then we could get to Grundy before the courthouse closes. I already talked it over with your Dad and he thought it was a good idea."

Lucinda's eyes widened angrily, "Oh well, if you've talked it over with Daddy, why ask me? All of you already know what's best for me, so sure, I'll be delighted to help." Lucinda jumped up from the table, taking her plate to the dishpan on the stove and almost ran from the room.

Nancy followed her, "Lucy, honey you're not being fair to Jeff. He's trying to work and get all of this taken care of at the same time. You need to be working with him instead of getting mad at him. It weren't his fault that his truck broke down, and you said he was good to you. Now, don't you think you ort to try to be good to him?"

Lucinda was too miserable to be agreeable. She gathered her things and started out but turned and hurriedly went back to put her arms around Nancy, giving her a fierce hug, "I know, Mommy, but I'm just so mixed up."

With a hug Nancy assured her, "It'll be all right, Lucy. It's just marriage jitters."

Lucinda went to the kitchen, told Jeff she was ready, and as she went toward the door Jeff was right behind her. The rain began before they got out of Brushy Ridge and was pouring by the time they reached Estep Ridge. Lucinda didn't care if a flood came, a tornado, or any kind of delaying disaster, but knew they would do no good. Jeff was trying to do what Burb and Nancy said was right, but she also knew that he was happy in doing it. Jeff was getting what he wanted and part of her wanted to believe he caused it, but she knew it was just an event that had played into his hands. "Why couldn't it have been something I wanted?" questioned Lucinda in a tormented mumble.

Jeff glanced at her warily, "We may have to live in my room until school is out. Can you do that?" he asked.

"How would I get to school from Bradshaw? You're having trouble getting me out of the ridge," said Lucinda snidely.

"Well, I'll take you to school each morning. I just don't know how to get you back in the evening," Jeff mused aloud as he splashed through the pouring rain gripping the steering wheel.

"Couldn't we just pretend a while and not get married at all. You could stay at our house and take me down in the mornings and I'd walk out in the evenings. That way, you'd find out how hard it is to be married. You may want to change your mind," proposed Lucinda.

Jeff slowed down and pulled to the side of the road, "Lucinda, how long do you think your Mom and Dad will want me to stay there, if we aren't married? I don't want to do that anyway. Nor do I want you walking eight miles every day alone on a road with no houses. Anyway, your Dad insists that we marry this week."

Seeing Lucinda's mulish countenance, Jeff begged, "Honey, please don't make it more difficult. I can't see how a few months can make much difference. I've told you I'll see that you get to summer school. I know you love teaching and I'm willing to help you. Honestly, Lucinda, I don't know what else to do and I won't change my mind."

"Okay, okay, let's go, I don't care anyway. I'll go with you this evening to get everything done that you and my folks cook up. God, I'll just do what everybody tells me, and then maybe people will be satisfied," growled Lucinda, almost in tears.

Jeff reached toward her but Lucinda flinched away, "Lucinda, I love you and I want to marry you more than anything but I swear, you make me so mad. I'm glad, yes, but this wasn't my idea and you know it. Don't be mad at me. I couldn't help that damn truck breaking down." Suddenly Jeff leaned over, lifted her chin and kissed her. Without meaning to, Lucinda responded. He leaned closer and mumbled, "Honey, it will be all right. It will be better than all right. It will be wonderful. You'll see. I'll make you happy if it kills me."

Lucinda pushed away but felt a little better. She knew Jeff loved her and she did enjoy his kisses. Maybe everything would be okay, if she could push these doubts and Jason out of her mind.

When they arrived at Dora's and Uncle Jake came to the door, he gaped in surprise, "Where you fellers been? You ain't slipped off and got hitched, have you?"

"As a matter of fact, we did get married, Mr. Kinnard," lied Jeff with a big grin. His pretense had Lucinda staring in red-faced amazement.

Dora came to the door with a big smile on her face, "Well, it's about time you talked some sense into that girl. Come on in and have some breakfast. It's on the table."

"Thanks just the same, Dora, but I have to get back. I do have a favor to ask though. Can Lucinda come here at this time each morning for a while? This all happened so fast, I just haven't had time to get the bugs out yet," explained Jeff.

"You know you can. This girl is welcome here anytime day or night that she wants to come and now so are you," laughed Dora.

Jeff leaned over and kissed Lucinda on the mouth. She blushed vividly and dropped her head. After Jeff thanked Dora for her help, he ran off the porch and got into his truck.

CHAPTER 31

Dora ushered Lucinda into the kitchen, pointed to a chair before going to make hot chocolate. On the first morning of her stay with Dora, Lucinda had tried hot chocolate and it became her favorite drink.

Uncle Jake came ambling in to the table to finish his coffee and hear what had happened. Lucinda repeated the rehearsed tale, "You know how Jeff has begged me to marry. I finally felt sorry for him, and when we went to the concert, we got married. Some concert- huh!" As she hoped they would, Uncle Jake and Dora accepted her story without question. She apparently was very convincing, for both Dora and Uncle Jake thought it was grand and were glad she was married. Lucinda sighed with relief and began to relax, but not for long.

Uncle Jake felt it behooved him to give her some sage advice, "Now, girl, from what the younguns around here say, you're a good teacher so don't you get yourself in the family way right off and have to quit teaching."

Lucinda turned red and stammered, "I'm not going to...." She started to say, "Do anything like that," but caught herself in time.

Dora jumped in with, "Good Lord, no! Don't quit, cause there ain't many good teachers no more and younguns need a good teacher to learn. I'll bet Garson Lester has learned more this year than he's ever learned before."

Lucinda smiled in appreciation at the thought of little Garson who had blossomed this year. From being unable to read at all when school started, he could now read second grade books. It was like learning was bottled up inside him and suddenly a door sprang open. Even though all her students had learned, Garson had improved the most.

Before she left for school she packed all her belongings to be picked up later. Leaving her little room was heart wrenching. She had been happy here and she didn't feel like she would be that happy again.

When she arrived at school the children were all agog as to what had happened to her. The news of her marriage and the truck breaking down created excitement and questions in all the students except James Estep. She was floored by the look of anger and disillusionment on his face. She realized that she could no longer rely on his support with the other children. He didn't say anything but was sullen the rest of the day; so much so that the other children noticed it and steered clear of him.

Mr. Estep came by that evening at three o'clock, got out of his jeep, came to the door and explained that Jeff had asked him to bring Lucinda out with him each evening. As soon as the last child walked out, Lucinda locked the door and hurriedly climbed into his jeep. Mr. Estep was his usual jovial self, laughing about how proud and happy Jeff was about marrying the teacher. "You've married a good man, Miss Harmon - uh, uh, what are you going to be called now?"

"I'll just leave it Miss Harmon since school is almost out anyway," replied Lucinda. At Sam Vencill's store, she got out and turned to thank Mr. Estep just as Jeff's truck pulled in.

Jeff quickly helped her in and pulled out, spinning gravel, headed for Grundy, Virginia. "What in the world are you doing, Jeff Marshall? Slow this thing down before you wreck and kill us both," demanded Lucinda.

Jeff slowed a wee bit but kept up a faster speed than usual, "The courthouse closes at five o'clock so we don't have much time. It's already 3:30, but don't worry, I'll be careful."

Jeff asked what Dora and Uncle Jake thought about their marriage and Lucinda snapped, "Oh, they're just like all my folks, they think it's just grand, also."

Jeff made no comment but concentrated on the road down the Slate Creek side of Bradshaw Mountain. As they leveled out at the bottom, he glanced at Lucinda, "Do you feel calm enough to talk now? I wish you would be reasonable. You would have had a bad name, because Wilfred did a good job of spreading the news. He made a big deal about that motel. I guess your Dad was right. It is mostly used for 'one-night-stands.'"

"What in the world are 'one-night-stands?'" asked Lucinda, staring at him innocently.

"Lord, Lucinda, for a woman who's been to college, you sure are ignorant about life. A 'one-night-stand' is a place where prostitutes- uh, supply their favors," Jeff said grinning broadly.

Lucinda looked out the window and mumbled, "Well, I didn't know," but when Jeff burst out laughing, she snapped, "You can laugh if you want to but I didn't go to college to learn about that stuff."

Jeff slowed and gently drew her to his side, "It's all right, honey. I'm kind of glad you don't know much. I'll just have to hone my teaching skills." He hugged her tightly but abruptly released her as a car swerved into their path, causing him to hit the dirt to avoid it.

"Would you like to go on a short honeymoon to Bristol or some place? I could get us a nice room in a good hotel and we could look over the town then go to a movie. Would you like to do that?" questioned Jeff.

Realizing that this would delay the inevitable, Lucinda said, "Sure, but no dumps like we had to stay in last weekend. We'll just have to come back to your room anyway and I don't think I'm going to like that very much. If I couldn't be gone every day, I'd go nuts."

Jeff seemed confident about finding another place, "The only thing that will keep me from getting us a nice place is if another strike comes. Then I'll be out of work and walking the picket line. We won't strike if we get a decent contract, but we won't sign it if we don't."

"Couldn't you go on to work anyway? I don't see any sense in you staying out of work just because the rest of them want to," said Lucinda.

"Be a scab! No Siree, I'll not do that. The union takes care of the miners and I'm going to obey the union. If everybody else can get by, so can I. I always have."

"You've not been married before. How are we going to buy groceries and pay the rent? I'll be in summer school and I can stay over there, but you may be set out in the road," stated Lucinda.

"No, you won't stay over there, Missy. I can tell you that for sure. I'll spend everything I have saved before I'll let that happen," stated Jeff with a startled glare.

They had reached Grundy and soon pulled into the courthouse parking lot. Jeff got out, put some coins in the meter, took Lucinda's arm, and walked beside her up the steps into the Clerk's Office. When the worker approached and Jeff made his request, she began filling out the forms. When she asked Lucinda for her name and age, she looked suspicious. Lucinda said she was nineteen and the woman smiled and said, "You look about fourteen. Did you bring your birth certificate?" When Lucinda said she didn't, the woman said, "I'm sorry, but I have to have proof of age."

"She's a school teacher, so she'd have to be 18, don't you know that?" demanded Jeff.

"I'm sorry, Sir, but without a birth certificate or one of her parents, I can't issue a license. That's just the rules. I didn't write them; I just carry them out."

Jeff turned in disgust, saying they would be back the next day. They went out and Jeff stood fuming, "That's the pits. It makes me want to bite nails. Aw, come on, we'll go to the hospital to get our blood tests. They may want written permission from your parents for that, too."

They didn't have any trouble at the hospital and were soon finished. They were assured the tests would be back Thursday evening or Friday morning. Jeff asked about preachers who performed marriage ceremonies. The nurse said, "The Church of Christ on the outskirts of town is where lots of people go. Preacher Greenleaf is the pastor and is there most of the time. I don't reckon he lives there but he's sure there a lot."

When they left the hospital, Jeff asked Lucinda if having Preacher Greenleaf to marry them was all right with her. Lucinda shrugged indifferently and Jeff asked, "What about ten o'clock Saturday morning, if the Preacher can do it then?" When Lucinda wanted to know why so early, Jeff explained that they needed some time to get to Bristol, find a room, eat, look around town, and see a movie. "That way we won't be rushed and will have Saturday night and Sunday to spend together before coming back to the room."

Lucinda felt nauseous and jittery on the inside again. She miserably thought that her life wasn't her own anymore. But had it ever really been under her control; she had always been a robot with her family pulling the strings. Always, Burb or her brothers and sisters told her what she should do, as if she didn't have a brain. It was different when she worked in Welch, and when she was in college, but it started all over again as soon as she moved back home.

They found the church and talked to Preacher Greenleaf, who agreed to their plan for the ceremony. They left the church and went into a restaurant on Main Street and sat down at a corner table. The nauseous feelings that had plagued Lucinda since they first pulled into Grundy, came back now in full force. She jumped up and ran towards the sign saying "Restrooms," and Jeff followed her.

He heard gagging noises from inside and said through the door, "Honey, what's wrong? Are you sick?" When Lucinda didn't answer, he motioned to a waitress, "My fiancée is sick, will you go in and check on her for me, please?"

The waitress came out and told him Lucinda had been sick but was coming out as soon as she washed her face. Jeff stood waiting and when he saw Lucinda's ashen face, he took her hand, "Why didn't you tell me you were sick, Honey? Do you want to go to the doctor or what can I do?"

Lucinda told him she would get some Pepto Bismol to settle her stomach. She thought it was nerves, with all the things that had happened in the last few days. Jeff ordered two plate lunches and told the waitress they would be back, but were going next door to the drug store. When they returned, the waitress had their plates ready and brought them over. Lucinda managed to eat most of the creamed potatoes, and after the waitress told her that coke would settle her stomach, she drank some of it.

By 8:30 they were back at Burb and Nancy's telling them about not being able to get their license. Burb shrugged that off as a part of life and said they'd know better next time. Jeff worriedly told Nancy about Lucinda's sickness, and Nancy was concerned. "Lucy, it's just nerves. I know this is all new and strange, but everything is going to be all right. You told me you loved Jeff and I know he loves you, so it'll be fine. You're just on edge for nothing. Take some more of that Pepto Bismol and try to get a good night's sleep, and you'll feel better in the morning."

Lucinda went to bed hoping Nancy was right and it would be all right. Again she found herself begging the Lord for some relief from all this anxiety. She went to sleep with a plea in her heart.

Lucinda found Jeff at the table when she got there the next morning. She had hoped to avoid him but for Nancy's benefit, she smiled at his welcome. She knew this had to stop if she was going to marry him, and since it had gotten as far as it had, she didn't see a stopping place. She sat down beside him and tried to eat. She managed a few bites of oatmeal and drank a small glass of milk. When she brought her things from her room, Jeff was waiting and she noticed that he had a lunch pail in his hand. "Did you pack yourself a lunch? I could have done that if you'd asked me, Jeff," said Lucinda.

"I didn't do it either. Your Mom packed it for me. I thanked her, for I certainly didn't expect it. I didn't take a lunch yesterday, but Joe, my buddy, gave me a sandwich. I've not wanted much to eat in the last few days, to tell the truth. I guess we're both suffering from nerves, aren't we?" smiled Jeff kindly.

Lucinda patted his arm and then went out and got in the truck. In fairness, she knew that Jeff was doing everything he could and she realized she should act better than she was, but her mind was in such turmoil. She would have felt better if she could have talked to someone but that would create a real stir. She wondered what would happen if she suddenly said, "I can't marry you, Jeff, because Jason might come back." The results of that were too terrible to even contemplate. Jeff would be worse than the time she broke up with him, and her entire family would be bawling her out and telling her she was acting like a baby.

Jeff stopped on the hill above Dora's and enfolded Lucinda in his arms, "Lucinda, I love you more than life. Please try to relax and not be so worried. I promise you that I'll be the best husband any girl could ever have." He looked so torn and upset that Lucinda hugged him close, to be kissed passionately.

She got out, with the assurance that they could get everything right this evening since Nancy had produced Lucinda's birth certificate. Burb had also written a note saying that he gave his permission for the marriage. Jeff swiftly kissed her again before he left and she walked into Dora's kitchen smelling her usual hot chocolate.

She arrived on the school grounds to the sounds of curses, yells, and crying. Tinker Dawson and Joe Baker were in a free-for-all, with James, the normal peacekeeper, looking on. Lucinda ran to the boys and pulled at Tinker's shirt saying loudly, "You boys stop this right now! What is this all about, and James, why are you standing there letting these boys fight?"

"I ain't the teacher. Get that red-headed feller you married to come down here and help you," snarled James as he walked behind the school house.

Lucinda was perplexed by James attitude. Surely, he didn't think she would date him. She wondered what else was going to go wrong because of this marriage. She would have to live in one room with a man for probably a long time, especially if the miners went on strike. Jeff should look for work at something else but Lucinda knew he wouldn't. It was almost like the union was his God. Jeff may not even believe in God for all she knew.

CHAPTER 32

That evening, Jeff was waiting when she arrived at the Vencill store. She thanked Mr. Estep before slowly getting into the truck headed for Grundy again. Going down Slate Creek, Lucinda suddenly thought about another pitfall. "Jeff, have you told your family about this- this marriage?"

"No, not yet, and I don't think we should. Let's just wait until it is over with? Dad and the girls will be pleased, but Mom will get all upset. She wants all her children to have a big church wedding. Lucinda, I wish we could have, for your sake, I really do," said Jeff.

Lucinda didn't care what kind of wedding it was if she could just put it off for a while. She really didn't know why she felt this need to wait. She hadn't seen Jason in almost two years. She hadn't even heard from him in over a year. It was common sense to realize that Jason was not coming back and she should have been convinced. She just couldn't understand what her problem was, since she really did care for Jeff. Trying to act reasonable, she said, "I dread your mother's reaction when she finds out and I can't stand much more this week."

Jeff decided that they should wait a few weeks. "Can we run to Bradshaw when we finish over here?" asked Jeff. "I want to check on some things and get some clean clothes and you may want to buy something like a pretty nightgown," said Jeff hesitantly.

"No, I have pajam - well, maybe I'll look around while you're getting your stuff. Sometimes, Lacy Wright's or Jones Department Store gets some nice things."

The lady at the courthouse accepted the birth certificate saying, "Well, this proves you're nineteen, but Honey, nobody would believe it by looking at you. Maybe,

it's because you're so small and that innocent face just —
well, it makes you look younger than you are. I wish I had
that problem," she grinned as she handed them the
license. She informed them that the preacher had to fill
out the enclosed form, give them the original, and mail the
copy back to the court house. Then in a few days they
would receive a beautiful official Marriage License with a
seal. "This license is legal and has a seal, but the other one
will be the one you want to frame, or most people want
to."

They thanked her and left with the license placed
securely in the inside pocket of Jeff's jacket. They decided
to wait until they got to Bradshaw and then eat at the bus
terminal, since it was only 4:30. Everything seemed so
much better this evening and Jeff was so relieved and
happy. When they got in the truck, Jeff nestled Lucinda
close. He kissed her, crushing her to him, as he whispered,
"Three more days and then you will be all mine. Mrs. Jeff
Daniel Marshall, how does that sound?"

"Daniel! I didn't know you had a middle name. I
guess I never asked, did I? Some people don't have middle
names, but all our family does. I guess it sounds all right. I
like the name of Daniel."

Jeff began kissing her again and trailing his fingers
down her back but when he moved his hand lower than
her waist, Lucinda pushed away and said, "Let's go."

They pulled into the bus terminal just as a bus had
arrived from War and the first person Lucinda saw was
Mrs. Justus and her husband, Carl. She hadn't seen them
since they moved just before Christmas. Mrs. Justus was
helping him off the bus and Lucinda went over to her.
"Hello, Mrs. Justus, it's good to see you."

Mrs. Justus looked at her for a minute and then said, "Oh, you're Miss Harmon, the teacher Mindy talks about so much." Lucinda introduced Jeff as her husband and they stood talking a minute before Jeff left, telling Lucinda to go on in the terminal and find them a table.

Lucinda asked Mrs. Justus about Billy and Mindy and then inquired about Mr. Justus' eyes. "That doctor that treated him in Korea is back in this area. He's an eye specialist now and works at Grace Hospital. Carl had an appointment with him because Dr. McCall looked him up when he first come back to Welch," bragged Mrs. Justus.

Lucinda began to tremble and felt dizzy. She grabbed Mrs. Justus' arm to steady herself. Mrs. Justus saw her pasty face and became agitated, "Here, Miss Harmon, you're sick, ain't you? Let me help you inside. Carl, send somebody after her man."

Lucinda walked unseeing into the terminal and slumped into the first seat she could find. Deputy Stevens was there and came over when he saw Lucinda. Taking the seat across from her, he said, "What's wrong, Lucinda? Do you want some water?"

He ordered some water, when Lucinda nodded. She opened her mouth to drink and vomited all over the floor. She dropped her head, embarrassed and crying.

Just then Jeff came through the door and stopped in horror, "What happened? Did someone say something to her or do something to her?" he demanded.

Lucinda held up her hand to quiet him and shook her head as a waitress came over with a mop and pail to clean up the mess. "I want to go home, Jeff," begged Lucinda through chattering teeth. He immediately pulled off his jacket and put it around her. "Sure, Honey, we'll go but I think you should see the doctor first. He helped her up and, keeping his arm around her, walked her out the

286

door and down the street. When they passed his truck, she said, "Here's the truck."

"I know, Lucinda, but you need to see the doctor first. I'm afraid you may have an ulcer." Lucinda drew back in alarm. "Come on. I'll go in and stay with you." Lucinda walked on like a zombie, too numb and miserable to care.

Dr. Mitchell was new, but Maggie Barker was an old friend, and when Jeff walked in with Lucinda she immediately went back into the doctor's office. She soon came out and motioned Jeff to bring her on in. The doctor asked Lucinda what was wrong, and Jeff, fearing that Lucinda would vomit again, told him she had been having trouble with her stomach for the last few days. "I don't know what caused this episode," said Jeff worriedly. The doctor took Lucinda's hand and asked her if anything unusual had happened today. She said no, that she had been talking to a former parent and had suddenly felt faint. Then the doctor asked her when she'd had her last period. Lucinda turned red and dropped her head as she mumbled 28th of March. "I guess I'll need to examine you, you may be pregnant," stated the doctor.

"No, I'm not, I'm not that kind of girl," blurted Lucinda as Jeff cut in with a grin, "We've only been married a week Doctor, and I know for sure she is not pregnant. I think it may be nerves or an ulcer. I think getting married and having to adjust to being married and still trying to work is just difficult for her."

The doctor seemed to think he was probably right and gave her a bottle of green colored medicine after he had loosened the cap and given her a spoonful. "That should calm you down but it will make you sleepy. Take a teaspoonful three times a day until you feel better." Turning to Jeff, he said, "Take her home and put her to bed and let her rest." The doctor turned, hiding a grin as he winked at Maggie Barker.

Jeff assured the doctor that he certainly would as they left the office. Deputy Stevens met them at the truck and wanted to know what was wrong. "Have you two been married longer than you're telling," grinned Jack wisely.

Worry about Lucinda had made Jeff short tempered and he muttered, "Hell no. Just get that nonsense out of your head. It's all nerves, I think. Coming back from a concert married and having to tell her folks, having to leave Dora's, and having to tell those kids that she won't be back next year just got to her. We went to Grundy on Monday and the same thing happened but she made it to the bathroom that time."

"Mrs. Justus said she seemed fine," explained the deputy. "She said they were talking about Mr. Justus's eyes and the doctor coming back that treated him, and suddenly Lucinda started to sway and caught hold of Mrs. Justus' arm. It scared that woman to death but she helped Lucinda into the terminal and put her in a chair. When I walked over to find out what was wrong, she just suddenly vomited," said Jack worriedly. He also advised Jeff to take her home and let her get a good night's sleep. "Where are you all staying anyway, with her folks, I guess?" questioned Jack.

Jeff told him yes and that he was going to take Lucinda home and see if her mother could get her to eat something. Jeff drove slowly with an arm around Lucinda who slowly relaxed and nodded off with her head on his shoulder. As he drove, he wondered how in the world he was going to get her to accept married life. He wanted to believe Lucinda loved him but something was holding her back, probably that damn doctor still yet. Suddenly he recalled Jack Stevens saying, "that doctor coming back" and froze in terror. Did Jack mean that doctor that Lucinda had liked? He was so glad they would be married in three more days. He drove on, realizing that the next few months were not going to be easy unless some miracle happened. Jeff wondered if there was a God and if there was, he sure wished he would help him figure an easy way to work this out.

When they arrived at Burb and Nancy's, Jeff lifted Lucinda's head, kissed her, and she opened blurry eyes. "What is it, Jeff? What do you want?" asked Lucinda.

"You went to sleep, Honey, but we're back at your Mom's and we need to go in. Do you want me to carry you? I can, if you want me to," offered Jeff gently.

Lucinda lifted her head and looked around, "No, I'll walk, but I feel so sleepy. You may have to help me," she mumbled.

Jeff told her to sit still and he got out and went around to her door and helped her out. She walked through the gate and up the walk leaning heavily on Jeff. Nancy met them at the door full of concern. Jeff explained what had happened and that she had been given some nerve medicine. "If you can get her to eat something, I think it would help. We went on to Bradshaw to get me some clean clothes and were going to eat there but Lucinda got sick. So, she hasn't eaten this evening. The doctor said the medicine would make her sleepy and it sure did. She slept all the way up the mountain."

Nancy warmed up the food left from their supper, since they had just finished, and put two plates on the table. Lucinda looked around sleepily and then said she had to go to the bathroom. Realizing she would be too unsteady to make it around the hill on her own, Jeff started forward but Lucinda smiled mistily, "Sorry Jeff, you can't go with me. It's girls only." Jeff looked at Nancy and smiled as he whispered that she didn't even realize what she was saying. Nancy shook her head smiling and took Lucinda's arm as they went out the kitchen door.

Lucinda ate and was soon in bed where she slept soundly all night but awoke at her usual time of six o'clock. She swung her feet to the floor and stood up as the thought, Jason is in Welch, hit her like a ton of bricks. What in the world would she do now? She had her blood test, her license to marry, and everybody thought she was already married. She went to the kitchen for water to take her sponge bath and hurried through it, before she ran around the hill to the toilet. She met Jeff on the way back. He stopped her, put his hands on both sides of her face, and kissed her. She couldn't believe she could enjoy Jeff's kiss the way she did, when she couldn't get Jason out of her mind. Jeff wanted to know if she felt better and she assured him she did.

They hurriedly ate their breakfast, grabbed the lunches Nancy had packed for them, and went out to the truck. Lucinda sat beside Jeff, deeply engrossed in her problem. She didn't even notice when Jeff's hand dropped to her knee, as he shifted gears. Jeff looked at her, puzzled by her non-reaction since always before, she had immediately rebuffed him. He moved his hand a little higher and suddenly she looked down and gasped, "Jeff Marshall, keep your hands to yourself, please."

"Okay, then tell me what's wrong? I've had my hand on your leg for at least five minutes, and you didn't even notice. So, what's bothering you, or is it the medicine?" questioned Jeff.

Lucinda said it wasn't the medicine because she had forgotten to take it. "It's probably good that I did forget it because I can't teach and sleep at the same time.

Jeff, everything just seems to be piling up on me and I can't think straight. I'm so confused," she moaned.

Jeff was so worried. He was afraid she would be sick again and he didn't know what to do. He couldn't afford to miss any more work. He was getting married and the threatening strike loomed on the horizon. Trying to put off his worries, he said, "You didn't get to buy anything in Bradshaw yesterday. Do you want to go to back again this evening?"

Lucinda said yes and Jeff didn't get out when they got to Dora's but told Lucinda that if she felt ill during the day, to send for Mr. Estep. He kissed her quickly and felt pleased when Lucinda kissed him back and clung to him momentarily. He was reluctant to leave but since he was already late, he put the truck in gear and roared away.

Dora had her hot cocoa ready, but Lucinda refused, telling her about her latest stomach upset. Dora laughingly asked if they had been married longer than they were telling. Lucinda shook her head, remembering that the doctor, and Deputy Stevens, had thought the same thing. She assured Dora that it was not what she was thinking. "I'm not that fertile, my friend," she laughed, thinking Dora was the only person she knew with whom she could talk about anything personal. She wished she could tell Dora about Jason being in Welch but Dora thought she was already married so she couldn't tell her. She had begged the Lord to give her some kind of sign and he did but it was too late- just two days- no, a week too late.

Lucinda thought she acted normal during the day but when James Estep said, "What's wrong with you, Miss Harmon? Have you been drinking or just so crazy about that red-headed feller you're not listening?"

Lucinda apologized, explaining that she had been given some medicine for her stomach and it was making her sleepy. That seemed to satisfy the other children but James watched her knowingly the rest of the day.

She was glad when three o'clock rolled around and Mr. Estep's jeep pulled into the yard. On the way out of the ridge, they talked about the warm spring weather and how the trees were 'putting out.' "I've got lettuce big enough to eat, and green onions, too. I told the Missus that nothing tastes as good as soup beans, kilt lettuce and onions, and a big hunk of corn bread," said Mr. Estep, smacking his lips.

Lucinda told him it was also one of Burb's favorite meals, but that her dad also wanted salt bacon with the other ingredients. Mr. Estep eulogized the merits of living on a farm as they made their way to Sam Vencill's store. Lucinda smiled and nodded in agreement as she listened but had her mind on other problems. She wondered how long Jason had been in Welch and why he hadn't tried to contact her. To tell someone you love them and then never contact them just didn't make any sense. She wondered if he had been lying to her when he had declared that he loved her and would as long as he lived. Maybe he was just a city feller, amusing himself, as Gordon had said, or maybe his mother had convinced Jason that she was the wrong girl for a big city doctor.

On Friday evening, she found out why he hadn't tried to contact her. She had thought the Lord had sent her an answer, even if too late. On that Friday evening, however, all doubt was removed. She knew for sure, that the Lord had sent her proof positive.

CHAPTER 33

Lucinda wanted to go to Bradshaw, thinking Jason might come down there, but also dreaded going. Surely, if he had already been in Bradshaw, Maggie Barker would have known. But what if he came while she was there? What in the world would she do? Did she have the nerve to back out now and tell everybody they had been lying? That would really ruin her name because Wilfred had done a good job of circulating the motel story. To back out now would also destroy Jeff. The Board of Education might not even hire her next year if she got a name of being immoral. Even with all that dread, she still wanted to take the chance to see Jason. Even if she went ahead with the marriage, she would love to see Jason just one more time. Why would the Lord send Jason back when all these other things had already happened? Was the Lord trying her faith? She would have loved to talk to Preacher Hiram. But she'd never heard of any of the Primitive Baptist people going to any of their preachers with that kind of problem.

When she arrived at Sam Vencill's store, Jeff was already there and acted funny. She wondered what was wrong. Could somebody, maybe Gordon, have told Jeff that Jason McCall was in Welch? No, Gordon didn't know about Jason. She hadn't told anybody what Mrs. Justus had said. So that must not be it because Jeff wouldn't just act funny if he heard that; he would go wild with jealousy. Lucinda shivered in dread as she got in the truck.

Jeff had seen the shiver, "Are you feeling all right? We don't have to go to Bradshaw if you don't feel good. In fact, we probably should wait until you feel better."

"I'm feeling all right, Jeff. I just felt a little cold but I'm okay now," said Lucinda as she quickly shut the door.

She slid across the seat to his side, since it was expected, and he put his arms around her and sat looking at her intently.

"Why are you looking at me like that? Have I done something wrong?" questioned Lucinda hesitantly.

Jeff grimaced and shook his head, as he started the truck, assuring her that she had done nothing wrong. "I'm just worried because you've been so sick." They drove into Bradshaw talking very little but Lucinda kept looking at Jeff warily. She sensed that something had happened, or something was said, that had Jeff bothered. He didn't act angry though, so it couldn't be that he had heard about Jason, or at least she didn't think so.

When they parked in front of Lacy Wright's store, Jeff got out and went around the truck to help her out. As he closed the door, he saw Deputy Stevens coming up the street and quickly told Lucinda to go on in since he needed to talk to Jack for a minute. Lucinda wondered why the rush but went on in and began looking for a dress. She found a pretty, light blue, voile dress with a satin underskirt that was her size. It was $30 and Lucinda wondered if she should spend that much money when she needed to save for summer school. Mr. Wright, the owner, came over and said, "That's just the dress for you. It looks like a prom dress or a bridal outfit. But, since you're already married, you won't need it. That's too bad though because I marked it down, since not many people are that size."

"How much is it now, Mr. Wright?" asked Lucinda eagerly, telling him that she would be going to a dinner dance with her sister-in-law next month. This was true but Lucinda had forgotten about it since so much had been happening. The dance was a good excuse for buying the dress now, though. When Mr. Wright said it was now $25 she told him she wanted it, and then went back to the lingerie section just as Jeff came in.

Looking back, Jeff saw her and came back to that section, making it very embarrassing for Lucinda. She turned to go back up front but Jeff said, "Lucinda, here is what I'd like you to have. Do you like it?"

Lucinda looked at the pale peach satin nightgown with the matching robe. They were the prettiest things she had ever seen, but she couldn't look at Jeff to tell him. Dora had told her that a woman should have a pretty night gown when she got married. She had also said it would be taken off her. Lucinda turned scarlet at the memory of that conversation. Jeff saw her face and decided he'd best just get it himself. He put them on his arm and went to the front where Mr. Wright was waiting with her dress. The dress was already in an opaque zipper bag and when Mr. Wright was going to take it out for Jeff to see, Lucinda stopped him. "No, I'm buying this myself and I don't want him to see it, not yet, anyway."

Mr. Wright grinned and accepted her money before he turned to Jeff, "Oh! I see you've bought the important stuff," as he laughed merrily. Lucinda turned away and, taking her dress, started out of the store to be stopped by Jeff. He told her to wait, since the truck was locked. That puzzled Lucinda since people didn't lock anything on the mountain, but maybe towns were not as safe.

Jeff came out of the store smiling and went to his side of the truck. The smile quickly faded and he constantly looked up and down the street, as he was unlocking the door. He reached across the seat, opened Lucinda's door, and took her package as she got in. He started the truck, and said, "Let's go to the Sunset Drive-In tonight instead of eating in town. After we're married, we'll probably never eat in a drive-in again." Knowing that Jeff usually wanted to hang around town and talk to people he knew, and definitely did not like drive-in restaurants, Lucinda was puzzled. She looked at Jeff wondering at his unusual behavior. He may think I'll get sick again and embarrass him. She quickly agreed to go to the drive-in. That settled, Jeff shifted into gear and drove to the lower end of town, turned and went speeding back up the street. At the intersection of Route 80 at the upper end of town, a man tried to wave him down, but Jeff wouldn't stop. He just threw up his hand and drove on.

"Jeff, was that man a friend of yours? He acted like he wanted you to stop," said Lucinda. Jeff drove on, telling her the man was Jeb Sweeney who was probably drunk and wanted to give him a drink of moonshine.

There was a big wide space on Hall Hollow curve and Jeff pulled into it, stopped and cut the engine, then gathered Lucinda close and began kissing her. Lucinda wondered if he had also been drinking as he became more amorous. Finally Lucinda pushed him away, "Jeff, what is wrong with you? Now, you know how I feel and you know I will not do anything wrong. So, why are you acting like this? Sometimes, you almost scare me."

"God, Lucinda, don't ever be afraid of me. I wouldn't hurt you for the world. There's been so many things going wrong, when I think about it, I get scared something will happen at the last minute. You won't change your mind, will you, Lucinda? You wouldn't do me like that, would you?" His abject pleading tore at Lucinda's heart. She couldn't see how she could refuse him but then she had begged for a sign and the Lord had sent Jason back. She couldn't stand to see Jeff looking so anguished and fearful. She was having a hard time keeping her tears at bay since she really did care for Jeff. She wondered how

296

in the world a girl could love one man and have such tender feelings for another. She quickly decided to bide for time, at least for right now.

"What brought this on, Jeff? We bought a wedding dress and you bought that beautiful nightgown and I thought everything was fine. Now you're acting like this. I think you're just hungry, so let's go get something to eat," smiled Lucinda as she leaned over and kissed his cheek. That seemed to satisfy Jeff because he pulled out and drove on up the mountain with Lucinda snuggled close. Lucinda could still feel the tenseness in him, however.

After they got up on the mountain, Jeff seemed to relax. They went to the Sunset Drive-In and ate, and the rest of the evening was spent in friendly conversation. Going down the ridge later, Lucinda asked Jeff how big his room was. Jeff described it and Lucinda was amazed. "Jeff, that room is barely big enough for you. Where will I put my things?"

Jeff assured her that it was big enough and that it also had a private bathroom. "We, at least, won't have to jump out in the dark, rain or snow, and run a mile around the hill to sh- do our business," he grinned. He apologized, explaining that he had planned to find something much nicer if they had waited until August but now they had to improvise. Lucinda knew this was true and thought, if she didn't back out, she'd be gone in the daytime and Jeff would be gone part of the night so they could make out. Besides, she would be away at college most of the summer. When she mentioned this to Jeff, he became upset, saying he didn't want to talk or think about it until the time came. They arrived back at Burb's, disgruntled and agitated. Both had decided to go to bed as soon as they got home and Lucinda did. Jeff, however, lingered, talking to Burb, after Nancy and Lucinda said good night.

The next morning, Jeff was at the table as usual when Lucinda entered the kitchen. He smiled and moved over to give her room on the bench. He gave her a gentle kiss and handed her the oatmeal, as he said, "I was an old bear yesterday, Lucinda. I'm sorry. If we don't hurry and get married, we'll both be taking nerve medicine."

He patted her hand, then suddenly got up and brought her a glass of milk and her medicine. Lucinda would have forgotten it half the time if Jeff hadn't reminded her. In the mornings, she only took a half dose since she didn't want to be groggy and sleepy all day. When they rose to leave, there was only one lunch on the table by the door. "Is this my lunch or yours? I'll pack the other one," said Lucinda, starting to lay down her things.

"No, I told your Mom I've got some things I need to see about so I'd just buy a sandwich," explained Jeff as he opened the door and walked behind Lucinda to the truck. Lucinda wondered why he wanted to buy his lunch if he just needed to see about something, but didn't say anything.

They rode out of the ridge in companionable silence until Jeff said, "Your Dad will come for you this evening. I might be late getting to Vencill's and you'd have to wait.

Lucinda smiled in appreciation and began to tell Jeff how James Estep had changed since their supposed marriage.

"That big old kid's got a crush on you. He'd better not get fresh with you or I'll hew him down to size."

Lucinda assured Jeff that James was too afraid of his dad to try anything but was just being sullen. She related several incidents in which, at one time, James would have intervened but now didn't. Lucinda hated that James felt this way but knew of no way she could change it. She also told Jeff about little Garson and how proud she was of his accomplishments. Jeff hugged her close and told her he was very proud of her. Lucinda kissed his cheek thinking how good it felt to have someone like Jeff who always seemed to be proud of her. He never seemed to think she did wrong, even when she knew she had.

All day long Lucinda worried with how to deal with her dilemma. The Lord had answered her prayers and sent Jason back. She couldn't help but question why he hadn't tried to contact her if he still cared. Maybe he hadn't had time. She wished she knew how long he had been in Welch but didn't know anyone she could ask. Time is what she needed. Surely the Lord would work something out and every minute that she wasn't working with one of her students was taken up with silent prayers.

At three o'clock Burb's car pulled into the school yard and the children wanted to know who that old man was. When she told them it was her father, they were amazed that a man that old could drive. Lucinda thought Burb would be upset if he knew the children thought he was old. Burb was in his late sixties, but Lucinda had never thought of him as old, even with his sparse gray hair. Burb walked tall and proud with his shoulders back and head held high. She just couldn't think of him as old. However, both of his parents had died in their sixties and they were considered old.

James wanted to know why she was riding with her Dad. She explained that her husband couldn't be there on time to meet her and James scowled and walked sullenly up the road kicking at rocks along the way.

Burb asked if she was looking forward to tomorrow, and Lucinda told him she was worried and scared to death. "Cindy, Cindy, I don't understand you a tall. You're marrying a good man. I can't say I like his politics or his ideas on unions, and I don't think he's got an ounce of religion about him," Burb stated thoughtfully. "Still, from all accounts, he is a good man. I know for certain that he loves you. You're just young and petted. I guess we've sheltered you too much."

Lucinda agreed that she had probably been sheltered too much and didn't know much about life. She knew her sisters were fine and they were raised just like she was. Silently, she wondered if any of her sisters had ever had the problem she was dealing with. She knew that Odell had married to get away from home, or really Burb's strict demands. Lucinda wondered if Odell had cried and worried the way she had. Did she love Bud? They had five children. Even if she didn't love him, she still had five children with him. So, you didn't have to love a man to have his children, mused Lucinda silently, and in the next breath asked the Lord to please help her.

Lucinda missed Jeff when she got home and he wasn't there. She wondered if they had put him on the 'hoot owl' shift. She thought he would have told her if they had or maybe they just told him when he went in to work today. She asked Burb if they had moved Jeff to another shift and Nancy said, "No, he just…" but stopped when Burb interrupted with "No, I don't think so. I think he's trying to work out some kind of surprise for you." He glared at Nancy, shaking his head, but since Lucinda had gone to look out the window, she didn't see him. When she turned back into the room, Burb smiled as he told Nancy how he had been bragging on his future son-in-law. Nancy declared that if he had, he must really think Jeff was great. He'd be the first son-in-law she'd ever heard him brag on.

CHAPTER 34

Lucinda helped Nancy get supper. They were just putting it on the table when Bud and Odell's car came down the road. The children started piling out of the car almost before they stopped. Quickly, they ran to Burb who first hugged and then slapped each bottom playfully, telling them to hurry and wash for supper. They ran to Nancy, not even listening to Burb's orders, letting everyone recognize that even though they loved their Grandpa, their Grandma was super special.

Odell hugged Lucinda, wistfully smiling, "I wanted to come and spend some time with you before you became an old married woman." She hugged Lucinda again and looked at her closely, "It's going to be all right, you know. I wish I had a man as crazy about me as Jeff is about you."

After supper was over, Odell told Bud to go to the car and get the newspapers that she had brought for Burb to read. "I don't have time to read them and most of the time, I don't even get to look through them. I don't reckon Bud can read," laughed Odell. "If he can, I've never caught him at it. But then, I don't see him that much," she added with a tired grin.

She had five young children to get ready and off to school each morning, plus straightening the house before going to work. Lucinda wondered how she did it all. They washed the dishes talking and laughing, or, at least, Lucinda was trying to laugh. Odell, always very sensitive to others, said, "Lucy, you're not still grieving over that doctor are you? I hope you're not. I'd hate to see Jeff hurt."

They were interrupted by Burb's, "Looky here, Cindy. Here's why that doctor didn't never get in touch with you." He came into the kitchen holding the newspaper spread out in his hands, "A marriage announcement and a picture. Here, see it for yourself." He laid the paper on the table and Lucinda and Odell looked down on Jason's smiling face beside a girl in a white wedding gown. Lucinda felt faint and had to sit down and Odell began to read aloud. "Dr. Jason Charles McCall was united in marriage to Miss Miranda Janet Washburn, both of Pittsburgh. Doctor McCall, who specialized in eye surgery after a stint in Korea, was sent to Welch for a period of one year to finish out the training he left when he was drafted."

Lucinda felt waves of blackness wash over her but took big gulps of air and suppressed it. Gathering every ounce of strength she could muster, she said, "Well, I figured something like that had happened." She got up and made her way out the door and around the hill to the toilet. Then she broke down and cried. She could see through the cracks and warily watched for anyone coming that way. Twilight was approaching as she made her way back to the house. She wanted to avoid facing anyone since her eyes were red and swollen. Luckily, nobody was in the kitchen and she washed her face and hands, rubbing them vigorously. The light hadn't been turned on but the fading sun still threw its lingering rays across the kitchen. Burb was as careful about the use of electricity as Uncle Jake Kinnard. When Nancy came in wanting to know what had taken her so long, Lucinda rubbed her stomach and shook her head. "Have you took your medicine? You ain't, but you're goin to," said Nancy as she went to the cabinet and brought it to the table.

Odell came in looking solemnly at Lucinda but not saying anything when she saw Nancy with the medicine and a spoon. "Lucy girl, you'd better get a hold on them nerves. Life's tough but you have to stand it. Be like me, just be too tough to let it get you down," Odell said with a laugh, as she reached down and hugged Lucinda, whispering, "Be happy, little sis." Lucinda realized that Odell knew how much the news had upset her but wasn't going to say anything.

Nancy dropped the used spoon into the dishpan on the stove and went to hug her grandchildren who were preparing to leave.

Lucinda stood up and hugged Odell furiously but with tears in her eyes, "Odell, I've prayed and prayed for the Lord to send me a sign. He did, didn't he?"

Odell looked down at the newspaper still spread out on the table and shook her head, "Yeah, Honey, I think he did," and then whispered, "I'd not say much about this if I was you, though. I promise I never will." Lucinda hugged her again and then stayed in the background until they left.

Jeff still hadn't come but Lucinda hadn't even thought about him. She told Nancy she was going to bed and after folding the newspaper took it to her room. She carefully cut out the picture and announcement and then, going back into the kitchen, she wadded the paper up, lifted the stove eye, and put it into the stove where it burst into flames.

She then went to the door and told Burb and Nancy good night. They asked if she was going to wait up for Jeff and she said no. "I guess he must be on another shift or something. Anyway, I'm tired, so I'll just go on to bed."

Burb and Nancy looked at each other and Nancy started to speak but Burb shook his head. Lucinda had been afraid to lift her head in the bright light of the naked bulb hanging from the ceiling and didn't see this visual signal. She knew that soap and water would not conceal her swollen eyes and red nose.

Lucinda looked at the wedding picture for a long time and then folded it into a small square and slipped it inside the lining of her new suitcase bought to take to the concert. She had found a small slit where the lining was not sewn and intended sewing it back herself and now she was glad she hadn't. Finally she went to bed and lay for a long time thinking about Jason. She wondered why he wanted to put his wedding announcement in the Welch paper. If he had been from this area, she could have understood it. Finally, she decided he must have wanted her to know. Tonight when she prayed, she thanked the Lord for giving her positive proof that marrying Jeff was the right thing. Then she made up her mind that she had committed herself and it was what the Lord wanted her to do. "I'll make a good marriage, no matter what it takes, Lord. Please, help me to put Jason completely out of my mind. I want to be a good wife to Jeff, so please help me Lord. I'll need you every day," she prayed before she finally drifted to sleep.

Lucinda awoke with a start as she felt lips settle on her own. She started to struggle before she realized it was Jeff and then opened her eyes. "Good morning, blue eyes," whispered Jeff as he kissed her again. Seeing that Lucinda was puzzled as to why he was in her room, he lifted his wrist and pointed at his watch, "It's seven o'clock and we have a lot to do before ten, so rise and shine, sweetheart. Let's get this show on the road," he said as he leaned down to kiss her again. Lucinda impulsively reached up her arms encircling his neck and he moaned in pleasure as he kissed her hungrily.

Nancy came to the door which was ajar and said, "I got breakfast ready, so get a move on." Jeff looked around and grinned sheepishly, "I just came in to wake her. I figured it would be all right since we're getting married in a few hours. I haven't been here but about three minutes," he added just in case Nancy thought he had spent the night.

Nancy went back to the kitchen smiling. *"He's a good man,"* she thought, *"and he'll make my baby a good husband. I'm going to miss her but that's what I wanted for her, a man to take care of her and be good to her."* Nancy, who had already given up her other eight children in marriage, was sad to see the last one go. "It shore ain't easy being a mother. It wouldn't be so bad if a person could stop lovin' 'em when they get grown." Nancy often talked aloud to herself when she was trying to deal with a painful problem and this was no exception. So she talked, as she put the finishing touches to the breakfast table.

By 8:30, Lucinda and Jeff were in their truck and ready. Ellen and her husband, Benny Pruitt, had come to take Burb and Nancy with them to the wedding. When Lucinda had walked out of her room dressed in her new blue dress, Jeff gasped in appreciation and everyone else said she looked beautiful. Lucinda turned and went to the kitchen to take a dose of her medicine. Jeff came behind her and laughingly said, "You reckon it would hurt me to take a little of that?" Then he took it from her saying, "I'm going to put this in the truck. You may need it toni- uh, while we're away. Lucinda went back in her room and donned her long blue spring coat, picked up her purse, and left the room. She knew if she looked around, she would begin to think about leaving it for good. She was already fighting tears and she didn't want to start that again. She walked out the door thinking, 'Please Lord, help me. Just help me get through this.'

They arrived in Grundy at a quarter past nine to meet Preacher Greenleaf pulling into the church parking lot. They all got out and marched solemnly into the church. By this time, the medicine was taking its effect and Lucinda floated serenely down the aisle beside Jeff. She stood quietly, answering clearly, and repeating everything the preacher told her to. When it came to the 'I do' she said that strongly and firmly as she looked Jeff in the eye.

Jeff seemed nervous and stammered a time or two and when he said, 'I do,' Lucinda saw tears glistening in his eyes. When the preacher said, "I now pronounce you, Jeff Daniel Marshall and Lucinda Marie Harmon Marshall, man and wife and now you may kiss the bride," Jeff pulled Lucinda to him and tenderly kissed her as tears broke free and washed down his cheeks.

Preacher Greenleaf patted his shoulder, smiling. Burb, Nancy, Ellen, and Benny all hugged Jeff first and then hugged Lucinda, saying how fortunate she was to find someone who loved her so much. Lucinda had already taken a half teaspoon of her medicine before Jeff had seen her that morning and then a second dose before they left. Now everything seemed just fine. She had done what everybody wanted her to do and even what God wanted her to do. She was happy, but she wanted to cry, and so she did. She didn't cry like she had last night. Now, she didn't really know why she was crying since she wasn't sad; she was just so sleepy.

Ellen had taken several pictures during the ceremony. Now she posed Lucinda and Jeff by themselves, then with Burb and Nancy, and finally with Preacher Greenleaf. When the license was filled out, and Jeff had paid the $25 required by the preacher, they filed out of the church. Lucinda hugged everybody again and went with Jeff to be helped into the truck.

When Jeff got in the truck, he looked at Lucinda and crushed her to him as he really cried, "Honey, I have been terrified that something would happen or maybe you would back out. This has been an awful week for me." He straightened up, wiped his eyes and started the truck and with a smile said, "Let's go, Mrs. Marshall. We have places to go and things to see."

Before they had passed the intersection at Vansant, Lucinda was asleep with her head resting on Jeff's shoulder. In a semi-wakefulness state, she heard Jeff say something like Lebanon and eating lunch. She was too drowsy and mumbled something about waiting. He looked down at her, smiled, and drove on to Abingdon before he tried to wake her.

When she was fully awake, Lucinda sat looking down at her hand, gazing at the wedding band that Jeff had put behind her engagement ring during the ceremony. Now she remembered the words that had been said and remembered that Jeff had given her a ring. She leaned over and looked at his left hand, and sure enough, he had a wedding band on, too. She asked Jeff when he had gotten them and he said he'd had them since Christmas. "That was when you asked me to marry you. You mean, you bought my set of rings and one for yourself at the same time?" asked Lucinda.

Jeff told her he had gotten a really good deal and bought all three together. "I didn't think you would think about getting me a ring, so I just kept it and didn't say anything about it. I wanted to show people I was married too," smiled Jeff.

They stopped at a family diner on Main Street in Abingdon before they drove on to Bristol where Jeff had reserved a room at a Holiday Inn. Lucinda was pleased that it was really nice; not like that terrible room in Iaeger. Jeff held her close and kissed her and would have lingered but Lucinda urged him to hurry since she'd never been in Bristol before. They wandered in and out of the numerous shops and Jeff bought Lucinda a pair of house shoes when she mentioned that she didn't have any. Lucinda didn't want him to waste his money, since she had lived all her life without house shoes, but he only laughed and told her that a lot of things would be different now that she was his wife. They ate supper about seven o'clock and then went to the Paramount Theater and saw *Abba Dabba Honeymoon* starring Debbie Reynolds.

When they came out of the theater, it was 9:30 and Jeff said he thought they should go to the hotel. Lucinda didn't want to but knew it was inevitable and so went along without saying much.

In the room, Jeff held her a long time, then kissed her tenderly and told her she needed to go in the bathroom and put on her gown that he had bought her. Without Jeff knowing it, Lucinda had slipped the nerve medicine into her purse and this she took with her into the bathroom. Lucinda was tempted to take an extra dose of her medicine but only took a little more than a teaspoonful. She took a long time, delaying as long as she could and came out shivering. She turned quickly when Jeff came to take her in his arms and jumped into the bed and pulled the covers snuggly up around her neck. Her heart was beating wildly and she couldn't control her shaking. Jeff came to bed and took her in his arms and she didn't resist, she was shaking so badly that she couldn't have if she wanted to. "Honey, I forgot your medicine. I'll put my clothes on and go back down and get it."

Knowing that tonight had to happen, she told him that she had already taken it and she would calm down in a while. She kept as still as a statue when Jeff began to caress her and determined that no matter what happened she was not going to resist or say anything. She didn't, even when she hurt, but Jeff was so gentle and loving that after a while, she drifted off to sleep. Sometimes she felt like she was half awake but she felt very warm, protected, and loved. Sometime in the night she remembered telling Jeff that it wasn't too bad but she was so drowsy that she didn't know what wasn't too bad.

She awoke the next morning to see Jeff sitting on the side of the bed without his shirt on and then she realized that gowns did go missing when one was married. She dropped her eyes and refused to look at Jeff when he leaned over to kiss her. "Don't, I want to get up. You shouldn't have taken my gown. Why did you buy it if I wasn't going to wear it?" mumbled Lucinda.

Jeff snuggled back into bed and laughed as he told her that she did wear it for a while. He began to kiss her and Lucinda pushed him away and, wrapping the cover around her, swung her feet over the side and got up. When she looked back, she saw her first naked man and gasped in surprise as she also saw blood on the sheet before she ran to the bathroom. Well, she thought as she washed and brushed her teeth, what I dreaded most has already happened, so the rest should be easy.

Jeff ordered breakfast to be sent to the room and Lucinda donned her gown and robe. She had intended to put on her clothes but Jeff wouldn't let her have them. He said they had paid for the room until five o'clock and they were not giving it up until then. Soon breakfast was brought and Lucinda found that she was hungry. She still couldn't look at Jeff and hoped he didn't mention last night but she wasn't to get her wish, for as soon as the bell boy had departed, Jeff said, "Are you really sore, Lucinda? I tried to be gentle but you're so little."

Lucinda told him she was okay, but didn't look at him and told him she'd rather not talk about it. They ate, talking about everything under the sun, until Lucinda asked, "Are you back on the night shift? You didn't come in until after I went to sleep on Friday night."

Jeff chewed a few seconds and then reached over and lifted her chin, "Lucinda, I didn't tell you because you've been so upset, but the miners are on strike. They have been since last Thursday. That's one of the reasons I was so scared when we went to Bradshaw on Thursday. I was afraid someone would come up and blurt it out and you would call off our wedding."

Lucinda looked shocked, "What are they striking about now? You may as well not have a job if they're going to strike every time the moon changes."

"No, Lucinda they are right to strike. A man got hurt and they made him stay down until the shift was over. I'll admit he wasn't hurt bad but still they should have brought him out. If the company is allowed to get away with that, they'll do worse next time. I was at a union meeting Friday night and it didn't break up until ten o'clock."

Lucinda questioned Jeff about paying the rent and buying food. He didn't seem concerned but said he had some money saved. Lucinda said, "Jeff, why don't you find work in something else and quit the mines? We never will have a house or anything else with them striking so much."

This seemed to upset Jeff as he told Lucinda that he was part of them. "I'm a coal miner and a union man, Lucinda, and we stick by our own. You don't leave your family when they have a problem and that's the way the union is. We all work for everyone's benefit."

"Well, you go right ahead and stick by the union and I'll go right ahead and teach school. I'll be getting a payday and if you're good, I may even buy you some food," laughed Lucinda until she saw the look on Jeff's face.

CHAPTER 35

The closer they got to Bradshaw, the more Lucinda noticed the tension in Jeff which she couldn't understand. "Are you already having regrets, Jeff?" asked Lucinda playfully.

"That'll be the day, Sweetheart. No, Ma'am, I certainly do not regret marrying the love of my life," said Jeff with a wolfish grin, pulling her more snugly to his side. "I was just dreading your reaction to our living quarters," he quickly improvised.

Lucinda explained to Jeff that she had married him for better or worse, richer or poorer, in sickness and in health and so whatever came along, they would cope. Jeff smiled and said, "Please, Lucinda, always remember those words, no matter what happens."

That was such a puzzling speech, 'no matter what happens' that Lucinda wondered if he knew something he wasn't telling. Maybe he had seen the same newspaper she'd seen or maybe somebody told him about Jason being back in the area. She decided she wouldn't say anything unless he mentioned something because she could be wrong. Anyway, the Lord had answered her prayers. She had no doubts about that anymore. She couldn't have possibly gone through the marriage and everything, the way she had, before seeing that newspaper.

Lucinda wanted to put to rest any uneasiness he might be having and get rid of his jealous thoughts. "Jeff, I know you are jealous and think I don't love you at times but I want to assure you that I live up to my commitments. If I give my word, I keep it. I promised you and God that I would be faithful to you and honor you and I'll keep that word. Now, I want you to put all that behind you. You said you wouldn't be jealous once we were married so, now, prove it."

They had pulled in beside the rooming house as she finished and Jeff gathered her in his arms alternately kissing and thanking her. He was smiling as he said, "Mrs. Marshall, do you wish me to carry you up the stairs or just wait to be carried across the threshold?"

Lucinda laughed and got out of the truck intending to run up the steps in front of him. Deputy Stevens came around the truck just as she slammed the door. "Jeff, you stay gone more than you stay home since you married. Some of the miners have been looking for you. They're having a meeting down at the union hall so you'd better scoot on down there, my friend."

Jeff frowned, "Tell them I'll be along shortly. I have some things I have to do. Lucinda will be staying in my room from now on and I have to give her some space."

Jack raised his eyebrows, "Fell out with the in-laws already? That was quick."

Lucinda started to explain, but Jeff waved him away, and taking her arm, walked up the stairs beside her. From the landing he looked down at Jack, "Like I said, I'll check in on the meeting later." Then, fishing the key from his pocket, he unlocked the door, then plucked Lucinda from the landing and carried her across the threshold.

He dumped her unceremoniously on the bed. "I've finally got you in my bed," he said and laughed as she scrambled to the back side and onto the floor. Before he could give chase, she scampered to an open door that she hoped was a bathroom. Surprisingly, the bathroom was fairly large, compared to the room which was about a 12 x 14 in Lucinda's estimation. There was a small closet on one side of the room, a dresser, a chest of drawers, a nightstand, and, of course, the bed that took up the rest of the space. There was a space in the middle of the room and one small space under the windows. Standing in the bathroom door, Lucinda surveyed the room, "Jeff, we need a chair, sofa, or something. There's no place to sit down. Where will I grade papers, write, or- well, we just need a chair, at least. Don't you think so?"

Jeff sat down on the bed and pulled her into his lap, "Now, here's a chair." He then lay back on the bed, pulling her with him, "And here's a sofa and uh! What'd you do that for?" huffed Jeff as Lucinda poked him in the stomach and jumped out of his grasp.

She scurried into the bathroom, slammed the door shut, and yelled, "Go on to your meeting, Mr. Union Man. I want to get cleaned up and try to get ready to go to work tomorrow. You can stay here and play nurse maid to the union." She waited for a while and then cracked open the door. Jeff was standing watching something from the window. He had such a fierce look on his face that she thought there was an accident on the street and started over to see what it was.

Hearing her, Jeff turned, "I thought you were getting a bath. Go ahead, but lock this door as soon as I leave, and don't let anyone in. If anyone knocks, don't answer the door. Don't look so scared. You'll be okay, but some of the guys I work with might think I'm back and come up. I don't want them in here if I'm gone, okay?"

Jeff left, saying he would bring supper back from the bus terminal. Lucinda wondered why he wanted to carry food up here when it would be easy to walk down the street. She locked the door behind Jeff and went into the bathroom, found some Comet cleanser and gave the tub a good scouring. She ran water into the tub and sank blissfully into the soothing warmth, hoping to relieve her soreness. Lucinda thought back on her talks with Dora and silently thanked her and her college roommate for sex education lessons. She still didn't know much but felt Dora's information and her medicine had helped her over the first hurdle. Now, she might even read the book Jason had given her if she could hide it from Jeff.

By the time she had washed her hair and put it up in curlers she was beginning to feel hungry. She looked at her watch and realized it was 8:30. She wondered if Jeff was going to get back before the bus terminal closed and what would she do if he didn't? Then she heard someone on the steps and held her breath but relaxed when Jeff turned the key in the lock and opened the door. A box which emitted a delicious aroma was on the floor at his feet. He picked it up and came in, slamming the door shut with his foot. "You're right. We need some chairs. We could even use a table." He stood holding the box, looking around until Lucinda took it from him and hurriedly put it on the corner of the dresser since it was hot.

"Let's have a picnic," said Lucinda as she spread a clean towel on the floor. "What are we going to drink? You forgot drinks, didn't you? We'll have to drink water, but that's okay. Come on, let's eat. I'm hungry." She opened the box and took out a plate of food wrapped in a dish towel and sank down on the floor.

Jeff went into the bathroom, washed his hands, and filled two cups from the bathroom holder with water. He brought them back and dropping to the floor he leaned over for a quick kiss, "You even look good with those rolling pins in your hair."

Lucinda was busy eating but she rolled her eyes and wiggled her head, making the curlers bounce and jiggle. She wondered why she felt so relaxed because she hadn't taken any of her medicine today at all. When she commented about that to Jeff, he thought it was because all that indecision was over with and, "Besides, you have a good husband." Jeff looked soberly at her, "Lucinda, I will try my best to make you happy. We'll have to get used to each other's ways. I might sometimes be short or even aggravated, but that won't mean that I don't love you. Hell, I'm the proudest man in the whole world and if this strike would get settled I'd be happier still." He sat munching for a while then said, "Honey, how would you like to move someplace else? I mean like maybe over around Logan or somewhere in that area? I could probably get a job at Coal Mountain. We would be close to Margie, and you like her. I'll bet Sam Duncan could help you get a school over there. What do you think?"

"I don't know. What brought this on, anyway? I have to finish out this year at Estep School and then I have to go to summer school. We can't make a move now. This is the first time you've mentioned moving. Has something happened? I guess your union buddies told you the strike was going to last a long time, huh?" Lucinda looked at Jeff speculatively. He had been looking for a house in Jolo, Bradshaw, or Raysal and she had written asking for a school in this area. She hadn't mailed it yet but planned to this week.

Jeff told her that it was just something he had been thinking about this past week. "Bradshaw is all right but it is almost impossible to find a decent house to live in. The company might let me have a coal camp house if one ever comes empty, but I doubt you'd liking to live in a coal camp."

Lucinda didn't feel like she was going to like living in any town. She needed breathing room and a place to walk. Also, she needed to smell the mountain air and hear the wind whistling through the trees. She loved all of McDowell County, but especially Bradshaw Mountain and

316

always had. From the top of the mountain she could look out over the whole world, it seemed. When the fog gathered in the valleys on cool nights, on the following mornings she could look down on a blanket of soft cottony clouds and feel isolated from the world around her. The sunsets on the mountain were spectacular, especially in the fall when all the earth was dressed in yellow and crimson. She'd often wished she had a camera and could capture some of the breathtaking scenery of every season.

Lucinda looked at Jeff smiling, "You're right. I don't want to live in a coal camp. I really want to live on the very top of a mountain, where the birds sing, and the dogs chase, howl, and bay at the moon, and cows bawl, and well, just..." She stopped because Jeff was laughing at her.

"What's so funny? I'm just telling you what I like," Lucinda said when she'd swallowed her last bite.

"I wasn't making fun of you, Lucinda. I just didn't know you were so fond of outside toilets, mud, and rutted roads." Jeff looked at her with his heart in his eyes. He acted as if he had gained a treasure and Lucinda reveled in his admiration.

Surely God had intervened, thought Lucinda, because things happened just at the right time to get them married before anything else could happen. Now, Lucinda believed that the truck breaking down was meant to be. If that was so, then God must have chosen Jeff for her. That being so, then maybe he will keep Jason out of my mind, thought Lucinda.

The miners being on strike solved the problem of getting Lucinda to and from school. Jeff also worked it out for his stint on the picket line to be during the day while Lucinda was in school. In this way, Jeff could also come back for her in the evenings. On Monday after school, they went to Dora's for the few remaining items left in her room. Then they went on to Burb and Nancy's for the rest of Lucinda's clothes, and also the loan of two chairs. They were just plain old ladder backed porch chairs, but at least they had a place to sit. Later that week, Margie came over bringing a folding card table. Now their supper, brought from the bus terminal, could be eaten from a table. They found they both liked doing jigsaw puzzles and spent happy hours chatting and working puzzles.

The following week they went to Jeff's parents' house. Everybody was really surprised but happy, except Mrs. Marshall. She was astonished that they would get married and keep it a secret. When Jeff told them how it had happened, Mr. Marshall and Margie broke out in gales of laughter. "A shotgun wedding for nothing," giggled Margie as Mrs. Marshall sat scowling and looking very angry. "What kind of people would want their daughter to get married because she'd had to stay out all night? Didn't they believe you that nothing happened? I thought you weren't getting married until August. Now, what will I tell everybody?"

"Tell them I couldn't wait to make Lucinda my wife and I begged her into marrying early, which I did," smiled Jeff, lacing his fingers through Lucinda's and kissing her nose.

Lucinda bristled at the aspersions cast at her parents and said, "Mrs. Marshall, my parents have raised five daughters and they have all had very good names. They just wanted the family honor to be intact. They're not as awful as you seem to think."

Calming down, Lucinda realized that it wouldn't have mattered when they married. Mrs. Marshall just didn't want Jeff to marry her. She wanted Jeff to marry that Clary girl.

They spent the rest of their visit talking about the strike and what kind of agreement the union would accept. Mr. Marshall said he hoped they got this one settled pretty soon because in July the contract was up for renewal and that usually led to a lengthy strike. Lucinda wondered who was benefiting the most from all this striking. It didn't seem like the miners were. She promised herself to learn as much as she could about both sides of the issue this summer.

CHAPTER 36

Lucinda was busy and happy. She had another month of school and then she would go to summer school. Now she dreaded going because she knew she would miss Jeff. He was so good to her, but if they went anywhere, it was either Grundy or to Gilbert and Logan. "Jeff, why is it that you don't want me on the streets in Bradshaw. I'm hurried to the truck each morning and rushed back to our room in the evenings, and we never go to the bus terminal to eat. I want to know why you're doing this," demanded Lucinda adamantly.

Jeff grinned and said, "Too many of my old buddies think you're pretty and I don't want to have to whip them." Lucinda studied him warily, thinking that his jealousy was going to be hard to live with.

The first Saturday night in May, Lucinda told Jeff she wanted to go to meeting the next day with Nancy and Burb. Jeff dropped his head and acted pitiful, "What will I do by myself all day?"

"You could go too, you know. You act like you don't believe there is a God. Do you believe in God, Jeff?" asked Lucinda doubtfully.

"I didn't, but some of the things that have happened lately have made me wonder. Maybe I'll just go with you and see what the attraction is," grinned Jeff and Lucinda threw her arms around his neck and kissed him. "Heck, I may even join the church if I get this kind of reaction," and began tickling her.

Sunday morning they pulled into the church yard and got out, surprising many of the members and regular attendees. Burb was already in the row designated in Lucinda's mind as 'deacon's row' and he only raised his hand in greeting. Nancy, however, slid over and made

320

room for Lucinda and Jeff beside her in the second row on the right side of the building. When Jeff looked around and saw that only women were on that side, he whispered to Lucinda that maybe he was in the wrong place. She held his hand and told him it was all right since there were no assigned seats. "This is just the way the men and women have always seated themselves. Its habit, I think, but nobody will say anything."

The first song made Lucinda feel like she could fly away. "Come Thy Fount of Every Blessing," seemed to be a beckoning call from the heart, or at least Lucinda's heart, and when the next line said 'tune my heart to sing thy praise,' tears rushed to her eyes and she was caught up in the praise of God. Jeff had been watching her and knew she was feeling deeply about something but didn't know what it was so he held her hand tighter and didn't say anything. After two more songs the congregation stood and either hugged each other or shook hands. Lucinda was rejoicing so much that she didn't notice Jeff's reaction when she was hugged by both men and women as he was, also.

Then some young visiting Elder rose to open the service and pray and Lucinda kept her eyes right on him and listened attentively. He seemed scared to death at first and then it was as if suddenly something took over and he spoke with power and authority. Aunt Rhoda Wagner began to shout and so did several others and Uncle William Blakely hobbled up and hugged the young man. Jeff scowled fiercely, watching Lucinda's rapt gaze at the young man.

When the Elder knelt to pray, Lucinda bowed her head and tried to thank the Lord for answering her prayers and being so watchful over her. The service seemed to move along quickly but Lucinda was eager to see Elder

Hiram take the stand. His silvery white hair made a halo around his head and he began in a soft clear voice to talk about God's called and chosen church. "Now, little children, the kingdom is within you 'God within you- the hope of Glory' so then this building is not the house of God but you, God's men and women, are the house of God. God set up his church in Wisdom for the scripture tells us that 'Wisdom hath built her house and those that labor, labor in vain in building' so then we have nothing to do with building the church. That is the Lord's business, but I tell you that once he writes his law in your heart and engraves it in your mind, then you have a work to do. You see little children, where there is no law, there is no transgression. Sin is a transgression of the law and if you don't have a law, you can't transgress it now, can you? The thing we lack is faith to believe and because of that we fail to do the things the Lord bids us to do. We don't have the faith to believe that the Lord intervenes in our lives, but my children, I tell you He does. He does his will in the armies of Heaven and amongst the inhabitants of the earth and none can stay his hand nor say, 'Why doeth thy?'"

Lucinda sat thinking that she had doubted that the Lord would send her a sign right up until the sign was given, 'the newspaper,' and then she had no more doubts. Silently she again thanked the Lord as the congregation rose and sang the final hymn. She started to the front, not really knowing why, but Jeff's tight grip on her hand held her back. It also killed the spirit or whatever had her compelled to go and she stood wondering what was happening to her.

Burb and Nancy asked Jeff and Lucinda to go home with them for dinner and they agreed. When they got in the truck, Jeff was quiet as he started the engine and pulled out into the road. "What's the matter, Jeff? Didn't you enjoy the service?" asked Lucinda.

Jeff said he didn't know because he had never been in anything like it in his life. He couldn't understand why they didn't have a piano or a choir or the reason they had so many preachers. Lucinda tried to explain but Jeff said it seemed to him that having only one preacher would be a lot cheaper. Paying all those preachers had to make it hard on the congregation was Jeff's thinking.

Lucinda was astonished, "We don't pay our preachers, Jeff. The Lord rewards them for feeding the flock."

"Don't pay them! How do they live? I never heard of not paying somebody. Why do they do it if they don't get paid?" said an astonished Jeff.

Lucinda did her best to explain but he kept saying things that were getting her upset and about to make her angry so Lucinda told him to just forget it. She couldn't stand for somebody to belittle or put down her faith and that was what Jeff seemed to be doing. He glanced sideways at Lucinda and then pulled her closer to him, "Honey, I don't understand one thing about it but I could tell you really loved it so that makes it fine with me. I may not go with you much but I don't mind you going. I don't care much about all those men hugging you, though," he said with a scowl. "There at the end, what were you going to do, Lucinda? You know, when you started toward that old preacher?"

Lucinda sat puzzled herself, and told him she wasn't sure if she was going to do anything, that it was just some compulsion to move. He said, "I hope you weren't going to join them. I mean, if you did, you'd be away from me too much."

Lucinda dropped her head in resignation as she realized that Jeff didn't want her to be anywhere or do anything where some man would have the opportunity to look at or touch her. Getting married hadn't helped that one little bit. He didn't seem to get mad at her but he wanted to hit out at the men. Knowing the Lord had already helped her with one problem, she thought she should pray about this one, also.

The last of May was getting closer, without Lucinda even thinking about it. She was embroiled in doing the final testing, counting textbooks and library books, and storing everything away as the days flew by. Suddenly it was the third week of May and after this week, she would only have one more week of school. Jeff had gone to the union hall every day but they were still on strike.

Twice they had been to Odell's house and she and her husband were talking about moving to Michigan to get work. Lucinda's brother, Ernie had written to say Odell and Bud could stay at his house until they could get a place. Odell said if Bud didn't find work soon, they just might move to Michigan. Bud had tried working in a garage, driving a bus, and working in a grocery store but even with Odell working, they just couldn't make ends meet. Lucinda knew that Bud drank all the time and he also played poker several nights each week. She was puzzled as to why Odell put up with it and wondered if she really did love Bud. Bud had suggested to Jeff that he should go with them since he wasn't getting any work. "You wouldn't be going against the union cause you wouldn't be in the coal mines," said Bud and Jeff said he'd like too but Lucinda wanted to go to school.

One evening, Lucinda told Jeff she wanted to go into Lacy Wright's store and also the drug store. Jeff looked worried for a minute but agreed, saying he would go with her. Again, she wondered why he was so watchful of her here in Bradshaw? He wasn't like that when they went to Logan, Gilbert, or Grundy. She got out of the truck and felt a total blackness envelop her, momentarily followed by a brief dizziness. She didn't say anything because it soon left and she walked by Jeff's side across the street and into the store. A sense of foreboding came over her however, which she attributed to the brief dizziness. Inside, Jeff went to the men's aisle while she ambled slowly through the lingerie aisle. She bought a new slip and some wash cloths and as she passed the personal items she suddenly thought, she hadn't had her period that month. That sense of doom was still with her so she let the thought skitter through her mind without dwelling on it. She thought of all the trauma and worry she had been through as she went on with her shopping. When she was finished and had paid the girl at the counter, Jeff took her parcels and they walked outside. On the sidewalk they met Mr. Estep, and Lucinda was pleased. She hadn't seen him since she married and she happily shook his hand, saying, "Mr. Estep, it's so good to see you. How have you been?"

"Not too good, Miss, uh I mean Mrs. Marshall. This strike is wringing me out good. It's a good thing we raised a big garden or it'd be hard to feed that big crew of mine," stated Mr. Estep as he shook her hand. He told her she was looking good but he believed she had lost a little weight. "It ain't hurt your looks none, cause you're still as purty as a picture."

Lucinda smiled and thanked him then stood, hesitating as if expecting something. Confused, she shook her head wondering what was wrong with her; she couldn't shake this strange eerie feeling. Jeff was still talking to Mr. Estep so she started slowly on up the street to the drug store. As she neared the drug store, she again felt dizzy and hurriedly walked toward the door. The door swung open just as she lifted her hand to push it inward, almost hitting her in the face. Lucinda's hand thrust out to keep from being hit and then stopped dead as Jason stepped out the door to stop in front of her.

Jason stood frozen in place and Lucinda stared from a face which had lost all color, "J-Jason," she mumbled through chattering teeth. Jason, still standing like a statue, recovered enough to breathe, "Lucinda," just as Lucinda crumpled slowly towards the sidewalk. Jason reached for her before she hit the pavement and bent to lift her up, only to be shoved aside as Jeff scooped her into his arms, snarling, "Keep your hands off my wife, you damn son-of-a-bitch."

Jason turned red, "Your wife? When …" Seeing others watching, he said, "You don't understand, I'm a doctor."

"I know who you are and you'd better get away from my wife and make sure you stay away from her. Do you hear me?" Jeff threatened as Lucinda began to moan and mumble. He turned quickly and marched down the street with Lucinda held tightly in his arms. Deputy Stevens had also been in the drug store and coming out had witnessed the entire scene along with several others. He looked at Jason who was still standing as if hit by a ton of bricks.

"They've not been married but about a month and I'm afraid Jeff is a little over protective. I'll say one thing though, if ever a man loved a woman, Jeff Marshall loves that girl. He begged her to marry him from the time he met her but she wouldn't agree. Then a little over a month ago, they just up and married one weekend. I'm sorry about the way he acted because he's really a fine fella."

Jason turned to Deputy Stevens, "I suppose he is. I think something must be wrong and I was going to check her but I don't guess I will now. I hope he takes her to see the doctor. Do you think he will?" asked Jason with concern.

Deputy Stevens assured him that Jeff would do anything in the world to keep Lucinda, safe, healthy, and happy. Jason smiled grimly and thanked him as he walked hurriedly down the street to his car, got in, and went speeding out of town throwing gravel right and left.

Lucinda roused just as Jeff got her to the top of the stairs. She turned her face against Jeff's shoulder and began to cry. Jeff cursed loudly and put her down to open the door but held her firmly against him. When the door was open, he picked her up again and carried her over to the bed and laid her down. He wet a wash cloth and came over and washed her face and she opened her eyes and looked up at him. His face was still red and he was struggling to control himself. Lucinda knew it was a shock to see Jason but didn't feel like that was all that caused her to faint. She put out her hand and pulled Jeff down to her and kissed him, "Jeff, did you know who that was? I mean, the man I met there at the drug store."

"Hell yes, I know him. He's that damn doctor. He's been hanging around here for about a month now. Why do you think I've been keeping you off the street as much as I can? That son-of-a-bitch was here in town the first night we came back after we were married. He's got no business down here and he only comes in the evenings. I'm going to knock his damn brains out and then he'll stay where he belongs," threatened Jeff angrily, hugging Lucinda tightly to his chest.

"Jeff, I want you to listen to me. It was a shock to see Jason and I would be a liar if I said I had never cared for Jason, but remember, I married you. I will be faithful to you regardless of whether you believe me or not. We have to trust each other, and unless we do, our marriage is doomed before it can get started," stated Lucinda solemnly.

Jeff hugged her furiously, "Honey, I know you'll be faithful but I can't stand the thoughts of that man ever kissing you." He shivered. "It just makes me so mad I can't stand it. I want to hit something." Lucinda wondered if Jeff would ever get that angry with her and then put it out of her mind.

Seeing that he was still angry, she continued, "I was feeling dizzy before I saw him, though. In fact, I've felt dizzy all day. When I first got out of the truck this evening, everything went black for a second. I think something else is wrong but I don't know what." Jeff removed the washcloth and felt her head in concern, "I'll take you over to Doctor Mitchell in the morning unless you want me to get him to come up here tonight."

Lucinda told him no, that she just wanted to drink some milk and go to sleep. So, Jeff left her and went down the street and came back with sandwiches and a quart of milk. Lucinda ate about half a sandwich and drank some milk. Still feeling a little woozy, she quickly brushed her teeth and climbed into bed, leaving Jeff sitting by the window.

When the doctor examined Lucinda, Jeff stood by, glaring resentfully and Maggie Barker smiled knowingly at him. "This is very impersonal for a doctor, you know. This is just a part of his job just like your job is mining coal, so relax Jeff."

Again the doctor asked when she'd had her last period and she said March 28th. The doctor grinned and said, "Well, it seems you're about six weeks pregnant, young lady." Lucinda's eyes were as round as saucers and her face was rosy red, "We've just been married about six weeks, Doctor. I can't be pregnant, can I?"

"You must have married just before your cycle was due to start, didn't you? That's what usually happens," smiled the doctor, assuring her that she seemed to be healthy, and asked about morning sickness. Lucinda told him she hadn't felt any different at all until the evening before when everything went black for just a moment. She also told him about fainting later that evening. The doctor gave her a prescription for some vitamins and told her if she had trouble with morning sickness, to eat some salt crackers when she first got up.

Jeff had stood transfixed and now he said, "But I've been using protection- well, I have, all except the first night we were married."

The doctor assured him it only took one time, especially at certain times of the month. "She's so little, Doctor. I'm afraid for her to have a baby," said Jeff worriedly. "If I caused something to happen to her, I couldn't stand it."

The doctor patted his shoulder, telling him that she seemed healthy and small women didn't have any more trouble than large women. "The best thing you can do is cheer her up and take good care of her. Bring her back next month, but I'd make arrangements for her to have the baby in Grace Hospital. Dr. Glovier is a great obstetrician and he is chief man in that department. Jeff and Lucinda made their way back to their room very subdued. Lucinda plopped down on the bed thinking Jeff is out of work, I'm pregnant, and we don't have a house. Then she thought about a baby and was glad, but scared. The next thought was Uncle Jake telling Jeff, "Keep her pregnant and she can't go to school," and she jumped up ready to do battle but became so dizzy that she slumped back down.

Jeff saw her stagger and turn deathly white and was instantly at her side, "Lucinda, are you about to faint again? Here, lay down and I'll get you some water. Do you want to go back to the doctor," said Jeff, hovering like a mother hen.

"Just get away from me, Jeff Marshall. You did this deliberately to keep me from going to summer school. Well, it is not going to work. I'm going to summer school whether I'm pregnant or not. I don't care if I'm big as a cow. I'm going." Lucinda turned away from him and began to cry.

Jeff stood in stunned silence. "Lucinda, please believe me. I don't - didn't want you to have any babies at all. I wanted to keep you for myself and not share you with anybody. I didn't mean for you to get pregnant. I don't want a damn baby." He sat down on the bed and dropped his head in his hands.

Lucinda turned over and sat up, "You don't want our baby. What kind of person are you? Here I am pregnant and you curse it and tell me you don't want it. I've married a monster."

Jeff raised his head and then suddenly had Lucinda clasped tightly to him, "Honey, I'm so tore up I don't know what I'm saying but I swear to you that I did not deliberately get you pregnant. I'm as surprised as you are and I promise you that you can go to school, unless you're too sick to go."

Lucinda was so tired and mixed up that she couldn't even think straight, so she said, "Let's just go to sleep and talk this all out tomorrow," then turned and crawled into the bed.

Jeff went into the bathroom and stood looking out the window. He had told her the truth; he didn't want any children. He wanted Lucinda all to himself; not sharing her with anyone. Then there was that damn doctor.

"I've got to get away from here," he mumbled in desperation. "There's no way I'm going to take her to Welch and to the same hospital where that son-of-a-bitch works." Then he began to think seriously about going with Bud and Odell. He'd have to talk Lucinda into going, however, which would mean she couldn't go to summer school. From what he had just heard, that did not seem very likely. He finally went to bed and pulled Lucinda close in his arms, then hugged her fiercely. Lucinda moaned and mumbled something and he loosened his hold and finally slept.

Later that night, Lucinda asked God to let her baby be all right and not to let her run into Jason anymore. She knew the Lord had wanted her to marry Jeff. If that's what God wanted, then why is he letting Jason come around and why doesn't he let me forget him altogether? I'm married to Jeff, and I know it's wrong to be thinking about Jason. That's all over and- it can't be. I'll just have to bury him in the back of my mind and forget about him. Lord, please help me, was her last waking thought. She snuggled closer to Jeff, who mumbled in his sleep and tightened his arms about her.

CHAPTER 37

Lucinda had morning sickness and got thinner than ever since she couldn't seem to hold anything down. Every time she was sick she resented Jeff and then felt bad for feeling that way. They visited Odell's several times since Bud had already left for Michigan. Lucinda loved Odell and knew Jeff liked her, but wondered why he was visiting her so much. Odell always shared the news from Bud with them. "Bud's planning to find work before he gets a house and comes back for us," explained Odell as she started begging Lucinda to make the move to Michigan with her. "Cindy, I'll be so lonesome for home, but it won't be so bad if I have some of my folks with me."

Jeff was afraid to say too much since Lucinda already acted upset with him, but when Odell begged, he added, "Honey, if I could get a job up there, I wouldn't be in the mines. You've always begged me to leave the mines and I'd have to if we lived up there. You're not able to work. It really hurts me to take you to work and have to stop every morning because you're sick."

"The doctor said that would stop in a few more weeks and then I'll be all right. I'm going to summer school, so get moving out of your head. I'm not going," stated Lucinda adamantly. However, Lucinda was torn because she did want Jeff out of the mines. Also, she didn't want to see Jason. She was married to Jeff and that must be the way it was meant to be. That should have made her happy, but it didn't. If they ran into Jason very often, Jeff would certainly end up in trouble.

Lucinda had already registered for summer school and had paid the registration fees. If she went to school four summers and took extension classes in the winter, she would still have four more years before she would get her degree. Having a baby or not, she felt that if she didn't go to school, she would be losing complete control of her life. She'd had it all worked out, but now, every way she turned she ran into a mountain.

It was not Bradshaw Mountain, but a mountain of conformity, of subjugation of wants and dreams, and worst of all, a mountain of self-denial which loomed higher and higher. When she tried to tell Odell and Jeff that moving away would destroy all her dreams, they assured her that she was young and had plenty of time. "You can finish after the baby is born, and if you're in Michigan with me, I'll even baby sit for you," offered Odell.

She could see her life stretched out before her, with her doing everything someone else wanted. She hadn't helped herself by marrying Jeff. Now, she would just be doing what he said, instead of what her family said. She just closed her ears to Odell's pleas and told Jeff she wanted to go back to Bradshaw. For the first time in her life she felt rebellious, and assured herself that other people didn't know what was best for her. How could they know how she felt inside? She had never questioned before but now she did, which surprised her.

As her problems seemed to mount, she found her thoughts dwelling more and more on the church. She questioned herself whether she only turned to the Lord when she had problems. She didn't think that people should only go to the Lord when they were in trouble and this made her doubt if she really loved the Lord. Even as a child she had talked to the Lord and thought she loved him, but now she wondered if she was just using the Lord instead of praising him. She felt ashamed as she realized that sometimes she even resented his interfering in her life; like letting her see that newspaper and letting Jason come back here. Now she even dared to question whether the Lord did interfere in the natural lives of his people. He didn't make a bunch of robots; people were born with a brain and undoubtedly they were meant to use it. She kept those thoughts to herself, however.

Jeff tried his best to be friendly and cheerful but Lucinda could see that he was deeply troubled. Lucinda also wondered why he hadn't mentioned about her going to see the obstetrician in Welch. More and more he begged her to move to Michigan, just like he had begged her to marry. Sometimes she still wondered if he planned the breakdown on his truck. Common sense told her that he couldn't have, but it sure helped him get what he wanted. Finally, Lucinda decided that Jeff just wanted away from Bradshaw or any place where Jason might show up.

She hadn't been thinking much about the baby and, in a way, kind of resented it. She was so sick every morning and knew also that Jeff didn't want it. One day she was on Bradshaw Mountain and asked Jeff to drive her to the cemetery where her Grandpa was buried. She told Jeff she wanted to go there by herself and he waited in the truck. She sat down by Grandpa's grave and began telling him all her problems. She knew that Grandpa couldn't hear but neither could anyone else. "Grandpa, I've made a mess of my life and now I don't know what to do. I wish you were here to help me," mumbled Lucinda as she pulled at tufts of grass that had sprung up around his headstone. She must have stretched too far for she felt a twinge run across her belly and quickly put her hand over her tummy. Suddenly, she felt such love for this child. A child that would have nobody to love it unless she did; Jeff was jealous of it, and she hadn't wanted it, and it was their baby. She began to cry and beg the Lord for forgiveness. She had been thinking about what she wanted, and not giving a thought to what her baby might need. "I need to grow up," said Lucinda as she stood up and smiled down on her Grandpa's grave. When she walked back to the truck, she saw Jeff standing, anxiously awaiting her. "Jeff, we didn't plan this baby and you don't want it, but I love it and I'm going to do what's best for it. You've been thinking about yourself, and I've been thinking of what I want, but from now on, I'm going to think about my baby. I hope you will, too. This baby is a part of me and you and we should both love it."

Jeff looked at Lucinda keenly, then slow tears seeped from his eyes, "Honey, I knew that my crazy jealous talk had bothered you and I've been so ashamed. I was afraid to try to talk to you because you've been so edgy. I was afraid to make it worse. Lucinda, I may not have wanted us to have a baby, and I'm still afraid for you, but I do love anything that is a part of you. Don't worry, I'll love our baby." Seeing Lucinda's happy face, he enfolded her in his arms and they both wept.

Constantly Odell begged her to move with her to Michigan. The week after she found out she was pregnant, she visited Nancy. Nancy was pleased but also thought she should move to be near Odell. Lucinda wondered if Odell had told Nancy about her running into Jason and fainting. If Odell told, then it may have been the reason that both Nancy and Burb joined Jeff and Odell in pointing out the advantages of moving to Michigan.

Nancy said, "Lucy, Honey, I just want you near some of your family while you're carrying this baby. I got to be with Odell once and, of course, with Oprey cause she lives here on the mountain. I allus wanted to be with my girls but I couldn't. If you'd move to Michigan, then Odell could be with you."

Burb said, "Cindy girl, you're just too little and puny to try to work and carry a baby so I think you ort to go somewhere so Jeff can work" Turning to Jeff, he said, " Seems like that strike ain't never goin to be settled. Besides, the coal boom is over. I think Rockefeller sold out to the coal companies out west and left us hanging. He's trying to say our coal's got too much sulphur. That's just an excuse to help his companies out west."

Jeff started to refute his statement but then thought that he needed Burb as a friend until he convinced Lucinda to move.

Lucinda had started going to meeting every Sunday with Burb and Nancy and the more she went the more she wanted to go. Jeff hadn't gone with her except for the two times they went up on Crane Ridge. Then he took a book and stayed in the truck and read. Each time, Lucinda found him asleep when the service was over. On the first Sunday in May, she went to the top of the mountain to Bee Branch Primitive Baptist Church. Jeff drove her there but went on down to Burb and Nancy's house to wait for services to be over.

Preacher Hiram seemed to be more eloquent and more blessed than Lucinda had ever heard him. On the final hymn, she completely lost sight of where she was. She was caught up in the love of God and was in such a blissful state that she never wanted to come out again. When she realized where she was, she was at the pulpit holding Preacher Hiram's hand and telling him she wanted a home with the church. Preacher Hiram asked her to tell of her experiences with God and Lucinda began to tell of how the Lord had always heard her cries and now she wanted to come home.

"I just need to be a part of this family of believers, if you'll have me," she whispered. Lucinda's request was put before the body and she was received as a candidate for baptism. Preacher Hiram then asked when she wanted to be baptized and who she wanted to baptize her. "I want to be baptized as quickly as I can get to the water and I want you to baptize me," smiled Lucinda joyously. She told them she wanted her membership where Burb and Nancy had theirs, at Bee Branch Church.

Someone must have gone down the ridge and told Jeff because he showed up at the river. Lucinda wasn't concerned about Jeff or anyone else. This was a special happening between her and the Lord and when Preacher Hiram led her out into the water she felt she had on a special wedding garment. She was to be the bride of the Lamb and gloried in it. When Preacher Hiram crossed her hands and raised his hand to Heaven, such a peace swept over her that she went into the water and out feeling she and the Lord were one. She felt like shouting aloud but this was too much to utter with words as her heart swelled with love. She walked to the shore touching and hugging everyone she saw as if she were touching the hem of His garment. Someone put a towel around her and over her head but she didn't come down to earth until Jeff put his arms around her and held her close. Suddenly, she looked up at him and seeing his look, wondered if he was angry with her.

When Jeff helped her to the truck, he was upset. "Lucinda, you shouldn't have been out in that dirty, filthy water in your condition. These people let their sewers run straight into that river and there's probably glass in the water. You went in barefooted, didn't you? I noticed that as that old preacher was leading you out in it. I started to run over with your shoes but there were too many people in the way. Why didn't you tell me you were going to do this?"

Lucinda just smiled and told him she didn't know she was going to and she was sorry if he was upset. "Nothing would have harmed me today, Jeff, because the Lord was with me. I know He is with us all the time but today I felt Him all around me and, Oh Jeff, I've never been this happy in my whole life," breathed Lucinda exultingly.

She had been baptized in the Dry Fork River at Bradshaw so she didn't have far to go for dry clothes. Then they went back on the mountain to Burb and Nancy's for dinner. Burb and Nancy now had a telephone; a party line, but still a phone. Odell met them at the door beaming from ear to ear, "Bud just called and he has a job in the Ford Automobile Factory in Toledo, Ohio and he says they are hiring and Jeff could get a job at the same place."

Lucinda knew she only had a few more days of school and then go to Concord College. She felt that if she didn't go to school this summer she would be making a big mistake.

Jeff knew that Lucinda really wanted to go to school. Going to school wouldn't have been so bad if he could have gone with her, he thought, but what if she met somebody- some educated man. Then, too, she would be away from him. The biggest reason Jeff wanted to move was that he did not intend for Lucinda to go to that hospital in Welch, yet he couldn't tell Lucinda that. She'd see that doctor every time she went and Jeff couldn't stand it. If ever in his life he had hated anybody, he hated that doctor and often wished that he had gotten killed in Korea. So, he decided that if there was any way possible, he would move to Michigan and never return to West Virginia.

Lucinda felt sure that Jeff must have enlisted the help of every member of her family, for in the following days every one of them added their voice to Jeff's. Gordon came up to the room one evening and went on and on about how important it was for her to be free of worry while carrying a baby. Further, he said that she had promised to love, honor, and obey her husband and she knew that Jeff wanted to move to Michigan. "Lucinda, how do you think Jeff feels, not having any work? He's a proud man and it is really getting to him that you are working and he isn't. You know there's no work around here except the mines and now they are on strike, and probably will be all summer."

The next day, Ellen came to Burb and Nancy's while Lucinda was there and added her advice to that of all the others. "A woman's place is with her husband, Lucy. A man feels proud to be able to take care of his wife and Jeff can't get any work around here." That same evening, Oprey came and spoke longingly of how she wished Jess wasn't crippled. "We'd be away from this mountain so fast we'd only leave our dust." But the clincher was Preacher Hiram. He came to dinner at Burb and Nancy's on the Sunday after school had closed for the year, and said, "Sister Lucinda, I'd hate for you not to get to attend your meetings but, Child, your place is with your husband. You and that baby you're carrying both need him. The Lord can visit you no matter where you are, and your husband will bring you back as often as he can so you could attend some meetings."

Jeff shook the Preacher's hand, "I sure will, Preacher. If she'll go, I promise I'll bring her back about every three months, at least until time for the baby." He looked across the table to Lucinda, in her usual place on the bench next to Burb. "I will bring you back Lucinda, but we do need to go, so I can get some work. Please say you'll go."

So in one year's time, Lucinda finished her first year of teaching, married, became pregnant, united with the church, and now she would be leaving. Again, she was being pressured to do something that she did not want to do. She sat looking at everyone with her mind racing madly. Maybe some miracle would happen. Suddenly she didn't want the kind of miracle or answers she'd had before. Her heart had kept telling her to wait. She had prayed and then saw that picture in the newspaper. But now Jason was back in the area; he was married and she was, too. What a mess her life had turned out to be was Lucinda's prevailing thought.

Like her beloved innocent McDowell County, she too was young and innocent and had so much to learn. Somehow, she, like the county, had to learn who really cared for her and who was using her to get what they wanted. She had thought that living on Bradshaw Mountain caused all the problems women had, but now she saw the true mountain. This mountain she now faced was going to be much more difficult to scale. Somehow she had to learn to make wise decisions for herself and stand by them regardless of pressure from others. She had to learn to be like the mountain oak tree which bent before any wind but didn't break. She had to gain the confidence to believe that she could conquer any mountain, no matter how difficult.

Here I am then, thought Lucinda, ready to leave West Virginia, and I thought I wanted to but I don't. Now, in her innocence, McDowell County and Bradshaw Mountain seemed to be shelters, places of safety, and the place where the Lord had made himself known to her. Someone had said that lives make a change every ten years and it seemed to be true. She'd had no hopes of going to high school and then the truant officer forced

Burb to let her and Ellen go. Finishing high school was the only hope of education she had, but now she had attended college. Was it all going to end here? It looked as if, after all her struggles, she would not be finishing college.

She hadn't heard from Concord College and she knew she couldn't get a school without going to summer school. Jeff didn't have any work, and they didn't have a place to live, and he didn't want her to see Jason. Lucinda thought she might as well go, since everybody seemed to want her to. She turned to look at Jeff who was waiting expectantly, "I don't know why you aren't smiling, Jeff Marshall. I'll be going and you'll be getting everything just the way you always wanted it, won't you? You wanted me to marry early, you didn't want me to work, and you didn't want me to go to college. With this move, you'll have it all your way and I won't be getting to do one thing that I hoped and dreamed about. I guess everybody will be happy though, everybody but me. I never mattered before, so why should I now?" she sneered as she walked out the door.

That night Lucinda resisted all overtures of peace from Jeff and they arose still being very polite to each other. They had planned to leave from Burb and Nancy's and when Odell arrived in her dark blue Kaiser four-door sedan, they were ready to leave. They stowed most of the belongings of both families into Jeff's truck since Odell's car was full of children.

Lucinda looked back with longing as they pulled away from her childhood home. It won't look the same, if I ever get to come back, thought Lucinda. McDowell County is also allowing others to decide its future, mused Lucinda. The county is the 'billion dollar coalfield' and yet where is the money going. We don't have any good highways, county sewage systems, or county water systems, so whoever is 'minding the store' as Jason called it isn't doing a very good job. Going through Bradshaw, she wondered how many other miners would leave because of the strike. She then stiffened her back and looked straight ahead. "You have to stand whatever comes along, Cindy, but it's up to you how you want to stand it," her grandpa's voice came unbidden into her tired and weary head.

There was no turning back now. She was married to Jeff. Jason was also married. She didn't have her degree. She was pregnant, and couldn't go to summer school. Jeff loved her, and he would be good to her, unless he became jealous, and even then she didn't think he would physically abuse her.

Lucinda counted the times that the Lord had heard her pleas and she silently offered her petition. "Lord, please help me be a good wife and mother, and Lord, please make a way for me to finish my degree," breathed Lucinda. Seemingly gaining renewed strength, Lucinda clinched her teeth and inwardly vowed that she would get her degree. Then she slid across the seat close to Jeff who quickly smiled and gathered her close as they drove away together.

ACKNOWLEDGEMENTS

In First Timothy, second verse, The Bible says that, "I exhort therefore, that first of all, supplications, prayers, intercessions, and giving of thanks, be made..." In my case, thanks must first be given to our Creator and Maker for any talent for writing that I may have been given.

A second group that I must thank is composed of my much loved grandpa, my parents, and my wonderful brothers and sisters for being the kind of people that helped to mold and shape me into what I am today.

Next, I sincerely thank my own family, my husband and children, who are the mainstays of my life. I especially want to thank my first grandson, Matthew Asbury, a student of University of Virginia at Wise, Virginia for his insight and editing on particular passages of this book.

I thank all the people of McDowell County, West Virginia whom I became acquainted with and grew to love. That rich heritage gave me a history from which to draw while writing this book.

This is not an autobiography, but I have taken attributes and personalities from many people and made them a person in my book. If someone reads this book and says, "That's me," they will be mistaken. Lucinda is not me, and yet she experiences some of the things that I experienced. The only true names of real people include Sarah Lester, now dead, whose desire to educate her children I so much admired, second, the late Colonel Ballard, who, without knowing it, did play a part in my actual life. Another name I used, Sir Marget, was the mountain version of Sarah Margaret, a wonderful sweet neighbor that I loved. I think it wonderful that my uncle,

Luther Horn, and my neighbor, Jess Compton, are famous in having hills in McDowell County named for them.

I truly appreciate David E. Cramer, staff engineer for the West Virginia Department of Transportation, for the invaluable help with accurate routes and dates for certain events.

My former boss and friend, Claude Banner, an exemplary citizen of Welch and McDowell County is due my heartfelt thanks for taking the time to send me information on Welch and spending numerous hours getting me straight on places in McDowell County.

Another person who answered my questions is my nephew, Jerry K. Horne, who served in McDowell County as a Justice of the Peace, principal of Iaeger High School, assistant superintendent of McDowell County Schools, and a county commissioner before he retired.

Appreciation and gratitude are given to my brother, Gilbert Horne and his wife, Edna, who helped me, not only on this book, but really were the cause of my beginning to write for publication. They took me to present my work when I had no way to go.

My dear sister, Rosa Mullins, helped me to go to college where I learned about writing. Without the loan of her dresses, I couldn't have gone. Thanks so much, Rosa.

I would be very remiss if I failed to thank Howard Dorgan, Professor Emeritus of Appalachian State University in Boone, North Carolina for his encouragement and help in trying to find a publisher. Professor Dorgan is well-known for his studies and books on religions in Appalachia and for his devoted help to Appalachian Studies.

My deepest appreciation and thanks go to my precious friend and fellow author, Lee Smith. She is a famous Appalachian writer, whose books include: *Fair and*

Tender Ladies, Family Linen, Black Mountain Breakdown, and *The Last Girls* as well as other works. She critiques my synopsis and gave valuable suggestions on the rest of my book, plus tried to help me find a publisher.

I also want to thank Pat Connor of West Virginia University Press for his valuable comments about my book. Even though he could not publish my book, he took the time to have it read and reported on the worth of the endeavor.

A very special tank you goes to Dr. Robert J. Higgs, Professor Emeritus of Appalachian Literature at East Tennessee State University, who did a critique of my book and wrote a detailed review. He is the author of many well-known works such as: *The Machine in the Garden in Anes Station, Southern Humor: The Light and the Dark,* and *War in the Stadium: Metaphors and Machines in the Fields of Strife, Friendly and Otherwise* and other publications.

Thanks to Dr. Jerry Beasley, president of Concord University, for taking the time to write the introduction to this book and for being a friend for many years.

This book would probably have never been finished were it not for Dr. Thomas McKnight's Reminiscence Writing Class at Southwest Virginia Community College. Two members, Kathleen Taylor and my precious, sisterly friend, Jo Osborne, deserve my undying love and gratitude for their editing skills and willingness to help.

The talents of Rhonda Wolford Whited, Art Gallery director of publicity and installation at Southwest Virginia Community College and assistant director at the Appalachian Arts Center, has made the cover of my book a pleasure to the eye. I most humbly thank her for her service.

I must not leave out Professor Greg Horne of Southwest Virginia Community College who critiqued the first few chapters and pointed me in the right direction.

Many, many thanks are due Barbara Smith, freelance writer, editor, medical ethicist, and Professor Emerita and Former Chair of the Humanities at Alderson-Broaddus College, for her advice on the publishing of this book.

Last, but not least, I wish to thank my editor, Rachel Riggsby. She spend many hours editing and also in long discussions with me on the phone about my book. She is not only my editor but a true friend.

CPSIA information can be obtained
at www.ICGtesting.com
Printed in the USA
LVHW010932230821
695886LV00001B/51

9 781523 493241